BLUE SKIES

ALSO BY T. CORAGHESSAN BOYLE

NOVELS

Talk to Me (2021)

Outside Looking In (2019)

The Terranauts (2016)

The Harder They Come (2015)

San Miguel (2012)

When the Killing's Done (2011)

The Women (2009)

Talk Talk (2006)

The Inner Circle (2004)

Drop City (2003)

A Friend of the Earth (2000)

Riven Rock (1998)

The Tortilla Curtain (1995)

The Road to Wellville (1993)

East Is East (1990)

World's End (1987)

Budding Prospects (1984)

Water Music (1982)

BLUE SKIES

A Novel

T. CORAGHESSAN BOYLE

Liveright Publishing Corporation

A Division of W. W. Norton & Company
Celebrating a Century of Independent Publishing

Copyright © 2023 by T. Coraghessan Boyle

For information about permission to reproduce selections from this book, write to Permissions, Liveright Publishing Corporation, a division of W. W. Norton & Company, Inc., 500 Fifth Avenue, New York, NY 10110

For information about special discounts for bulk purchases, please contact W. W. Norton Special Sales at specialsales@wwnorton.com or 800-233-4830

Manufacturing by Lakeside Book Company
Book design by Beth Steidle
Production manager: Julia Druskin

ISBN 978-1-324-09302-2

Liveright Publishing Corporation, 500 Fifth Avenue, New York, N.Y. 10110
www.wwnorton.com

W. W. Norton & Company Ltd., 15 Carlisle Street, London W1D 3BS

1 2 3 4 5 6 7 8 9 0

For Marie Alex and Griff Stevens

Blue skies
Smiling at me
Nothing but blue skies
Do I see.

—IRVING BERLIN

PART I

1

THEY WERE LIKE JEWELRY

THEY WERE LIKE JEWELRY, LIVING JEWELRY, AND SHE COULD see herself wearing one wrapped round her shoulders to Bobo's or the Cornerstone and sitting at a sidewalk table while people strolled by and pretended not to notice. It would make a statement, that was for sure. She'd put on a tube top so you could see the contrast it made with her bare skin—black, definitely black, and she'd wear her black jeans too and maybe her fedora—and she'd just look down at her drink or up at Todd as if nothing were out of the ordinary. And he'd go along with it too, she was sure he would—they were in that phase of their relationship where he'd given her a ring and they'd moved in together and she could have just about anything she wanted.

Except a baby. *Are you joking, or what? I'm no way even close to being ready for that, and plus the expense, Jesus.* He wouldn't let her have a dog either—or even a cat. He was allergic. Hair. Dander. Fleas. And did she have any idea of what his parents had to spend on inhalers and injections and the rest of it when he was a kid? She didn't. And at this point she didn't care. Talk about impulse buying—the minute she walked through the door and saw them glittering there in their plexiglass cases she knew she had to have one.

The shop was called Herps and it was located on the fringe of the shopping district, where the fast-food places were and the auto supply and a couple hole-in-the-wall Haitian and Cuban restaurants. She wouldn't even have noticed it, let alone pushed through the door, if she hadn't been so bored. Todd was having the car detailed and he couldn't just leave it there and trust them to do the job—no, he had to look over their shoulders while they plied their rags and toothbrushes and sealants, making sure they were on top of it. That was just the way he was, a perfectionist, and he liked to say that the two of them were a good match because she was an imperfectionist. Which might have been passive-aggressive but really wasn't far from the truth. So opposites attract—wasn't that the way of biology?

She'd been looking for a bar, thinking a mojito would brighten her afternoon, when she saw the snake there in the window, thick as a truck tire and stretched out on an artificial branch canted up off the floor at a forty-five-degree angle. It was chocolate-colored, with gold lattice-work that ran the length of it like a pattern in a catalogue. Its eyes were hard cold beads. Its tongue flicked in and out. Most of all, it was *present* in a way most things in this world definitely weren't. She stared at it for a long moment, falling into a kind of trance till the reflection of a car wheeling by on the street behind her brought her out of it. Of course, she'd seen snakes before—at the zoo, in the nature films on TV, smeared across the blacktop on one country road or another—but she'd never really looked at one, not until now, when the abstraction and the actual fused into an idea, a want, a need, a sudden need so pressing it constricted her throat. She paused a moment to dig the Dasani bottle out of her purse and take a long lukewarm swallow before she swung round and stepped inside.

The place was dimly lit, all the light radiating from the individual display cases. The cases lined the walls and stood end to end on low tables in the middle of the room, some with lizards or frogs or turtles isolated inside them, but most with snakes, which lay there motionless like so many bolts of material in a fabric shop. There was a smell too, subtle and dry, a smell of process, and she thought about that, the snakes unhinging their jaws to take in their prey—mice or rats, wasn't it? Or rabbits for the big ones. And then what? Shitting, she supposed. Snake shit, and what was that like? Was that what she was smelling? They must have pissed too, though she'd read somewhere they reabsorbed most of their moisture. Or maybe Cooper had told her, her brother the biologist, who knew everything.

The snakes barely stirred, but for the one right in front of her nosing in slow motion at the clear plastic lid of its container, so calm and unhurried it could have been narcotized. It was a snake in a box and it had nowhere to go—the box was everything, the box was the world— which somehow struck her as sad. Shouldn't they have more room—a terrarium where they could stretch out to their full length, with rocks and dirt or at least sand? Didn't snakes like sand? Or was that only desert snakes? The term *sidewinder* came into her head along with the quick flash of an image from a nature show, a dun snake looping across a barren landscape, the engine of its own intention. But this one, the one before her, was beautiful, they all were, as if somebody had dipped a brush in acrylics and traced the lines that radiated in a widening V from their mouths to draw reticulate patterns across their backs and down their sides. She was drifting from case to case, peering inside, *shopping*, when a guy was there suddenly, appearing from a door in back she hadn't noticed, and she realized he must have been watching her on closed-circuit TV, maybe from one of those ergonomic office chairs you could push all the way back till you were practically levitating because there was no reason for him to be on his feet in a deserted store in the middle of the day.

"You looking for anything in particular?"

He leaned a hip casually against the waist-high table supporting several of the cases in the aisle, his face lit from below like a Halloween trick, the brightness settling in his nostrils and sharpening the tip of his nose. He was about her age, or maybe a year or two older, and he wasn't chunky or fat but just undefined in the way of a whole generation of guys who played video games compulsively through all the hours of every day of the week, of which Todd, thankfully, wasn't one.

"I don't know," she said, "tell me about them. I mean, they're gorgeous. Are these the prices here, these numbers on the side?"

"Oh, yeah, sure, but if you see something you really like, I'm always willing to bargain—I breed them, you know? That's my thing in life."

"This one, for instance," she said, leaning over the case nearest her, where a milky pale snake maybe two feet long and decorated with neatly defined bars the color of lemon peel lay inert on its belly, looking at nothing. "What's his story?"

"That's a banana-coral glow. A ball python morph?" He swept a hand in the air. "All these right here? They're all balls. I just got back from Repticon over in Kissimmee—the big expo?"

She nodded, though she had no idea what he was talking about. He was trying to sell her something and she was going to buy it. These were the preliminaries. Part of the price was to listen to him talk.

"And I just laid them out, even my rarer hybrids, in case somebody stopped by. The really primo ones go back over to my house when I close up at seven, but I am in business and most of what you see's for sale."

"It's pretty," she said, then pointed to another, this one the color of dried blood with a black imbricate design like something you'd see in a print top at Anthropologie. "This one too. But the one that really caught my eye is the one in the window, which is too big, I know, but do you have any like that—I mean, that pattern—of maybe this size?"

"Well, yeah, a couple, but most people want balls. They're the fad right now." She followed him across the room to another table, where there were four cases containing snakes just like the one in the window, only smaller, much smaller—a tenth the size, a twentieth, even. They were somehow . . . cute, if you could describe a snake as cute. Self-contained, sleek, vibrant—she couldn't find the adjective, except that at this size they were proportional, just right. Neat, as her mother would say. "Are they babies?"

"More or less. These are Burmies, Burmese pythons? They banned them for a while a couple years back because of the problem down in the Everglades."

"They got loose, right? Didn't I hear about that?"

"People can be totally irresponsible, let's face it—just look at the thousands of dogs and cats that have to get put down in the shelters every year—but we got that overturned. Owning a snake is a basic constitutional guarantee—life, liberty and happiness, right? And nothing'll make you happier than having a snake in your life, and while the anoles and the bearded dragons and all that are fine in their own way, for kids especially, a snake's the real deal, you'll see." He paused. He had a polkadot kerchief knotted round his neck—to soak up the sweat, she supposed. It was hot outside, hotter in here. He took a minute to unknot the kerchief, slap it against his thigh two or three times as if that would do any good, then stuff it in his pocket. "First time, right?"

"Is it that obvious?"

"No, no, it's exciting," he said. "It's like, welcome to the club. And I love the Burmies, don't get me wrong—they make great pets, but they do tend to get big." He was gazing steadily at her now, delivering his pitch, and she wondered if her face was flattened by the lights the way his was, which, of course, it must have been—which only added to the sense of intimacy, of initiation, because this was cool, so very cool, a whole new world opening up to her on a day that was otherwise as ordinary as the two poached eggs on wheat toast she'd ordered at the diner before they brought the car in.

"So what's the difference, if I take one of these four here—they're all the same, right? I mean, is one healthier than another or different to your eye? Which one would you pick?"

"Your choice. They're all from the same mother."

It took her a moment. "You mean the one in the window?"

"As I say, they get big. You keep it for its life span—and you're going to want to, I promise you, because it's a trip and you're really going to get attached to it—but say that's twenty years, or even twenty-five at the outer limit? This little guy here"—he tapped the near case with a forefinger—"could wind up nineteen, twenty feet long, though they average out at something like twelve or thirteen." He paused, gave her a steady look. For some reason, an image of that mojito she'd been looking for appeared dead center in her mind, frosted and festive. She could feel the sweat on her scalp. Her throat was dry. Her shorts clung to her as if she were dancing a slow dance with an invisible partner. "The balls are smaller," he said. "Which, truthfully, is why they're more popular right now. That and the really cool morphs people've been creating."

Todd was going to be surprised. Todd was going to smile and say, "Cool," but underneath it he was going to resist. Or maybe not, maybe he'd get into it with her, maybe she'd buy him one too and he'd wear it along with her when they went out, just to show off a little, and why not? Why not be different for a change? There was more to life than work and takeout for dinner and Netflix and sitting out on the deck watching the tide carry the beach away as if they were already a hundred years old. But she was getting ahead of herself. And really, Todd didn't need the attention—he got that at work. She tapped the case in front of her. "That's the price here, in Magic Marker? Three-fifty?" The snake seemed to glance up at her then, though its eyes were so opaque she really couldn't tell.

"Yeah. And these are a real bargain. Compared to the balls."

"You're willing to go down, right?"

"Make it an even three," he said.

IT WAS PROBABLY HOTTER INSIDE than out, but at least it was out of the sun. The minute she went through the door, riding the high of her new purchase, the sun started building invisible walls all around her. This was fall, hurricane season, and though she loved it, loved

Florida, loved Todd, she missed California on days like this when you were instantaneously converted into a sweat machine and the air was so heavy it was like walking neck-deep through a river that kept fanning out in front of you as far as you could see. Her legs went dense on her. Her tee was glued to her back and her bra straps were like wet rawhide. *Mojito*, she murmured, repeating it under her breath, *mojito, mojito, mojito*, as if she were playing a game, and she began to laugh to herself as cars punched through the wall of light one after the other, their windows rolled up, air-conditioners cranked.

But wait—was that a bar across the street? It was. A place called Cora's, neon sign, double door with awninged windows flanking it, no tables outside, just an expanse of blotched and spat-over sidewalk. A parrot screamed from one of the battered-looking palms that limped down both sides of the street. And here was a jetliner, fat as a blimp, just hanging there in the sky on its descent to the airport. She didn't like going into strange bars alone, guys hitting on her, old men too, or just the way they looked at her, but this was an emergency, wasn't it? And a celebration. She'd have a drink and then call Todd and tell him she had a surprise for him, and if he wasn't done yet and the place was tolerable—really, all that mattered right now was air-conditioning—maybe she'd have another.

The snake was in a cloth bag imprinted with the name of the store just like any other purchase, except, of course, that you couldn't put it in a plastic bag because it wouldn't be able to breathe, as the guy who'd sold it to her—R.J.—had explained, though it should have been obvious. He'd sold her a tank for it too, a hundred gallons, which seemed too big until she thought of the mother in the window, and she'd taken three bags of aspen- and coconut-fiber bedding, as well as a dozen frozen mice for food (*fuzzies*, the next stage up from *pinkies*, which were newborns without fur, another thing she'd just learned today), all of which she and Todd would pick up on the way home. That was fine, and she was already thinking about where she'd set the tank up, in the living room next to the TV where everybody could see it or maybe in the bedroom where it would be the first thing she'd see when she opened her eyes in the morning, aside from Todd, that is. But Todd didn't glisten. Or writhe. Except when they were having sex—and then she was laughing again because the snake's name had suddenly come to her. She'd call him Willie. And if people asked her about it—and they would—she'd just widen her eyes and say, *It's a private joke.*

R.J. had offered to hold the snake for her till she came back, but she'd shaken her head no. She wanted the thrill of carrying it with her like any new purchase and though it couldn't have weighed more than a can of tomato paste, she was enjoying the solidity of it there in the bag dangling from her right wrist as she debated whether to cross the street here or trudge all the way up to the light . . . but Jesus, it was hot. Which must have been nice for Willie, but it was killing her. She shot a glance both ways, timing the traffic, then crossed the street in a quick skipping stride, pulled open the door of the bar and ducked inside.

She liked the place right away, mainly because it was deserted but for the bartender—a woman, middle-aged, with coral earrings and a generic Northern European face not much different from her mother's, actually, who would turn out to be none other than Cora herself—and a couple, also middle-aged, sharing a plate of taquitos at the bar. All three of them gave her a nod of greeting as if she'd been coming here at two in the afternoon every day for the past six years. Which made her feel she'd lucked out as she made her way up to the bar and took a seat two stools down from the couple, giving them their space, and waited for the bartender to ask the question to which she'd had the answer for the better part of the past hour now. The music was unobtrusive—jazz of some sort—the air-conditioning set so low it was practically arctic, and all the usual bottles lined up on a tier of shelves behind the bar, including, she saw right away, the Flor de Caña white rum that was the only rum on the planet as far as she was concerned. For mojitos, anyway.

She'd gulped half her drink down before she realized what she was doing—she was that thirsty—then asked for another and a glass of ice water and took out her phone to call Todd.

"Hey," he said, picking up on the first ring.

"You done yet?"

"I don't know, Cat, another half hour maybe? You okay? Where are you?"

"A bar."

"A bar? Isn't it a little early in the day?"

"I've got a surprise for you."

"Really? Like one of those surprises where you saved a hundred dollars because the dress you bought was on sale? That kind of surprise?"

"No. It's something for both of us."

She could hear noises in the background, the usual thumping and banging, men's voices, oldies rock echoing hollowly off the walls, and she thought he was going to say something more, make another snide comment or at least ask what it was, but he didn't, so she just said, "Call me when you're done."

SHE TOOK HER TIME WITH the second drink, playing with her phone and idly fishing through the nuts in the smudged glass dish on the bar in front of her. There was a soccer game on TV, not that it meant anything to her—it was just there, always there, in every bar extant, imprinting images on your brain through every minute of the day. And night. They played soccer at night too, at least somewhere in the world, and of course there were rebroadcasts for the convenience of those who'd missed out on all the excitement first time around, twenty-two guys in shorts eternally kicking a ball around a field as green as crème de menthe. A drink she hated. How could anybody ever drink that? Or chartreuse? Or Pernod? Or, even worse, drink it and watch soccer?

She'd hooked her purse over the back of the stool, but she kept the cloth bag in her lap, where she could feel the weight of it and communicate a little of her body heat to the snake—to Willie—in case the air-conditioning was too much for him, but then she didn't know what constituted too much since all this was new to her.

The thought made her impatient. She wanted to get home, see him, admire him, play with him—or at least handle him to establish trust, which was the first step, reinforced by food. Snakes couldn't love you the way dogs or cats could—their brains were too primitive to foster any higher emotions—but R.J. had assured her that it would definitely recognize her and come to regard her if not with love, then equanimity, which was as much as you could hope for. "Can I take him out in public?" she'd asked. "Drape him over my shoulder, I mean? You know, like you see in ads sometimes? Or this one girl I saw in South Beach?—I think she was a model, but she had a snake wrapped around her and it was really, I don't know, eye-catching."

R.J. had shrugged. "They can get used to anything."

So now, because Todd wasn't here and wasn't answering her calls and because she was excited and bored in equal measure and maybe a little drunk, she loosened the string at the neck of the bag and ducked her head down to take a peek inside and admire her purchase. The snake was right there, coiled up and staring at her, utterly calm and unconcerned. If he was cold, he didn't show it, but then she realized she wouldn't have known one way or the other—what was he going to do, shiver?

When she glanced up, Cora was right there in front of her, leaning over the bar to get a better look at what she had in her lap. "*Herps?* Don't tell me you bought yourself a snake? From R.J.?"

She nodded. The couple—speedboat tans, hair dyed the exact same rusted-out color as if they'd gone halves on a box of Nice'n Easy—swung their heads round.

"I've got two balls myself. Mohave mystics? You know mystics?"

She felt a secret thrill. She had a snake in a bag—not even on display—and already she could feel the power of it. "No, I'm sorry," she said. "This is like . . . my first?"

The admission took the power right out of her, but it didn't seem to faze Cora. Cora wore a ton of lipstick. Her grin was emphatic. "Well, don't be shy, let's see it."

"You mean here?"

"Where else? I'm a certified ophidian lover and Lois and Larry here love everything—right, Lo?—after the second drink, anyway." There was a mad spike of laughter that ended with Lois coughing into her fist. Up on the TV, the soccer ball got kicked around. "Come on, come on," Cora insisted, "don't keep him to yourself, let's see him already . . ."

The drinks, magnified by her dehydration, were having their effect, but she hadn't reached the point where she could just randomly stick her hand in a bag that contained a live snake, so she said, "You sure?"

"If it's a baby python, believe me, he's not going to bite you. Unless you've got a Gaboon viper in there—and I know for a fact R.J. doesn't handle anything with fangs." She shot a look to the couple. "Thank God for small blessings."

Another jag of laughter. This was fine. This was convivial. This was just what she wanted. She pulled back the flap of the bag and slipped her hand inside, not knowing what to expect—pythons could bite, after all, though their teeth were for gripping only and canted backward to ease the swallowing of their pinkies and fuzzies or whatever it was, or so R.J. had told her. What she felt—the snake's body, its living body—was as smooth and frictionless as leather, no different from the snakeskin purse she had at home ("This small but mighty accessory has the power to take any look from zero to 100 in *seconds*"). In the next moment, it was gliding up her wrist and then her forearm and when she withdrew her hand from the bag, the snake came with it as if it were an extension of her own body, its head weaving and driving forward so that she had to bring her other hand into play while Willie kept shifting back and forth, flicking his tongue and weaving and coursing and trying to climb a ladder in the air only he could see.

"Whoa," Lois said, bringing both her feet up off the floor and hooking her heels over the rung of her stool. "You're not going to let that thing loose, are you?"

The jazz, whatever it was, seemed to time its beat to Willie's movements and she shaped her hand into a funnel and he went right through it and into the funnel of her other hand and then back again. She felt like a juggler, felt connected, transported, as if this were what she'd trained her whole life to do, and yes, she was going with the flow. Literally.

Cora said, "He's beautiful. Love the pattern. But that's not a ball, is it?"

"He's a Burmie," she said, and felt the thrill go exponential—from now on she'd be explaining this and all that went with it to everybody everywhere she went, and talk about a conversation starter . . .

"They get really gigantic, you know that—R.J. explained that, didn't he?"

She grinned. "The bigger the better, right?" The truth was, she couldn't really picture it, this little thing that was no thicker around than a sausage and barely two feet long growing up to be a replica of the truck tire in the window across the street, but then that was life, wasn't it? Wasn't that the point? She herself had grown up to look like her mother, at least to the extent that everybody was always saying they must be sisters, which might have been flattering to her mother but was like poison to her, especially when she was a teenager. But here was Willie, who kept stitching the air with the insistent needle of his head, and now he wanted the bartop and not knowing what else to do she gave it to him and in the next minute he was working his way up Cora's arm and Cora was saying, "Yeah, well, he really is a cool snake, absolutely, and I wouldn't want to put a damper on things, but I tell you I would have gone with a ball myself."

After that, Willie had about sixty seconds more of fame and glory and then Cora handed him back to her and she slipped his head into the funnel of her palm, fed him back into the bag and ordered another drink, which Cora said was on her.

☀

SHE NURSED THE DRINK, played with her phone, called Todd three times—without success, because he wasn't picking up. She was tipping back the dregs, tonguing her way around the shreds of muddled mint, starting to get angry, when Todd finally showed up. In the interim, two younger guys in Marlins caps had come through the door in a quick pulse of light and wordlessly occupied stools at the far end of the bar. Far from hitting on her, they never even gave her a glance. Which was the way she wanted it, of course, but it was somehow disappointing too, especially the way she was feeling. The snake was in the bag. She was no longer the center of attention. And she was drunk at three-fifteen on a Saturday afternoon.

All the excitement she'd felt had drained away, which was depressing, and she'd begun to relive old resentments and bugaboos of one sort or another, maybe even muttering to herself for a minute or two there, but then Todd stepped through the door and everything changed—she had a surprise for him and within the hour they'd be at home setting up the terrarium, which, she realized, was going to go perfectly with the Klee reproduction her best friend Melody had given her when she graduated college, or at least Willie was. He was like a reverse image of the design and the perfect shade too—only the painting was static and he wasn't. The plastic arts, and what could be more plastic than this?

She watched Todd standing there just inside the doorway, trying to get his bearings. She didn't wave, though she wasn't angry, not now, not anymore. He slipped off his sunglasses and the look on his face went from mild annoyance (*Is this the right place? She did say Cora's, didn't she?*) to an inflection point of relief and recognition—here she was, foregrounded against a wall of coruscating bottles, Saturday, party in progress, love and all the trimmings like something out of a movie. He gave a little wave and came across the room to her, leaning in for the quick peck of a public kiss. "Sorry, Cat, but they just didn't get it right, or not the way I wanted it, and I had to—" He paused. "Is that your second?"

"Yes," she said, which was true if you were counting from two.

"I guess I've got some catching up to do," he said, waving a hand for Cora, who was deep in conversation with the two Marlins fans at the other end of the bar.

"This is my fiancé, Todd Rivers," she said when Cora came to take their drink order, and she couldn't help holding up her left hand to show off her ring, a two-carat ideal-cut diamond set in platinum that had belonged to Todd's mother. Who was dead, dead now three months, which was why they were living in Florida in a beach house they could never have afforded on their own even if they lived a thousand years. So what if the beach was eroding? At least it was a beach. Which was a whole universe apart from the one-bedroom apartment in Sherman Oaks she'd had since college, featuring a panoramic view of Ventura Boulevard and the fifty thousand cars that scraped and glinted and honked their way by each day. She was sorry Todd's mother was dead. Sorry she was going to miss the wedding. Sorry for Todd. But to get a chance to live right on the beach with the ocean on one side and an inlet on the other? That made up for all the sorrow she could even begin to conceive of.

"What're you drinking?" Todd lifted the empty glass and took a sniff. "Don't tell me it's Flor de Caña again, *please*. How many times do I have to"—here he looked to Cora and shook his head. "There's only one *ron* for me, Bacardí. The Reserva Ocho. Do you have it back there?" There were four *r*'s in this speech he could rattle his tongue over, and he took advantage of every one of them, though he didn't speak more than ten phrases of Spanish. She didn't begrudge him for showing off. He was a Bacardí ambassador. That was how they paid their bills. Before they were through he'd buy a round for the bar on his ambassador's account and give Cora his business card. Like a salesman. But he wasn't a salesman, he was the next rung up and making good money, which made life even better when you got to live rent-free in your own house with only property taxes and utilities to worry about.

When Cora drifted down the bar to mix their drinks—yes, she was having another—she took hold of Todd's arm and leaned into him, pressing her forehead to his shoulder and then thumping it twice as if her head were the axe and his body the tree. "I like Flor de Caña, okay?" she said. "So shoot me."

His face went dark. "You know it's a business thing, don't you? At least in public?" The truth was, and this was a secret even the torturers wouldn't get out of her, Todd didn't even like rum. When she first met him, his drink was vodka and tonic, but that didn't make sense anymore because the Bacardí was free and at that price he found he could just as easily drink rum and tonic, with a twist.

"Just teasing," she said, and that was the truth. She was soaring, so happy in that moment she seemed to be looking down on the room from a great wings-spread height, the couple shrunk down to half their size and the two guys at the end of the bar all but invisible. The walls dissolved, the ceiling lifted off, the sky gleamed. She could see all the way across the street and down the block to where Willie's mother lay wrapped round the artificial branch in the store window. "Don't you want to see what I bought?"

He tried to hide the look of alarm or annoyance or whatever it was—he was a good actor and a good guy and he loved her, he did, she knew that, knew it as well as she knew anything. Love was a negotiation, she knew that too. "Yeah, sure," he said, giving her his big smile, his ambassador's smile, the smile of a Saturday afternoon when all they had ahead of them now was leisure and pleasure and more of the same. "Sure, what is it?"

"A snake," she said, letting go of his arm to bring both hands to bear on unloosening the string of the bag in her lap.

"A snake? You got to be joking."

But here was Willie, weaving up her arm and stabbing his head at the ladder only he could see and Todd said, "Jesus, fuck," and pushed back his stool. She almost laughed. His face was so comical, all popped-out eyes and shrinking mouth—if only he could see himself, she thought, and she felt the power all over again. "Put that thing back in the bag, will you? You can't—what are you thinking?"

"It's okay, Cora doesn't mind—she's got two of them herself. Todd, isn't he beautiful?"

"Put it away."

The walls and ceiling fell back into place and the speedboat couple reinflated as if they were blow-up dolls. The thought came to her that Todd was being a jerk. She hadn't complained when he went out and spent a full third of his mother's life insurance payout on his top-of-the-line Tesla or when she'd had to tear up her roots to move out here to Sweatlandia or anything else. She made her hand into a funnel and Willie slid into it and she put him back in the bag. There was a fresh drink sitting on the bar at her elbow. She stared into Todd's eyes, made a mock toast and drank off half of it before setting the glass back down on the bar.

"Jesus," he repeated, "you amaze me, you really do. A snake? Who buys a snake?"

"Lots of people. Cora does. Just ask her."

"I'm not asking her, I'm asking you. Where're you going to keep the thing? Who's going to take care of it? Huh? Tell me that?"

Cora was watching them from the far end of the bar, which was embarrassing. They were fighting in public, and over what? She'd meant to surprise him and he was spoiling everything.

"I thought next to the TV, actually, where we could watch him during commercials or when the movie gets boring, like that HBO thing about the race car driver you insisted on watching, because really, come on." She reached for her drink, snatching it off the bar as if it were about to explode, and so what if she spilled a drop or two? So what? "And if you want to know, I bought this walnut stand for the terrarium that'll be perfect there where your mother's ugly lowboy is, and why anybody'd ever paint over natural wood is beyond me. And I bought bedding for him and fuzzies and all the rest, a snake hook too. And don't you worry, I'm going to take care of him a hundred percent. I mean, I thought you'd be happy, Todd. I thought he'd be for both of us."

"Right," he said, "like you took care of the houseplants."

"I told you, they got overwatered. It was your mother. Years of it, the potting soil all leached out—"

"Fuzzies," he said. "What the fuck are fuzzies?"

ON THE DRIVE HOME, the clouds wrote various messages to her, most of them positive. She was feeling better, much better, the purchases loaded in the trunk and Todd making the car sing with the rush of air through the open windows. Everybody argued. Couples who claimed they didn't were liars, the sort of people who seemed just like anybody else on the surface, but cast their ballots for racists and xenophobes in the privacy of the voting booth. She and Todd had already made up— the best way, with a long mutually communicative kiss in the lot out back of Herps, his body pressed to hers up against the door of the car that was so flawless it was as if they'd just driven it off the showroom floor. The air felt good on her face. It was richer than California air, denser, with a smell of the tides that made her feel as if she weren't in a car at all but on a sailboat cutting across the bay. She was half-drunk still, though she'd switched to water, thankfully, when Todd ordered his second round, and as the tires thrummed and the clouds spoke to her and the radio gave her a song she couldn't get enough of, all the excitement she'd lost hold of came rushing back.

The fact was, she couldn't wait to set up the terrarium and let Willie explore his new home—the rocks, the imitation branch, the bedding and what they called a hide, which was like one of the tunnels for the miniature train set she and Cooper had had when they were kids and was designed to give the snake a little privacy so he could feel secure. Curl up in there, close his eyes—but snakes never closed their eyes, did they? They didn't even have eyelids. But of course snakes slept just like anything else—maybe they even dreamed, who knew? Snake dreams. If you'd told her when she got out of bed this morning that she'd be entertaining the concept of snake dreams, even putting the two words together for probably the first time in her life, she would have laughed aloud. And what was that all about? She didn't know. She didn't care. She could see the evening playing out before her like a movie projected on the concave surface of the windshield—she'd call for pizza, make a salad, sip a glass of wine and just sit there and watch Willie coil and uncoil and flow like a ribbon in a steady breeze while the light softened and faded over the bay and then she'd flick on the bulb in the terrarium and watch him some more.

Todd wasn't maybe as enthusiastic as she was, but he was coming around. He'd bitched about the cost—"Three hundred bucks for a *snake*?"— but when he saw how much it meant to her and had a beat or two to consider how many times she'd given in to him over these past months and how little a thing this was, really, he'd backed off and before long he was tapping his fingers on the dash and singing along with the radio, all sunshine and love. At home, first thing he did was pop the trunk and carry the stand up the stairs, where he helped her shift the lowboy out of the way. Then he went down for the terrarium while she carried up the rest, including the star of the show—Willie— and the fuzzies that had to be kept frozen till it was time to defrost one of them for his weekly dinner. ("Never microwave a fuzzy," R.J. had warned her. "The insides could still be frozen and that'll kill a snake, if you can picture it, since they're cold-blooded and they can't evacuate it till it's digested, right? So the danger is their body temperature drops beyond what they can survive with. Best thing is to heat up some water or better yet chicken broth, for the flavor, and pour it over your fuzzy to thaw it gradually. That's what I do, anyway.")

It didn't take her long to set things up, the hide propped against the rear wall that featured a faux-rock backdrop that was meant to make the terrarium look like a cave—not that any of these snakes had ever seen a cave before, but it was aesthetically pleasing to the owner, to her, who wanted to imagine the whole thing a scene out of nature, like the dioramas in the natural history museum, with the exception that everything depicted there was dead and stuffed. Water bowl in the corner. Bedding artfully scattered across the floor, though of course Willie would rearrange it to suit himself. And he'd crap in it too, which was why she'd bought three bags of it just to save her an extra trip. She'd picked the rocks out individually from a barrel in the back of the store in order to give the terrarium a more realistic look, and while Todd went into the kitchen to open the wine, she got down on her hands and knees and tried arranging them in various configurations till she was satisfied. Finally, she eased herself down on the Persian carpet the moths were starting to get to in a major league way—fingertip-sized patches gone bald no matter how many times she sprayed and vacuumed—and took a minute to admire her handiwork. It was perfect, a world of her own into which she could insert her imagination and bring something wild into the house other than flies or palmetto bugs. Or moths. And where did *they* come from anyway? Cooper was always bemoaning the decline of flying insects throughout the world, which was a terrible thing, of course it was, but what about carpet moths? Mosquitoes? No-see-ums? She wouldn't miss them, that was for sure.

From the kitchen came the glug and splash of the wine as Todd poured them each a glass, the homiest sound in the world, and she held on to the moment, gulls crying out like the sentinels they were, pelicans riding a string in perfect equipoise over the crenellated surface of the water below.

"I'm ready," she called. "It's the big moment. Come on, let's see how he likes his new home."

Todd drifted in from the kitchen and handed her a glass of wine— a Paso Robles zin he got by the case that was so full-bodied you could almost chew it—and she took a sip, set the glass down on the floor and rose to her feet. Willie was an S-shaped lump in the cloth bag, as well behaved as you could hope for, just lying there patiently on the coffee table where she'd left him. She lifted the corner of the terrarium's mesh top, unloosened the strings of the bag for the final time and laid it inside on the glass floor amid the shavings, letting Willie do the honors himself. If she'd expected him to be tentative, it was just the opposite—he slid out as if he were being extruded from a piping bag and began exploring the terrain, happy to be free of the bag, sure, but more especially that plexiglass display case R.J. had squeezed him into, which really couldn't have been all that much fun for him, talk about artificial.

"Ta-da!" she sang, and turned to Todd to give his bicep a squeeze and pull him to her for a kiss, a deep kiss, a soul kiss, and in the next moment they were all over each other. She didn't know what she must have smelled like, sweating all day like that, but this was the moment and she was in it, and she tugged the tee up over her head and he helped her with her bra and then they were down on the rug. Of course, the pizza guy rang the bell right in the middle of it and Todd had to pull out of her, step into his shorts and go to the door, but she didn't move and he came right back to her and it was all the hotter because of the interruption, if that made any sense. Then it was the pizza with artichokes and prosciutto and more wine and they both felt so hot they did it again, right there in front of the tank.

FIRST THING IN THE MORNING, even before putting the coffee on, she went to check on Willie. She was feeling fine, considering how much she'd had to drink the day before, though she had the beginnings of a headache and there was a faint acidic gnawing down there deep in the diamond mines of her stomach that the coffee was only going to make worse. Normally she'd fix herself eggs and a medley of fresh fruit—papaya, kiwi, honeydew, blueberries or raspberries or whatever looked good in the market that week—but she thought maybe she'd go for a muffin, blueberry, with a sprinkle of sugar, just to settle her stomach, and skip the coffee. The air was thick enough to sit on. Everything smelled of rot. Under the impress of her bare feet the floor felt vaguely vegetative, as if a miniature forest had sprung up overnight—mold, the ubiquitous mold the whole state must have been built on. Outside the windows the sky was dark and close and the sea hissed at the shore and somewhere there was the high whine of a speedboat breaking through the endless sound loop of gulls keening and squalling as they picked over whatever the tide had brought in. From the bedroom came another sound of nature—Todd's cascading snores that were like the last gasps of a drowning man, or no, a manatee, if manatees could drown, which she didn't think they could.

If he slept on his side, he was okay, but the minute she left the bed, he'd roll over onto his back and start in. He was only twenty-six, but the doctor said he had sleep apnea and lectured him about drinking, how drinking only made it worse, but for Todd—and her too, she'd be the first to admit it—drinking was a way of life. They weren't athletes, either one of them, not since high school, anyway, when she'd been on the cross-country team junior year and Todd had played baseball, she thought it was, though they walked on the beach once in a while or swam out beyond the breakers when the mood took them, but there was no tennis or jogging or anything like that in their lives. They liked bars. And while they didn't go out every night, they wound up having drinks at cocktail hour because that was a way to relax, that was what cocktail hour had been invented for, plus Todd's profession involved drinking and hosting parties to promote the brand. If he snored, it was no big thing. Except when she couldn't sleep. Then she'd shove him and he'd gasp as if she were pushing him off a cliff and thirty seconds later he'd be snoring again.

The tank was dark because she'd shut out the light when she went to bed, even though in a state of nature Burmies were mostly nocturnal, but then they wouldn't have had an infrared heat bulb in a state of nature either. Or a night-light, for that matter. She went to the tank and flicked on the light, then settled down on the carpet so she could watch him in the way other people might have watched TV, which made her feel good, superior, really, because morning TV was nothing but crap anyway. The only thing was, she didn't see him right away. She shifted closer, till she was inches from the tank, studying every angle of it, and, of course, snakes could hide in plain sight, which was what their ravishing patterns were all about—camouflage—but still she didn't see him. She tapped the glass, thinking he must be in the hide, but nothing happened. Finally, and she didn't really want to disturb him but just couldn't help herself, she rose to her feet and unlatched the mesh top, not even noticing that the fastener in the far corner had worked loose because she was new to all this and wouldn't have caught such a minor detail anyway, especially on a morning when she hadn't had her coffee yet and probably wouldn't have any at all, for the sake of her stomach. In the next moment, she reached down for the hide and lifted it out of position, expecting to see Willie coiled up there in the vacant space beneath it, sleeping late, lazy snake, lazy, lazy, lazy—but he wasn't there.

2

ENTOMOPHAGE

BECAUSE OF HER SON, BECAUSE HE WAS AN ENTOMOLOGIST and because she loved him and because it was the right thing to do, Ottilie decided to add insects to her diet. She'd resisted at first, but Cooper had worn her down. The death of the planet, that was his theme. The Anthropocene, our species a curse, et cetera. The polar bears. The monarchs. The frogs. "The planet's dying, can't you see that, Mom?" he'd asked—or actually, demanded—the last time he was over for dinner, which was almost two months ago now, plenty of time to consider all the angles.

She saw it. And she felt guilty about her part in it, every child of Western industrial society burning through thirty-five times the resources as the average Indian or African, but there wasn't much she could do about it aside from cutting her credit cards in two and recycling every scrap of everything that came into the house. She had no problem with the latter proposition—as it was, she rigorously separated items for the recycler and composted the better part of her organic waste. It was the former that gave her pause, because you had to buy things just to keep the economy going and she'd gone paperless on her credit card statements and all her other bills too, so that was a step in the right direction.

"But actually, the planet's not dying," she'd said, glancing up from the cutting board on which she was dicing peppers, onions and eggplant for the marinara sauce she was preparing for dinner (with the turkey sausage unincorporated in deference to her son, though he'd already complained twice about the smell of it frying in the pan). "Latest I heard it's got at least four and a half billion years left before the sun swells up and boils us all like lobsters in a pot. Or five. Didn't I hear five?"

"Come on," he said. "Cows. Pigs. Goats. Jesus, we're chewing ourselves into oblivion."

"Your father just isn't into vegetarian, you know that."

"That's what I'm saying—you need the protein content, B_{12}, choline, amino acids." He'd given her a long look. "Especially as you age. Both of you."

So she went online and bought herself an Entomo Farms cricket reactor in order to produce her own endless supply of high-fiber, low-fat protein while ever more efficiently recycling her kitchen scraps into the bargain. A click of the mouse—and yes, a credit card number—and four days later a three-foot-high box appeared on her doorstep along with a padded envelope stamped LIVESTOCK that rustled and chirped when she picked it up. The reactor was made of plexiglass so that you could watch the life stages of the crickets as they progressed from eggs to larvae to adults, as if the farm itself were a science project—like the ant farms that were all the rage when she was a girl. Only in this case, it was crickets, and the crickets would be harvested as food by way of reducing the methane load produced by the earth's billion or so cattle and the felling of all those forests to provide pasture for them. Not to mention sparing sentient creatures the horror of the slaughterhouse, which was another argument Cooper had used to soften her up. And yes, she'd seen the films of chickens dangling by their feet on a disassembly line, awaiting the whirring blade to decapitate them, and the steers taking the blow to the head while their knees buckled and they pitched forward in dark avalanches of flesh.

So she felt good about herself as she sorted out the individually plastic-wrapped components, studied the directions and put the thing together, including the drawers for her kitchen scraps and the tray at the bottom to collect the frass, which, according to the promotional literature, made an incomparable high-grade fertilizer for houseplants or for use in the garden. *Are you an avid gardener? Do you grow begonias? Tomatoes? Zucchini? You'll be amazed at the way they'll thrive with even a few teaspoons of this end-product added regularly to your soil.*

Following the directions, she fitted the components together, filled the feeding station with scraps of lettuce and potato peels left over from last night's dinner, then set the reactor in the double sink preparatory to releasing the crickets inside their new home, where they would chirp and breed and begin producing up to a pound of what she'd have to get used to calling meat per week. It was exhilarating, as with any new project, especially one as green and self-redemptive as this, and the most exhilarating part of the process was the final step, the crickets themselves. There they were, scrambling and frantic-legged, all bunched up in the bottom corner of the narrow extra-long plastic bag in which they'd come. They chirped, twitched their antennae, fought for purchase. She shook the bag a few times to dislodge the more adventurous ones and concentrate them before removing the twist tie, upending the bag over the reactor and letting gravity and cricket initiative do the rest.

The sun slanted through the kitchen window, picking out the coffee maker and toaster oven on the countertop, both of which she was going to have to slide down to make way for the cricket farm. Everything was awash in a soft reddish glow, the light refracted through the particulate matter drifting high in the atmosphere from the fires in the Bay Area, and though she knew it was only a matter of time before the chaparral in the hills here in Santa Barbara went up in flames, as it seemed to do every other year, she couldn't help thinking it beautiful. It was different, anyway. A change. The skies had been clear for months, since the end of the rainy season in March, each day a replica of the previous one, which made for a kind of tedium of the usual and a daily reminder of the drought that had been ongoing for four years now—or was it five? Cooper obsessed over it, but aside from being more water-conscious it really hadn't affected her and Frank all that much, especially since they'd uprooted the lawn and had it replaced with the wood chips Frank had insisted on spraying with fire retardant just to be on the safe side. She leaned in close a minute to watch the crickets—her livestock, think of that—as they poured themselves in and out of the empty egg cartons she'd arranged inside to give them cover, as per the instructions, then slid the toaster oven over till it was hard against the coffee maker, lifted the reactor out of the sink and set it in place on the counter.

That was when she noticed that two of the shiny black insects had somehow got loose during the transfer and were in the sink still, circling the slick porcelain contours in confusion before settling in the moist confines of the strainer. She wasn't squeamish, or not particularly, but now she was flashing on the student apartment she'd shared with three roommates who could have been cleaner and the cockroaches that came boiling out of every crevice once the lights went off, and why couldn't you eat them too? They didn't look all that much different from the crickets, actually. But then crickets were sanitary, weren't they? And she'd always associated their song with the countryside, with nature, whereas cockroaches didn't make a sound and they lived in filth and brought that filth into your house, spread it across your countertops, onto your food and into your mouth. But cockroaches were one thing, as Cooper could tell her (*Periplaneta americana*), and crickets another (*Acheta domesticus*), and she was committed to them now.

But how to capture them without injuring them? This was her breeding stock, after all, and though they'd be sacrificed in due time, this wasn't the time. She watched them huddling there in confusion, their antennae registering what must have been an irresistible taste and scent of the waste particles adhering to the stainless steel strainer, but their brains, if they had brains—did they have brains?—telling them they were separated from the colony and that at least for the moment, under these new conditions, separation spelled danger. She reached for one of them where it was crouched over the twin carets of its folded legs, attempting to pinch it ever so lightly between her thumb and forefinger, but it was too quick for her. In the next moment it was clinging to her forearm, making use of the fine hairs there by way of anchorage.

Up to this point, the crickets had been mostly theoretical—a picture online, a recollection of the bugs Cooper kept in jars as a boy, furtive things in the garden that never revealed themselves and fell silent when you came too close—but here it was, right here, under her gaze, clinging to her as if to some monument of flesh. Which was what she was in its eyes, a carnivore the size of a tree that really couldn't have meant it any good at all. Its feelers faintly twitched, but otherwise it was absolutely still, as if the leap from the drain had exhausted its energy. She had to admit it didn't look particularly appetizing, but neither did its fellow arthropods creeping across the floors of the oceans and rivers of the world, crabs, lobsters, crayfish, the relationship so close the promotional materials made a point of mentioning that people with shellfish allergies should proceed with caution.

When she took hold of it this time, it didn't resist. It felt prickly, horny, like one of the burrs she removed from the dog's coat after a walk in the woods, but it didn't attempt to bite her—the worst it could do, she'd read, was to exert a faint pinching pressure with its mandibles, but this one seemed content to let her have her way with it. Or maybe it was dazed, that was all. It had come from some breeding facility in Oakland, scooped up she supposed out of the only home it knew, squeezed into a mailer and released here, in her kitchen, which must have been as alien a space to it as the surface of the moon was to us. No matter. She screwed off the lid of the reactor to a rasp of deflated chirps and scrambling legs and dropped it in. Then she went for the other one.

❀

FOR THE FIRST COUPLE OF weeks, she experimented with various recipes, mostly simple things like cookies and brownies, using cricket flour she bought online from a company called Little Bits, but also home-made pasta, and one night, tortillas, the concept of which appealed to her, even if she wasn't yet brave enough to use a handful of sautéed crickets instead of grilled chicken strips for the filling. She suddenly saw the future in that moment, even as she rolled out the tortillas and a piano piece tinkled from the radio in the corner and the fluorescent light hummed over its chemical load—"And what would you prefer, señora," the waiter at Casa Lorena would ask, "tortillas of *maíz, harina*—or *insectos?*" She'd glance up from her margarita and pronounce, very carefully, so there would be no misunderstanding, "*Insectos, por supuesto.*"

In due course she'd make and sift her own flour and try out some of the simpler recipes in Michel Horan's *Cuisine de divers insectes—grillons poêlés rôti* or maybe the tempura crickets, which required nothing more than a tempura mix, hot oil and a dipping sauce of soy, wasabi and finely diced parsley, the parsley an essential ingredient in so many of the recipes as a way of neutralizing what the online forums called "cricket breath." And there was another concept for you, and a whole market just waiting to be exploited by the Wrigley Company or the breath-mint manufacturers. What would she say to Frank, "Don't kiss me, I've got cricket breath"? Well, yes, and that was the point, wasn't it? No different from onion breath or garlic breath, or, for that matter, bourbon breath. Sure. And people would move on from there till insect cuisine was as pedestrian and widespread as sushi or oysters on the half shell, just another high-protein food to process through the digestive tract till the residue dropped into the toilet in the morning and got flushed into the sewage system to emerge as fertilizer for plants and trees and the insects that fed on them, insects infinite and various and packed with the essential amino acids that were the foundation of life.

For his part, Frank seemed game enough. He'd been subjected to their son's arguments just as she had, and he agreed with Cooper—and, more importantly, with her—that reducing their carbon footprint was an existential imperative for the whole species, let alone any grandchildren Catherine or Cooper might one day produce, if they were lucky. If she herself was lucky too, because each of us on this earth was the singular end product of millions of years of evolution and she definitely did not want the germ line to die out, not after it had come this far. As for the cookies, she didn't say a word about them because that would have spoiled the experiment—she'd just left them out on the kitchen table, seductively arranged on the Blue Danube platter her mother had handed down to her, which had been handed down from her mother in turn. He came into the kitchen after he got home from the clinic to pour himself his nightly inch of bourbon, no ice, discovered the platter of cookies and was already chewing his second before he thought to ask what the occasion was and she'd said, "I just felt like baking."

On the night of the tacos, though, it was different. He'd been asking her daily about the crickets (*our livestock*, as he invariably referred to them, delighted with the joke the Entomo Farms people had provided him with), bending at the waist to tap on the plexiglass and watch them leap and tumble and pullulate—that was the word, exactly—and wondering when the harvest was due and how many meals she thought it would take to recoup their investment. It was a joke, a further joke, a joke on top of a joke. She waited till they'd finished the meal before asking him how he liked it.

It took him a minute. "Don't tell me that was crickets," he said. He gave her a grin. "Tasted just like chicken to me."

"The *tortillas*." She reached for her wineglass.

"I don't know," he said. "Good. Was that cricket flour?"

She swirled the wine in her glass—a zinfandel Cat and Todd had sent them direct from the winery—then tipped back the glass and finished what was left of it. On the floor, twitching in his sleep, lay the dog, oblivious to the origins of whatever scraps might be coming his way. "I'm thinking of having a dinner party," she said. "Cooper and that girl he's always finding an excuse to talk about, Mari? The one he's been working with at the field station?"

"The acarologist."

"And definitely Peter and Sylvie. We owe them. They've had us over the last two times or—I don't know—more. So I'm thinking six. Keep it small. What do you say?"

"Ticks and mites," he said, tracing the bottom of his wineglass with his thumb. "Little bloodsuckers. That'll make for some great conversation."

"I've only talked to her on the phone—the last time Cooper came home? I'd like to meet her face-to-face." She glanced up, her attention snatched by a silken fluttering at the window—termite alates, attracted to the lamplight before dropping their wings and pairing off so they could have their night of sex and give rise to the next generation. She wondered if she should get up and spray them with something—not Raid, which killed the whole planet, but Windex, which worked just as well and was basically only ammonia and water. Cooper had explained to her that it was the tiny black ant-sized termites she had to worry about, not these big lumbering ocherous things that mainly infested dead stumps out in the yard and emerged each fall to establish new colonies, but still, they *were* termites. And what did termites do? What was their modus operandi? They turned the world to dust—and frass, more frass.

She picked up her glass, saw that she'd left the bottle on the counter, and set it down again. "I think he's serious about her, though of course with him it's always hard to tell."

"*Cuisine d'insectes*," he said. "That ought to be perfect."

"You read my mind."

"You've got the crickets for it, at least. And if you want to serve a tick dish for the guest of honor, you can just pick them off the dog—Jesus knows he's got enough of them."

"Come on, Frank, give me a break," she said, but she said it with a smile.

☀

COOPER'S GIRLFRIEND BARELY CAME UP to his shoulder. She looked too young to have a Ph.D., almost like a teenager, though she was twenty-eight, same age as Cooper. Her father was Phillip Ajioka, a distinguished professor at the university—in economics, not the sciences; she'd looked it up—and so she guessed it ran in the family, which was fine, which was great, and she wasn't prejudiced, not in the least, but if she pictured grandchildren, she pictured height, height above all else. Especially if they turned out to be boys. Was she getting ahead of herself? Had it been wise to have a glass of wine—all right, two—while putting the finishing touches to things? Was her mind careening all over the place? Maybe. Maybe so. She was no Mrs. Dalloway. Or maybe she was, come to think of it.

The two of them came early, before Frank got home from his office, and while the dog fawned and tail-thumped and spun round their legs in tighter and tighter circles, Mari managed to say, "Nice to finally meet you," and handed her two big green sweating bottles of what turned out to be chilled sake. "I hope this'll be okay? I have to confess your son sort of gave away what cuisine we're having tonight, and I just thought, well, we could pair these with it?"

"Absolutely," she heard herself say, though she'd already picked out wines to go with each of the three courses, not that it mattered all that much—but sake, the notion of it, that was inspired. If it went well with sushi, with *ebi* and spicy crab roll and lobster *maki*, then it should be the perfect complement to the *chapulines* she was planning on serving as finger food, not to mention the fritters she'd made from her own livestock and the entrée of mescal-worm tacos, the segmented bodies of which she was planning on disguising with shredded lettuce and a creamy chipotle sauce. And if anybody asked, she'd call them *gusanos*, which had to sound more appetizing than worms. Or better yet, go French: *les vers*.

The dog chuffed and grunted and flopped over on his back as Cooper bent to thump his belly and rib cage for him, stirring up dust, unfortunately, but then one of the primary functions of dogs was to transport dirt and communicate it to the people they liked best. Which she was all in favor of—the epidemic of allergies and asthma in children these days was largely attributable to the antiseptic environments they were raised in. One immunologist she'd read about offered a simple three-word prescription, "Get a dog." At any rate, Mari didn't seem to mind. She smiled. "I've got two dogs myself."

Ottilie said it again, "Absolutely," though it struck her in the next moment as a howling non sequitur, and so she covered herself by saying, "They're making an insect-based kibble for dogs now, did you hear about that?"

Mari nodded. "Yeah, I've heard about it. Anything to spare the cows, right?"

And then once more: "Absolutely."

The *chapulines* were a hit. She made no attempt to disguise them—grasshoppers, from which she'd removed the wings and legs, then fried in oil in which she'd previously sautéed garlic, onions, serrano chiles and cilantro. Simplest thing in the world. Pat them with a paper towel to soak up the excess oil, upend them over a serving bowl, sprinkle with salt, add a squeeze of lime and set them out on the table next to the twin ice buckets, one of which contained a California viognier the girl at BevMo! had been high on, and the other Mari's *onikaroshi* sake, and forget pretzels or potato chips or even crudités with a dip, because here you were getting not only a unique food experience (with a satisfying crunch and a nutty flavor, like pistachios, or better yet, cashews), but a protein boost too. Which was what she told Sylvie as they stood there under her Kichler chandelier, balancing wineglasses on their palms.

Sylvie was wearing a black cocktail dress and a pair of opal earrings Ottilie had given her for her birthday. "Yes," she said, "I see your point. And they're good, very good, don't mistake me, but they are insects, after all, and who really wants to eat insects? Unless you have to. In

France . . ." she said, and Ottilie tuned her out. When she came back to the conversation Sylvie was talking about the fires up north and how the only truism seemed to be that things always got worse. She almost said, "Absolutely," but then caught herself.

At dinner—she'd made a salad of escarole and home-grown cherry tomatoes for balance—she was enjoying the fact that both Sylvie and Peter, having got by the *chapulines*, didn't seem to realize that the fritters were cricket-based and the tacos, which they both had second portions of, were not *tacos del mar* but *tacos de la tierra* and that what they took to be bay shrimp were not bay shrimp at all. Of course, Cooper and Mari were in on it, but she didn't feel obligated to broadcast the news in the least because this was the truest test—taste—and if there was any hope of feeding the nine-point-seven billion mouths the planet would have to support by 2050, then everybody was not only going to have to get used to this sort of cuisine, but enjoy it, relish it, crave it, right? Wasn't that right?

Frank was the one who gave it away. In the interval between the time everybody had pushed their plates to the side and she got up to put the coffee on and bring in the liqueurs—and her cricket cobbler—he raised a glass of sake and proposed a toast. "To the bugs of the world! May they keep on stuffing our tacos and *frittering* our fritters!"

Peter, a steady and committed drinker, raised his glass, but then slowly lowered it again, as if he couldn't decide what to do with it. He looked to Frank, then her. "You mean—?"

She could foresee taking them all out to the kitchen to marvel over the cricket reactor and to lecture them too, but not yet. She just gave first Peter, then Sylvie, her best enigmatic smile, and said, "Dessert, anyone?"

THE PATIO WAS STREWN WITH wind-borne debris when she slapped through the screen door for her morning swim. She'd gone to bed not long after the party broke up and though the winds had evidently raked the property and rattled the windows through the course of the night, she'd managed to sleep straight through. Mercifully. It was calm now, cloudless, the sky pushed back to its limits. Leaves crunched underfoot, twigs, oak galls, eucalyptus buttons and whatever else was light enough for the wind to displace. Her method was just to plunge in, though lately, with nights in the low fifties, the water had gotten unforgivingly cold and she'd begun to think again of installing a heater, though it was wasteful in the extreme, burning through twice or three times the natural gas of even the furnace she was reluctant to turn on except to take the chill off the house on winter mornings, especially when it was raining, but then it hadn't rained in so long she'd practically forgotten what rain was. She and Frank had talked about installing solar panels, which would cut their dependence on fossil fuels, which in turn would please Cooper, who'd been badgering them about it since he was a teenager, and the electricity could be used, at least in part, to heat the pool, couldn't it? Win-win? She thought maybe she'd phone a couple of installers after breakfast, at least to get a price.

This morning, though, no matter the temperature of the pool, she couldn't go in without first clearing all the crap off the surface, a job she hated, though she was too independent to hire a pool man, which was also a ridiculous waste when she could just do it herself—and he wouldn't have been here now anyway, would he? A branch from some sort of tree she didn't even recognize was propped up on the coping at the far end, its leaves half-submerged, and a ball of tumbleweed was jammed up under the diving board. The filter basket was choked and the glaze of debris on the surface was so interwoven and continuous it looked as if somebody had backed a dump truck up to the pool overnight and filled it in. She took a broom to the patio, then started the process of flinging the skimmer net out to the limit of its telescoping pole and dragging it back across the surface of the pool, maneuvering it like a twirler with a supersized baton, scooping and dipping till her upper arms ached. When finally she was done, it was past nine and the sun was high enough to make her sweat under the arms, so she stripped down to her two-piece, steeled herself, and dove in.

It was a shock. For the first few frantic strokes she couldn't catch her breath, but after the second lap her body adjusted and by the third her circuits were flooded with the dopamine rush swimming always gave her and her mind drifted away. She thought of everything and nothing, her arms digging, her feet churning, and then Mari's face floated up in her consciousness and she was back at the party. At one point, setting down his half-eaten taco to pat his lips with his napkin, Frank had turned to Mari and mentioned that he was seeing more tick bites among his patients than usual, especially for this time of year, and wouldn't that have been more prevalent in spring? Had she noticed any—and he couldn't resist the pun—*uptick* in their populations lately?

Mari laughed. She was pretty enough, Ottilie supposed, with her standard-issue straight black hair and big liquid eyes that always seemed trained on you as if you were the single significant point in the room, the kind of girl who might have been a rare beauty but for her buck teeth and a tendency to slouch, which, unfortunately, made her seem even shorter. Not that it mattered. If Cooper liked her, if he liked her doll-like hands and feet and the way her lips were perpetually parted by those protruding teeth, then that was his taste. She was bright, obviously. She had a sense of humor. She liked bugs.

Mari said, "Not that I've noticed, but you're right, this low humidity does tend to stress them. They need moisture. They thrive on moisture."

"Which is why they like us, right?" Sylvie put in. "We're just big sacks of water, aren't we?"

"And blood," Frank said. "And yes, my friends, I don't just tap knees and peer into ears and strap on the blood-pressure cuffs, I perform tick-ectomies too." He let out a laugh. "You'd be surprised."

"It's the white-footed mouse," Mari said. "That's the major host, not the deer, so *deer tick* is really a misnomer. We've trapped some out at the reserve that had as many as a hundred *Ixodes* nymphs on them. The black-legged tick? The one that carries Lyme? Which can represent a serious blood loss in a creature that weighs less than an ounce."

"Black-legged tick, white-footed mouse," Frank said. "Sounds like they were made for each other."

Nobody laughed, but it was funny. Frank was funny. The more he saw of the world, of his patients, of disease, the funnier it all seemed. Cooper looked pleased with himself. This was just the sort of conversation he relished, and it gave Mari a chance to shine. "Parasites," Ottilie said, as if she'd been musing on them all evening. "How did you ever get into parasites, instead of, oh, I don't know, beetles or butterflies or something?"

Mari shrugged. "I guess I just like bloodsuckers."

The water was cold, but cold was what she had and what she wanted because it made her come alive, and though her face was numb and her hair a sodden flail beating at her shoulders, she kept going. She was aiming for fifty laps, and she wasn't just swimming for recreation but to keep her weight in check, which tended to be a problem no matter what she ate, insect-based or not. Unfortunately, she almost always lost count, her mind in another place altogether, so when she thought she'd reached fifty she added one more just in case, then heaved herself up out of the pool and took a moment to sit there in the sun, her feet in the water still, and let her body decompress.

She watched a lizard chase another up the side of the fence. A dragonfly hovered over the diving board like a red spike driven into the air. Two tiny yellow-cheeked birds flitted across the coping to snatch a drink from the filter basket at the far end of the pool, their heads dipping and snapping back again till they sprang into the air and shot away. She looked down at her feet, distorted by the lens of the water, kicked out her legs and flexed her toes. She'd done her toenails for the party in Dior Vernis, the brightest shade of red she could find, but wound up wearing closed-toe heels, so nobody saw them anyway. Except Frank. In bed. And he was asleep and snoring before he'd had a chance to get much of a look, if he was even interested.

She might have sat there longer, feeling good, feeling blessed, but the mechanical world suddenly flared up on her, somebody's car alarm walloping to life out on the street and a leaf blower rising to a screech in the exact same moment, as if they'd timed it. Reluctantly, she pushed herself up, toweled off, then crossed the patio to the back door, where the dog sat watching her, his nose pressed to the glass. She was going to feed him, then make herself some scrambled eggs and toast—sliced from a loaf of sourdough from the local bakery where they used standard insectless flour, because balance was everything and she wasn't about to become a fanatic. Or not yet, anyway.

Though it was Saturday, Frank had gone into the clinic to try to catch up on his paperwork. His PA had quit on him during the latest surge of the pandemic, and while the replacement—a girl all of twenty-three years old—seemed to be working out, the backlog was crushing and Frank was doing what he could to help her catch up. So the house was quiet save for the percussion of the dog's nails on the kitchen tiles as she fetched his dish and went to the broom closet to plunge it into the forty-two-pound bag of Purina Dog Chow, "with real chicken," she kept there. She liked the assurance of "real chicken"—what was the alternative, ersatz chicken? non-chicken chicken?—but of course whatever it was it just kept the slaughterhouses in business. She'd ordered two bags of insect kibble from a company called Cricket Concern, which the company assured her was on the way and had been on the way for something like two weeks now, which made her wonder just how reliable they were. The dog—Dunphy—regarded her with patient eyes as she mashed one of the leftover fritters into the kibble for the extra protein, then set the dish down on the floor beside his water bowl and went to the refrigerator for the eggs.

That was when it came to her that the house wasn't just quiet—it was without a soundtrack altogether. The Japanese, or at least some of the Japanese, or so she'd read, traditionally kept caged crickets in their homes for the comfort of their music, a way of isolating nature when nature itself was in retreat. She'd been charmed by the notion. The buzzing and chirruping of the reactor was a plus as far as she was concerned, though for the first few days Frank had complained about it, pro forma. And now, suddenly, the crickets had gone mute.

She bent at the waist to study the plexiglass farm. Whereas before the crickets had been in perpetual motion, a film clip of furious unceasing activity, now they lay still. Puzzled, she unscrewed the top and reached a hand inside. None of the insects vaulted out of the way or clung to her fingers and she saw the reason in that moment, even as she turned over the egg cartons at the bottom and sifted through the scraps of wet newspaper she'd laid there to provide them with moisture. They were dead, that was the problem. Every one of them. Hundreds of them. Dead.

There was a hand in her throat making itself into a fist. The morning collapsed around her, light puddling on the floor as if it had nowhere else to go. She didn't feel sorry for the crickets or the waste of money or even the fate of the natural world, but for herself, only that.

3

FIELD STUDY

MARI WAS DRESSED ALL IN WHITE—LONG-SLEEVED SHIRT buttoned to the collar, white jeans tucked into white sweat socks and secured with rubber bands, a Panama hat with a white strap tied in an exaggerated bow under her chin. She'd put her hair up in a topknot so that only the odd strand, animated by the breeze, poked out from under the brim of the hat, jumping and flailing at her ears. Her backpack was vanilla-colored. Her sunglasses had white frames. The only items she was wearing that weren't white were her hiking boots.

Cooper eased down beside her on the split-log bench out front of the field station. He could feel the blood whispering through his veins, quickening now with the anticipation he always felt when he was about to go into the field, an anticipation intensified by her presence, by the smell of sage and sunbaked dirt drifting across the field to him, not to mention the two lattes that were fueling it all. He was going to have to piss. Coffee did that to him, the surest diuretic, but he would hold it till they were out of sight of the building and he could contribute his waste fluids to the soil and save the 1.28 gallons of water the toilet consumed per flush.

"You're slipping, aren't you?" he said, pointing to her boots. "Strictly speaking, shouldn't they be white too?"

You wore white in the field so you could spot the ticks on your clothing and intercept them before they got more intimate with you, and even then you had to rely on your visual acuity, because the nymphs were no bigger than so many grains of cracked pepper. To that end, he was dressed in neutral colors himself, bleached-out blue jeans that had been patched in both cheeks and an old dress shirt he had no use for anymore.

"White hiking boots? That must be some kind of oxymoron." She was spraying an organic insect repellent around the uppers of both boots, her face locked in concentration. "And Kuru doesn't make white anyway, so I had to settle for these."

"What are they, yellow?"

"Yellow? You are so naïve, my friend—no apparel company would ever call anything just plain yellow. Who's going to buy yellow? How sexy is that?" She handed him the bottle to apply to his own boots, which were just boots, cracked and worn and the color of dead leaves. "These are GoldenWheat, of course, all one word. Trademarked, I'm sure."

"So you're saying I don't have a future in marketing?"

"Sorry to disappoint you," she said.

They were in that stage of their relationship, four months in now, where everything she did, every motion—the tilt of her head, the way the tendons worked in her wrists as she reached down to slip her boots back on, the clench and release of her lips when she spoke and breathed and smiled and frowned—screamed sex at him. "Damn," he said. "Now what I am going to do in life?"

"My advice? Stick to bugs."

❉

THE WIND HAD BLOWN THROUGH the night and leached every-thing of moisture. There was a tree down in the oak grassland out back of the station, not an oak but an invasive eucalyptus, trees notorious for shattering—and burning. Mari called them candles. "There's another candle down," she said as they skirted coyote brush and toyon and cut through the high grass, chaff and seedpods clinging to their pants, boots crunching, the hot breath of the planet roaring in their faces. He was sweating. His throat was already dry. His skin itched. "What fun!" he said, throwing it out there just to see where it would land, then stopped to piss on the bones of the dead tree.

Mari had no comment. She kept walking, her legs dividing the light in neat triangles, the grass fanning out at her heels, the only sound the faintest rumor of a jet threading its way through the distant arch of the sky. Lashed to the top of her pack were the two rolls of white flannel and the bamboo poles they would use to fashion their drags. Bug collecting. It was as low-tech as you could get—attach cloth to poles, drag through vegetation, pluck off ticks with forceps and secrete in two-millimeter vials containing one hundred percent ethanol, then head back to the lab. Or bed. Or wherever else you wanted to go, like the tavern at the top of the pass where there would be a band and danc-ing and a more potable blend of alcohol. Inside the pack were a bota bag of wine, two cheese, avocado and alfalfa-sprout sandwiches, her collecting kit and a top she was planning on changing into when they got back. His own pack contained a farrago of things that might come in handy whenever he picked it up and wherever he was going—his kill jars for lepidoptera (you never knew what was going to turn up, even though this was Mari's show today), his net, binoculars, canteen, snakebite kit, field knife, compass, a change of socks that should have been changed out six months ago, sunblock, duct tape, a bottle of nail polish remover for killing specimens and the shredded remnants of a geologic survey map or two.

They were going to conduct their drag today on one of the grids Mari had been sampling weekly since the first of the year, doing a population count, after which she would select a few of the adults and nymphs to test for Lyme and whatever else they might be carrying. Today's sector lay three miles northeast of the field station, in the foothills of the San Rafael Mountains, which rose up abruptly in a long dark wedge of Jurassic rock that ran north for fifty miles. He shook himself off, zipped his fly and hurried to catch up with her.

By the time he came abreast of her he was sweating from the effort and though he wanted to make a joke about abandonment and Porta-Potties or whatever else popped into his head, he just fell into rhythm beside her and they walked on in silence till they were nearly into the chaparral that wrapped itself like a collar around the base of the ridge. "Just up there," she said, pointing. "You know the spot." She turned to give him a glance from under the brim of her hat, which pulsed and flapped in the wind, making a light show of her face. "I liked your mother," she said.

"I like her too," he said. "Sometimes."

"It was cute the way she was trying out her recipes—and the look on the one guy's face, what was his name?"

"Peter."

She let out a laugh. "That was worth the price of admission."

"It was. And I give her credit for trying."

"The tacos were respectable, good actually—and the fritters were, I don't know, *fritters*."

"She calls them critter fritters."

"A little greasy, didn't you think? But the cricket cobbler, wow. Of course, anything with that much sugar in it and a big glob of whipped cream . . ."

His phone had buzzed in his pocket on the way to the field station that morning and though his instinct was to ignore it he saw that it was his mother calling and picked up. "They all died," she said.

"Who?"

"My crickets. I went into the kitchen after my swim and there were all these shiny black corpses. And to think we ate them."

"Probably CPV—cricket paralysis virus? It's not going to hurt us, only the crickets. And I thought the breeders were using the Jamaican subspecies now, which are supposed to be immune?"

"Sylvie called. Peter was vomiting all night."

"Is he allergic to shellfish? That could be it, because Mari and I are fine. Mom, the whole meal was really, I don't know, three stars."

There was silence over the line. Then her voice came back to him: "What am I going to do now, though? I've already invested in the reactor, but more than that, it was the idea of it. It made me feel good about myself. As if I was doing my part."

"I wouldn't use it again for crickets, no matter how much you scrub it, because the pathogen that causes the disease could linger there and you'd just go through the whole thing over again. My advice? Why not go with mealworms?"

"Aren't they for fish bait—or what, feeding your pet lizard?"

"Less chitin, more meat, and they don't make any noise. They're shrimpier, like the mescal worms you put in the tacos last night. And they're not susceptible to any colony disorders, not that anybody knows of, anyway. Think about it."

"It's only bugs, right?"

"Right," he said. The onus was on him, since he was the one who'd talked her into it in the first place. "Only bugs."

He was striding through the grass, appreciating the way sun and shadow played alternately over Mari's face, but at the same time watching out of the corner of his eye for moths and butterflies, though he didn't expect much with this wind. And the monarchs, where were they? This was the time of their fall migration and though he and Jerry

Brickman, his dissertation adviser, hadn't conducted the annual transect yet, he'd seen precious few of them. Which was beyond worrisome,
considering they were reaching the point of no return, one more species sinking into the void, their numbers down ninety-seven percent
over the last forty years—what was he going to study when the only
specimens were the ones mounted on frames in museum galleries?
Or worse, private collections? The thought depressed him and so he
stopped right there in the middle of the field while the sun blasted him
and the wind sucked the moisture out of his pores and made his eyes
sting. He waited till she turned to see what was keeping him. "What
did you do with all my butterflies?" he demanded, trying to be funny
when it wasn't funny at all.

"It's just the wind," she said.

"I hate the wind."

"Me too. And the ticks probably aren't that crazy about it either."

THEY WOUND UP EATING THE sandwiches and passing the bota bag
in the car as they climbed back up out of the valley. The field trip had
been a loss, the wind flapping the drags like banners and flinging dirt in
their faces till the uselessness of what they were doing became apparent
and they turned round and headed back. Mari recorded zero specimens,
but zero was a viable number too, if not all that illuminating. After that,
things began to look up—no matter what the ticks' itinerary was, he
was taking her to the tavern. To dance. And drink. And worry about
nothing but being alive in the moment. Saturday. Saturday afternoon
on planet earth.

The sandwich was in his lap, the radio cranked. He squirted wine
down the back of his throat with one hand, steered with the other,
manipulating the sandwich as best he could. The switchbacks sprang
up and ducked away, gusts rattled the windows, windblown debris
crunched beneath the tires. He'd sweated through his shirt, his throat

was thick with phlegm and his nose running from some sort of allergic reaction kicked into gear by all the dust he'd breathed in, and what
he was picturing was something cold and celebratory—rum and Coke,
plenty of ice, served up in a plastic cup, though he thought he might have
a beer just for the immediate slaking action of it, even if it too would be
delivered in plastic, since glass had proven problematic for the management of this particular establishment over the years.

He parked on the dirt shoulder between a pickup and a Porsche,
then he took hold of Mari's hand and they crossed the road, went up
the two worn steps and into the cool shadowy interior of the bar, where
it felt ten degrees cooler than out in the lot. The appeal here was rus-
ticity and the take-it-or-leave-it attitude that went with it. There was
no table service, that was part of the charm, just line up at the bar, get
your drinks and either squeeze into one of the six inside booths or carry
them to the blistered picnic tables just outside the propped-open door.
Everything was finger-greased, even the floors. Stumbling had occurred.
Fights. Droppage. Hence, the plastic, and forget the Pacific Gyre and the
polymerization of petroleum pumped out of the earth and the fact that
recycling was in its death throes. You want a drink? Here's your cup.

The band was one that played here on a rotating basis and it featured
a female guitarist who wrestled the neck of her instrument between her
legs and flipped it over her back because she was a showman ("*Woman*,
Mari corrected him, "a show*woman*") and because she had to have been
bored with the rock and blues standards she must have played sixty thousand times in waking life and another sixty thousand in her dreams. Still,
the whole point was to kick back and dance, the world gone Dionysian
after the long bleak pandemic lockdowns, and the rhythm was all that
counted. She had a bass player who must have been sixty, white-bearded,
with a skull shaved down to a patchwork scalp like something out of a
medical text, and though he barely moved, he stepped into the chords
as if he were going up and down a flight of stairs, endlessly rebounding
the beat till whatever song it was fell off in the clobber of drums that
signaled it was over. The drummer was another woman, also older—old,

actually—and she hammered the beat right into your pores while you stomped and flailed and sweated, and what else could anybody want?

Mari, dancing, compacted her gestures, getting a maximum of action out of a minimum of effort, while he was riding a pogo stick launched by the wine and now the rum. He circled her, twirled her, clasped her to him and thrust her away, thumped off people's backs and flailed his elbows as if he were trying to fly. He was all rhythm, no mind, which was just the way it should be. On the slow songs, he clutched her to him as if he could mold her flesh and remake her bones. He caught a whiff of the stale ashes in the big fieldstone fireplace at the far end of the room, the spills of gin and spiced rum on the bartop, barbecue potato chips, the shampoo she'd used on her hair that morning, and he closed his eyes, locked in sync with her, the heartbeat of the bass rocking them back and forth in a slow sweet shuffle. When the band took a break, it didn't seem right, everything falling away into the absence of that last ringing chord, but bands took breaks, that was the way the world worked, so he scooped up their drinks and steered her out the door and into the dirt lot under the shade of the trees.

"You know, all things considered, I wouldn't mind being a tick," he said, staking claim to the first unoccupied table. "I'm serious," he said, giving her a grin as she slid in beside him. "No work, no worries. You just sit there and wait for a meal to come along."

She was still wearing her hat, the white jeans and hiking boots. She'd gone into the ladies' and changed out the long-sleeved shirt for the Lycra top she'd brought along in her backpack. It featured alternating bands of red, pink and black. "My rock-and-roll top," she'd proclaimed, doing a little spin so he could appreciate it. "Or maybe R&B, call it R&B." Now she tipped her plastic cup to him and said, "Good for you. But be prepared to starve to death. Don't forget, your whole existence is based on luck—and over the course of your lifetime you have to find three hosts to get through metamorphosis. Most ticks starve to death."

"And yet there they are," he said, "as predictable as anything else. You start with a life-form that makes its own food through photosynthesis, which leaves a niche for something to come along and eat it, which leaves a niche for something to eat whatever eats it and then, as if anything's going to go to waste, you get the parasites to complete the circle. And parasitoids for the parasites. And the Lyme spirochete going along for the ride."

"Evolution in all its glory," she said, and gave him a bucktoothed grin that made him think of nothing so much as reproduction in his own species. He touched his glass to hers, plastic to plastic.

"You up for another round?" he asked, already rising from the table.

The sun was in the trees. People shuffled back and forth, murmured, lifted their drinks, laughed. And she was there, right there, poised over her elbows in her rock-and-roll top, smiling up at him, a snapshot of everything right with the world. He was feeling no pain. And if by the time they were ready to leave his blood-alcohol level was above the 0.08% California law allowed, he'd just follow the weekend bikers down the hill and let the cops sort them out while he slipped right on by, herd-protected.

When he got back with the drinks, there was a couple sitting across from her, the guy in a denim jacket and a Dodgers cap, the girl in a long lime-green dress and calf boots. The girl was saying, "And they have to be attached for how long?"

Mari glanced up at him as he set the drinks on the table and settled in beside her, then turned back to the girl. "Twenty-four hours. Minimum. When they feed, the bacterium migrates into their salivary glands, which is how it gets in you. They puke, actually, and that's where the transfer happens."

"That's disgusting," the girl said. "My daughter—Macy?—she had one on the back of her neck, but there was no bull's-eye, it's got to be a bull's-eye, right? So we really just pulled it off and threw it in the toilet, though Jeff"—here she looked to the guy—"said you're supposed to hold a match to them till they back out, but I just couldn't do that to my daughter—"

"Okay, fine, but the bull's-eye isn't infallible. Just remember you're not going to have a problem with Lyme unless you don't notice it from thirty-six to as much as forty-eight hours. But listen"—she dug in her purse and came up with one of the stamped, self-addressed envelopes she carried with her everywhere—"do me a favor? Any tick you find, whether it's on you or your daughter or your dog or cat, just stick it to a piece of Scotch tape and drop it in here. It's part of a survey? We want to know what species are where."

He was going to interject a joke here, just to lighten things up, because not everybody was necessarily as fixated on arachnid parasites as she was and he didn't want her to come across as a science nerd, or not exclusively, but he didn't have the chance because one of the weekend bikers sitting at the next table over gave out with a sudden curse, jumped to his feet and began jerking round in a tight circle, kicking up dust and gravel with the heels of his boots. He kept reaching over one shoulder in a furious backward brushing motion and slapping at his forearm at the same time. "Motherfucker," he sobbed in a high corkscrewing wail while the woman who'd been sitting next to him—rings, tattoos, leathers—sprang up herself. "Oh, shit," she said, "not again."

"The fucking EpiPen. For fuck's sake, where's my fucking EpiPen?"

Everybody near them, forty or fifty people, including the bouncer, who'd positioned himself on a stool outside the door to check IDs and take surreptitious sips from a flask, began swatting at the air, alternately cursing and shouting. "Yellowjackets," Mari said, tipping back her cup even as the couple across from them leapt up, windmilling their arms. He was about to concur with her assessment, the scent of charred meat rising from the grill in the courtyard enough to inflame every *Vespula* wasp within a radius of half a mile, but then he caught himself. A blur had appeared, a swelling blur of motion that was suddenly affixed to the crotch of a branch overhanging the roof of the bar, humming, buzzing, rapidly accreting. "It's a swarm," he said, and she said, "This time of year?" and then they were both on their feet.

Behind them, the woman was shouting for a doctor—"Call an ambulance, for Christ's sake, somebody call an ambulance!"—but that scene would play itself out in a way that didn't involve him, whether the EpiPen turned up or not or one of the bikers was a doctor in disguise or the ambulance made the half-hour trip up the winding road in record time or something a whole lot grimmer intervened, anaphylactic shock, asphyxiation, death. There was nothing he could do about it. He wasn't his father. He'd never saved anybody from anything and hoped he'd never have to. But the bees, that was another story. The bees he knew.

THE CARDBOARD BOX—DOUBLE-WEIGHT, imprinted with the logo of a produce company—he found in a pile of trash out back of the building, along with the plastic milk jug he was going to need for a scoop, but he didn't pick them up, not yet, because he was busy shoving his way through the back door and into the kitchen, looking for a brush, a broom, a dustpan, anything he could manufacture into a tool for the task at hand. He was in a state, but it wasn't the biker he was concerned about or the possibility of other people getting stung or who was allergic and who wasn't—it was the bees he wanted. Honeybees. Free for the taking.

His eyes ransacked the room: industrial-sized pots set like stones on a blackened gas range, stainless steel refrigerator, the sink, the dishes, pans hanging from hooks twisted into the ceiling—and a flyswatter, which he considered and rejected in the same moment. Bent over the sink, splashing water on his face, was a big-bellied man he took to be the chef, and just beyond him, in the corner, leaning up against a calendar featuring a naked woman in a snowdrift tipping a cocktail the exact color of her nipples toward the camera, was a push broom. He leaned in and grabbed it, even as the man at the sink swung round on him, soapsuds drooling from his beard. "Hey, you can't be in here," the man sputtered, "this is—" but he was already out the door.

By this point, the shouting had stopped. Everyone had drawn back in a ragged circle, waiting to see what came next. Bees thickened the air over the table where the biker lay flat out on his back, but the bees weren't interested in him or anybody else—they were coalescing in a bright trembling stream, moving as if magnetized toward the crotch of the branch overhanging the roof, the ball of them swelling and swelling again. A voice announced, "I'm a nurse," and here was a woman in shorts and a T-shirt featuring a bright red lollipop of a heart with the injunction BE KIND superimposed across it, pushing her way through the crowd to bend over the biker, who'd stopped cursing, stopped kicking out his legs, stopped moving.

Cooper unscrewed the flat head of the broom and dropped the handle at his feet. While he'd been enlivening the chef's day, Mari had gone to the car for his backpack, and now he rummaged through it till he found his knife, which he used to cut a rectangular hole an inch high in the face of the box. Then he hacked the bottom out of the jug to fashion his scoop and dropped the knife back in his pack. "You're going to need gloves," Mari said, but he waved her off. "My hat," she said, "take my hat at least."

There was no sound yet of the ambulance. The bees hovered, jays shot through the trees like flung stones, a kid who might or might not have been stung was howling at the fringe of the crowd while his mother pressed him fast to her thighs. Everybody was watching the nurse, who'd stuck her fingers in the biker's mouth to clear his tongue and begun pumping his chest in a steady practiced rhythm. The bees were no longer a problem—and if the biker hadn't slapped the one that landed on his arm they probably wouldn't have been in the first place. They were interested in one thing only—finding a confined place to construct a new hive, and if that turned out to be a cardboard produce box, at least temporarily, so much the better. Why they were swarming this late in the season, unless their hive had been disturbed, was a mystery. Maybe it had fallen off the back of a truck when a beekeeper was moving his hives down into the valley to overwinter or the gusts had toppled the snag the bees had been living in. No matter—here they were and he was going to get them.

"I'm going to need a ladder," he said, turning to Mari. He didn't have time to worry about how ridiculous he must have looked in her hat, which was two sizes too small—it would keep him from getting stung on the crown of his head and offer at least some protection for his face, and that was the best he could do at the moment. "You see a ladder anywhere?"

The bass player was standing in the doorway of the tavern, blinking out into the light. "What is it?" he murmured. "Heart attack?" Distantly, chopped into segments by the baffle of the switchbacks, came the first ricocheting wail of a siren. The nurse, exhausted, stepped back from the biker and a skeletal man in leathers took over for her, pumping in a hard cyclic way, up and down, up and down.

"What about one of these tables?" Mari pointed to the table where their drinks stood like artifacts and half a dozen disoriented honeybees, wings folded back, crept uncertainly over the weathered surface. "Could we move it up against the wall? Would that work?" And then, to the bass player, "Would you mind giving us a hand here?"

Perched atop the table, Cooper was no more than two feet below the bright boiling mass caught up on the tree limb, close enough to do what he had to do. Mari handed him the box and he flipped open the top and set it down on the roof an arm's length from the swarm, then braced himself for the stings to come. Wielding the brush with his left hand and the improvised scoop with his right, he made a quick plunge into the heart of the swarm, came up with a ball of bees which he hoped contained the queen, and dumped it into the box, then immediately made a second plunge and a third, brushing the excess insects into the scoop as best he could. He was stung immediately, stung repeatedly, of course he was, but he didn't have a bonnet or a smoker or gloves or a deluxe polycotton bee suit to protect him, stung on his hands, his face, through his shirt, yet he kept at it till the better part of the swarm was in the box, the four flaps of which he shut on them even as he flung away his tools and leapt down from the table.

He was the focal point now and everybody was watching him as if he were a geek in a sideshow, which wasn't far from the truth, and when he was back down at their level and the bees were in the box and more pouring in through the opening he'd fashioned, a spatter of applause started up and swept through the crowd till it became an ovation. The bass player ducked his patchwork head and said, "Man, you are one crazy motherfucker," and Mari smiled and said, "Well done, you," before slipping into the bar for ice to press to the welts rising on his hands, his neck, his face. Later, in the privacy of his apartment, she would examine him intimately and tally up his battle wounds, which burned and itched under their load of histamines—"Twelve," she would announce, touching each one with her lips. "A nice round number."

At the moment, though, he felt nothing but exhilaration, and he turned to the crowd and took a bow before downing the remains of his rum and Coke and easing onto the tabletop to remove as many of the stingers as he could locate. He'd been stung before. He'd be stung again. When he was twelve he'd kept his own bees and was stung so many times he'd built up a resistance to the venom, but within the year varroa mites killed off his hive and after that he went into a spider phase, then a beetle phase and finally fell under the spell of the lepidoptera that had got him through college and into grad school.

Eventually, the ambulance pulled up out front, the paramedics took charge of the victim, who seemed to be breathing, thankfully, and the band strapped on their instruments and went back to work pounding the blues. Dusk was settling into the trees. Inside, people were dancing again, but he was done dancing for the day. The bartender sent out a round of drinks on the house, which was nice, and for a long while he and Mari sat there at the picnic table, watching as the remnant of the swarm fed itself through the aperture he'd cut into the box. A couple of people stopped by to thank him, and the girl in the green dress called him a hero, a real true hero. He took his time over the drink, relishing the moment. Soon, he would climb up on the table and retrieve the box, secure it with duct tape and carry it to the car. Mari tipped back her beer and set the empty glass down on the table. *"Apis mellifera,"* she said.

"Man's best friend. Except for dogs, but dogs don't make honey, do they?"

"So what are you going to do with them?"

He shrugged. "I was thinking maybe I'd give them to my mother."

IT WAS PAST NINE BY the time they got back to his apartment, which was a converted two-car garage behind a fifties ranch house on a street where you could still see the stars at night. There were only forty-five hundred people in town, though that number swelled with tourists on weekends, but there were no sidewalks or parking meters or other outward manifestations of the madhouse society that was America today, and that suited him just fine. You could breathe the air out here. You could collect insects. Listen to coyotes doing their thing at two a.m. He ordered take-out Chinese and they ate in front of the TV, watching a sci-fi flick about androids who came equipped with genitalia by way of providing their human owners with a sexual outlet in a world so overpopulated people had taken to eating one another just to clear some space. It was a comedy. Or so it seemed. His interest in any future scenario never extended much beyond the setup in any case—what *would* it be like in twenty years, fifty, a hundred? Was there any hope? Or was it all a wasteland? And if so, what kind of wasteland and what lived there?

"Another dystopia," Mari said, delicately pinioning a square of tofu with her chopsticks and lifting it to her lips.

"What else?"

She didn't answer. On the screen, a pair of androids, both female and both with exaggerated figures—tits, that is, enormous tits—chased each other around a track, setting new records for speed with each revolution. It made him think of sex, as it was calculated to do. Mari was spending the night, and in an hour or however much longer they could put up with the movie, they'd be in bed.

He pushed himself up from the couch and took his plate to the kitchen and laid it in the sink, then made a detour into the bathroom to dab another round of calamine on his beestings, which had begun to itch all over again. It wasn't till he was standing in front of the mirror, twisting one shoulder to assess the welts on his back, that he noticed the dark spot on his right forearm, midway between wrist and elbow. His first thought was that it was a mole or a fleck of dried mud, but when he ran a finger over it he felt it tighten its grip and all he could think was, *Mari's going to be pleased.*

4

HIGH TIDE

"IT HAPPENS," HE SAID, "DON'T BEAT YOURSELF UP OVER IT. If I had a hundred bucks for everybody that lost a snake, I'd be down at the dealership buying myself a Tesla like that Model S you guys have. That's my dream car, actually."

It was just past noon, four days after Willie had gone missing. She'd looked all over for him, everywhere she could think of, even the hard-to-access places, like the air-conditioning ducts and the inner rim of the fan in the shower and behind the big top-of-the-line Viking range Todd's mother had installed in the kitchen six months before she died (and which she herself loved, after spending the last five years working around a rusty grease-clogged two-burner the size of a chopping block, not that she did all that much cooking, but still it was a comfort just to have it). He could have gotten into the walls for all she knew. Or outside. There was a discolored spot in the weather stripping beneath the door leading to the deck and when she got down on her hands and knees and put pressure on it with her index finger, it gave way like a flap of wax paper.

"What if he got outside? Is that it? Kiss him goodbye?"

R.J. was wearing a T-shirt that featured a full-color life-sized depiction of a Burmie, its head rising almost to the collar and its coils wrapped around front to back, armpits to waist, as if it were in the act of crushing whoever was wearing it. She loved it. Wanted one for herself. Did he have a stack of them around somewhere, she wondered, part of his sideline, sell people the snake, the tank, the fuzzies—and tees too?

"Pretty much," he said. "I mean, they're real escape artists—all snakes are. If he gets out, he's going to find an environment for himself. Or make one."

"But what about in winter, when you get those cold snaps and the oranges freeze and everybody goes into panic mode? Which, I have to admit, I've never had to deal with yet because we just moved here like three months ago. From L.A.?"

He shrugged. He was giving her a look that was half-amused, half-come-on, and yes, he was scoping her out, his eyes diving down the front of her dress and making no attempt to hide it. Which was fine with her—that was why she'd worn the dress in the first place. She was hoping to negotiate a discount on Willie's replacement—Willie II—and while she knew there were no guarantees when you bought anything alive, whether it was a pet snake or a parakeet or even a houseplant, she felt, very strongly, he'd be sympathetic and do the right thing. He said, "You never know, because the Burmies that've got loose and established themselves are a couple hours south of us, but with global warming and everything moving north, I wouldn't bet against it."

"I just hate to think of him suffering or starving or whatever."

He gave her a grin, full-blown, his eyes sparking and dimples showing, nicest guy in the world. "No worries there. You got rats around the house, lizards—birds, even? He'll eat anything that moves, and that means right on up the scale as he establishes himself in a hole or drainpipe someplace and grows into his adult proportions, because no matter what neighborhood you live in there's always cats and dogs, right? Shih tzus especially. Oh, they love shih tzus."

She grinned back at him, flirting now. "Better than fuzzies, right?

"Right. And you don't have to defrost them."

The shop wasn't as cluttered as it was the first time she'd stopped in, the plexiglass cases mostly gone now and the specimens arranged in terrariums that looked a bit more homey. She saw the balls on display and a few other snake species, but no Burmies. It was just as hot as it had been last time and she was sweating, though outside the temperature was in the low eighties, a preview of winter when the whole state would sink under the weight of the tourists flocking down from the north. Snowbirds, they called them. Practically every shop she went into there was somebody with a Florida twang proclaiming, *The snowbirds are coming*, or *You better pick it up now, honey, before the snowbirds get here*, as if the zombie apocalypse was on the way.

"Okay," she said, "I guess you know why I'm here?"

He kept the grin in place. "I think I can guess. And it's the right move, it is."

She ran a finger over the terrarium nearest her, where a pair of green lizards clung to the glass like refrigerator magnets. "Maybe I missed it," she said, "but I don't see any Burmies out. Have you got any in back, maybe? And this may sound strange because I had him for such a short time but I got attached to him, I did, and I want the nearest thing to him I can get. If he's not coming back, I mean."

"Most likely not," R.J. said, shaking his head from side to side as if to confirm it. "But who knows, he might surprise you. And what's the worst thing that can happen—you wind up with two snakes? Truthfully, snakes can get lonely too."

THE SNAKE HE SHOWED HER was older than Willie, maybe eighteen or twenty inches longer, and fatter around the middle by a good three times, which seemed to her perfect. He had the same dazzling pattern, the same flick of the tongue, the same otherworldly eyes, and if Willie was too small to drape around her neck and have any effect on anybody, this one was ready to wear. (She had to laugh at the thought, as if Burmies were just another accessory, which they weren't, she knew that, but so what? *Prêt-à-porter.*) They were in the back room of the shop, where he had his desk and a couch and the closed-circuit TV she'd known would be there ghosting pictures of the empty store. The desk was a welter of papers, catalogues, invoices, display cases and rolls of packing tape, with a landline phone and a big yellow DeWalt staple gun to anchor it all. Stacked up on shelves against the wall were a dozen or so unlit terrariums infested with dark shadows and across from them, side by side on the concrete floor, were two cages of feeder rodents, mice in one, rats in the other. The smell was compacted in a funk of overripe wood shavings, shit and urine and sweat—or no, maybe not sweat, because rodents didn't sweat, did they?

He'd flicked the light on in one of the terrariums and said, "I've got this one, the only one I have on hand right now, and it's a beautiful snake, as you can see."

It was. And she wanted it.

"To be honest with you," he said, watching her watch the snake, "this is a return. Like a customer bought him six, seven months ago and he's moving out of state, or so he says, so I took him off his hands." He opened the tank from the top, lifted the snake out with his hook and offered it to her. "Go ahead," he said, "let him feel you."

She cupped both hands under his middle, which was the way you were supposed to do it, and eased him from the hook. Like Willie before him, he worked his way up her right arm, then her left as she held it out to him, and finally he coiled himself around her wrist like a big glowing bracelet. "How much?" she asked. "Considering I just bought Willie here four days ago? I mean, shouldn't I rate a discount?"

"How does half-price sound?"

She gave him a smile. Ever so gently, but firmly, because he was all muscle, Willie II tightened his grip on her forearm.

"If you'll let me buy you a drink, that is. You up for a drink?"

She wasn't exactly taken by surprise—there had to be a trade-off, as in any negotiation. Half-price sounded pretty good to her. So did a drink. Todd wasn't going to be happy when he found out about it—the cost, that is—but she already had the setup and the fuzzies, so what did he expect? Besides which, Todd was in Boston, co-hosting an event for the New England Bacardí reps and he hadn't taken her along because the company wouldn't spring for her airfare, which was always first class, the only way Todd would fly, and she figured he owed her. "Sure," she said.

R.J. rocked back and forth on his feet, still holding that smile. "Cool," he said, then lifted a hand and gestured at the couch. "Or maybe you want to just stay here for a while, get acquainted—"

The look she gave him was like a towering red stop sign three stories high because what did he think she was? She was going to put out— for a snake? Maybe he'd got mixed up somewhere there between looking down her dress and drooling over the Tesla in the lot out back, but he was reading her all wrong and she was about half a beat from walking right out the door, snake or no snake, when everything in his face changed and his shoulders drooped till he was one big sack of apology and inoffensiveness and he said, "With the snake, I mean. Willie II, right? Isn't that what you're going to call him?"

HER DRINK WAS A MOJITO, of course, with Flor de Caña, not Bacardí, and within two minutes of sitting down at the bar, and without even asking, Cora set it in front of her. R.J. didn't have to ask either: Cora brought him a Sierra Nevada in the bottle, no glass, and a shot of Patrón Silver.

"How are you, honey?" Cora asked, leaning into the bar on her elbows. "How's that cute little Burmie R.J. set you up with? Are you loving him or what?"

She felt herself choking up—and why she should get emotional over such a trivial thing, especially with Willie II in a cloth bag on the seat of her car in the lot across the street, was totally unaccountable. There was a sadness to life that everybody had to deal with in one way or another, the inevitable sense of loss that crept up on you at the strangest times. She'd glance up at the ceiling fan whirring overhead till it didn't seem real or watch a ray of sun slant through the window in a shower of dust particles and feel as if she were about to break down. Or shadows, the way shadows leaned out away from everything when the sun was going down, the relentlessness of it, day after day, sun and shadow, sun and shadow. Hormones, that was what it was, every human feeling controlled by the drip of chemicals in our bloodstreams, and that included love and hate and everything in between. Prolactin, that was the one. She'd looked it up. And whether she needed Xanax or Ativan was another story because she'd been there and done that. In a small voice, she said, "He got lost."

"Oh, I hear you," Cora said, "but don't give up hope. Tiny? That's my female Mohave? She was gone for three days once and then I came home from work—from here—at like two a.m. and there she was, stretched out on top of the TV. Which was on—and I hadn't left it on."

"Woo-woo-woo," R.J. said, spinning a finger in the air.

"No, I'm positive, I really am."

"Come on, now, don't get all *Twilight Zone* on us. Snakes just live in their own world, that's all, and when we're not around they've got their own agenda. Call it snake life." He paused to sprinkle salt on the webbing of his left hand, then licked it off, knocked back the tequila, and sucked the lime wedge that came with it, his lips drawing back in a grimace over the sting of the citrus. "Anyway," he said, "whether Cat's Burmie shows up again or not, she's got a new one— bigger, better, with as crisp a pattern as you can imagine—out in her car right now."

"Well, good for you," Cora said. "Stick with the agenda, I like that. I'll bet this one lasts till you're my age, what do you say?"

What could she say? You lose something, you replace it—and toast the effort with a mojito. "Yeah," she said, "me too."

There was soccer on the TV, just like last time. Four middle-aged Cuban men in matching gray suit coats came in and took a seat at one of the tables against the far wall and Cora went over to take their orders. R.J. was saying something about a band she'd never heard of and she countered with a band he'd never heard of, which was good, which was fine, just the way it should be, because they could turn each other on in a way that went beyond Spotify and its robotic playlists. It turned out he liked the same sort of things she did, the retro blues and soul a lot of young bands had turned to in the wake of rap saturation. He'd once been in a band himself. Sort of ska meets power pop. Guess what he'd played?

"I don't know," she said, shaking her head. "Bass?"

"Vocalist. I was the front man. We never went anywhere or cut a record or anything, but we could have. It's like what everybody does, right? Like it's an American birthright. What about you—were you ever in a band?"

She loved music. Listened all day every day, especially when Todd was off on one of his trips, but she didn't have an iota of musical talent. She laughed. "I can barely carry a tune."

He winked one eye shut and stared down the neck of his beer bottle, then lifted it to his lips and made a flute of it, tooting a few barrelhouse notes before setting it down and waving for Cora's attention. "You up for another?" he asked.

There was nothing for her at home. She hadn't gotten a job yet, though she had some applications out and was picking up a few little things here and there online, but her ambition was to be an influencer and she was working on building up followers, though it was a slow process, at least so far. She was thinking maybe of coming up with some sort of daily montage that would be like an establishing shot in a movie, as well as a way of showing off where she was living—palm trees, ocean, beach—which to most people was exotic. Exotic sold. But then so did the prosaic, if it was done right. There was one guy who traveled all over the country, and the first thing he posted every morning was what he was going to wear that day—cool outfits, always, just folded over a vacant chair in one hotel room or another, and that became his personal iconography, which got him a sponsorship from Zara. She needed something like that—Willie, maybe. Maybe Willie was the key. Or Willie II, that is. But it was just past three on a day already stacked high with meaningless hours and while she was looking forward to seeing him settle into his new home, which would complete the circle, at least for now, R.J. had assured her he was perfectly fine in the cloth sack, so there was no rush on that score. She shrugged. "Yeah," she said, "I guess so."

"So I was all of nineteen when our guitar player, who'd been my best bud since we were in junior high, quit and moved to San Jose, and that was it for the band," he said, holding up two fingers for Cora, who slipped behind the bar and made them fresh drinks. "It was kind of sad, really, but it worked out okay in the long run because I found my true calling."

"Which is?"

"Snakes. What else have we been talking about?"

Halfway through the second drink, he shifted his stool so their legs were ever so slightly touching. She'd never cheated on Todd and she wasn't going to cheat on him now, but she did bring her face close to his so that his cobalt eyes came soaring to hers like the sky when you come up after a dive in the deep end of a pool. He kissed her. She liked the taste of his tongue. They made out a bit. The soccer players kicked their ball around. In the far corner, two of the Cubans lit cigars, though smoking was prohibited. The question was: One more drink or take Willie II back home?

What came next was a moment of brain freeze, nothing happening on any conscious level. Her ears felt stopped-up. Her body was limp. The music—still jazz, still unidentifiable—tinkled and whined in the background till it brought her back and she found herself staring perplexedly into R.J.'s face as if trying to make out who exactly he was. *Willie II*, her brain told her. *Home. Safety. Wine.* She didn't want to drive drunk, did she? And this had gone far enough, hadn't it?

"You know, R.J.," she said finally, pushing back her stool, "this has been fun, really fun." She rattled the ice around in the bottom of her glass, then finished off her drink. "But really, I've got to go. Todd'll probably be home by now"—she gave him a grin—"and I can't wait to surprise him with Willie II."

THE BAY SPARKED AND GLITTERED in the windshield as she turned off the highway and took the peninsula road to the house. It seemed full right up to the brim, almost on a level with the car itself, and she couldn't help thinking of Todd's joke on the subject, which she'd heard him use on his clients half a dozen times now—"Jesus," he'd say, "I don't know who they're paying to keep the water topped off, but whoever it is they're doing a super job." The problem was flooding, of course. She'd never had to think about rising seas when she was living in the Valley— the whole notion might as well have been lifted from a sci-fi movie—but when you were lucky enough to live on the ocean, it was something you had to be aware of. And she probably should have parked the car up on the ramp Todd had built for it, but she really didn't want to bother because she was just going to go in and relax a minute, and if that was the rum talking, so be it. She was thinking she'd put on some music, pour herself a glass of wine and introduce Willie II to his new habitat. Which would provide her with her entertainment for the evening before she settled in with a Netflix series she was getting addicted to and then maybe she'd call Todd, though he'd probably be right in the middle of his event at that point.

All right. She parked the car by the stairs up to the first floor (the house was raised on pilings five feet high, same as most of the houses on this stretch of beach, which was nice, because it eliminated worry during the extra-high tides that came with the full moon each month), cradled the bag with Willie II inside it and went up to see how the rest of her day was going to go. She loosened the string at the neck of the bag and folded back the flap of material there before laying it carefully on the floor of the terrarium, figuring the snake might be more comfortable if he took his own sweet time to slide out and explore his surroundings. For a good five minutes she waited for that to happen, but he seemed content to stay where he was, so she left him there, with the top closed and all the fasteners secured—and double-checked, thank you very much—and went into the kitchen to pour herself a glass of wine and see what she wanted to microwave for dinner.

She'd had Todd take her to Trader Joe's the week before to pick up a couple of frozen dinners so she wouldn't have to go out and eat alone while he was gone—or cook anything if she didn't feel like it, which she mostly didn't, whether he was home or not. Sipping the wine, she pulled open the freezer door, and the first thing that spoke to her— right there on top, in its neat nut-brown package—was chicken tikka masala, as good a choice as any. Or no, the best. Just what she wanted. She felt her glands clench at the thought of it and realized in that moment she hadn't had anything since her bowl of Catalina Crunch that morning, lunch having been replaced by her two mojitos, which might not have given her all that much nutrition (beyond the mint, that is), but had done wonders for her mood. The wine was helping too, but she needed to put something on her stomach—and here was the solution, three minutes in the microwave, stir the sauce to distribute it, then another ninety seconds and *le dîner est servi*. If only everything in life were that simple.

She pulled over a footstool so she could eat in front of the terrarium and hadn't taken two bites before she was rewarded with the sight of Willie II emerging from the bag. His head was broader than the late Willie's, but of course he was bigger and older, and yet even his colors seemed more striking—or was she misremembering? He did a slow striptease until he was free of the bag and nosing around the enclosure, claiming it for his own, every detail of him, every scale, glowing under the heat lamp as if he were lit from within. She couldn't help congratulating herself on her purchase. She was a snake lady now, no doubt about it. Other women were cat ladies or horse ladies or in the case of biologists like Cooper's new girlfriend, tick ladies. But not her. No, she was a snake lady. Which was cool, *molto* cool. It gave her an identity, which would make her stand out as an influencer, because how many snake ladies could there be out there?

She sat watching the snake as the last of the light closed down over the bay and the pelicans made their way in formation to wherever they went at night, then got up, scraped the remains of her meal into the trash can, poured herself just a touch more wine and sat back down again. She purposely left the overhead lights off so the terrarium was the focal point, shining and swelling till it was a world in itself. All the while the snake roamed tirelessly round his new home, the pointer of his head drawing the long unfurling necklace of his body over the shavings and the hide and the strategically arranged rocks, tongue flicking and flicking, and was he picking up the scent of Willie? Why not? Snakes had an excellent olfactory sense, or so Google had told her.

She thought of calling Todd, but the wine took her out of herself and she forgot all about it until she got up to pour herself another glass and saw her phone lying there on the counter where she'd left it after texting photos of Willie II to her mother. (But not Todd, not yet—Todd she was going to surprise. Again.) If she was drunk, it was his fault. He shouldn't have left her, especially with everything that was going on, though they'd agreed the wedding was going to have to be a pretty basic affair out of respect to his mother, which took some of the pressure off, yes, but they were hardly even settled in yet and she was still navigating Florida and the Floridians and keeping a checklist of how even the simplest things here were totally different from the way they were back at home. Todd kept saying they really had to scale it all back, considering, and she told him she was okay with that. She still wanted to walk the walk in her gown with her bridesmaids and the flowers and decorations and her mother's friend Dr. Lisa Clevenger, the Unitarian minister she'd known since high school, to perform the ceremony, though—even if the reception wound up being in her parents' yard and they'd already pushed back the date out of respect to Todd's mother.

She felt a sudden flare of resentment, slid back the door and went barefoot out onto the deck and into the full blast of tropical funk that smelled like foot odor, like fungus or a bad case of halitosis, everything stinking and rotting. And why was that? Wasn't the ocean supposed to smell clean? Was it another red tide, was that it? Or something washed up dead under the pilings, which had already happened twice since they'd moved in, the first time a manatee that was like a huge fat man in a rubber suit and then a shark, she thought it was, seething there under a scrum of crabs till the tide came in the night to carry it away. She threw her head back to look up at the stars, but there were no stars. Just haze. Fog. Whatever. The first couple of mosquitoes came out to welcome her and she slapped them, hard, harder than she had to, and maybe she got one of them and maybe not. She slid back the door, stepped inside and slammed it shut.

Willie II, apparently satisfied with his explorations, was lying there quietly, bunched up on himself, watching her. She watched him back, interspecies surveillance, rocking to and fro on the twin pillars of her legs, and then she loosened the fasteners, lifted him out and went into the bathroom with him to see how he looked against her skin and the dress she was still wearing because she hadn't bothered to change yet. It wasn't really the right color—a black-and-white zigzag from H&M—and she thought maybe a solid color, plain black or maybe even an earth hue, green or beige? She set him down in the tub where he immediately began snaking around—how about that, a snake *snaking* around?—and went to the closet to try on a couple outfits, which wasn't a problem at all because each time she came back in and wrapped him around her shoulders, he was compliant, if not downright sluggish, his head weaving in the slowest of slow motion on one side, tail just barely twitching on the other. The thought came to her that there might be something wrong with him—she wasn't going to have to take him back to R.J. and ask for her money back, was she? But no, she told herself—he was fine, just calm, that was all. One cool snake. Which was what she'd been looking for to begin with, a snake she could wear round her neck without having to worry about him.

The best look, as she'd suspected, was black, her satin off-shoulder top with black jeans, and maybe she might want to go with a pair of gold heels to match his markings. How much time passed, she didn't know, but somewhere along the line she got out her phone and snapped a few photos, and then, since it was right there in her hand, she called Todd.

"Hey," he said, picking up on the first ring. There were party sounds in the background, live music, cocktail murmur, the braying laugh of somebody drunk on Bacardí.

"I miss you," she said. Willie II looped a coil round her neck and she gently removed him and laid him back in the tub, where he began exploring all over again.

"Yeah," he said. "Me too. But no worries. I'll be home day after tomorrow, right? You'll be there for the flight—four p.m., Delta?"

She didn't answer. Of course she'd be there—what did he think, she was going to forget?

"So who's at the party?" she asked. "What's it like?"

"You know. The usual. A fairly young crowd, though, which is cool."

"You wearing your tuxedo?"

"Yeah. It's that level. Stirred, not shaken, you know?"

"I'm jealous."

"No worries. Actually it's kind of"—and here came a female voice drifting into range, cloying, annoying, floating high on free rum and canapés and the sense of entitlement that comes with the full treatment, saying, *Todd, that is like so delicious; what's in it again?*—"I don't know, kind of boring." And then to the possessor of that voice, the woman, the partygoer he was paid to suck up to, "Here, I've got the ingredients printed out for you on my card? It's simple, really, anybody can make a Bi-Black. Orange, cinnamon, and our Black Bacardí, which we age one to three years in our super-special charred oak barrels for the flavor and color."

How did she feel in that minute? Sick. Angry. What bullshit. And of course he always had to pronounce it Bacar-*dee*, which might have been right but really did smack of pretension. "You still there?" she said.

"Call you back later," he said, and broke the connection.

SHE WOKE TO THE SOUND of rain rat-tat-tatting on the roof. Her eyelids weighed a thousand tons each. In the middle of the night somebody had shot an arrow through one ear and out the other, and while she was going to need aspirin for that, if not something stronger, it seemed to have sharpened her hearing somehow, as if the thrust of it had cleared her eustachian tubes. Every whisper of the house came to her, muted creaks and groans, the drumbeat of the rain, the refrigerator starting up. And something else too, a repetitive thump and whoosh that didn't seem to be coming from the beach but from a deeper place, a more intimate place, right beneath her. Her next thought began with an image—of the car sitting in the drive rather than up on the ramp where Todd insisted it should go, every night, no matter what, Rule #1—and she let out a curse. Todd was going to kill her. What had she been thinking? What was wrong with her? Shit. Shit. Shit.

In the next moment, dressed only in shorts and tee, she was out on the deck in the rain, peering down at the yard, which was no longer solid ground alive with cycads and lantana and nasturtiums, but a roiling extension of the bay, which was itself an extension of the ocean, one continuous sheet of water that gleamed dully under a dull sky. And the car? Todd's pride and joy? It was an island.

She kept telling herself it wasn't that bad as she thumped barefoot down the stairs and into the bath-like water, which was only shin-deep and only as high as what, the rocker panels, okay, but not up to the doorframe yet, not inside anything . . . But the keys? Where were the keys?

She charged back up the stairs, cursing herself all over again, spent five minutes looking for her purse, which, when she found it kicked under the bed alongside her shoes, turned out not to contain her keys, and how could that be? It took another five minutes of ransacking the place till she thought of the black jeans and yes, there they were in the right front pocket and how they'd got there she had no idea except that maybe she'd gotten a notion to move the car the night before and then somehow let it slip her mind . . . because she'd been drinking. Because she'd been drunk. And careless.

Okay. Down the stairs, through the water, hit the remote and very gingerly pull the door open because the sea with all its jellyfish and seaweed and everything else was right there ready to spill over and ruin the carpet and rust out the floorboards and who knew what else. She held the image of a bowl in her mind, a bowl pushed down in the sink till the dishwater spills over its sides, then slid in, pulled the door softly shut, started the engine and very slowly backed the car round and started up the road, pushing a low rippling wave before her as if she were piloting a boat. Very slowly, very, very slowly, as if she were balanced on the rim of the world, she crept up the drive till the wheels contacted the fractionally higher level of the roadway and then kept going. The turnoff was flooded, but she inched her way through and onto the highway, which was above water, thankfully, though there were no shoulders and the ditches shone greasily under a load of sea wrack decorated with disposable cups and fast-food wrappers. There were pelicans in the middle of the street, along with some bedraggled shoulder-humping thing that might have been a nutria, which she had to honk at before it would move. The way she was feeling—the frustration, the anger—she would have run it right down if it hadn't dodged out of the way at the last minute because this was ridiculous, no coffee yet, no breakfast, and she was playing chicken with a rodent?

She parked in the Chick-fil-A lot, got out and walked round the car, inspecting it. The rain was still coming down, but it was lighter now, almost a drizzle. Her hair was wet, her tee too. But the car (it was red,

Red Multi-Coat, officially, Todd's choice) seemed fine—spattered and dripping, but fine. She opened both the back doors and laid a hand on the mats there, which were dry. Everything inside was dry—presumably, she hoped, the engine too. Especially the engine. But she didn't know where the latch for that was and didn't really want to know, but it was fine, she was sure it was fine, and before Todd came home she'd run the car through the car wash so there'd be no trace of sand or salt or anything else and whatever her faults were—her *imperfections*—he'd be none the wiser, at least not this time.

She walked home through the rain. It was only a mile or so, maybe a mile and a half, she'd never really clocked it, and once she got to the peninsula road, she cut through the yard of the first house on her right (no, she didn't know the people, had never seen them or anybody else there, not even a gardener), so she could walk on the beach. The roadway had been hard on her bare feet, the macadam strewn with fragments of driftwood and palm fronds and whatever else the sea washed up, which made her wince and curse out loud because she was in a mood and hungover and breakfastless and only wanted to get back and shower and eat something, anything, just to push back at the queasiness she'd felt since she first opened her eyes on this disaster of a morning.

She might have enjoyed the walk under other circumstances, but she didn't enjoy it now. She just sloshed through the water, nobody around, no cars moving on the street, no boats out, nothing before her but a gray sheet of drizzle running to showers and then rain, tropical rain, coming at her in bursts. It was disorienting. She knew where she lived, right there at the end of the peninsula where the little bridge spanned the inlet, but somehow, with everything so transformed, she walked right past the house and didn't realize her mistake till she came to the inlet and could walk no farther. It was only maybe a hundred yards, but still . . .

As she went up the outside stairs she was entertaining notions of something like a smoothie, ice crushed in the blender, orange juice, two spoons of plain yogurt, a scoop of Häagen-Dazs Dulce de Leche and maybe, just because of the day she was already having, a shot of Todd's top-end Bacardí—the Gran Reserva Limitada he was so proud of. Yeah. Sure. Why not? Everything was just more of the same anyway and he wasn't here now and wouldn't be here tonight either.

At the top of the stairs she took a minute to swipe at her feet and ankles with the towel they kept on a hook there to keep from tracking half the beach into the house every time they went outside. She was thinking nothing, totally absent in the moment, so when she replaced the towel on the hook she didn't at first register what she was seeing there, the sudden flash of it that at the same time managed to be so dull as to blend in with the flat edge of the clapboard it was stretched across like a bead of caulking. She was startled, but only for an instant. "Willie?" she said.

He flicked his tongue. She held out her hand. And here he came, snaking his way up her bare right arm as if he'd never known anything else.

5

APIS MELLIFERA

THE WINDS—THE SUNDOWNERS THAT SCOURED THE CAN-
yons and left black lines of grit on the windowsills—kept blowing
through a second night, rattling the windows and flailing the trees and
recoating the pool with a fresh layer of debris. Which she'd have to clean
out all over again before she could take her swim. Frank was sleeping in
and he could do that, his prerogative after putting in a full work week
at his practice. She eased out of bed at her usual hour, six-thirty, careful
not to disturb him. He was lying on one side, turned away from her, the
comforter pulled up over his ears, his visible cheek drawn taut under a
fuzz of white stubble, lips puckered round a pipestem of air. Here was
her husband, her sleeping husband, who'd lain beside her in this bed and
how many others like it in student housing and hotels and motels and
vacation cabins for something like two-thirds of her life now. Frank.
Sleeping in. She tiptoed out of the room, Dunphy rising from his bed in
the corner to follow her down the hall and into the kitchen.

After feeding the dog and pouring her first cup of coffee, she found herself standing barefoot on the cold pool coping for the second morning in a row, flinging the skimmer net out over the surface to harvest the debris and dump it in the mulch pile, where it would cook down into the grainy dark loam she worked into the soil of her garden. Cuttings, leaves, coffee grounds, the deliquescing goop of her dead crickets—it was all part of the mix, life to death to life again. She worked mechanically—fling out the net, draw it in, upend it over the mulch, repeat. She'd been at it awhile before she noticed the ripple of vibration on the far side of the pool, a butterfly—orange and black, the iconic colors—in the process of drowning. This was a monarch, a species in catastrophic decline, and her son's chief obsession these past few years. Each fall, during the monarchs' annual migration, he'd spend weeks helping conduct transect surveys stretching across the Santa Ynez Valley, counting their numbers, and each fall he was increasingly despondent over the result. Which only confirmed his direst predictions—the food chain imperiled, the world in collapse—and pushed up his hectoring a notch, as in we all have to do our part or there's not going to be an ecosystem left to worry about anymore. Or food. Or civilization. Doom atop doom.

Well, at least this one wasn't going to drown, not on her watch. She maneuvered round the pool, carefully dipped it out of the water with the edge of her net and set it on the flagstones in the sun where it could dry its wings and then take to the air again. And mate. And lay eggs—and with a little luck give rise to the next generation. She stood over it a moment, watching it adjust itself to the new conditions, solidity, oxygen, warmth, the world as it was meant to be. At her son's prodding, she'd devoted half her garden space to wildflowers and half of that to the milkweed the monarchs needed for survival. She was just about to fling the net out again when a flash of reflected light caught her attention and she glanced up to see a car wheel into the driveway.

It took her a moment to realize it was Cooper's car, the electric Outlander he hadn't washed since he'd bought it, his bug collector's car, the one he used for bumping over dirt roads and accumulating dust. She felt her mood lift—this was a real surprise. It wasn't her birthday, was it? Or his? Or some sort of anniversary? No, not even close, but she couldn't imagine what he was doing here at this hour—he lived on the other side of the coastal range, in Santa Ynez, out near the field station, and he'd always been a late sleeper, especially as a teenager, when it was a trial just to get him up for school in the morning. He climbed out of the car, the sunlight sparking in his hair, and then the door slammed and the far door swung open, somebody else there—Mari, stepping out into the light—and then her door slammed too. But here was the puzzle—neither of them started up the walk but instead went round back of the car, where Cooper flung open the rear liftgate and two dark forms—Mari's dogs, Scotties—sprang down onto the pavement and Cooper reached in back to fumble with something, a box, two boxes . . . and what was he doing, unloading groceries from Costco?

She called out then—"Hello! Good morning!"—and watched them both swivel their heads in surprise. They hadn't seen her there behind the standard five-foot fence required by the building code as a way of protecting children and non-swimming adults, though every creature of the chaparral—including deer—either climbed up the slats or vaulted it at will. Over the years she'd found drowned lizards, mice, birds, even a baby opossum once. Cooper looked startled—or no, sheepish, as if he'd been caught out, which was even more puzzling.

"Hi, Mom," he said. "I was going to surprise you—*we* were." He cradled a produce box to his chest, its flaps secured with strips of shiny silver duct tape. Mari smiled and gave an abbreviated wave. Dunphy, who couldn't see them because of the interposition of the fence, let out a perfunctory bark and began whirling in a circle, whining in the highest register he was capable of, which had no visible effect on the Scotties—they ignored the greeting or incitement or whatever it signified in the language of dogs and floated across the former lawn as if propelled by the wind. Actually, blessedly, there was no wind to speak of—it had died down till it was no more than a breeze reshuffling the fronds of the twin palms Frank had planted years ago to frame the front door.

"So, Mom," her son said, striding across the yard with the box held out in offering, "I've got a present for you."

☀

THERE WERE BEES IN THE box—you could hear the low-threshold hum of them if you leaned in close, which she did. The other box was a ten-frame beehive, painted white, which Cooper and Mari laid atop a platform of concrete blocks to keep it up off the ground and make it easier on the beekeeper's lumbar region when it was time to tend to it and extract the honey, whoever that beekeeper might be. Her first instinct was to refuse: What about the neighbors? What if someone got stung? What about lawsuits? But as her son leveled a patch of ground at the far end of the garden and set the concrete blocks in place, she relaxed into the idea. By the time he and Mari had set the hive on the blocks, facing south, for the sun, all she felt was a growing sense of excitement, as she had with the crickets before them. This was perfect. Just what she needed. She could pollinate her flowers and her zucchini and muskmelons and all the rest and at the same time provide habitat for yet another declining species.

"You've got blotches all over your face," she said, raising a hand to keep the sun out of her eyes.

He gave her a sidelong look, then went back to what he was doing—daubing the entrance of the hive with a mixture of beeswax and lemongrass, which, he'd explained, would help induce the hive to exchange the cardboard shelter for the wood. "It's nothing," he said, grinning. "Just a couple of beestings." He'd been down on one knee, working the mixture into the wood, and now he rose to his feet. "It's this I'm worried about, actually," he said, rolling up his sleeve to display the underside of his arm, which was mottled and swollen and as red as if he'd burned it on a stove. He exchanged a glance with Mari, brought the grin back into play. "Or concerned, I mean. Is Dad around?"

"He's sleeping in. The paperwork, you know? There's no end to it.

And the new PA he's breaking in, who's good, he says, but maybe not quite up to speed yet." Then she took hold of her son's wrist and ran a finger over the inflammation, thinking of all the hurts and abrasions she'd tended when he was a child, the Mercurochrome, the Band-Aids, the ice packs and compresses, nothing to worry over, a nick here and there, the price of being alive—and a doctor in the house if things got out of hand. The skin was rough under her touch, rippled like an alligator handbag, and there was a tiny whitish crater dead center in the middle of his forearm as if a wound had healed over and left a raised scar. "Don't tell me that's from bees? Looks like you burned yourself."

"A tick," Mari said. "Just like we were talking about at dinner the other night. Karma, right?"

"More like voodoo, if you ask me," Cooper said, releasing his arm from her grip with a casual flexion of his wrist. "They'll be sticking pins in me next."

"No, no, that's your effigy, the doll," Ottilie said. "They stick the pins in the doll, not you." Here she was offering clarity when the metaphor was all that mattered. Live by the bug, die by the bug. But she wasn't really alarmed, not yet. People got bitten by ticks every day—and stung by bees—but only one in fifty thousand was going to die from it.

"It's infected, obviously, and I'm no doctor," Mari said, "but this looks more like cellulitis than Lyme." She paused to glance out over the yard to where her dogs were rooting in the bushes, crapping and pissing and kicking up wood chips with their hind paws. "Which can be dangerous. *Is* dangerous."

"You'll need an antibiotic. Your father will know." She turned to go back to the house—for Frank, to haul him out of bed, because she didn't like the looks of this at all—but Cooper held her back, his hand at her elbow.

"Yeah, okay, great," he said. "I'm going to need Dad to write me a prescription, and I'll tell you, this does itch like holy hell, but don't you want to see your present first? In action? The real deal? The honeymakers themselves?"

She hadn't really thought of the honey—it was enough to imagine bees pollinating not only her vegetables and flowers and fruit trees but the neighbors' too—yet the idea appealed to her. Why not? It would be one more step toward food independence—and she hadn't given up on insect protein, already having put in an order for a mealworm farm and a second cricket reactor to replace the contaminated one. And bees were edible too—one of the recipes in the Horan book was for "Three Bee Salad," which included adult bees, bee pupae and bee larvae, so there was that if nothing else. But let them thrive. Let the world renew itself. Honey. Her own pure backyard honey. "Yes," she said. "Yes, please."

Her son propped up the produce box on a pedestal of concrete blocks, angling the face of it so it was no more than a foot from the hive. Then he peeled back a strip of tape to reveal a rectangular slit cut in the cardboard and the dark forms of the insects clustered there, already fumbling out into the light. Some crawled. Some flew. Some shot away as if they wanted nothing to do with this hive or any other, but the majority of them—the seething yellow-and-brown bulk of them—discovered the beeswax with its lemongrass-oil attractant and began feeding themselves into the hive in an ever-thickening stream. "It's like magic," she said. "Like a magic show."

Cooper grinned, pleased with himself. And then, as if he were unconscious of it, he dropped his arm to his side and started itching.

SHE MADE EVERYBODY BREAKFAST—nothing fancy, just omelets with a little Asiago and tomatoes and peppers from the garden, toast, juice, coffee—while Cooper consulted with his father. No insects, not this morning, not with her crickets dead and her bag of frozen *gusanos* all used up, though she still had half a pound of cricket flour left and could have made pancakes, she supposed, but ultimately it was too much bother—this was a time to be sociable, not laboring over a griddle. Mari offered to help and she let her dice the peppers and grate the cheese while all three dogs, companionable enough, nosed around the kitchen. The classical channel was playing a Mozart piano sonata. Sunlight shimmered at the windows. Mari, working the edge of the knife like a lever in quick clean strokes, looked up and said, "It's ironic, isn't it?"

"What?"

"That Cooper dates an acarologist and winds up hosting a tick. And a bacterium?"

She shrugged, smiled, felt an upwelling of goodwill—here was her future daughter-in-law, or potential daughter-in-law, gracing her kitchen on a sunny morning and making small talk while the oil sizzled in the pan and the coffee sent up its promissory aroma. "I guess we should be thankful you're not a bacteriologist, then, right?"

Mari laughed and shook her head, the black silk of her hair fanning round her shoulders. "Sometimes I feel like one. You can't believe the strains my beloved little bloodsuckers are harboring these days—and your husband's right, we are seeing more tick bites year-round, and whether that's an effect of climate change or the loss of woodlands or something going on in the microbial world we can't even guess at, nobody knows."

"But it isn't pretty, right?"

Another shake of the head. "Uh-uh, but it makes me think I made a wise career choice. Did you know I was really into parasitoid wasps as an undergrad? That was my thing, and the field's hot right now, seems like everybody wants in . . . but then I found my mentor—Dr. Liza Blassy-Epstein? At UC Santa Maria? She really opened my eyes to parasitic arachnids."

What could she say to this? Her future daughter-in-law was a science nerd and so was her son, and in his own way, her husband too, but if you weren't a science nerd yourself it might be hard to appreciate the subtle advantages of specializing in acarology over, what, parasitoid *waspology*, if there even was such a word? But it was all right. It was fine. And it certainly wasn't Mari's fault that one of her study subjects had bitten and infected Cooper with something that was probably fairly routine but oh so potentially dangerous, what with MRSA infections popping up all over the place, and just listen to Frank talk about that—methicillin-resistant *Staphylococcus aureus*, which means untreatable infections down the road as the bugs vitiate one antibiotic after another and nobody's investing in new ones because drugs like Viagra and Rogaine and Xanax and OxyContin are so much more profitable. What if that was what Cooper had? And even if he didn't, having to take antibiotics—any antibiotics—was a disaster for your intestinal biome, which, scientists were discovering, had an influence on everything from strengthening your immune system to boosting brain and heart health.

Mari ran a finger over the flat of the blade to dislodge the remaining pepper fragments, rinsed it under the faucet and set it carefully on the drainboard. Then she picked up the cheese grater. "Really," she said, "after that I never looked back."

And Cooper? He'd never looked back either, and that was a happy thing, both of them anchored in their work. Bug people. They were both bug people. And what was wrong with that? Better than being drug addicts or gamblers or, what, insurance salesmen, stockbrokers, *politicians*. To be able to observe the world minutely, that was the thing, especially as the world shrank and all the big charismatic animals—the lions, gorillas, elephants—vanished. E. O. Wilson, the patron saint of entomologists and her son's personal deity, said in an interview she'd read somewhere that if he were starting out all over again, he'd study microbes. That was where the action was, right at the frontier of a whole new world, go smaller, go deeper.

A murmur of voices came to her from the living room, where her own entomologist was having his father examine his infected arm, speaking of microbes. Frank would write a prescription to clear it up. And they'd all sit down and eat breakfast.

Unfortunately, she'd lost the thread of the conversation, so she just said, "Yeah, that sounds great," and then, "Let's just sauté the vegetables and we're all set to go."

☀

AT BREAKFAST, COOPER KEPT THE sleeve of his sweatshirt rolled up because it was painful to have the material come into contact with his infected skin. Frank had given him an antibacterial cream and called in a prescription—to be picked up and started immediately after the meal. He'd also drawn a jagged looping line around the inflamed area in black Magic Marker. When she asked what it was for, he looked up from his coffee and gave her a signal with his eyes, a signal that meant not here and not now, which sent a chill through her, because what was this? Why so secretive? He said, "Just routine. We want to see if it spreads." And here he looked to their son, who was performing the delicate operation of slathering his omelet with ketchup and easing it between two slices of whole grain toast. "Send me a picture tonight. And first thing in the morning too. If it spreads—or if you start running a fever—you get in the car and come straight to me, okay?"

"It's only a tick bite."

Mari, the acarologist, the science nerd, the daughter-in-law-in-waiting, made as if to say something, but didn't. She cut a wedge of omelet with her fork, then set it down and lifted her coffee to her lips. Her eyes were huge. They missed nothing.

"Are you *listening*? This isn't something you can fool around with." Frank looked angry, the muscles clenching in a tight weave just above the bridge of his nose, and his anger scared her. "If you don't see results with the clindamycin within twenty-four hours, you let me know right away. Did you keep the tick? In case we have to test it to see what it injected you with?"

"I've got it," Mari said. She tried for a smile, but then seemed to think better of it. "It's part of my collection now—and I didn't put it in ethanol but just stuck it in a vial, so whatever it's carrying should still be active," and then she and Frank went back and forth with a point-for-point recitation of jargon as if they were auditioning for a quiz show, and

Ottilie tuned them out. She turned to Cooper and asked what he was planning on doing for the rest of the day.

"Me?" He shrugged. "Take a walk on the beach, I guess. No ticks there, right?"

"Not unless they live on starfish."

"But at some point—after the drugstore—I'm coming back here so we can go online and order you your beekeeper's outfit," Cooper said. "And a smoker too." He paused to lift the sandwich to his mouth with both hands and take a dripping bite of it as if he were ten years old still. There was ketchup on his face. And his knuckles. And a bright red spot of it on the tip of his nose. "You're going to look great in one of those hats with the gauze over it, absolutely," he said, chewing. "You'll be the fashion plate of the bee world."

"Am I really going to get honey?"

"Are you kidding? You won't be able to give it all away."

TWO DAYS LATER, COOPER WAS in the hospital.

It was three-thirty in the afternoon when the phone rang. She'd spent the morning in the garden, pruning, pulling weeds and recalibrating the drip system since there was no rain in sight and this was the time of year when the plants were most stressed. She'd gone grocery shopping in the afternoon and had a long talk on the telephone with Cat about the wedding and its cascading details, which was now rescheduled for the Monday of Thanksgiving week, then spent a good half hour perched on a wooden stool contemplating her new beehive, gratified to see the workers sailing in and out of the entrance, the returning ones so furred with pollen they dwarfed the ones heading out. Inside, they'd be making their wax honeycombs and the queen would be laying eggs, the business of eternity, and there would come a point when there'd be honey for the taking.

The odd thing was that it was Frank on the phone, because he never called during the workday. "Don't get excited," he said, "because every-thing's fine and it's only a precaution, but I decided we'd better put Coop in the hospital."

"What are you talking about? For what?"

Frank was good at disclosure, which was one of the things that made him so effective in family practice (and trusted and liked too, his patients forever coming up to them in the street or at the movie theater or supermarket, and they could hardly go out to a restaurant without somebody sending a round of drinks to the table), but like all doctors, he could play it close to the vest. Even with his own wife. "The infec-tion was spreading, when the clindamycin should have knocked it right back, so I want him on intravenous just to speed things up."

"My god, *spreading*?" she said. "I thought you said it was nothing—he's not . . . you're not telling me there's anything wrong, are you?"

"Standard procedure with an infection like this. We get him on the IV and you'll see dramatic improvement—"

"What are you saying, dramatic improvement? Over what? Is he sick? Is it a fever?"

"Yeah, he's fighting an infection, so yeah, he has a fever—which I didn't like. I took him down there myself and got him hooked up, and called Manny Profar in to see what he thinks at this point . . ."

"I'm going down there right now."

"Why don't we both go, after dinner? Give him a chance to rest up and let the antibiotic go to work."

All she could do was repeat herself: "I'm going down there right now."

6

BUG BOY

THERE WAS A NIGHT WHEN HE WAS TWELVE OR THIRTEEN, somewhere in there—the first flush of adolescence, the period when all that mattered was being cool, being accepted, being popular—an unstoppable Saturday night during an interminable school year. His mother had made a roast for dinner, a bloody slab of which he had to eat around because he was just beginning to know enough to be adamant about things, especially cruelty to animals and the damage commercial meat production inflicted on the environment. He ate pan-roasted potatoes, he ate salad and a slice of sourdough toast, drank two cans of Dr Pepper and left the meat for the dog, after which he took his skateboard and went down to the 7-Eleven to hang with some of the kids from school. Or one, actually, Jerome Kittleman, who was a math whiz and a bit of a geek, like him, but who also did things like fractionally reduce his parents' marijuana and alcohol stashes without sanction—or compunction. "Do you want to get high?" was what Jerome had said to him over the phone, and he said, "Yeah, I guess so," and Jerome said, "The 7-Eleven?" and he said, "Yeah, sure, okay."

In a previous era, three or four years before this particular night, the lot out back of the store had been a point of convergence for older teens, the ones with girlfriends and cars who'd installed Kicker speakers that tore the bottom out of the night when they humped in off the boulevard, but whoever owned the store had put in megawatt lights and rigged up speakers tuned to the classical channel by way of discouraging them. That left the field to the younger kids, like him. And Jerome. And half the junior high soccer team. And girls too, at least once in a while—when they weren't at the mall. Actually, he didn't mind classical music all that much—and you had to find someplace to go on a Saturday night or you'd just sit there in your room playing video games till your eyeballs froze solid in your head and your muscles turned to mucilage.

Half a dozen kids were hanging around out back with their skateboards, doing kickflips and ollies off a makeshift ramp, but he didn't see Jerome there so he went inside and bought himself a wild cherry Slurpee and two single-server bags of Cool Ranch Doritos. He started in on the chips right there at the checkstand while harassed-looking adults shot in and out the door with twelve-packs, baby diapers, hot dogs and taquitos, then he paid and went back out into the night.

Everything smelled like the bottom of the ocean, a dense churning fog coming in off the water to saturate the air (May Gray, they called it, to be succeeded by June Gloom), which got the crickets going so affirmatively they poked all sorts of holes in the music leaching out of the store's speakers and made the clack and thump of the skateboards seem like the unnatural intrusions they were. The fog reduced the *rap-rap-rap* of car tires to white noise and the discontinuous wheeze of the automatic door faded away to nothing. The crickets ruled. And because it was warmer than usual, whole cohorts of insects were gathering around the lights, more than he'd seen in months, it seemed. That caught his interest. More so even than the crudely wrapped joint Jerome showed up with or the unspoken dare of the ramp and the society of the other kids, the cool kids he'd come here to be cool with.

Jerome said, "I have this jar I poured some of my dad's single malt scotch into?"

They were leaning against the wall, listening to Beethoven or whoever it might have been, and Jerome opened the flap of his backpack to display a mason jar almost full to the top with mahogany liquid. "What's the difference?" he asked. "I mean, single malt, double malt, whatever?"

"I don't know. It's just that this is the best—or that's what my father says."

"Your father? He doesn't know about this, does he?"

"No, no, no—and if he did he'd be pissed. This is the good stuff, trust me. It's expensive."

"Like how much?"

"I don't know, a hundred, hundred fifty? I could google it, but are we going to drink or what? Why don't we just drink it?"

He watched Jerome turn away from the lights to unscrew the lid, tip the jar to his mouth and take a quick abbreviated swallow. "Whoa, that's good," Jerome said. "I mean, *yeah*."

Cooper didn't like the taste, which was harsh, hot, chemical. He'd done this before a couple of times, with Jerome and Peter Sacker, his only other close friend, who'd unfortunately moved to Seattle three months ago, and he'd tried beer, wine and tequila, and each time he could hear his mother's voice in the back of his head telling him how there was a history of alcoholism on both sides of the genetic divide, hers and his father's, and how liquor had cut her father's life short, which was why he'd never even got to know his own grandfather. It was the kind of thing parents told their children, a formality almost, and whether it was true or not he had no way of knowing, but he trusted his mother and loved her and though he'd never seen her drunk, or not the sort of drunk depicted in the movies or that you saw with bums on the street or loudmouths waiting for their cars at valet stands, he'd watched her slide into another persona altogether over cocktails at a restaurant or when she and his father had friends over to the house, as if she'd temporarily lost track of who she was. Was that such a big deal? Not really. She didn't stumble or curse or break things or vomit, or not that he knew of, anyway. She drank and so did his father—as did ninety percent of the rest of the adult population, judging from the billboards you saw along the boulevard and the ads they ran during the football games on TV. Now, with the crickets outdoing one another and Beethoven stuck like glue in the speakers and Jerome staring into his eyes, he forced himself to take a swallow or two and a hit off the joint, but when a couple of the other kids drifted over to see if they could get in on the action, he went round to the front of the store as if drawn by a higher force and started digging through the trash bin that stood just outside the door.

What he was looking for was discarded cups with the tops still on so he could select a couple and make use of them to trap and sort out some of the species swarming the lights. Amid the moths and beetles he'd seen a few pale nocturnal *Ophionine* wasps, which were related to the more colorful diurnal ones that mimicked tarantula hawks but were more muted and maybe rarer, and he thought he'd like to collect them and bring them home. And there was a stick insect and a couple of ant lions in their winged phase. And more too, as he saw when he came back round the corner with six empty plastic cups, lids intact. By this point, his brain had gone into another place altogether and maybe the liquor and the pot had something to do with it, but that didn't matter. Here he was, looking up at these distinct species, common and not so common, all of them crowding the light—and more coming. It was like a treasure hunt. And all of a sudden he was on it.

At some point, after he'd managed to trap two of the wasps—and in a separate cup, the stick bug, which was huge, close to four inches, which meant it must have been a female, and if it was a female she might have eggs inside and could lay them in a terrarium so he could watch them hatch—he became aware of a tonal shift in the group gathered around Jerome. He'd been so absorbed in what he was doing he hadn't noticed that one of the girls from school, Reina Swazy, had joined them, drawn to the smell of the pot and the sight of the furtive mason jar going hand to hand. It was her voice that clued him in. She had a very distinctive voice, totally different from the piping trills and squeals of most of the other girls at school—her voice was low-pitched and hoarse, as if she had a perpetual sore throat. She had big eyes. And breasts. Bigger breasts than practically any of the girls in their grade. He was balanced on the bumper of somebody's SUV, one hand braced against the wall, trying to get closer to the light, when he heard her voice, swung his head round, and saw her there.

"Hi," she said, appending a giggle to the greeting as if there were something funny about saying hello to a classmate in a foggy 7-Eleven parking lot on a Saturday night in May. The crickets sang their mating song. Beethoven tightened his grip. The fog metamorphosed from silver to gold in the glow of the fog lights somebody had left on in their car when they ducked into the store. "What are you doing up there?"

The question took him by surprise—wasn't it obvious? She was wearing a short skirt and a bleached denim jacket that from this angle narrowed her shoulders down to nothing so that she was all head and face. And lipstick. And eye shadow. "Collecting specimens," he said over his shoulder.

There was a snicker from one of the guys huddled around Jerome, somebody he didn't recognize. "*Specimens?* Specimens are in the zoo, if you want to know." A pause. "Which is where you belong. What are you, like five years old?"

Reina didn't say anything, but one of the other kids, passing the joint back to Jerome, let out an ostentatious cloud of smoke and said, "Bug Boy."

In an instant, the others had taken it up—"Bug Boy, Bug Boy," they chanted—and though he tried to ignore them, that wasn't working, not at all, because the one who'd started it whipped across the pavement in a fluid display of poise and agility and kicked over each of the cups in turn as if he were slicing soccer balls through the goalposts. Which meant that all the specimens were lost, but for the stick insect, as Cooper was later to discover when he found it clinging to the lid of the cup, and that was something at least, the biggest one he'd ever seen. And he told himself he could always come back later—or another night. It was no big deal, but then it was, because in the space of thirty seconds he'd acquired a new nickname, one that would chase him down the corridors all through junior high and beyond, a negative, an embarrassment, until finally, by his senior year when he'd grown past all that pettiness and bullshit, he accepted it, embraced it even. Bug Boy. It was an honorific, that was what it was. He went out after school one afternoon and had six T-shirts printed up at a silkscreen place, each with the hugely enlarged face of an insect front and back—mantis, wolf spider, cabbage moth—and the legend, in crisp crimson letters, stamped over the right breast: BUG BOY.

Of course, it didn't help him any that night. That night he was humiliated, which was made all the worse by the presence of Reina Swazy, and this brought up the question of what was cool and what wasn't. Who decided? Was there a panel of exemplary teens out there somewhere who passed down edicts? Why was it cool to go fishing or hunting when collecting insects was a one-way ticket to geekdom? He jumped down from the bumper of the SUV, which turned out to be a well-timed move because the two guys associated with it, twentysomethings who each had a twelve-pack of Bud Light tucked under one arm, came round the corner in the next instant—and who knows but that they might have taken umbrage with his making use of their bumper and launched him into a whole other stratosphere of humiliation. But that didn't happen. He just stood back as if it were the intermission of a play while they climbed into their car, set the beer down on the floor and slammed the doors shut. Then the car backed out, cut the front wheels with a metallic screech and squealed out of the lot, speakers thumping.

He was faced with a choice: hang around on the fringes of the group till the moment passed or collect his cups on the off chance any of the insects were still secreted inside them and head on home alone. Reina said, to no one in particular, "Is that scotch? I mean, scotch is the best, right?" Somebody laughed. Jerome said, "Single malt," and Cooper bent to pick up each of the cups in succession, luckily finding the stick insect (*Phasmatodea*) stretched across one of the white plastic caps. He fitted the cap on the empty cup that was lying next to it, said nothing to anybody, not even Jerome, then ducked round front of the store and walked home.

☀

THROW YOUR SHOULDERS BACK, stand up straight, that's what everybody told him, his mother and the gym teacher especially, but an entomologist does just the opposite—you hunch forward, you look down instead of up—and if that meant you were going to go through life in a slouch, then so be it. He read E. O. Wilson's *Naturalist* and found a hero. Then he read *The Ants* and *The Diversity of Life* and everything else Wilson had written. And Thomas Eisner. And Howard Ensign Evans. He catalogued all the insects in his yard, on his block, in the chaparral behind his house. He grew up. Went to college. Discovered his métier. Went to grad school. Did field studies in Costa Rica and close to home too, in the Santa Ynez Valley. Met Mari. Took a windy-day hike with her through the dead stiff grass of the preserve and acquired an infection transmitted through the bite of a tick, ran a fever and wound up in the hospital with his mother sitting in a chair by the bed in a room with a window that looked out on the south slope of the mountain range where the ticks lived in numbers uncountable, where they congregated in the posture known as questing behavior, their front legs spread wide in anticipation of a meal coming to them, a living moving blood-infused thing they could hitch a ride on, then absorb their fill before dropping off into the undergrowth to lay their eggs and produce still more ticks.

There were no ticks in the hospital room, no bugs of any kind except for the odd fly or two, but he'd hardly have noticed because a different kind of bug was methodically replicating itself throughout the cells of his right arm and provoking the immune response known as a fever and that fever tipped the world on its head so that he couldn't really follow natural processes or even, for long periods, know who he was or where.

Walls. He was inside, within walls, but the walls were pulsing in the way of living organs, as if he'd been swallowed and digested and processed down to the cellular level, to blood cells that were his own and everybody else's too, all the human race just a feast of meat for the insects and bacteria and bigger animals too, four-footed creatures bearing the faces of hyenas and civet cats gnawing at him and whispering behind his eyelids. Somewhere in there voices came to him, voices in discussion, arbitration, argumentation, voices that were hushed for the most part, but that rose in hot furious sweeps of agitation, his mother's primarily, but his father's too.

If he'd been awake to the world he might have registered terms like *MRSA*, *blood culture, sepsis, bullae, compartment syndrome, necrotizing fasciitis*. He might have detected the desperation in his mother's tone, his father's anger and bewilderment, Dr. Profar's insistence, the nurses' hushed acknowledgment that things had gone so far beyond the manipulation of IV lines, bedpans and soiled sheets they were all but helpless. And Mari? Where was Mari? Not there, not that he could tell or remember—off with her ticks somewhere, he supposed. Too embarrassed to show her face. But no, no, she was right there, dead center in the middle of the dream he was having, her crisp precise biologist's intonation telling him she wasn't going anywhere, though in fact she was or rather he was because they trundled him down to surgery where the anesthesia they gave him went to war with the fever and he saw things and dreamed things until everything in his mind had a desperate red clawing edge to it.

When he woke he was back in the same sterile room. His mother was there, his father, Mari. The mountains were outside the window. A fly hovered. He was thirsty, had never been thirstier. "Water," he said. "Mom, I want water, ice water. Or Coke. Or Dr Pepper. Get me a Dr Pepper, Mom. My throat is, is . . . my throat . . ."

So that was an afternoon. The rain his mother had been hoping for hadn't come and the sun affixed itself to the window like a spattered egg. There was wind out there—he could see it in the way the palms thrashed back and forth, then stood motionless again, then thrashed, then stood motionless. He was hot, then he was cold. He saw that there was a glass of ice on the aluminum tray by his bedside and a can of Dr Pepper rigid in the shell of itself and giving up the scent of its twenty-three natural and artificial flavors, cherry foremost among them, right there next to it.

He went to reach for it but couldn't quite manage, something wrong somewhere along the line, the signal from the motor neurons in his brain short-circuiting before they reached his hand, his right hand, the one he'd always favored, the one he'd shifted with when he'd learned to drive on his father's old M3, the one he wrote with, ate with. His mother looked as if she'd just been hit by a bus. Mari's face was a dead thing. His father said something that had the term *prosthetic* in it and his mother, her voice a thin bleat of lament, said, "All that matters is that you're here."

The fly—and what kind of hospital was this when they couldn't even keep flies out?—described a lazy arc round the bed, hovered over the mouth of the open can, then settled down there to drink its fill.

7

WILLIE II, WILLIE I

SHE PICKED UP TODD AT THE AIRPORT AND THEY WENT straight home and straight to bed, which really helped clear her mind. If she'd been at all jealous—*Todd, that is like so delicious; what's in it again?*—she got all the reaffirmation she needed. If anything, he was even more passionate than usual—and he was the best lover, totally involved, totally giving, whereas most of the guys she'd dated before she met him seemed more interested in whatever game was on or *Call of Duty* or just sitting around drinking beer with their college buds than in her. Until the mood took them, that is, and whether that lasted for ten minutes or twenty, counting foreplay, they were up out of bed three minutes later clicking their game controllers or watching hoops on TV with the sound muted—or in the case of Tim Potter, a lit major she'd gone out with for six months sophomore year, plunging right back into whatever novel he was reading almost as soon as he came. And it wouldn't have been so bad if he had any kind of taste, anything he could *share*, but it was all fantasy and sci-fi, psionics, gengineering, wormholes and the like.

The night before, though she'd told herself she was just going to stay in and be patient and wait for Todd, she'd wound up feeling so bored—or antsy, *antsy* was a better word—she decided to go down to Bobo's for a drink. She walked, because she didn't want to risk getting the car any dirtier—or worse, saltier. In California, all the cars were pristine, even old cars like the restored '72 GTO Todd had had before he met her, of which she'd seen glossy color photos at least ten thousand times, but here a good proportion of them were rusted-out, ugly shredded holes poked through their fenders and rocker panels (and if she didn't actually know what a rocker panel was, she knew it was one of the first things that gave way, or so Todd had told her, the sharp jab of his index finger flagging one example or another as they drove down the street, the point being that California was so much better than this, at least when it came to cars).

It wasn't a question of the water—it had magically receded overnight—but the roadway itself. The blacktop was still strewn with debris, each passing car grinding it into a finer paste, which was just a recipe for concentrating sea salt and other corrosive chemicals. She was planning on driving the car just one more time—to the car wash and the airport, period—and then have Todd take over and let him worry about the composition of whatever crap was streaking the fenders. The car was parked up on the ramp and that was where it was going to stay. And when the mood took her to see what was happening down at Bobo's she put on her lip gloss and mascara and the black jeans and blouse, slipped on her teal walker booties and was already half out the door when she thought of Willie II.

She'd introduced him to his new terrarium mate, Willie I, the wanderer, the night before, though she'd been careful about that, thinking they might get violent or that Willie II might even attempt to cannibalize his namesake, but she finally decided he wasn't big enough, at least not that she could gauge. Willie II had already been fed—by R.J., the day before she bought him—which meant he would have been good for a week or more, but who knew what shape Willie I was in, since he'd been out there on the deck or wherever and she'd never had a chance to feed him. Even once. She put him in a cardboard box while defrosting a pinky for him in a pan of chicken broth and then kept an eye on him till he began to show an interest in it and finally, opening wide and wriggling his body with a soft silken swish of his tail, he got it in his mouth and then his throat, until eventually it appeared as a lump working its way through his gut, one long interval after another. Then, and only then, did she put him in the terrarium with Willie II. If she expected trouble—violence, hissing (if snakes even hissed, which Google told her they in fact did)—she was pleasantly surprised. The two of them explored each other without prejudice and even for a while intertwined themselves before Willie II undulated his way up the artificial branch that cut a diagonal from floor to ceiling of the terrarium and went to sleep.

In the morning, there was no change. Willie I was still bloated, Willie II still asleep. She couldn't really tell—she was new to all this—but they seemed happier, if that was possible, or maybe calmer, which was a kind of happiness or at least a reflection of it. Could snakes be happy? Why not? They had heat, food, a decent place to live—and companionship. They weren't twisting neurotically around the enclosure, wondering where they were, but just living in harmony with themselves and each other as if this really were a cave in the jungle someplace, but a cave with all the stresses removed and food delivered up on a regular basis. Though they really couldn't have known that yet. But they would. Just give them time.

All day, off and on, she kept watch over them, though most of the time she was perched on a stool at the kitchen counter, posting pictures of herself and Willie II and collecting like after like, which made her own mood soar. She'd stumbled onto something here—an identity that would elevate her as an influencer, that would be her tag, her entrée, the Snake Lady here to sell your line of tops or jewelry or designer tees or whatever it was. Great. Fine. Excellent. But before long she began to feel the faintest twitch of regret at having no one to share it with, stuck home alone without Todd, without anybody, and the regret morphed into resentment. Todd wasn't home and she was. Todd was still in Boston and she wasn't. And the cure for that, at least temporarily, at least for the space of a drink or two, was Bobo's. When she decided at the last minute to take Willie II with her she realized she couldn't just let him ride her shoulders the whole way—it was too long a walk—so she lifted him out of the terrarium and let him glide down her forearm and into a straw shoulder bag she liked to use for toting things, especially on shopping expeditions or when she went to the grocery, and then she was out the door and down the steps and into the night.

BOBO'S WAS PRETTY LIVELY FOR a weekday night, which was just what she wanted, really, some *life*, and what was wrong with that? The hostess, a Black girl named Daria with a shako of teased-out hair that stood a good twelve inches up off the crown of her head, led her to her favorite table in the far left-hand corner of the patio. In the past weeks there'd been a couple of occasions when she and Todd had hung at the bar with her when she got off work and Cat was thinking of inviting her and her boyfriend over someday for dinner or at least cocktails. She could use a girlfriend. Or two. Or three. She'd washed up here in Florida without knowing anybody and Daria was a prime candidate, her age exactly, and smart and funny and she really had style. "So where's Todd?" Daria asked, laying the menu down on the table though it wasn't really necessary since Cat had it pretty well memorized and probably wasn't going to order food anyway.

"He's hosting? Up in Boston? He'll be back tomorrow."

"Cool. You want the usual? I'll just tell Kelsey and save her the trip—unless you want food? You want food?"

She shrugged. "I don't know, I already ate, actually" (another frozen entrée, Salvo's Vermont Cheddar Mac and Cheese, which had tasted like cardboard saturated in grease and made her feel as bloated as the snake she'd left behind in the terrarium). "So maybe I'll just start off with a cocktail and take it from there."

A guy who looked vaguely familiar—had she seen him here before?—was perched on a stool with his guitar singing into a microphone and two couples were dancing in a slow shuffle around the flagstones of the patio, older people, in their forties she guessed, with graceless bodies and adhesive feet, but the bar behind them was crowded and young and she could see guys there taking furtive peeps at her and all she could think was, *Wait till they see Willie II.*

It took a second drink for her to work up the courage to lift Willie out of her bag and drape him around her shoulders. She felt shy and daring all at once, like at Halloween in the moment before walking into a party with your costume on and not knowing whether people were going to get it or not. For his part, Willie II was cooperative, as if he didn't mind being on display—he didn't keep snaking out his head or trying to climb an invisible ladder the way Willie the First had the day she'd bought him and showed him off for Cora. Which was perfect, just how she'd pictured it. And sure enough, within five minutes two of the guys who'd been standing at the bar were hovering over her table making appreciative noises.

"Oh, wow, cool," the taller of the two said. He was wearing a Tommy Bahama shirt in a black-and-white floral print and he had his hair slicked tight to his head, gangster-style. "What is it, a python?"

She nodded. Smiled. The question made her feel good, made her feel special: she had the knowledge and he didn't. "Uh-huh," she said. "A Burmese? They call them 'Burmies' for short."

The other one, shorter, heavier, Cuban or maybe Dominican, in a Jaguars jersey and a gold bracelet, gave her a smile to show he was impressed but not afraid, or not all that much. "Does it bite?" he asked.

"You got nothing to fear unless you're a mouse," the taller one said. "You're not a mouse, are you, Jaime?"

"Not if you ask my mother. But really"—he turned back to her, grinning, one hand lightly braced on the edge of the table, getting comfortable—"does it?"

"His name's Willie," she said, taking a sip of her mojito. "Willie II, actually—Willie I couldn't make it tonight . . ."

"All partied out, huh?" the taller one said.

"Yeah," she said, "something like that." The night clung to her, everything smelling of alcohol, cookery, flowers in bloom. This was Florida, and all at once, she realized, she was at home in it.

"Can we buy you a drink?" the taller one asked (his name was Brandon, as she was soon to discover, and he was two years out of college and working for a famous architect she'd never heard of).

"Sure, why not?" she said and then Jaime pulled over a chair and they both sat down and she told them all about Burmies—and what she didn't know she made up.

It was fun, a distraction anyway, and Willie II behaved himself perfectly, even after both the guys had asked if they could touch him and ran their hands down the length of him as if they were caressing a pipe bomb that might go off at any minute, nervous but too macho to show it, and that was fine. They were both cute and they were talkers, both of them, which she liked, but she *was* wearing her engagement ring and they could see that plainly when she stroked Willie herself until a point came when they remembered they had to be somewhere else and thanked her and said they hoped they'd see her again—was she a regular here? well, okay then—and she watched them make their way back to the bar, hover there, then pass on out the door and into the street.

SHE'D HAD THREE DRINKS AND was about to ask for the check and call it a night when without warning Willie rotated his head and bit her just above the wrist, at the same time wrapping himself firmly around her forearm. It wasn't anything savage or violent, just a sort of exploratory bite, and it felt like a dozen tiny pinpricks as his teeth punctured her skin ever so delicately. She knew enough not to jerk her hand away because any number of his backward-slanting teeth would come along with it and she didn't want to hurt him, plus there was the embarrassment factor. Nobody was watching her at the moment—she saw Daria flit by the bar with her menus and a couple trailing behind her, and the rest of the crowd had settled into that postprandial, third-cocktail torpor that meant the evening was winding down and whatever had been of interest earlier had lost its novelty. The guy was still playing his guitar, but he wasn't singing, just doing instrumentals now. Nobody was dancing. There were only three other occupied tables out on the patio and the people there took no notice of her. Thankfully.

It didn't hurt, not after the initial pinpricks, but Willie had hold of her and showed no sign of letting go, though she began stroking his neck in the hope of relaxing him. He must have smelled her, must have known she was made of meat just like the pinkies and fuzzies he consumed but he must have known too that she was a hundred times too big to be prey. His eyes revealed nothing. His mouth was like a spring trap, stretched open wide. He didn't wriggle, didn't move, just stayed right there as if he'd been glued to her arm, and yes, it was embarrassing above all. She had a scarf in her purse and she discreetly fished it out and draped it over his head so no one would see what was going on, not even Daria when in the next moment she caught her eye and waved for the check.

She watched Daria change direction and cross the patio to her, propulsive in her heels, till she was standing over the table and smiling down at her as if nothing were amiss, as if she didn't have a snake attached to her arm and wasn't trying to hide its head under a silk flowered scarf. "Kelsey says you don't owe anything, not even a tip. Your fans—those two guys? They took care of it."

"Okay, great, thanks," she said, massaging Willie's head under the cover of the scarf. There was blood there, she could feel it, tightening, crusting, which made it even more embarrassing—and what if Daria wanted to sit and chat?

"And the snake, you didn't tell me about *him*—he's really something. So incredibly beautiful. I mean, that *pattern* . . ."

"Yeah," she said. "I just got him, though I don't think Todd's going to be all that happy about it, if you want to know the truth."

Mercifully, because she really had no idea where this was going to end, if she'd have to walk home with Willie attached to her arm and somehow get out the door without everybody tsk-tsking and giving unwanted advice along the lines of, *Rub vinegar on his tail* or *Sometimes if you just squeeze them behind the head*, Daria said she was still on duty ("There's like this party of eight coming in at ten?") and drifted back across the patio.

So she had her snake and he was beautiful. But he was a snake and snakes' brains didn't really work in any logical way, as she was discovering to her mortification, and what was she going to do? With her free hand she lifted her drink, rattled the ice cubes and drained the glass, which gave her an idea—ice. What if she applied the ice in her drink to the back of Willie's head by way of letting him know that what he was doing had consequences, that the whole world wasn't heat lamps and ticking mammalian flesh and pan-warmed fuzzies? So that was what she did. Lifted the edge of the scarf, brought the bottom of the glass into contact with Willie's head and held it there like a compress for ten seconds, fifteen, twenty—and then, small miracle, he got it, got it all the way, and in the next moment released her so she could put him back in the bag, stroll out the door as if nothing were out of the ordinary and walk back home amid the seething insectoid racket of the Florida night.

TODD DIDN'T HAVE MUCH to say about Willie II one way or the other—he just accepted him as a fait accompli and, if there were a balance sheet here, maybe the cost of keeping her happy. And of course she wanted to keep him happy too—that was what this was all about, love, living together, the wedding—but she had her own life and her own needs and he was just going to have to get used to that.

"They get along okay?" he asked musingly, as if he were interested.

They were drinking wine, his second day back, the sun incinerating the horizon and a creeping band of blue-black night ready to put the cap on another day. They'd both taken the day off, which hadn't been all that big a sacrifice for her since she wasn't making any money anyway, or not yet, and they'd gone to an upscale place in St. Augustine for a lunch that lingered for nearly three hours and was as close to perfect as she could hope for. She'd had an entrée-sized conch salad and he had grilled pompano, and the view out to the ocean, though not all that much different from the one they had here, managed to be special, very special. Little white boats, sailboats, there were sailboats out there catching the wind and the high hard light of the early afternoon, a whole flotilla of them—somebody said it was a regatta and the idea appealed to her, all those amateur sailors chopping the water into neat grids, back and forth, racing for the pure fun of it. Regatta. She loved the word, repeated it under her breath half a dozen times, and when her lips opened on the first syllable it tasted just like a mojito.

"I thought maybe they'd fight or something, but as far as I can see— so far, I mean—they're like buddies. R.J.—the guy at Herps?—he said snakes get lonely too, so there they are, buddies."

"Seems far-fetched to me. Sounds like a salesman talking."

"Yeah, but I didn't know Willie I was going to turn up again and you know how upset I was when he just disappeared like that . . ."

He didn't acknowledge this, just sat there sunk into the lounge chair, his face pink with the declining sun, the wineglass in one hand, the other trailing on the bleached-out boards of the deck, which really could have used a good coat of sealant, as if she didn't have enough to worry about already. Upkeep. Upkeep was all-important if you wanted your home to last. "Anything to watch on Hulu tonight?" he asked.

She was going to say she wouldn't mind going back to the sci-fi thing, the one where the world ran out of food, though she'd have to admit she was a couple episodes ahead of him because she couldn't resist watching it while he was away, but she didn't have the chance because the phone rang and it was her mother on the line and there was something wrong and she knew that just from the way her mother pronounced her name, her full name, not Cat but Catherine, in a tone shredded with hurt and anxiety.

For a full minute she just listened, the details accumulating like the pebbles that become stones that become boulders in the roaring froth of a mudslide, though what she was hearing was so far out there she just couldn't grasp it. "A tick? What do you mean—it's like minuscule, it's like nothing."

Todd heard the alarm in her voice and, from the chair, he mouthed, *Babe, what's the problem?*

She put her hand over the phone and jerked her head toward him: "It's Coop. He's—"

Todd was on his feet now, the glass still clutched in his hand. He crossed the deck to her. "What? He's not hurt or anything, is he? Was it an accident? Did he have an accident?"

Her mother filled in the details. "We almost lost him," she said, choking down the words, and then the details came, one on the tail of the other in logical progression till the picture was complete: her brother, Cooper, her big brother whom she loved as much as anybody in this world, even as much as Todd, had lost his right arm from the elbow down, which was something she couldn't picture, not at all, because how could you picture an absence?

When her mother was done and she'd asked all the questions she could think of till she was asking them for the third and fourth time, finally she asked the key one, the only one that mattered in the bleakness of the moment: "Is he there? Can I talk to him?"

They were at the hospital. Three to five days, the surgeon said. Cooper was resting. Her mother repeated herself: "I thought we were going to lose him, Cat, I really did."

"Okay," she said, "okay. What about Dad, let me talk to Dad—"

"I just stepped out a minute to go down to the cafeteria—he's up in the room with your brother. I'll tell him to call you."

"Okay," she said, "okay," and her mother broke the connection.

When she turned back to Todd the sun was gone and the air had turned chilly enough so that she wanted to go in and get her jacket. She didn't think about what this was going to do to the wedding, which seemed more and more like a random term written on a scrap of paper whirling down a storm drain, didn't think about herself at all, how could she? Her brother had lost his arm. Her brother was a cripple. She thought of people she'd seen over the years just walking down the street or at the airport or in a restaurant, young guys too, casualties of the war on terror, and how no matter what they did to act normal or how they tried to disguise it, anybody looking at them couldn't help but shudder. It was horrible. Awful. Beyond awful.

She went into the house, her hands shaking, and poured herself another glass of the red. Todd followed her, numb-faced. "Jesus," he said. "I can't believe it. I mean, it's crazy."

She didn't happen to notice what was going on in the terrarium because all that was so beyond irrelevant in the face of this and she was already picturing herself on a flight home, because no matter what Todd said, she was going. In the depths of the terrarium, where the heat lamp glowed and the water bowl trembled ever so fractionally with the activity of Willie II, who was using it as a counterbalance, a primal scene was being enacted: the larger snake, the older one, the one with the brighter pattern, was in the process of unhinging its jaws and working the smaller one, Willie the First, into his alimentary canal.

"The next flight," she said, "I'm out of here, I'm sorry, and I mean, you don't have to come, I know you've got work, but for me, it's my *brother* . . ."

Todd—he was the best—came over and held her and though she never cried because she wasn't one of these weepy manipulative types making life a nonstop drama for everybody concerned, she cried now, and she didn't even know what she was crying for. Todd said, "Of course, babe, no doubt. Take as long as you want."

"I just have to go," she said.

"It's okay," he said, rocking her back and forth. "Everything's going to be fine."

"Fine? His arm's gone, don't you get it?"

He held tight to her.

"It's not going to grow back," she said.

"No," he agreed, "it's not."

She wanted to tell him about the lizards in the backyard at home, how they could lose their tails and have them regenerate miraculously, but that was irrelevant because Cooper wasn't a lizard and it wasn't a tail he'd lost but his arm, his right arm. She tried to imagine how it would look, a bandaged stump like a roast wrapped up in butcher's paper, or some sort of prosthesis, skin-toned plastic or whatever it was, and then she was seeing him at the wedding, Todd's best man, the ring bearer, standing there with the sleeve of his tux hanging empty at his side. She said, "We're going to have to find another date."

"For what? What are you talking about?"

"The wedding," she said.

8

NO MATTER HOW MANY BLOWS

LIFE WENT ON, OF COURSE IT DID, NO MATTER HOW MANY blows you had to take, and this was as bad as it got, this brought her to her knees. Her son, her only son, was maimed. For life. For all his days, even if he lived into the next century, a father, a grandfather, a great-grandfather, a centenarian, he'd be less than whole, incomplete, crippled, the sort of figure people shun in a crowd or pity or mock or just turn their backs on. A week ago he was fine, healthy, perfectly proportioned—handsome as a movie star, actually, her son, her shining son—and now she could hardly bear to look at him. She would have given her own arm, both her arms, if she could have spared him that. But she couldn't. They had to take a scalpel and a bone saw to him to save his life and she knew that, Frank explained it to her, over and over, but the minute they wheeled him into the operating room something got inside of her and started gnawing. She couldn't sleep. Couldn't think of anything but that raw bandaged stump where his arm used to be. After three days of sleeplessness and a tension she'd given birth to that froze her muscles till her whole body was cramped like a spring compressed and compressed again, Frank gave her a sedative, though she hated the idea of it, of blunting her emotions as if she could lock them away in some pharmaceutical drawer and pretend life was all blue skies and sunshine.

The day after that, Cat flew in and she picked her up at the airport and brought her straight to the hospital. Cooper was sitting up in bed, leafing through one of his insect tomes, the TV tuned to a football game, sound muted. He looked good, all things considered, even if he did have to spread the book open flat on his tray table instead of holding it up before him, and he managed a smile, or half a smile, when his sister walked into the room. This was meant to be a surprise, a way of bucking him up, and she herself hadn't said a word to give it away though she'd wanted to as she sat there for hours at his bedside trying desperately to bury the unmentionable with small talk, with chatter, a screed that was as meaningless as the sound of the surf or the wind in the trees, while Cooper stared right through the TV screen as if nothing would ever animate him again.

Cat never hesitated. She came sailing through the door and went right to him to lean over the bed and give him an awkward hug, the IV line and the tray table and the bandaged stump not even worth a second thought. She drew him tight to her, patting his back, and then he was patting hers, or trying to. "I'm not hurting you, Coop, am I?" she asked, drawing back and straightening up so she loomed over him, a tall girl, a pretty girl—her daughter, flown in from Florida with barely a trace of tan and dressed like a model in a magazine.

"Not any worse than Dr. Yang."

"Is he the one?"

Cooper stared at the television. "Yeah, he was the guilty party. The man with the saw."

"He's the best," Ottilie heard herself say, turning to her daughter. "Your father reached out to him personally."

"What are you talking about?" Cooper spat out the words. "We could've just got a guy from the meat department at Safeway—I mean, how much skill does it take to hack off somebody's arm?"

Cat's face was like a mask, pale and almost featureless. She was shaken and trying not to show it. "It sucks," she said. "I know that. I can hardly believe it. But everything's okay now, it's just going to—"

"Take time?"

Cat wasn't backing off. This was her brother. They'd been close all their lives, even through the hormonal storms of adolescence, and they knew each other's every least tic and mood. "Something like that. It's the clichés that count at a time like this, you know that."

"So you're saying I'm just going to have to learn to flick my net left-handed? Make it do loop-de-loops? Swish the air, swish, swish, *swish.*" He lifted his hand as if to demonstrate, but gave up and dropped it to the snarl of bedsheets beside him. "I'm a lefty now, right? Think I ought to practice my curveball, see if I can make the Dodgers?"

Cat let out a laugh, though she tried to rein it back in until she saw the way her brother was looking at her, which ratified it, made it okay, the release the three of them needed. "Why not? But let's face it—you never were much of a jock."

"Point taken. But what about my lifelong ambition to be a concert clarinetist?"

Ottilie laughed then too, the gloom lifting, if only for the moment. Cooper was alive. He was coming home the day after tomorrow. Life would start anew.

"I don't know," Cat said, leaning in to tap his shoulder, timing the punch line, "you could always take up the bugle."

His face dropped and for a minute Ottilie thought they'd gone too far too soon. The joke was grotesque, it was wrong, and she felt depressed all over again, but then Cooper dredged up his grin and said, "Different embouchure."

☀

THE TRULY GROTESQUE THING, the thing she couldn't bear though she didn't dare say a word about it, was the arm itself. Though he'd been all but delirious with a fever that spiked at 104, his eyes inflamed, hair slick with sweat, skin flushed and gummy to the touch—a sick child, *her* sick child—he'd insisted over and over on keeping the dead remnant of his arm as if it were the most precious thing in the world, as if it could come back to life like in some horror movie. "I'm not medical waste," he kept repeating, and "This isn't the Civil War" and "Promise me, promise me." She couldn't look at it. Didn't want it in the house. But he'd been so insistent, so distraught and traumatized, he'd persuaded Frank to bring it home from the hospital in a jar of formalin with a black plastic trash bag taped around it and he kept it by the bedside in his boyhood room, where he was staying until he could sort things out and get back to the business of his life.

All right. Fine. Her son's hand and forearm were preserved in a too-tall jar like an exhibit in a museum of curiosities, like the sheep fetus curled in on itself in the biology lab in college, wet flesh forever cramped and puckered, there for the edification of generations of students, probably still there, the jar speckled with dust and the smell neutralized in its chemical bath yet still somehow mysteriously present. She thought of the boy in Cooper's high school class—Ronald Fortier, wasn't it?—who rode up off the bump of a wooden leg with every other step, cancer having taken the flesh, blood and bone from him before it took the rest of him too midway through their senior year. He hadn't kept his missing leg, had he? And if he had, what good did it do him?

Still, if that was what Cooper wanted, as gut-wrenching as it was, then that was his prerogative, his choice—he was the one who'd suffered, not her. No, the important thing here was reestablishing a feeling of normalcy. Throughout their lives, before the kids had gone off to college, anyway, she'd made a point of seeing the family gathered together for dinner no matter the pressures of work and school and conflicting schedules—and so it was now. The first two nights they had takeout, Mexican and Chinese respectively, Cat's choice because the Floridians just couldn't seem to manage either one of them, at least not to her standards. Cooper was barely there but he did sit at the table with them and ply his fork left-handed without asking for anybody's help or attention or pity and if he drank too much you could forgive him that. (They all drank too much, actually, because what else could you do when anything you said was liable to set him off and any expression of sympathy or even concern just froze him into an ice sculpture? And your eyes— what to do with your eyes? You couldn't stare, couldn't watch him eat or fumble with his fork or even look him in the face for fear he'd shrink into himself—or worse, lurch up out of his chair and disappear down the hall.) They'd ordered tacos from La Fonda because tacos didn't need to be cut up—and with the Chinese, though they usually preferred chopsticks, Ottilie laid out forks only.

On the third night she cooked the meal herself, reprising the entomo-menu from the dinner party because she knew it would please him. In the afternoon, though he'd been loath to leave the yard or show himself anywhere in public, Cat had cajoled him into taking a hike on one of the trails up on the ridge where they used to go as kids, which was good, great actually, because it got him out of the house. If his sleeve dangled free, it wouldn't matter because there'd be nobody there to notice and at least he'd be out-of-doors, in nature, where he most wanted to be. It was a small step. And she had to bite her tongue to keep from lathering him with admonitions about tick repellent and staying on the path and tossing his clothes in the washer afterward and stepping directly into the shower. (But could he shower? Of course he could—he'd just have to be careful to keep the arm elevated and out of the line of spray. At least till it was healed over. And then there'd be a prosthesis which he could remove when necessary, and yet the mental picture of that, of some sort of mechanical arm lying there next to the sink or across the tank lid of the toilet, sent a shudder through her. But that was wrong. That was ridiculous. She wasn't squeamish, not when it came to her own son. She'd have to do better, she told herself.)

Mari brought sake again and she brought her Scotties too, which was a treat for Dunphy, a minimally motivated dog who lacked company and slept off the days as if they were going to last forever. She'd been to the house twice since Cooper's release from the hospital and though Cooper showed flashes of his old self and they spent their time sitting around the pool with Cat and a twelve-pack of beer, rock music spilling out of the radio and the birds darting over the surface in alternating bands of light and shadow so that the world was the best simulacrum of what it once was, it didn't seem to help. He sank back into himself. Became withdrawn. Sullen. Especially with Mari, as if he somehow blamed her for what had happened, but it was just bad luck, that was all. Catastrophically bad luck. He would have been out in the field anyway, whether he was chasing down ticks with her or butterflies or beetles or whatever else he happened to be collecting at the moment. That was his life and his profession too.

The trick at dinner was to try to bring him out without making him aware of it, but it wasn't really working because no matter what topic she latched onto (or Frank or Cat or Mari, who were all under the same constraints), Cooper kept tight-mouthed. Mari said the *chapulines* were even better than the first time and they all batted that around for a while—the temperature of the oil, the freshness of the grasshoppers, knowing when they were done and resisting the urge to overcook them, which would sap the flavor—but the spirit just wasn't there. Cat provided a running commentary on the cuisine, from the point of view of a neophyte. "I've never eaten bugs before," she said, "or at least not knowingly, but with some of the Haitian places down there, I'm sure I must've gotten a little gratis protein boost along with my griot and red beans," and "Jesus, Mom, I didn't know you were so into insects or I would have brought you a couple bushels of organic palmetto bugs harvested from under my very own refrigerator," which was good, which was normal, which made them all forget for seconds at a time that half of Cooper's arm was gone.

Frank, who was sitting at the far end of the table, Cooper and Mari on one side of him, Cat on the other, set down his glass of sake and gave their daughter one of his mock-sage looks, lifted eyebrows, pursed lips, eyes professorially fixed on her. "Cockroaches, you mean."

"Right," Cat said. "They're the size of bats in Florida."

"Well," Mari said, stretching the single syllable to two, "you've got to make use of whatever protein source you can. Really, get used to it—that's the world of the future."

"Not to mention the present," Ottilie put in. "Cooper's the one—you can thank him for this amazing cuisine, and really, could a meal be greener?"

Cat had been pouring sake with a free hand and her speech had begun to stumble ever so slightly. "I wish I could catch them all," she said, "and feed them one by one to Willie." She paused, as if calling up the image. "But really, he's too big to bother with anything that small." Another pause. "Did I tell you what happened to the first Willie? Or what we think happened?"

"Who's Willie?" Mari tightened her brow muscles round the interrogative, a grid of exaggerated lines blooming there—wrinkles, and in a girl so young, which seemed alarming. What was that all about? Too much time in the field? Too much squinting into a microscope or manipulating eight-legged images on a screen? Was she wearing contacts? The picture of her father online, Ottilie recalled, showed him in a pair of oversized glasses with lenses so dense they distorted his eyes.

"My Burmie."

"You mean a python? A pet python?"

In the next moment, Cat was passing her phone around the table, showing off pictures of herself with her snake wrapped round her shoulders like a mink stole, with the difference being that it was alive, of course, whereas the mink, foxes and chinchillas people used to wear were all dead. Which was barbaric, as far as Ottilie was concerned.

Society had wised up and turned the page on that. Thankfully. It had been years since she'd seen the images of the protests on TV in which demonstrators—college girls, mostly—stood jeering outside fur emporia and even, in one instance she knew of, had flung a bucket of blood at a woman coming out the door in an ermine stole.

Cat's phone went to Cooper. He took it in his hand, his good hand, his only hand. Stared down at it a long moment. "Don't tell me you're really doing this?" he said, jerking his head up to glare at his sister. "It's not some trick photo, right? This is you, in *Florida* of all places, with a *Burmese* python draped around your shoulders?"

Cat looked right into his eyes. She nodded.

"You know how fucking wrong that is? How fucking crazy?"

Frank, who'd been operating at half speed all night, his conversational tools dulled under the duress of having to pretend that everything was fine, that the medical profession was redemptive and their son the luckiest young man alive, said, "Come on, Coop, don't be like that."

Cooper ignored him. He was fixed on Cat, his face distorted with disbelief and outrage. "You of all people," he said. "If the average moron doesn't know any better, you certainly should. What do you think, animals are toys? Or what, fashion accessories? Is that what they are now?"

"I want to be an influencer," Cat said. "I love snakes. I love Willie."

"Mari, back me up here, will you? I mean, *Burmese pythons*? Can't you read—or the news, don't you watch the news? Are you living in a bubble or what?" He slammed his fist down on the table, glasses rattling, plates jumping, and then he was on his feet, looming over his sister, gesticulating in a whole new way, his anger out of all proportion to the situation, to Cat's sin, whatever it was in the grander scheme. "These things, these fucking things," he shouted, jabbing his index finger at the image on the phone's screen. "They've decimated the Everglades, hunted down every last thing that walks or crawls or flies. Right? Right, Mari? From muskrats to raccoons and egrets—and deer, even deer, for Christ's sake . . . Alligators! They're eating their way through the alligators now."

Mari nodded, but you could see she wanted no part of this.

"It's not like I'm going to let him loose or anything," Cat said, throwing it right back at him.

"What happens when it's twenty feet long and weighs twice as much as you? What are you going to do then?"

"Don't treat me like a child. You've kept animals in tanks and cages all your life and nobody ever—"

He was trembling. The stump of his arm jerked spasmodically. "Shit, shit, shit!" he shouted. "You just don't get it, do you?"

Cat glared back at him. "Apparently not." Her lips were drawn tight. "And by the way, fuck you."

"Yeah, and fuck you too," he said, swinging round and stalking out of the room, the empty sleeve dangling loose at his side.

THE FIRST THOUGHT SHE HAD in the morning, the thought that seized her and forced her eyes open, was that her son was a cripple and there was nothing she or anybody else could do about it. She resisted twisting round to look at the clock. Frank was snoring. The dog was snoring. It was still dark. She tried to get back to sleep, but her mind wouldn't let her. Still, she forced herself to lie there till the windows took hold of the light, then she got up, shuffled barefoot to the kitchen and put the coffee on. The empty space on the counter where the cricket reactor had sat was a reminder that the new one hadn't come yet, though ostensibly it was on its way to her via UPS, as was the mealworm farm and a two-pound sack of cricket flour to tide her over till she could get her own production up and running again.

The pool was colder than ever, but the shock was what she needed, like in the old black-and-white movies where the women fainted on cue and the heroes with the pomaded hair clasped them in their arms and slapped them back to consciousness. She counted off her laps, then lost count and flipped over and did the backstroke awhile, her face turned to the sky. The sky was deep and cloudless and she fell into a kind of trance, her arms and legs working mechanically, coming to only long enough to keep from cracking her head on the coping at the end of each lap. At one point she noticed two, no, three points of light hovering over her and realized they were worker bees traversing the pool to get to the penstemon she'd planted along the fence—*her* worker bees. They were still getting settled in, of course, and what with the trauma over Cooper, she'd all but forgotten them, and yet here they were, going about their lives in her backyard as if they'd never known anything else. It would be nice to have honey but the main thing here was that the bees didn't need any tending at all otherwise, which reminded her of the hive Cooper had kept when he was maybe eleven or twelve, as a case in point. The whole thing had been purely serendipitous. One day she went out to the trash can and saw a stream of bees working their way in and out of a quarter-sized circular hole in the plastic lid, which struck her as odd because bees weren't attracted to garbage the way yellowjackets were, but it seemed as if they'd somehow found it to their liking. She watched them a moment, fascinated, then very gingerly slid the can to one side and set another in its place, by way of sparing the garbagemen.

Cooper was thrilled. A wild swarm had taken up residence atop the trash! What could be better? When he briefly lifted the lid to show her, she saw that they'd built—or were building—honeycombs round the circular plastic walls. "Mom," he'd said in his piping tones, "we can have honey! We can sell it!" And Frank had said, "Great idea. You can set up a stand by the roadside with a big banner that says 'Pure Garbage Honey.' What do you think?"

"*Dad*, nobody's going to want that."

"Oh, I don't know. It's unique. A boutique item—you know what boutique is? I mean, anybody can offer the consumer clover honey or orange-blossom honey, but pure garbage honey? You'll corner the market."

The wonderful thing about a swim, even when the water was like glacial runoff, was the way it freed your mind at the same time it was

pouring endorphins into your bloodstream. She pulled herself up out
of the pool at the end of one of her miscounted laps, toweled off and
padded barefoot into the house, stripped off her swimsuit and took a
quick shower—very quick, because of the water restrictions the drought
had imposed, *yet again*—then went into the kitchen to feed the dog and
see about breakfast. Frank was already gone—he didn't take much for
breakfast, anyway, a piece of fruit, wheat toast, something he could gnaw
on in the car—but she thought she'd make cricket cakes and soft-boiled
eggs for Cooper and herself. She was mixing the batter with a wooden
spoon when it occurred to her to poke her head in the door and wake
him by way of easing him out of his dreams and into the world that was
moving forward whether he was ready for it or not. She propped up the
spoon in the batter and went down the hall, knocked lightly and pushed
open the door.

Her son wasn't there. His backpack was gone from where it had sat
in a jumble of clothes on the desk and the tall plastic-wrapped specimen
jar no longer stood on the floor beside the bed—which was made, if
haphazardly. She swung round on her heels and went to the front door
to see if his car was in the driveway, which she already knew it wouldn't
be. But why would he slip off like this without a word? That wasn't like
him. Or maybe it was. Maybe he was somebody else now.

She knew she should let it go, but she couldn't help herself and in
the next moment she was tapping his number on her cell. He didn't
answer. She called again. Still no answer. She was back in the kitchen
heating the griddle and wondering what she was going to do with the
pancakes, when he rang her back.

"Mom?"

"Cooper, where are you? You left already?"

"Yeah."

"To run an errand, or—?"

"I'm on my way home."

"But you didn't say anything—and when you didn't answer the
phone I didn't know what to think. Are you all right?"

His voice clenched. "It's not exactly easy to dig the phone out of your pocket when you're driving one-handed—you ever think of that?"

"But you're okay, right?"

It took him a moment to answer. She heard the swish of cars on the roadway and realized he must have pulled over to call her back. "I'm fine," he said.

"Yes," she said, "of course you are."

But she knew it was a lie.

9

THE WEDDING

HE WAS ANGRY, HE WAS HOPELESS, HE WAS ASHAMED, BUT he wasn't going to spoil Cat's wedding for her. She'd already postponed it twice, first when the groom's mother died unexpectedly (or rather, expectedly, since every living thing is programmed to die, but in this case at an unexpected time) and then again when he'd had his own brush with mortality. Though the last thing he wanted was to see anybody anywhere for any reason, he nonetheless found himself on this sunny December morning back at his parents' house poised before the mirror in the upstairs bathroom, trying to clip a black bow tie to the collar of a tuxedo shirt with one hand while the caterer invaded the kitchen and the band set up in the yard under a canopy they weren't going to need. At least not for rain. There was no rain in the forecast. There might never be rain in the forecast again. Today was the winter solstice, when the sun was supposed to be muted and feeble, but it was fixed there in a cloudless sky, temperatures in the eighties already and expected to rise into the nineties, breaking the high-temperature reading for the date, which had been set the previous year when the record from two years prior to that had been shattered. Great weather for a wedding, but not much else—or at least not anything that depended on water to survive.

Even before what had happened, he'd been growing his hair out for no other reason than that it felt good trailing down the back of his neck and falling loose across his brow, and now, once he'd got the tie clipped in place, he gave his head a shake to rearrange it. He didn't use mousse or spray or any other hair product because he didn't like the texture, the stickiness, the perfumed stink of it—even the unscented ones seemed to carry a freight of something that attracted midges and fungus gnats and agglutinated every speck of dander and leaf matter out in the field into dangling hair ornaments—but now he wished he had. As he'd come to discover, it was no easy trick brushing your hair one-handed, though he tried now, with mixed results. He was just patting it in place when the door pushed open and the startled face of Todd, his soon-to-be brother-in-law, appeared in the doorway. "Oh, man, sorry," Todd said, already backing away. "I didn't know anybody was in here."

"No problem. I'm just finishing up." He shook out his hair again, self-consciously this time. "How do I look?"

"Great. Really great." They'd been through the preliminaries when Todd had flown in three days ago, Todd grinning and ducking his head, fighting himself to keep from reaching out a hand for a brother-in-lawly shake and trying to hide his look of shock and confusion. At the moment, of course, Todd was dissembling. Lying, that is. How could he look great with an empty sleeve and a misaligned bow tie? But Todd was getting married and Todd was already stoned on something, his eyes lit from within and his pupils dilated like miniature bowling balls. His tuxedo was flawless, some custom-fit designer thing that put his own rented version to shame, but then tuxedos were as integral to Todd's profession as they were to James Bond's. Todd was a brand ambassador, for Bacardí. He hosted parties all over the country. And now, with Cat's help (and Frank and Ottilie Cullen's pecuniary input), he was hosting this one.

Cooper grinned till his lips ached. He was thinking the only way he was going to get through this was by hitting the champagne early and consistently. It was eleven a.m. The ceremony wouldn't start for two hours yet, but if Todd was already indulging, why shouldn't he? Just then the tip of his nose began to itch, a sudden maddening sensation as if he'd been stung—which he hadn't, thankfully, though his mother's bees were out there in the yard ready to oblige. His brain sent a signal to his right arm and his right arm rose as if to come into play before it dropped again to his side and the sinistral arm rose to take its place—and no, he hadn't experienced phantom pain in his stump. Or not yet, anyway. Small blessings. Small blessings, indeed.

"You cool with the ring?" Todd was asking. "Because we might as well"—he fumbled in his pocket and came up with a miniature black velvet box and handed it over—"I mean, before I lose it or something . . ."

Cooper took the box and stuffed it into his breast pocket even as one of the band members below announced himself with a sudden screech of guitar distortion followed by a jagged burst of laughter. A breeze sifted in through the window screen, though, sadly, screens were hardly needed anymore, even at night. Forget the moths, forget the beetles—they just seemed to have dwindled away. And whether that was a statistical blip or a function of population cycles or something a whole lot more ominous was anybody's guess. There weren't even any mosquitoes—the drought had seen to that.

"Cool," Todd said, giving him an automatic grin. He had something else in his hand now, a joint the color of a ripe banana and as fat as one of the *chapulines* frying in a pan in the kitchen (much to the disgust of the caterer, a stringy-haired woman in her mid-thirties with collagen-engorged lips and wraparound eyes who owned a bistro in Santa Monica and was doing the wedding as a special favor to Todd—along with a check for $18,000, that is). "You want a hit?"

He took the joint and stuck it awkwardly between his lips while Todd produced a vintage lighter embossed with the Bacardí logo and lit it for him. He filled his lungs dutifully—if his intention was to get wrecked, why not start now, especially since the groom had already left the gate ahead of him? It was tricky—still tricky—to rely on his left hand, but he managed to smoothly pluck the joint from his lips and hand it back. Todd took a hit and returned it, his eyes fractured with the effort his lungs and circulatory system were making in transferring the cannabinoids to his brain, where they were meant to enliven and dull him at the same time. "Amazing, huh?" Todd said, exhaling.

The bathroom, a relic of Cat's preadolescent taste, was tiled in pink, a color she'd insisted on for her eleventh birthday. It felt familiar and he was grateful for that.

"I mean," Todd said, "Cat and me? Finally?"

What could he say? He liked Todd well enough and this was a fine thing on a fine day, though when he handed the joint back this time he felt less exhilarated than just plain dizzy. It was early yet. Plenty of time to face the wedding guests and their wondering stares and furtive assessments, each and every one of whom you can be sure had been apprised beforehand about his accident or misfortune or whatever you wanted to call it. His abridgement. His curtailment. His winnowing. *Someday, son, somebody's going to cut you down to size.* He'd worn the shrinker sock over the stump and dutifully proceeded with physical therapy. Everything was going as well as could be expected—except for his brain, which pushed and pulled at him through every waking hour and mangled his dreams at night. PTSD. Combat veterans suffered from it, crime victims, the poor, the abused, the helpless. The acronym was on the counselor's lips, on his father's, lying in ambush.

His father had touted the advances in prosthetics and he'd had a preliminary fitting for a Hero Arm, "a multi-grip bionic arm with multi-grip functionality and empowering aesthetics" developed for mutilated veterans coming back from the Middle East and anybody else unlucky enough to be in their position, and in time he'd have an operation to reconnect his nerves so that it would work like an actual arm with the fine motor skills of the real thing. Almost. He didn't want a bionic arm—he just wanted his own arm back, but limbs didn't regenerate, not in the species to which he belonged. At least the Hero Arm made no pretense about what it was, unlike the brutally inert flesh-colored attachments of the past. It was made of Nylon 12 and came with an array of bright magnetic covers for the forearm that had nothing in common with synthetic flesh. This was an arm that announced itself. An arm that said fuck you to the world.

"Marriage," Todd said, musingly. "It's the ultimate, you know?" He was grinning, hadn't stopped grinning since this little interaction had begun, as if, for all his bravado and the armor of cool he wore 24/7 he didn't quite know how to behave in the presence of a newly abridged man on his very own wedding day. "And if you love each other, and we do, this is it. Right, bro? And in, what"—he rotated his wrist to check the big black-faced Alpina watch he liked to flash whenever he could—"one hour and fifty-five minutes, that won't just be a casual phrase anymore, know what I mean? *Bro-in-law?* You and me and Cat, right? Right?"

Down below in the yard, the guitar let out another screech, then thickened into a three-chord progression before choking off again. "Yeah," he said, "absolutely. But what I really want to know is, did anybody crack any of that champagne yet?"

CEREMONIES HAVE TO PLAY OUT at length and the duller they are the better, the whole point being to solemnize the occasion with cant, cliché and papered-over sentiments so that when finally the words are exhausted the release is nothing short of electrifying. After listening to the minister rattle on for a good twenty minutes ("Married life is full of adventures, surprises and memory-making—all made possible by the enduring power of love"), while standing there with the ring in his pocket and everybody's eyes on his empty sleeve, he was more than ready to celebrate something, anything, as long as a sufficient quantity of champagne was involved. He was sweating, woozy, half-plastered already, and when the time came to produce the ring, Todd had to nudge him to bring him back to life—and while he didn't drop it at the groom's feet as he was sure he was going to, the worry over it fairly well ruined things for him vis-á-vis taking any pleasure in his sister's big sacramental moment.

Then there was (more) champagne and the preliminary round of food and the band lurching into something with a bouncy preprandial beat to it. Mari, who looked like two scoops of ice cream in a vanilla gown that fit her like a wetsuit, leaned in to him for a kiss. The champagne went right to him. He wondered morosely if that was because there was less arterial terrain for his blood to cover—and if he was feeling sorry for himself, why shouldn't he be? He didn't want to look at anybody or be looked at in turn, but here he was, and next up on the agenda was the plate juggling. The dinner was going to be a sit-down affair, but the cocktails and hors d'oeuvres (tuna tartare cones, scallop-and-veggie skewers, prosciutto-wrapped persimmons, samosas with tamarind sauce and his mother's grasshoppers and critter fritters to round things out) required standing around with *two hands* in full operation, one for your glass, one for your plate, and while Mari stayed close to him, providing a running commentary and feeding tidbits into his mouth, she soon grew bored with that and so did he. "Look," he said, "I think I'm going to go mill—if that's okay?"

Her eyes assessed him, searched him, everything he did or said these days an occasion for analysis. "You don't have to worry about me—I can mill too. And later, you know, whenever, you just tell me when you want to go, no matter how early—or late." She grinned, pecked a kiss to his cheek. "I love weddings—did I ever tell you that?"

He went straight to the bar for a refill, the band's beat beginning to infuse him despite himself, his feet tapping and his head nodding autonomously as he held out his glass for the bartender. He was experiencing a variety of oblivion, no plate to hold, no apologies to make, the sun glazing his face and his mother's bees behaving themselves, when a voice came at him from his right side and he found himself staring into the face of Melody Foster, one of his sister's friends from high school he'd dated a couple of times senior year. Dated and penetrated, though they'd gone their separate ways to separate colleges and the years and the mileage had quashed whatever they might have felt for each other at the time. She looked good, very good, with her wide appealing face and eyes that disappeared when she grinned, which she was doing now. She didn't ask how he was, as just about everybody else had, essentially speaking in code because they could plainly see how he was unless they were blind, but just held her grin and said, "Tough luck, huh?"

He tried to shrug, but couldn't quite manage it. "Yeah," he said. "The toughest."

She waited till the bartender filled her glass, which she massaged between her hands as if she were molding dough, then took a quick gulp, dropped the grin and let her eyes widen. "Can I see it?"

"See what?"

"You know—your stump?"

He could have been offended, could have acted shocked, could have just turned away and ignored her, but suddenly none of that applied— this was his moment of truth, the tipping point between life as it had been and as it was going to be from here on out. He'd seen the counselor at the hospital and done his homework—books, pamphlets, the internet—and along the way acquired the relevant term, acrotomophilia, which denoted sexual attraction to amputees and by extension the erotic possibilities of stumps. Like his. Like the smoothed-over folded-up phallic terminus of what had once been his right arm. "What," he said, "here?"

Melody was living in New York now, working for some tech start-up, and she'd come in a week early for the wedding so she could get a little sun, which she'd succeeded in doing, her tan honeying her bare shoulders and descending to the tops of her breasts, which she was displaying in a low-cut electric-blue gown. "I don't know," she said, "why not? It's not like it's anything to be ashamed of, right? It's just life."

Sex. There was always a quid pro quo. And where was Mari? Milling. He scanned the crowd of wedding guests, heads and shoulders and laughing faces, and didn't spot her, but then she *was* petite, after all, so that was no surprise. "How about inside?" he said. "Where it's more private?"

✺

THE WIND CAME UP IN fits and starts but didn't begin in earnest till all hundred-and-some-odd guests were seated at the big long conjoined tables and digging into the first course—smoked salmon on crispy potato cakes with a dollop of sour cream and dill, served with a local sauvignon blanc the bridegroom himself had selected. There was patter, tranquility, a welcome breeze, and then all at once a gust whipped in out of the chaparral to seize hold of the canopies—the full-sized one that kept the band out of the sun and the more modest ones the caterer had erected over the bar and service area—and set them flapping like sails. Napkins and wedding programs went winging into the air, glasses rocked, hairdos jumped and lurched—and then nothing. Calm. The sun still held there in the sky, cranking the temperature, and all up and down the length of the tables people were anchoring their glasses with one hand and patting their hair back in place with the other. They'd been taken by surprise. But this was an outdoor wedding, with an open bar and the promise of gourmet cuisine, and they grinned at each other and winked and laughed and tossed quips back and forth. A little wind, that was all. Better than bugs, right?

He was seated at the head of the table with the wedding party—his parents, Todd's aunt and her husband (who were subbing for Todd's parents, both of whom were dead), the bride and groom, and Mari. Melody Foster, whose scent was still on him, was at the other side of the quadrangle next to the guy she'd come with, a big-headed dullard with erratic hair made worse by the attack of the wind.

Mari said, "I didn't hear anything about sundowners, did you? It was just supposed to be clear, I thought. And hot?"

This was a subject he could dive into, the erasure of norms, the destruction of the environment, meteorological chaos. "You can't even have an outdoor wedding, right? Not even in December. I mean, really, what's the world coming to?"

"Weddings don't count much in the grand scheme of things, is that what you're saying?"

"Not when everything's turning to shit before your eyes."

Her hair slashed across her face. She was giving him that maddening look of psychic dissection. "Sorry, but I can't agree. We need the rituals more than ever now. They're our guide, they stabilize us. Humanize us. Come on, it's your *sister's wedding*..."

Another gust hit then, a sustained one this time, the dumb force of it heaving at their torsos as if it meant to prostrate them. One of the waiters, plates shingled along the length of his left arm, took a direct hit and lost them all, crockery shattering on the flagstones and fragments of salmon and crispy potato cake flung out across the lawn like the refuse it had instantly become, dog food, bird food, beetle food. "Tell it to the Pacific Decadal Oscillation and the cranked-up CO_2 levels in the atmosphere and all the jerks and deniers and the paid shills of the oil companies and, and—" He was worked up, furious suddenly, pulse racing and heart slamming at his ribs, but here came the next gust, tearing the words from his mouth.

Everybody was stirring now, muscles tensed, faces frozen in mid-chew, and all at once Cat and his mother were on their feet, Cat rapping with a fork at the rim of her glass to get the guests' attention even as a fresh blast toppled one of the hired Porta-Potties with a plasticized shriek and the tablecloths jumped and tugged like tethered animals. "It's okay," Cat said, her voice unsteady. "It's going to be fine. Everything's going to be fine. We just have to—"

"The house," his mother called out. "Can we all maybe just adjourn to the house for a bit till this blows over? Or at least, at least—" A pair of tumbleweeds, Russian thistle, invasive in North America, came hurtling over the fence, jumped the band's canopy and sank into the pool. There was the low animal moan of eucalyptus trees chafing followed by the crack of unstable limbs and the whipping of leaves. People lurched to their feet and started for the house, hunched against the wind. There was no way all these people could squeeze inside and even if they could, where were they going to settle down to enjoy the three-star entrées the bistro woman and her staff had been preparing all morning? He could see that clearly, even if his mother couldn't—and the last thing he wanted was to be crushed up against the wall in the living room with all these people pressing in on him, or worse, going through contortions to avoid touching him as if mutilation were contagious.

With Melody it had been different. He'd followed her up the stairs and into his boyhood room (from which all traces of his teenage life had been removed but for the bed, the carpet and the desk so that it seemed almost a foreign space to him now), and guided her through the door with a touch of his hand at her elbow. She felt light, buoyant, willing. They stood in the middle of the room and kissed, kissed deeply, and the taste and smell and feel of her was like a sensory road map to the past, which was fine, which was all right, which wasn't wrong at all but the very opposite of wrong. Yet here was the truth—she wanted to see where he'd been hurt, where he'd never heal, and that took things in another direction. It was perverse. *She* was perverse. Even before she put her hand on his crotch to press his erection through the flimsy rented suit, he was having second thoughts. *Can I see it?* she'd asked. *It's not like it's anything to be ashamed of.*

It was no mean feat to slip the dress down her shoulders with one hand, but the brassiere was another thing altogether. He was hot and yet he wasn't. He went through the motions, molding her breasts through the silky cloth, but there were two breasts and he only had one hand, and in the next moment she was trying to roll up his sleeve, still clinging to him, still working her tongue in his mouth, but reaching for his arm now, and that was all wrong. He felt her hand there inside his sleeve, exploring, massaging, insinuating itself, and before he could think he was pulling away from her. "I don't know if I can do this," he said, his voice sounding as if it were coming from someone else altogether.

"Get over it," she said. "You know I had a boyfriend with one leg once? And don't give me that look—no, it wasn't Ronald Fortier, but this English guy I met that summer I spent in Europe?"

"Which leg?"

"I don't know. What difference does it make? One of them, that's all."

"So what are you saying—you're turned on by cripples?"

"Oh, stop it. You know I've always had a thing for you." From outside came the rattle of drums and the rising wail of the singer's voice working through a number so familiar Cooper could have sung it in his sleep except that he'd forgotten the lyrics and the name of the tune and even the band that originally recorded it—and they were one of his all-time favorites, weren't they?

"This very room," she said. "Right here, right on that bed. I lost my virginity to you, do you even remember that?" She gave him a loose wide-lipped smile. "Come on," she said. "I won't bite. Promise."

He was already shaking his head. "No," he said, "no, I don't think so."

She dropped her arms to her sides, her eyes locked on his. "Okay, I get it, I understand," she said, nodding vigorously, too vigorously, as if her head had pulled loose from the muscles and ligaments that anchored it to her shoulders. "All I wanted was to reconnect, you know? And I thought you—" She made a corkscrew gesture with one hand, communicating the remainder of the sentiment in semaphore. After a moment she said, "This girl you're with—I mean, are you two serious?"

THEY WERE ALL PACKED SHOULDER to shoulder in the hallway, the kitchen and the three downstairs rooms, clutching champagne flutes and cocktail glasses, wondering where the food was and trying to convince themselves they were having a good time. People perched on the backs of the sofa and armchairs and lined the steps going up to the second story, their legs gathered in the grip of their arms or folded under them in submission. The wind was omnipresent, raking the house with a hiss and clamor like a subway coming into the station. A drumbeat of fine particles rapped against the windows and at intervals there was the thump of something more substantial striking the roof. Cat, who was frantic, distraught, three-quarters looped and the molten center of everything, kept saying it was just like a hurricane, though as far as he knew she'd never experienced one—or not yet, anyway. The windows shuddered in their frames. Everybody was sweating.

Of course, there was no room for the band, and now, half an hour after the exodus had begun, he glanced out the window and saw the musicians fighting their way across the yard in a humped-over sprint, amps and instruments clutched in their arms, the rented canopy, shredded and frame-bent, left for dead behind them. Somebody turned on the radio, the volume just high enough to drown out the wind, because this was a party, still a party, lest anyone should forget. Hip-hop. Hip-hop was the cure for anything. As for the waiters—they were out there in the blow, trying to salvage what they could while the caterer bulled her way through the kitchen, shooing people, rattling pans, delivering orders in a voice of cold fury.

At some point he found himself in the hallway, leaning against the wall, Mari pressed tight to him in the crush. They were both drinking steadily. Mari's electric-blue gown was soaked through with sweat and there was no relief for that because you couldn't even think of opening the windows and there was no air-conditioning to turn on because air-conditioners were redundant here in the coastal zone. Or had been till now, anyway. And now was too late. Mari said, "Poor Cat."

He just nodded. He could have said, "Who would have guessed?" but he already knew the answer to that. The climate was changing, *had* changed, and the only reliable place for a gathering like this was an underground bunker.

His mother emerged from the kitchen then, trailing Peter and Sylvie, and came down the hall to him, her face flushed and her hair, which

had been done up in a French braid at the beauty salon, in a state of collapse. Her eyes were haunted. "That woman," she said.

"Who? Who are you talking about?"

"Noni."

He was puzzled. "Who's Noni?"

"The caterer? She's saying she's not going to be able to serve dinner
under these conditions, as if I had anything to do with it."

"Sue her," Sylvie said.

"She just refuses. *Force majeure*, she says. And I practically begged
her, Cat did too, just to use the oven to heat up whatever and lay it out
buffet-style if we have to because obviously we can't go back out there
and have a sit-down dinner—"

"Peter looked at the weather," Sylvie said, "and it's not going to let
up is what they say."

Peter's beard was beaded with sweat. If anything, his tux was an
even worse fit than Cooper's own. He was smiling though, enjoying the
chaos, bringing the party right home where it belonged. "It's supposed
to keep up till this time tomorrow—and the worst is yet to come, from
five on, they say."

Next it was Cat, still in her wedding gown, backing out of the
kitchen with a glass in one hand and a bottle of champagne in the other,
her voice raised and snapping like a whip at somebody in the kitchen, at
Noni, the caterer, whose face appeared in the doorway, snapping back.
"I'm sorry if you're disappointed," Noni shouted, "but I'm here, you see
me? I wasn't hired to serve dinner in a wind tunnel, was I? And I tell
you, even if I had a week, this kitchen's barely adequate—I couldn't
even cook for ten in there. Nobody could." Her voice rose up the ladder. "And I despise electric ranges, they're like the worst, they are the
worst, and no matter what I do this is going to be a disaster, okay, so
don't blame me!"

It was at that very moment that the power cut off, mooting the question and replacing the festive thump of hip-hop with the thin whining
protest of the security alarm.

☀

THEY WOUND UP EATING COLD entrées off handheld plates while standing or sitting wherever they could find room, which began to open up as one couple after another fought their way out the door to tip the valet, slam into their cars and swerve off down the road. His father rigged up a couple of portable solar lamps when the sun went down and his mother and Mari went round lighting candles to take some of the gloom off, but it was a full-on catastrophe no matter how you viewed it. By the time the cake was served and Todd and Cat posed for the ceremonial pictures, there weren't more than thirty people left to witness the event. The wind was the only thing now. It screamed. The windows flexed and bowed. Todd, whose tux somehow still managed to look crisp, raised his glass for a toast. "I just hope the rest of the marriage goes better than this!"

Cat looked wounded. Drunk. Beyond drunk.

"Right, babe?" Todd said, wrapping an arm around her and hugging her to him. Then he looked out over the huddle of faces and said, "It's got to be. And I'll tell you, all you great people who we love, we really, really love, if we can survive this we can survive anything, right, babe?" He let it hang there a moment, then gave her a long nuptial kiss.

There were cheers, whistles, a crash of applause, but there was something desperate in the performance. People looked on the verge of collapse, skin blotched, hair soaked through, sweat mapping their faces. The heat was staggering. Mari, still trying to make the best of things, fetched two slices of the cake (lemon-lavender, cricketless), handed him one and settled down on the floor beside him, the available chairs reserved for the elders—his parents, Todd's aunt and uncle, Sylvie and Peter, a grim-faced woman he'd never seen before who sat there fanning herself with one of the useless menus and gasping as if she were breathing through a snorkel. "I think we ought to go after this, don't you?" Mari whispered.

He was feeling good, or if not good, better, anyway, and if he was truly drunk for the first time since his accident, that undeniably had something to do with it. As did Melody Foster, who was seated on the floor in the near corner with her escort, date, whoever he was, and showing off her legs where she'd hiked up her gown in deference to the heat. Twice during the past hour she'd come up to press in close to him and Mari and run Mari through a version of twenty questions about everything from her college affiliation to her taste in music, books, movies and bugs. (*You're an entomologist too, so I hear? You know what we used to call Coop in high school?*)

"Give it a bit," he said, the plate propped in his lap, glancing to Melody Foster and back. "For Cat's sake."

If he was vaguely contemplating ducking out on Mari and slipping upstairs with Melody Foster again and letting her do whatever she wanted with his arm and the rest of him too, he didn't have the opportunity to see it play out because what had merely been bad to this point suddenly got a whole lot worse—there was a whiff of smoke on the air. Smoke. The windows were shut tight but there it was, unmistakable, and this wasn't the scorched metallic tang of a chop burning in a pan or a bagel in the toaster, but something denser, wilder, a fierce toxic strain broadcast wide and closing fast.

"Oh, my god," his mother said, and the whole room heard her in the stunned silence of the moment. "Is that what I think it is?"

The sirens started up then and his father threw open the back door, whether that was advisable or not, and before anybody could think, they were all out on the patio, the wind hurling debris at them and the smoke infesting their noses and mouths and throats. People cursed. The wind screamed. And the fire was already on the ridge behind them, turning night into day.

10

TAHOE

COUNTING BACK, SHE REALIZED IT MUST HAVE HAPPENED ON the honeymoon, which was five days in Tahoe at a resort one of Todd's contacts managed and was just exactly what she needed after the disaster of the wedding. People asked her why she hadn't picked Hawaii or Cabo like everybody else in the world, but after Florida, *living* in Florida, tropical was the last thing she wanted, especially at Christmastime. There was snow in Tahoe, there were pine trees, the air smelled of purity instead of rot and if she felt in the least bit chilled, they had a Jacuzzi in the room, which was one of three bridal suites on the property. They didn't ski, either of them—had never skied—so that wasn't an option, and though Todd liked to gamble and they did take in one of the shows at Harrah's, the main thing they did was relax. Mimosas with breakfast, then a stroll around the grounds, wine with lunch, which they took in the main dining room each day, at a table by the window where they could look out on the frozen landscape and feel all the cozier and above-it-all with a wood fire going in the fireplace behind them and the Jacuzzi right upstairs. They watched movies on the big flat-screen TV that took up most of an entire wall, had dinner sent up to the room, made love twice a day. It was as far from Florida as you could get and though Todd dutifully posted pictures of rum drinks and their meals and the scenery on his Instagram, he had a full week off, which meant she had him all to herself.

The following week, back in Florida for the heart of the dry season, when the bug counts were down and you didn't need an umbrella and a portable air-conditioner every time you left the house, she picked up where she'd left off with Willie II. She dressed in outfits that showed him draped round her shoulders when she and Todd went out and posted pictures wherever she could, blanketing social media and targeting certain specific products she felt she had an affinity with, apparel mostly, but also a couple of the vineyards she and Todd liked. As for Willie I, the wanderer, he'd vanished, and whether he'd somehow managed to escape again, or despite what R.J. had to say about it Willie II had made lunch of him, she couldn't say ("Everybody needs a little variety in their diet," Todd had said with a smirk, for which she could have killed him because it was no joking matter, at least not to her), though she held out the hope he'd turn up again—you never knew. Especially when it came to nature.

She was sure it must have happened on the honeymoon, though she didn't feel any different, not at first, anyway. It was the middle of February when she began to feel sick to her stomach at all hours of the day, especially in the mornings, and it had nothing to do with how much she'd had to drink the night before, or not that she could tell, anyway. She lost her appetite, then she was ravenous. Spicy foods killed her. And everything else seemed to sit on her stomach like landfill. The truth of the situation didn't really occur to her until one weekend when Todd was on the road again (in Hong Kong, of all places, which she desperately wanted to see, and no, she wasn't invited), and she bolted down a microwave dinner as if she hadn't eaten in a week and then promptly threw it up.

Birth control wasn't one hundred percent, she knew that, and she'd been forgetful sometimes—inconsistent, that is, lax—especially when she and Todd were out and about, and if this was what she thought it was, how was she ever going to break the news to him? She pictured him pacing back and forth across the carpet, counting off the reasons why they couldn't keep it, why he didn't want it, why she didn't want it, why it had to be terminated, aborted, got rid of. His look of umbrage. His icy frown. Mr. Perfectionist. She flushed the toilet, braced herself on the sink and reached for her toothbrush to get the taste out of her mouth. For a long while she stared at herself in the mirror, thinking the worst, but then it came to her that maybe she was wrong, maybe she just had a touch of something—the flu, she could have the flu, couldn't she? Or COVID, though she'd been vaccinated and twice boosted against the variants? Food poisoning? She back-scrolled through the meals she'd had over the course of the last couple of days, finally settling on the tacos from the food truck she'd got day before last on the street out front of the mall. Yes. Sure. That had to be it.

But what if it wasn't?

It was just past seven, dark out, her stomach in knots. She brushed her hair, put on some eyeliner and lipstick, grabbed her purse and a jacket and headed for the door, thinking the CVS would still be open—and beyond that she really did feel she could use a little company. She thought of Bobo's, the bar there with its high-backed stools and submarine glow and Daria to talk to or maybe Ricardo, the extra bartender they put on during the tourist season, whose voice was so mellow and melodic it sounded as if he were singing even if he was just asking, "You want that on the rocks, or up?" Willie II was lying quietly in his terrarium wearing a sheen of light and for a moment she considered taking him with her, but then she really didn't want the attention, not tonight. She just needed some space and maybe a sympathetic ear, though she wasn't about to reveal anything no matter what the pregnancy test said. If she was even going to try it. Which she might not—she was going to get it, yes, just in case, but she didn't know if she was ready to make that kind of leap, or not yet, anyway. Tomorrow. Tomorrow would be soon enough.

She decided against taking the car. There was a full moon climbing up out of the water, which meant everything would be flooded again, so she didn't want to risk it—and the walk would help her clear her head. As soon as she went out the door she saw that the beach was already awash and when she came down off the last step the water was up to her ankles, though it didn't much matter since she was wearing flip-flops anyway. She would have preferred walking along the beach, but at this point it wouldn't so much be walking as wading and she did want to get to the pharmacy before it closed, so she crossed the yard and started up the road, the night clinging to her, the insects providing the soundtrack.

All the houses along the beach were constellations of lights, porch lights, security lights and the myriad specks of red, green and blue appliance lights that winked from every window and leached power out of the grid continuously, 24/7, as if the supply were inexhaustible, and if she heard Cooper's voice in the back of her head that was okay, because he was right. The only thing that really mattered, beyond the refrigerator, the TV and the sound system, was air-conditioning. You couldn't live without air-conditioning here, that was her verdict. For his part, Todd was oblivious—electricity was like air to him. He routinely put the air-conditioner on its lowest setting no matter what the weather was and every night before bed she had to go around turning the lights off after him, but at least she tried to be energy conscious as much as possible—and they did have an electric car, after all, which cut CO_2 emissions but of course still required a power plant someplace burning something. Not coal, she assumed, but then who knew with Florida?

The drugstore was super-chilled and sterile, deserted but for two white-haired women, one fat, one thin, squabbling over whatever rancid label of wine the store carried. *You got to be crazy—I can't drink that crap. Oh, yeah? You didn't seem all that picky an hour ago at Ronnie's when you practically sucked the label off everything in his refrigerator.* She found the pregnancy test kit right away, but circled round it and picked up a few other things—detangler, moisturizer, a new shade of aubergine nail polish she thought she might want to try—before dropping it in her basket and taking it up to the counter. She didn't say a word to the checkout girl beyond "Hi" and "You too," after the things were bagged and paid for and the girl said, "Have a nice rest of your day."

Then it was Bobo's. Both Daria and Ricardo were there, but the place was busier than usual and she didn't get to say much to either of them. In fact, until a guy at the bar offered her his stool, she didn't even have a place to sit—and this was just a courtesy on his part, which she appreciated. He didn't loom over her and try to start a conversation as if she owed him something, as most guys would have, but called for his check, paid up and walked out the door. Which was good. It wasn't so much the conversation she needed at this point, she realized, but the atmosphere, the deep peace of being alone in a public space, part of the scene and outside it at the same time. And the rum. She needed the rum too. She might have looked composed on the outside but her mind was churning, going through all the permutations, because this was so much more than just the binary yes and no. This was her life. The rest of her life. When she'd sat down, she'd looped the CVS bag over the seatback along with her purse, and every time she leaned back it snapped and rustled, as if she needed reminding.

There was a movie playing on the TV behind the bar—not soccer, thank god—and though the sound was muted she got into that for a while, just by way of distraction. She'd seen it before but she couldn't remember what happened in the end and so it was almost like seeing it for the first time. If anything, the fact that the sound was off made it better, more mysterious—and it was a mystery, somebody murdered and somebody else trying to pinpoint the guilty party. She ordered onion rings and kept them down, which was a plus. She played with her phone. Thought of calling Todd, just to hear his voice, but the cost would have been ridiculous. After the third drink, she lost count.

It was past ten by the time Daria got off and came to sit with her and that was fine, another distraction, just what she needed to keep her thoughts off her present situation, though the longer she sat there the more she knew what the test kit was going to reveal and the angrier she got—and not at herself, but at Todd. Todd was going to say she'd tricked him or screwed up the birth control and he thought they'd agreed they weren't ready yet, right? Didn't they? Didn't they agree on that?

Daria saw right into her. "Something wrong?" she asked, sipping the Chardonnay Ricardo had set before her the minute she sat down.

"No, it's nothing—it's just Todd's away again, you know how it is."

"Really? Where's he this time?"

"Hong Kong."

Daria lifted her eyebrows. "Hong Kong? And he didn't take you along?"

"You have any idea what a ticket to Hong Kong costs? Plus we just got back from our honeymoon and the wedding and all that, so, really, here I am. Deserted again."

Daria knew the situation. Todd was away lately more than he was home. And she'd heard every sorry detail of the wedding a dozen times, from the way the caterer had bailed on them to the withering heat and the fact that even the cake was a disaster because the hillside was on fire and everybody had to evacuate before they could hardly even get to taste it and their first night as a married couple was spent not in the suite they'd booked at the Miramar—which had to be evacuated too—but in some random Best Western ten miles up the coast. About the only positive, aside from the fact of the ceremony itself—which was beautiful and nobody could take that away from her—was that the house hadn't burned down because of a shift in the wind that drove the fire away from them, even if someone else had to pay the price for that, twenty-seven homes lost, cars reduced to steel husks, trees to skeletons.

Some tune she didn't know was throbbing through the speakers, one of the synthetic hits that all sounded alike to her, not the blues, not soul, not anything that let you know you were alive—just rhythmic noise. The TV had the news on now, the co-anchors looking earnestly into the camera, their mouths mutely tightening and loosening between clips of the day's sorrowful events, people rioting somewhere or starving or wading through chest-high water, half of them waving guns and the other half looking as if they'd welcome being shot just to put them out of their misery. In the back of her head was the notion that she shouldn't be drinking, but that just made her feel as if she were jinxing herself, so she caught Ricardo's eye and tapped the rim of her glass.

"Full moon tonight," Daria said. "So here we go again. You okay over at your place?"

She swung round on the stool and stretched out her legs, grains of sand still sparkling on her ankles and between her toes. The beach. It came with her everywhere. "Well, I got my feet wet on the way over, if that's what you mean—and I definitely did not bring the car."

"I hear you," Daria said. "Good move. This is the world we live in, right?"

She felt herself slip out of her body for just a minute there, everything gone dreamlike on her. She realized she'd had enough to drink and wanted to signal Ricardo, though when she looked up she saw he was already garnishing her drink with a sprig of mint and a wafer of lime. She shrugged. "At least I get a little exercise."

"Tell me about it," Daria said, laughing, and held up her palm for a high-five.

The drink came. She drank it. At some point Daria wasn't there anymore and she paid the check and was halfway out the door before she realized she'd left the white plastic bag on the back of the chair, having automatically flung her purse over one shoulder after putting her wallet away and forgetting all about it, but here was Ricardo calling out her name and waving an arm in the air, the bag held out triumphantly before him. She thanked him with an off-balance hug and the quick peck of a kiss and then she was out in the night.

The parking lot was deserted but for a couple of cars that probably belonged to the employees, their finishes glinting weakly under the wash of moonlight. There was nobody on the street. The air was a surprise—it smelled fresh for a change, sucked in off the ocean on the shoulders of the tide, which had risen enough in the interval to convert the parking lot into a vast black puddle. This wasn't an encouraging sign, since Bobo's was on higher ground than the house, but there was nothing she could do about that beyond putting one foot in front of the other and sloshing her way up the street. A car drifted by, moving slowly, tires sucking at the water. A dog let out a series of staccato barks from behind the window of a darkened apartment. The bugs hissed and clacked and racketed. And she kept walking, almost enjoying it, the novelty of the night and the feeling of being marooned and thrown back on her own resources, which at the moment were considerable, her breathing shallow and regular, her legs right there to catch her every time she lurched into a puddle or pothole, the residuum of the rum providing all the fuel she needed even if she hadn't had anything to eat beyond a handful of onion rings.

The water was up to her shins by the time she turned into the peninsula road and she widened her stance the way you do when you're meeting resistance, but it was nothing, really, and she'd seen higher tides before, though this one seemed to be coming up still, which was worrisome. Was there a limit? What if it rose ten feet, twenty? What if it was like those CGI waves that just stood on end in the disaster movies? She passed the familiar houses, which remained darkened but for the sentry lights, wondering whether anybody was at home even as the term *evacuation* came into her head, a term she immediately dismissed because this wasn't so bad, it was nothing, but then she was thinking about how mild the hurricane season had been and what it would be like in a real blow and how they would manage to evacuate if it came to that—in a rowboat? They didn't have a rowboat. She made a note to herself: They should get one. Or no, a speedboat, which they could take out on the bay in the muggy weather and at least generate a breeze and wouldn't that be nice? Not to mention practical in case worse came to worst.

She was a long block from the house when her eyes picked out something moving in the road, a log rolling on the tide, wasn't it? She drew closer. It moved again, not in the direction of the flow, but against it, and what was that all about? The night was still, not a breeze even, the only sounds the trickle of the water and the incessant complaint of the insects. Curious, she pulled out her phone and shone the light on it so that all at once it fabricated itself out of spare parts and she saw what it was: an alligator.

She was drunk, or at least drunk enough so that everything seemed enchanting, the night, the water, *Florida*, but the sight of it gave her a start. It wasn't so much that she was afraid, just that this thing, this reptile, didn't belong there in the middle of her street at, what—she snatched a look at the time—twelve-thirty in the morning? It was wrong, that was what it was, like something out of a nature film on PBS transposed to her reality, and she stood there watching it for a long while before she clicked off the light, but that only made things worse because the reflection of its eyes, which had been like two holes bored into the night, disappeared along with the rest of it in a way that was unsettling in the extreme. She'd seen alligators before, of course, dull corrugated things hauled out on the green at the local golf course or the edge of somebody's lawn, a dime a dozen, and they hadn't made much of an impression on her one way or the other. They weren't beautiful like snakes, like Willie II and the ball morphs R.J. offered up for sale, but more like random piles of refuse washed ashore, which was fine for them, defensive coloring, she supposed, and they gave up their hides readily enough for boots and purses and the like, but otherwise they were just part of the background.

It hadn't been a good idea to stop walking because that allowed the mosquitoes to zero in on her, which they were doing now, even as her eyes readjusted to the moonlight and the alligator faded back into form-lessness. She didn't swat the mosquitoes for fear the noise might alarm the thing, but she ran a quick hand over her arms and legs to shoo them away and then started back up the street, giving the alligator as wide a berth as she could. Alligators weren't particularly aggressive, she knew that, though they routinely snapped up people's cats and Chihuahuas and on the rarest of rare occasions took hold of a swimmer's arm or leg, but still it gave her a bit of a jolt to be this close to one—and how close, exactly, was that? Twenty feet maybe. She flicked on the phone again and saw that it hadn't gone anywhere. There was the sudden flare of its eyes, the rippled length of it, the truncheon of its tail. Was it six feet long? Seven? Eight?

All right, okay, fine. She was past it now and walking as purposively as she could, given the fact that the water was up to her shins, but then she heard the sound of its claws digging at the pavement and when she looked over her shoulder she saw that it had swung round and was clumping along behind her. The light of the phone picked out the squat spread of it riding up off the surface of the road and thrusting forward at the same time, one push-up after another. *Lumbering*, that was the term that came to her—it was lumbering. The thing was, it seemed to be lumbering faster now, as if it weren't just coincidentally traveling in the same direction she was, but in fact homing in on her. She might not have panicked if she hadn't had that last drink—she wasn't a Chihuahua. And she could outrun an alligator any day, couldn't she? But she had had that last drink and all the ones before it and her perceptions were so skewed she didn't know what she was doing beyond moving her legs through the chop till the water got deeper and the thing let out a sudden explosive grunt and started swimming. Or maybe not. Maybe she was imagining it. Either way, in full panic mode, her knees pumping and feet slashing at the water, she ran frantically till she reached the stairway and charged all the way up to the landing at the top. It took her a moment to catch her breath. The sea rolled in beneath her, each wave jeweled in moonlight. There wasn't a human sound anywhere. When she glanced down the stairway behind her—could alligators climb?— she saw nothing there, not even a log.

She dropped her purse and bag just inside the door and went straight to the toilet, where she vomited up the onion rings in a slick of grease and mucus. And though she had to pee so badly she was in pain, she forced herself to hold it till she could dart back into the living room and retrieve the white bag with the pink CVS Early Result test kit stuffed inside beneath the aubergine nail polish, the moisturizer and the detangler.

☀

AS IT TURNED OUT, Todd had to take an Uber back from the airport. The street was still getting inundated twice a day on the high tide and she texted him when his plane landed to tell him she didn't think she should take the car and he texted back, *Yeah, good, will Uber.* He came in the door barefoot, his bag slung low on his shoulder, pants rolled up to his knees and his high-tops dangling from one hand, looking beat. The time difference between Hong Kong and Florida was twelve hours. For her it was four in the afternoon and counting down to happy hour but for him it was the middle of the night and she knew he never slept well on airplanes even if he did have a seat that converted into a bed. They hugged. She gave him a kiss he accepted without enthusiasm. He was slumped over. His shirt was wrinkled, his sport coat hung limp.

"How was it?" she asked. "What was it like? What's *Hong Kong* like?"

"You don't want to know. But Scott Cozzens—he's the regional head?—he was there with me and I gave my Bacardí spiel and the Chinese, though they're not supposed to be drinkers like us, really knocked back the Facundo Paraíso, which retails for like three hundred a bottle, so okay, we hosted some parties and laid on the charm and deepened our connections, right? Success on all fronts. But I am wiped. And I do not want to go to bed now and wake up jet-lagged at one in the morning. How about a cup of coffee? Maybe with some Kahlúa in it? Or Coquito. Babe, we have any of that left?"

Two nights before, the night of the alligator, she'd managed to unwrap the box just in time to position the test stick in the stream that came hissing out of her like the blast of a fire hose because she'd had to hold it so long, not wanting to use the toilet at the restaurant, not for that, and no, she couldn't wait till morning—what had she been thinking? Her fingers got wet. She almost dropped the thing in the bowl. When she was done, even before she flushed or got up to wash her hands, she reached out and laid the stick flat on the edge of the tub to wait the two excruciating minutes till the results showed. She timed it on her watch, the second hand creeping round and round again until a blue slash appeared simultaneously in both the control and result windows, settling the matter—and this was no false positive, she knew that without having to run the test a second time, though she would, and a third time too.

For a moment she was back in biology class, freshman year, human reproduction, the term *zygote* on the whiteboard as Mrs. Shapiro snapped her elbows and flashed her Sharpie and all the girls vied to fit it into various adolescent witticisms like, *My zygote is killing me*, or *Crap, I think I just strained my zygote*, because it was all so remote they couldn't imagine it applying to them in any present or even future scenario. What she felt now, though, was a surge of elation. She was married. She was pregnant. And she'd got pregnant on her honeymoon, which in a way was perfect. The fact was, she would never have married Todd in the first place if he was opposed to starting a family on absolute terms, which he wasn't—he just had a laundry list of excuses as to why he wasn't ready to go there yet, but it was juvenile and they both understood that. Time to grow up, right? And no better time than now.

She brought him the coffee, thick with half-and-half and sweetened with Kahlúa, and though she wanted something herself—a gin and tonic, maybe, in celebratory mode—she held off and had a club soda instead. "You hungry?" she asked.

"I don't know," he said. "Maybe."

"There's not much in the refrigerator, but we could call out if you want."

"Anything but Chinese," he said and they both laughed. She had something to tell him, but not yet. For now she was holding on to it, her secret, revolving it over and over in her mind until she got used to it.

She'd tell him when he was rested, tomorrow maybe—or the next day or the day after that, no rush really.

He had his feet up on the coffee table, shapely feet, strong and handsome like the rest of him. He was talking about Hong Kong now, filling her in on the odd details of the trip—*baijiu*, which was like vodka though it was made from sorghum, a sampan ride with an old lady who looked like a fossilized monkey at the helm, fried rice with your eggs over easy in the morning—but she was thinking *boy or girl*, thinking of names, baby names, and nothing as conventional as Catherine or Todd but something with some novelty to it, some individuality, something that would make their child stand out among the billions and billions uncountable staking their claim to the earth. Or what was left of it. The barren earth, the flooded earth, standing-room-only. The thought depressed her.

A breeze drifted in off the water. The sun slanted through the blinds. Todd got up and stretched, then went to the kitchen where she heard him filling a glass with cubes from the ice maker on the refrigerator door. When he came back he was sipping a drink, rum and tonic decorated with a wedge of lime. He made a slow circuit of the room as if he'd never seen it before, investigating the Navajo pottery she'd brought with her from California, the spines of the books on the bookshelf, even bending to peer into the terrarium at Willie II, whose front half was secreted in the hide so there wasn't much to see. Then he sank back into the sofa and floated the essential question: "Pizza?"

"I don't care," she said.

"What do you want on it?"

"Anything but pepperoni."

"You want to call or should I?"

"I'll call. You just got home—relax."

He tipped his glass to her, grinning. "That's what I like to hear. Spoil your man and you shall reap the rewards, oh, yes, indeed." But then his expression changed. He set his glass down on the table and gave her a quizzical look. "You're not drinking?"

PART II

11

SHE DIDN'T LIKE FLYING

SHE DIDN'T LIKE FLYING AND SHE DIDN'T KNOW ANYBODY who did, not even Sylvie, who'd once been a flight attendant for Air France but hadn't been back to her native country in twenty years because she couldn't stomach being crammed into an airplane anymore—and with a mask on, no less, because the coronavirus kept spinning out variants ad infinitum. There was no longer any pretense of service or legroom or amenities, even in business class. You were caged, you were trapped, and if you didn't like it you could hitchhike to Miami—or take a bus, a train, drive, all of which constituted their own forms of cruel and unusual punishment. There was alcohol, though, and from the moment they'd rolled the cart down the aisle, Ottilie had been numbing herself as the plane dipped and jumped and the seat belt light came on and stayed on and the cart disappeared and the meal service was discontinued and the tropical depression in the Gulf of Mexico steadily intensified and the flights behind them were being canceled one after the other. Though she didn't know that yet. All she knew was that she was here in this roaring sliver of time wedged in beside an obese snoring middle-aged man whose left elbow was practically in her lap and that she wouldn't be here at all but for the fact that Cat's due date was five days from now and she really had no choice in the matter.

The pilot kept shifting course and altitude, trying to avoid the turbulence, though he didn't say anything about it over the intercom. She felt it as a gradual veering, as if an invisible hand were guiding her by the shoulder, and this was interspersed with the occasional jolt of lurching up and dropping down again, various things rattling and humming across the breadth of the cabin and people retreating into themselves, but it wasn't anything she hadn't experienced before. Bad weather, that was all. Still, though she tried to blot it out with a book and a movie and scotch served up in the little 1.7-ounce bottles charmingly referred to as "nips," she couldn't help conjuring up images of her own frailty in the face of the forces arrayed against her and she wasn't able to concentrate on the book or the movie either and wound up paging through the airline magazine in which some previous passenger had already blackened in the crossword puzzle and unlocked the sudoku.

She was dozing, her chin pinned to her chest, when the intercom hissed to life and the pilot announced that they were being diverted to Atlanta, since the Miami International Airport, where she was scheduled to connect to Jacksonville, had been shut down due to adverse weather conditions. The man beside her snorted awake and gave her a look of bewilderment as if he wasn't quite sure where he was or how she fit into the scheme of things. "What?" he demanded. "What did he say?"

"It's the weather. We're being diverted to Atlanta." She was trying to think how far that might be from Beach Haven, which was an hour south of the Jacksonville airport, where a now-extraneous rental car awaited her. She'd been looking forward to the drive, actually, since she'd never been to Florida before, but she'd have to cancel that and take what she could get in Atlanta, where everybody would be scrambling for cars at the same time. And it was going to add hours to the trip.

The man—his head was shaved but he wore a full beard and a pair of those black plastic plugs that stretched your earlobes and hadn't been in fashion for twenty years—let out a curse and thumped his fist against the seatback, as if this were all about him. The engines roared. The winds buffeted. Every face in the cabin bore a look of outrage. Or fear. Or both. She felt she had to say something by way of commiseration—they were in this together, after all, at least for the duration. "It's a pain, isn't it?" she said.

"Damn straight it is. I've got to be in Jacksonville—and Atlanta, I don't know Atlanta from shit."

"There's nothing they can do about it, I guess, as frustrating as that is," she said, withholding the information that she too was going to Jacksonville—or had been.

He gave her a furious look. "Right," he said, snapping off the syllable like a rim shot. "And when was the last time any flight ever got anywhere on time?" His face was huge, perspirant, pop-eyed. "No matter the weather? It's always something—I had a flight turn back to the airport last week because the backup of some backup ventilation system wasn't working, as if anybody on the plane could give a shit. They just want to get where they're going. *I* want to get where I'm going—half the time I'm hoping the plane crashes, just to get it over with. Like now. Like right now."

"You don't mean that."

"It's a joke," he said.

The pilot came over the intercom then to remind them that they were to stay in their seats with their seat belts securely fastened and refrain from using the restroom as long as the seat belt sign was on. Which it was. In perpetuity.

"What really screws me over is I've got live freight down there in the luggage compartment," he said, adjusting his bulk in the seat, "and I need to get them where they're going because this puts them through a whole other level of stress. Which, believe me, ain't pretty."

As soon as she heard the term *live freight* she thought of her crickets in their plastic travel bag, her new crickets, the ones that were thriving in the new reactor—thriving to the point where she was harvesting so much meat she couldn't give it away. Not that anybody wanted it—which was a shame. There was waste everywhere. "Insects?" she asked.

He gave her an odd look, then let out a laugh. "C'mon, do I look like a bug guy? Though it takes all kinds, granted, and I know dealers that do these huge tropical stick bugs, tarantulas, scorpions, even beetles, which can be pretty cool. But me? I'm a snake man."

"Snakes on a plane?"

He grinned. "That's it. That's it exactly."

AT THE AIRPORT, SHE FOUND herself standing in line at the only rental car desk that was still open—Budget, though the reservation she was going to have to cancel was with Avis. She could worry about that later. For the moment she was in competition for whatever dwindling supply of cars was available, the people ahead of her focused on nothing but their own needs like all people everywhere, while Cat, nine months pregnant—with twins, no less—awaited her at the end of a maze of snaking interconnected roads in a place that was utterly foreign to her. With a storm coming. And Todd in New York and not due home till tomorrow.

She called Cat but Cat's phone went straight to message and the robotic voice that informed her the mailbox was full and could not accept any messages at this time, which turned the dial up on her anxiety level—as if it weren't high enough already. The employees behind the desk—there were two of them, heavily made-up young women sporting matching ponytails—moved at a glacial pace, while the line, correspondingly, seemed frozen in place. She dialed Frank next, though she didn't like to interrupt him at work—it was just past five here, which would make it two there, which meant he'd be seeing his afternoon patients. He picked up on the second ring. "You okay?" he asked.

She explained the situation to him.

"You sure you want to drive all that way? In the rain? With, what—a potential hurricane brewing?"

"Cat's there alone."

He was silent a moment. "And Todd—I thought he was due back tomorrow, or am I wrong?"

"They closed the Miami airport, I told you—they're saying the storm's building into a hurricane. He could maybe fly into Jacksonville, but if they close Miami why wouldn't they close that too? And then what's Cat going to do?"

"Well, what does she say about it?"

"I can't reach her, which really makes me crazy, to tell you the truth."

Another pause, longer this time. "It'll work out. Worse comes to worst—if she's early, I mean—she can take a cab to the hospital. Or a friend—doesn't she have a friend who can take her? In an emergency? And it's not an emergency, right—not yet, anyway?"

She didn't like any of this. And the more he talked, the more determined she became. Her voice rose, battling the connection, the ambient noise, the overheated buzz of the people in line ahead of her: "I'm driving down there if it takes me all night."

SHE GOT THE LAST CAR available. She didn't feel lucky, only capable, having sprinted through the airport to get here once she realized the car rental sites had all crashed. Until three years ago when she retired she'd run Frank's office for him, overseeing everything but the procedures themselves, hiring and firing, the supply chain, billing, insurance, even rotating the dracaena and umbrella plants in the waiting room, and if there was a problem—and there'd been nothing but, it seemed, even after they hired their first PA and settled into the office Frank still occupied—she was there to solve it. So yes, she got the last car. And yes, she was going to drive in the rain and wind and whatever else the weather threw at her and be there for her daughter.

The windows were black slabs. There were people everywhere, milling, grim-faced, the ones behind her giving her looks of undisguised hatred as she filled out the forms and waited for the nearest of the ponytailed women to hand over the keys. Just as the transaction was winding down, she felt a touch at her elbow and turned to see the man from the plane standing there, trying to work up the kind of grin that was meant to convey how harmless he was. He was more immense even than she'd imagined—you couldn't tell when he was seated, really, and, like a gentleman, he'd stepped out into the aisle and helped her lift down her roller bag, so she'd preceded him up the aisle and hadn't got a good look at him till now. He was wearing an open-collar shirt in a batik print that was like wallpaper and he was resting one hand on a shiny steel-tube rent-a-cart piled high with perforated white boxes stamped LIVE ANIMALS. "I was hoping you could help me," he said.

She was projecting images in her mind of the anonymous car, the rain, the dark lot and the darker road ahead of her, a road lit only by the headlights and the GPS display on her phone: she was in Georgia but the place she wanted to be, needed to be, was Florida. She was so distracted the question barely registered. "Me?" she said.

"I couldn't help overhearing you were going to Jacksonville, same as me. Or St. Augustine, actually. And they're out of cars." He gestured at the clean white squared-off boxes neatly stacked on the cart beside him. "These would fit in the trunk—you wouldn't even know they were there. And I'll pay the full cost of the rental—free, you get the car for free. And I'll help with the driving." He gave her a pleading look.

"You can't. The insurance . . . it's not allowed."

"Okay, then—I'll keep you awake. And when we get close I can give you directions . . . I mean, Jacksonville's not a problem." He held out his hand. Not knowing what else to do—and because she was polite, always, with everybody—she took it.

"Deal?" he said.

☀

THE CAR WAS AN SUV, which was a boon considering the conditions, but that meant that the snakes, as innocuous as they may have been—and drugged, for all she knew—were right there in the compartment with them. There was wind enough to stack the rain in horizontal sheets and they were both soaked through by the time they climbed into the car, her passenger having borne the brunt of it because he had to stand out there long enough to stack his boxes in back, ten or twelve of them, which had begun to turn from white to gray with the absorption of moisture. She wondered if that was going to be a problem. She wasn't particularly phobic—snakes, crickets, bees, it was all the same to her—but she just didn't want anything interfering with the drive, which was fraught enough as it was. There was the rain smell, the slamming of the tailgate, the shifting of the car on its springs as the big man settled into the seat beside her, then she put the car in gear and navigated the first hundred feet of what was some three hundred fifty miles to Jacksonville, plus the sixty or so from there to where Cat was.

Suddenly, the man let out a laugh. She glanced at him and saw that the top of his head was flush with the fabric of the roof. "What?" she asked. "What's so funny?"

"Snakes in a car," he said. "Or an SUV—snakes in an SUV." He waved a hand. "It's an old joke, forgive me. By the way, I'm Stoneman. And as you no doubt surmised, I deal in reptiles. And you are?"

She gave him her name and he said, "Nice to meet you," which made her feel rewarded somehow, the simple exchange of pleasantries in a situation that was anything but pleasant, and suddenly she felt glad he was there with her, this stranger, this immense stranger with the unfashionable earplugs and the snakes in their possibly disintegrating cartons. They were driving into a storm. The air stuck to her like glue. She had a steering wheel in her hands and pedals at her feet. "Have you ever been in a hurricane before?" she asked him.

"You kidding? You live down here, you better get used to them. But this isn't anything yet—it'll be a day or two before it hits us. If it does. A lot them keep on going out to sea where they're not going to do any damage. So we can hope, right? And again, no matter what the insurance says, you get tired I'll be happy to take over."

"Tired? We just got in the car."

"It's the flying wears you out. My first flight got canceled and by the time I sat down in that seat next to you I felt like somebody'd shot my legs out from under me." He shifted in the seat and she could feel the weight redistributing itself all the way down the chassis. "You just let me know," he said, and then he went silent. Before they'd gone five miles, he was asleep.

The rain came in waves, thumping and rattling one minute, whispering the next. She'd had a Lasik procedure a couple years back that sharpened her long-distance vision and the car—what was it, a Jeep?—had low beams that extended laterally so she could see both sides of the road, which gave her confidence. The GPS guided her through Atlanta and onto I-75 South and everything fell away behind her. Sirius gave her Bach's cantatas and Stoneman provided a steady dose of humanity at rest, his snores rasping along over the percussion of the wipers and Bach's celestial voices. The night closed in. The headlights fought it back. She could have been in a spaceship adrift in the void—or one of Cousteau's bathyscaphs, lighting up the seafloor and drifting, just drifting.

All that worked for a while, but then she began to encounter flooded patches, the water jetting up and pounding at the floorboards while she fought the wheel. Stoneman woke with a lurch at the very moment the term *hydroplaning* came into her head. He asked if everything was all right.

"It's the rain," she said.

"Rain? You call this rain? Believe me, this is nothing—and if anything heavy *is* coming our way, we'll both be asleep in our beds by the time it hits." He paused, the big pale globe of his head rotating toward her. "You're doing great, by the way, you really are."

Her anxiety level had fallen off a cliff for a while there, but it was climbing back up—if the roadway was flooded here, what was it going to be like to the south? "Thanks," she said. "I'm doing my best—and if it'll reassure you any, I've been doing this for something like fifty years now."

"Doing what—driving in Georgia? Or the rain? Or both?"

Something flew up out of the corner of her eye and she ducked it, but there was nothing there, just rain and a string of taillights winking red in the gloom. She feathered the brakes and held tight to the wheel. "I got my permit as soon as I could, sixteen years old and whipping around in my father's Mustang as if I was going to live forever—and I pretty much have, I guess."

"You've got a long way to go yet," he said, his voice so grainy and bottom-heavy it was almost tactile. "And so do I. Though the reptiles, they really have it down. Tortoises—you know how long a tortoise lives? They go a hundred years, easy. One of the Galápagos tortoises at the Australia Zoo—her name was Harriet?—lived to be a hundred and *seventy-five*. And that's reptile years, which have got to be like one for every fifty of ours because they take things at a crawl, not to mention they're the ultimate in solar efficiency. You take one of the ball pythons I've got there in back? He might eat once a week or even two weeks, whereas we've got to stuff ourselves three times a day just to keep the internal temperature cooking at a nice, even ninety-eight-point-six, right?"

"My daughter has a pet python," she offered. "A Burmese? She showed me pictures—it's really striking."

"They get big."

"This one's young still. She likes to wear it around her shoulders."

His comment was, "Cool," but suddenly he jerked his head round to stare at her. "Your daughter you're on the way to visit?"

She nodded.

"In Jacksonville?"

"Beach Haven."

"Wow," he said, mopping his beard with one big white hand that leapt and fluttered like a dove in the shadows. "You want to talk coincidence, I'll bet anything she got it at Herps, am I right?"

"I don't know where she got it."

"But not at a show, right? Because you can't trust the shows, where the quality—and condition—of the reptiles is always going to be suspect. But Jesus, I can't believe it. Did you know my little brother R.J. runs the Herps outlet in St. Augustine? That's what I'm doing here. We own it jointly, along with four other shops spread across the South, our own mini-franchise."

She didn't know what to say to this. It was conversation, that was all—and she was glad to have it in the dark tunnel of the night on an unfamiliar road with the trucks like drifting mountains coming up on her and the rain slashing at the windshield. It hardly ever rained anymore where she lived and now here she was, in the dark, fighting a whole season's worth of it.

"And we're doing great, if you want to know. You'd be surprised how many people want a good snake—or two or ten or even twenty, if you're talking hard-core enthusiasts. People want something real to look at, especially in a society as fake as this one, know what I mean?"

"I keep bees," she said, but he didn't seem to hear her.

"I'll bet anything she got her snake from R.J., I'll just bet. A Burmie, you said it was?"

SHE DROPPED HIM OFF IN the driveway of a long shadow of a house somewhere in the outskirts of St. Augustine. It was overhung with live oak and fringed with spikes of palm, which didn't look all that different from what you'd find in California, actually, but for the rain. Which had mercifully slackened off to a drizzle during the last fifty miles or so, giving her hope that the forecasters were wrong. She'd driven the whole way herself, with a pit stop at a McDonald's, where she and Stoneman both ordered McNuggets and fries and ate in the car because she was too nervous to waste the time it would take to sit there at a table when all she could think about was Cat. Whose phone kept going straight to message. "Pick up," she said under her breath, "pick up, already," but all she got was the robot. She had a nightmare vision of her daughter giving birth in the back of an ambulance, or worse, on the rug in her living room, all alone.

She waited there in the drive, the car running and wipers clapping, till Stoneman could rouse his brother and get some help unloading the car. He must have banged on the front door of the house for a full five minutes, a dull thump she could hear through the rolled-up windows like a distant bombardment. Nothing happened. She was getting impatient, getting nervous, when finally the porchlight flicked on and a man appeared at the door in a pair of shorts and a tee and in the next moment the two of them were at the back of the car, flipping open the tailgate.

She saw them in the rearview mirror as moving shadows, heard their voices blending in an easy murmur of familiarity. The chassis swayed ever so slightly as they leaned into it, removing the boxes, and then the brother's voice suddenly rang clear, "Jesus, one of them's loose, grab it, will you? Grab it!"

She jerked her head round and there it was, the snake—a snake—as thick and long as Stoneman's arm, uncoiling on the backseat, and Stoneman was wrestling with it, his face looming large in the shadowy interior while the snake, pinned by its head, thrashed its tail in a way that made her think to unfasten her seat belt and reach for the door handle. But Stoneman knew his business and it was all over in an instant. He had the thing clutched in both hands, stretching it like a length of hose, and here was the brother with a cloth sack, into which it vanished as if it had never been there at all.

"Sorry about that," Stoneman said, addressing her now. "But hey, Ottilie, I want you to meet my brother before you go," and if she was shaken she didn't want to show it, so she pushed open the door and went round back to where he was standing next to a man half his size who looked nothing at all like him. She shook the man's hand, which was wet with the misting rain. "Her daughter's one of our satisfied customers," Stoneman said.

"Good to know," the brother said, giving her hand a squeeze. She noticed that two of the boxes had collapsed so that you could see the plexiglass cases inside and the shadows of whatever they held. "We aim to please—and I tell you, there are no complaints. Everybody needs a reptile in their life."

"None of them are poisonous, are they?"

"Oh, we can do pit vipers, if that's what you're looking for, taipans, cobras, kraits, rattlers—which are as common around here as dandelions—but mostly, in the shop at least, we stick to things that aren't going to kill you. What did your daughter wind up getting?"

"A python, she said."

"Best bet. But let's get these guys in the house—can I offer you anything? A drink? Cup of coffee?"

"I really can't—I've still got half an hour to go, or so the GPS is telling me. And there's a hurricane coming."

"They're not calling it that yet," the brother said.

Stoneman said, "You'll be fine."

He handed her one of his business cards, which she accepted, but she tried to refuse the cash he pressed on her—it didn't seem right to take his money since she would have been passing through here anyway and he'd been a comfort even if he'd slept half the way. "No, no, I insist," he said. "A deal's a deal. And you really bailed me out there. So thanks." He bent awkwardly to give her a hug, his shirt wet as a dishrag, and then she was off down the road and into the night, the GPS on her phone shining like a beacon—or a guardian angel, that was what it was, her guardian angel made out of tempered glass, rare earth metals and silicon chips.

It was just past midnight. Except for the odd trucker, the road was all but deserted. She was making good time when the rain came up again, exploding with such force she had to pull over to the shoulder and let it crash down around her. Sitting there in the dark with her hazard lights flashing, she tried Cat again, and was so startled when Cat actually answered she thought it must be some trick of the microwaves. "Mom?" Cat's voice was small and distant. A sleepy voice. A child's voice. "Where *are* you?"

"I'm almost there."

"But you were supposed to be here hours ago—is everything all right?"

"Why didn't you pick up? I've been calling all night—"

"Is it the storm? Did you get stuck someplace?"

She felt a flash of irritation. "Why didn't you pick up?—you knew I was coming."

There was a long pause. Rain smeared the windshield, cleared, smeared, cleared, smeared. "I don't feel so great, actually."

"You're not having contractions, are you?"

"I don't know, yeah, I guess—and I went in to lie down and, I don't know. And I couldn't find my phone . . ."

"Are you timing your contractions? Because that's crucial."

"I have a phone app? But I don't need it yet."

"You sure?"

"Of course I'm sure."

"Todd's not there?"

"He's not due till tomorrow, remember, I told you? But who can say with this storm, which couldn't have been worse timing, right?"

She was already wheeling back out onto the road, the tires grabbing and the car shaking off the rain. A truck blared at her and a car coming up too fast behind her flashed its lights and she did something she'd hadn't done in years—she held up her middle finger right there against the rearview mirror where they could get a good look at it. "Just hang on," she said. "I'm coming."

☀

SHE'D JUST TURNED OFF THE interstate onto the two-lane highway that would take her to Cat, when the road ahead of her suddenly began to writhe and buckle as if it had come to life—which wasn't possible, which was an illusion, a delusion, a trick of her exhausted body and straining eyes. Instinctively, she hit the brakes, but that was unfortunate, because it sent the car into a spin, four-wheel drive or no, and she wound up in the middle of the opposite lane, her hands clutching the wheel in a strangler's grip and the engine stalled out. The landscape around her was flat and black and there were no lights anywhere—fields, farmers' fields. She was rushing with adrenaline, shaking with it, but there were no cars coming and she hadn't hit anything, so she thumbed the ignition button, goosed the engine back to life and eased over into her own lane in a kind of trance, and yet the problem hadn't gone away—the road pulsed all around her. It streamed and crawled in a thick brown slurry that was like mud, like a mudslide, but there were no mountains or even hills here that could have generated anything like this, so what was happening to her? The car crept forward in low gear and it was like riding over a conveyor of living flesh, of meat—or no, *fish*.

She picked out the eyes then, thousands of pairs of eyes glinting in the beam of the headlights as far as she could see. They were catfish, that's what they were, Siamese walking catfish. There'd been a documentary on the Nature Channel Cooper insisted they watch, a call to arms against invasive species that got her son—he was still in high school then—spewing epithets at the screen till she had to get up and leave the room because that was a version of him she didn't want to know about. Someone had apparently brought them here from Thailand for the aquarium trade—someone like Stoneman, it came to her, if fish were snakes, and what was the difference, really, when the result was the same? She flicked on the emergency flashers and eased the car forward a foot at a time until she was on the shoulder, the tires crushing the things to sludge even at a crawl. It was horrible. She didn't want any creature to suffer, not even an alien species that was actively degrading the ecosystem (and had got here through no fault of its own), and she felt the same way about her crickets and mealworms too—when it was time to harvest them, she put them in the freezer to lull them to their deaths in the most humane way possible.

Cat needed her. Cat was having contractions. Cat was twenty minutes away. Cat was in trouble, her only daughter, and the thought of it, of that very specific trouble and the multiple ways it could wrong, abraded her like sandpaper. The world was a reservoir of life and there was a storm coming to put it to the test. She wanted to wait until the migration, or whatever it was, played itself out, but finally—after sitting there for she didn't know how long, no end in sight, the field of grasping fins and flapping tails running on to the farthest reach of the high beams—she put the car in gear and started back up the road. She went slowly at first, tenderly almost, wincing as the fish squirted and popped under the wheels, but then she pressed down on the accelerator, picking up speed, letting the bodies lie where they might.

12

IT WAS A ROWBOAT

BEFORE SHE'D GONE IN TO LIE DOWN, CAT CRANKED THE hurricane shutters into place, even if the Weather Channel wasn't sure yet which direction the storm was going to take or how severe it was going to be. She hadn't felt like doing it, though thanks to Todd's mother, who'd had them installed, it didn't take all that much effort, but then she didn't really feel like doing anything of any kind, except the one thing that dominated her every thought. She wanted to get this over with. And she did not want a C-section. And she definitely did not want to give birth during a hurricane. She was having contractions—surges— but they were short and widely spaced, a little fist clamping and releasing deep inside her, what the books and videos called practice labor. Still, her body was definitely telling her something. She'd talked to her obstetrician on the phone first thing in the morning and she told her not to worry, it was perfectly normal, and reiterated that there was no need to go to the hospital till the contractions came every five minutes, lasted a full minute and kept coming for at least an hour: 5-1-1, that was the mnemonic key.

The wind was up. She could hear it slamming at the shutters. And what was it with the wind? First the wedding and now this. Was she just unlucky? Or was this the shifting baseline Cooper was always talking about, a new normal that superseded the normal before it, temperatures rising, California getting drier and the Southeast wetter and her twins coming into a world of wind and more wind? It was eerie and unsettling and she hated it. And she couldn't believe she'd lost her phone, which had to be around here somewhere. It wasn't as if she'd gone anyplace—and she'd had it before she fell asleep, taking pictures of the storm and a dozen selfies too and posting them to her Instagram, though she hadn't washed her hair and wasn't exactly looking her greatest. But she was bored. And cut off. And how could she resist posing on the couch with Willie II draped over her bump? This was what nine months looked like and she wanted the whole world to know it.

But the phone, where was the phone? She retraced her steps over and over again, going around in circles, exhausted, fully exhausted, until finally the phone began ringing in a distant mournful way and she found it in a clump of dust bunnies under the kitchen table. She was thinking Todd, thinking her mother, but she couldn't actually reach down and pick it up because the twins in their amniotic bubble were opposed to any kind of bending and her back was killing her, so finally she had to go down on her hands and knees to get at it, which presented her with the problem of getting back up again. Her feet gripped the floor. Her legs weighed a thousand pounds each. But then she was upright and the phone was in her hand and her mother's voice was scolding her over the line and she felt even tireder and sicker, if that was even possible.

"Okay, okay, Mom, I'm fine—I'm just exhausted, is all. And don't try to drive all the way in because the road's going to be flooded," she warned, taking charge of the conversation, "so just call me when you get to my street and we'll take it from there," but her mother said, "I've got four-wheel drive," and she said, "Good, because you're going to need it."

After she hung up, she tried Todd but the display read *Call Failed.* Which was frustrating, infuriating, pushing her right over the top—why he had to go on this trip so close to her due date she just couldn't fathom. (*No problem, babe, I'll be there in plenty of time—and your mother'll be there too, okay?*) What if the babies came now—what was she supposed to do, deliver them herself and use her teeth on the umbilicals? Shit. She wanted a drink. Badly. But of course she couldn't have one, even to calm her nerves, and hadn't had one—or only a couple—since the obstetrician confirmed what she'd already known and Todd had had his temper tantrum and then accepted it and apologized and played the hand he was dealt, Todd, who was off hosting in New York this time and wasn't reachable by phone or text and whether that was because of the storm she couldn't say, but every time she tried his number she got a *Call Failed* message.

She listened to the rasp of the wind, sinking into the chair in front of the terrarium to watch Willie II go about his business—and yes, he was restless, as if he knew what was coming, flexing his muscles and nosing round the enclosure, probing for a way out. He was bigger now, longer—almost eight feet—and so all the more satisfying to show off, which she'd continued to do religiously right up until she began to feel as if she were being buried under a mountain every time she got out of bed. He'd reached the stage where he was eating rats now, white rats, which she bought at Herps and fed him live, one every five days. At first she'd thought it cruel, like tossing a lobster in a pot of boiling water, but then she found herself getting drawn in, captivated by the interaction between Willie and his prey. Sometimes he struck as soon as she dropped the rat in the terrarium, while other times, depending on his mood and his level of hunger, she supposed, he remained absolutely motionless for whole blocks of time, all but inanimate, a feature of the environment no different in kind from the artificial branch, the rocks, the aspen bedding, until his head shot out and the teeth took hold. As for the rats, they couldn't have known what was coming. They were innocents, raised in a breeding facility in which predators weren't even a vestigial memory. They were meat. They were meant to die.

Her mother had said she was on the 206, and if she was going to ignore her and try to drive in anyway, she should have been here by now. Or called, at least. It was a worry, one more worry on top of everything else. She pushed herself up out of the chair with the notion of going out on the deck to scan the road for headlights, which would have been a plan, if not for the wind. As soon as she opened the door a gust grabbed hold of it, which threw her off balance so that she lost her footing and came down hard on her butt on the slick wet boards of the deck. The door slapped and rattled on its hinges, the wind drove needles of rain at her, the sea hissed, and for a long minute her ears rang as if somebody had clapped a pair of cymbals on either side of her head. She rose shakily to her feet and slammed the door shut, then peered over the railing to where the water rolled blackly through the yard, feeling a kind of rage that was new to her, a rage against what—the weather? The world that made it? Bad luck?

Her mother wasn't there. Nobody was there. Hand over hand, she pulled herself along the railing, panicking now, picturing her mother's car lying on its side in a ditch—and who was going to help her in this blow? The police? The fire department? The Coast Guard? She took hold of the door, but the door was immovable. She tried once, twice, three times, tugging at the doorknob while the wind tried to jerk it away from her till finally she won that battle and the door gave way under the counterbalance of her extra weight, the weight of the twins who were already supporting her before they were even born—good girls, the best—and she was back in the house, breathless and wet, hunched over the phone, dialing her mother.

"I'm almost there!" her mother shouted.

"There's no way," she said, and here came a contraction, tightening the screws. If she hadn't been scared before, she was scared now. "You'll never make it. The road's flooded—and the wind, it's crazy out there . . ."

"I made it this far and I don't care how high the water gets. I'm your mother. I'll be there. You just hold on."

She heard what sounded like static over the phone but was actually the boxed-in pulse of the car, the wipers, the wind, the roar of the defroster. "I left all the lights on. You can't miss it, okay?" Everything around her seemed to shift ever so slightly, as if she weren't in a house at all but the cabin of a boat at sea. "Hurry," she said.

☀

IN THE ENTRYWAY, HUGGING HER mother to her, the first thing she said wasn't, "Thank god you're here," but "You can't leave the car there, are you crazy?"

Her mother was sixty-four years old. She'd flown all day on a stomach-churning flight out of L.A., been rerouted to Atlanta, driven half the night through a storm and lugged her drenched roller bag up the outside stairway, fought open the door and slammed into the living room with the express purpose of rescuing her—saving her bacon, bailing her out, *mothering* her—and the first thing she could think to do was snap at her?

"Sorry, Mom, it's just—it'll get wrecked down there, believe me."

"Where am I supposed to put it?"

"Back up the road, at least—where you first turned in? Even there, I don't know."

"It's a rental. It's insured. And I tell you, I'm not going back out there again, not now, not in *this*—but what about you, are you doing okay? Because at this point that's all that matters." Her mother was standing in the entryway still, the bag at her feet. Her hair was soaked and snarled, her blouse misbuttoned. She looked exhausted. And old. So old it was a shock. "I mean, we won't be going to the hospital tonight, will we?"

She shook her head. "Uh-uh. No. I don't think so."

"Well, that's a relief. Five days to go still—at least officially, right? But that's always just a guess and with twins you never know because they do tend to come early—your doctor told you that, right? Or he factored it in—"

"She."

Her mother smiled. "Five-one-one, right?"

"I'm not a child. We went through everything, both of us together, Todd and I, a hundred times already. So yeah, absolutely."

"And you set aside an overnight bag and your birth plan? Which I guess we might have to amend since it doesn't look like Todd's going to be in the delivery room with you unless some kind of miracle happens—but I will, honey, I'll be there. Don't you worry."

They were silent a moment, listening to the wind rake the house. "And a car seat," her mother said. "I don't know about Florida but I know for a fact in California they won't let you leave the hospital unless you've got one, which we can put in my car, I guess, maybe in the morning, just to be on the safe side."

"Seats, Mom, two *seats*. And yes, Todd and I got them like a month ago, okay?"

She felt herself softening. Her mother was treating her like a child, but she realized that was exactly how she wanted to be treated right about now. All this—no Todd, the storm, falling on her ass on the deck, the fact that forty percent of twins are delivered by C-section, which meant a major operation and stitches and a scar—was too much for her, way too much. "I'm scared," she said.

"Don't be scared, honey. Everything's going to be all right, everything's going to be fine, I'm here now."

Her mother held out her arms and she moved into them, hugging her, rocking back and forth in place while the wind harassed the roof and the waves thumped at the pilings.

"You know what I'd really like?" her mother said.

"What?

"A drink. Can you make me a drink?"

☀

IN THE MORNING, THINGS WERE WORSE. She'd lain awake half
the night, oppressed by the wind, and when she tried to get out of
bed her feet didn't even feel attached to her. The twins, who'd been
so active the past couple of days, were quiet, which was either a good
sign or bad, she didn't know, and she was about to google it when a
surge seized her, longer, more intense. Only after it had passed did
she realize the sheets were wet, and then she was dialed in: this was it.
She caught her breath. Pushed herself up. Wind rapped at the doors
and rattled the shutters. The tropical storm she'd gone to bed with
no longer carried that designation—it was a Category 1 hurricane,
building toward Category 2 and maybe beyond, and it pulled the bottom out of everything. The trees were whips and the air was alive with
things that slammed against the house and crashed and grated along
the length of the deck. When she tried to turn on the bedside lamp,
nothing happened.

Her mother was in the guest bedroom across the hallway and had
insisted on leaving the door open, *just in case*, and she called out to her
now. There was no answer. Crossing the hall to investigate, she found
her mother sprawled diagonally across the bed, her bare feet projecting
from a snarl of sheets, and that was a kind of marvel in itself, her mother's feet, toenail polish faded, the soles lined and discolored, twin red
patches on her heels where the straps of her shoes had dug in during her
long day of humping through airport corridors, worrying the pedals of
her rental car and sloshing through a bayou just to get to the stairway.
She almost didn't want to wake her.

"Mom," she said softly, shaking her by the shoulder. "Mom, wake
up—it's time."

Her mother's eyes, the same pale faded blue as her own, jumped at
her out of a face that was still someplace else. In a wondering tone, her
mother said, "Cat, is that you?"

"My water broke."

"Okay," her mother said, her voice dense and throaty as she grimaced and pushed herself up. She held herself rigid a moment, then swung her legs over the edge of the bed, the thin cotton nightgown pulling at her knees as she bent forward and felt around for her shoes. "Fine. Good. How far away did you say the hospital was?"

The hospital was in St. Augustine, sixteen miles away. Todd wasn't here. Todd was in New York. Todd couldn't call, he couldn't take her to the hospital or hold her hand or time her contractions or coach her through so much as even a single moment of this. She eased herself down on the bed and sucked in a breath as the next surge came. Outside, the wind sounded as if it wanted to lift the roof off the house. "What about the car?" she said. "Did you move the car?"

"Give me a minute," her mother said, "I'm not even awake yet. But tell me, are you timing the contractions?"

"I don't know, yes. On my app."

"And they're regular now?"

She shrugged. "They slowed down again, which I hate—I just want to get this over with, *please.*"

"But not every five minutes yet, right? Of course, you never know. With you, it took forever—you just did not want to come into this world; Cooper came so fast they barely had time to check me in and get me to the delivery room."

"No," she said, "I don't think so, not yet."

"But your water definitely broke?"

She nodded. The room was so dark you could barely make out colors. They had no electricity. The shutters were down. The sun was someplace else, maybe California.

Her mother crossed the room to where she'd propped up her roller bag on the armchair in the corner and began sorting through her things till she came up with panties, bra, a pair of white shorts and a black rayon blouse. And an umbrella—a little purse-ready travel umbrella that was utterly useless, useless to the point of absurdity. Her mother stepped into the panties, then the shorts, turning away to pull the nightgown up over her head. "We still have time. No need to panic."

But Cat was panicking—or at least beginning to feel the symptoms of advanced emotional distress, because how were they going to get to the hospital if the roads were underwater? She repeated herself: "Did you move the car?"

"No, because I didn't think it was all that bad. I mean, there was water when I got out but it wasn't anything we couldn't drive through—and don't give me that look. I had to drive over catfish to get here—catfish, did I mention that? A whole school of them. Thousands of them. Catfish!"

If she wasn't so scared she would have been furious, but she was up now, up off the bed and shoving her way out the door, instantly wet, the wind slapping at her and snatching the air from her lungs, everything tightening inside her and the world glistening like polished iron as far as she could see. And the rain, the driven rain—it was like being in a car wash without a car, and was that funny, was that what she wanted? Was that what she'd tottered through nine months of bloating and gas and morning sickness for and no alcohol and the kind of weight gain she was sure she was never going to lose? Her mother was in the doorway behind her now, calling to her, but she ignored her.

Across the street, the palms were wading in water up to their knees, their tops seizing and releasing in the gusts—the ones that still had tops, that is, because half of them were just splinters now. When she got to the far end of the deck, fighting the wind the whole way, she peered over the rail to where the waves rose and flattened, pounding against the side of her mother's rental car, the wheel wells inundated, the hood awash in sheets of white foam.

That was bad. That made the fear come up in her and beat all the harder. And then she saw Todd's car, its custom cover in tatters and the rear end of it shoved askew so that one wheel was hanging off the edge of the ramp, spinning idly in the blow. Shivering, clutching at her shoulders, she jerked round and shouted down the length of the deck to where her mother stood huddled in the doorway: "Call the ambulance."

☀

SHE'D CHANGED INTO DRY CLOTHES, used the toilet, drunk half a glass of wine because at this point it didn't really matter, and now she was just present, stretched out on the couch in the living room, waiting. She felt like she was coming apart—twins, why did it have to be twins? The fist inside her clenched and unclenched and she repeated her meditation app affirmations over and over in her head, *You are calm, confident and in control*, but it wasn't really working. How could it? She had a whole new continent of anxiety building inside her. She thought of all the other expectant mothers counting their contractions in the birthing rooms at the hospital and sucking bits of shaved ice, rehearsing their own birth affirmations with their husbands at their sides while nurses and doctors hustled up and down the hallways and the walls stood firm and solid. There was an ambulance coming and it was going to try to get through, though there were no guarantees because the roads on the peninsula were flooded and trees were down and the storm hadn't even officially hit yet and it was going to get a whole lot worse before it got better. She waited a full forty minutes before her cell rang and one of the paramedics was on the line informing her that the closest they could get was half a mile away at the junction with the main road and that they were going to have to wait for a boat—the Coast Guard, the Coast Guard had a boat—and could she hold on? Or come to them. Was there any way she could get to where they were?

Her mother stood there listening to this, plucking compulsively at the hem of her blouse, and then she got on the phone and the conversation went back and forth and Cat lost track of things, just focusing on her affirmations and what was going on inside her. "Everything's going to be fine," her mother said, then handed her the phone and went out the door and into the rain.

Time dragged. She was alone in the house and about to give birth and she just couldn't understand what was going on. Todd had deserted her and now her mother had deserted her too and the only human entity she could rely on—the paramedic in the ambulance at the top of the road—was just a voice whispering through her cell phone. She tried not to think, just breathe. The house was dark. She was sweating. The snake in the terrarium on the far side of the room could have said something, but he didn't because he was just a snake and if he ever had offspring of his own they'd be extruded by his mate inside oval-shaped eggs covered in a thin leathery integument, no problem to him, no problem at all . . . and then her mother was there again, wet through, her hair snarled like the weed that washed ashore in big clumps on the tide, asking if she was okay and could she get down the stairs, could she do that?

Outside, everything stank of hidden rot. The wind was furious. The water at the base of the stairs was waist-high, with the odd wave climbing higher, slapping at the stairs and throwing her off balance. She clutched at the wooden railing, one step at a time, the steps slick under her feet. "Here," her mother said, "here," and at first she didn't understand because this wasn't what she expected, this wasn't an ambulance or a Coast Guard vessel with its dedicated crew and rows of bright orange life jackets neatly aligned along the passageway and an engine that could surge through anything the sea threw at it, but a blistered paint-peeled rowboat, jumping at the end of a rope tether. "Come on, Cat," her mother said, "get in. This is our lucky day."

13

PEELING A GRAPE

HE COULD MANIPULATE INDIVIDUAL GRAPES, EVEN PEEL them if it came to that—hallelujah and praise be—but why would anybody want to peel a grape? Grape skins were good for you, valuable sources of vitamins and roughage, but the truly significant thing about grapes was their juice, fermented and aged and poured into a delicate clear long-stemmed glass which you could hold, casually, in your right hand or your left as the mood took you or set squarely on the countertop while you sampled finger food or an Impossible Burger—let the winemakers worry about peeling grapes and their pinot grigio and blanc de noir. He could pluck an egg from the carton without breaking it too, but he really didn't want to do that either—he'd rather go to the café, order an omelet and let the chef do it, or if he was pressed for time, pull into McDonald's and pick up a veggie Egg McMuffin to eat in the car. Lately, though, he wasn't pressed for time—just the opposite. His dissertation was treading water because "Milkweed Patch Size Effects on Monarch Butterfly Oviposition Within California Fields and Road Verges" no longer held quite the sway over him as it had before his abridgement and if he went out to the field station it wasn't to pursue his research but to hang out with the people from all over the country who got grants to live on the premises and conduct research for various lengths of time, people who knew how to make their own fun in a place where night was a compartment of interstellar space and the nearest bar was twenty-seven minutes away, foot to the floor. They were mostly young. They had beer, brandy, pot and sometimes more interesting things, they talked biology and they didn't gape at his Hero Arm, which he kept covered up as much as possible in any case.

The operation he'd undergone was called targeted muscle rein-nervation and it allowed him to operate his bionic arm without having to consciously think about it, as long as the battery inside the forearm cover held its charge, that is. He'd chosen two covers, which he alternated depending on his mood. The first, the one he preferred, was a deep blue scalloped with red and reminded him of Spider-Man; the other, black-and-white, was more the style of the storm troopers from *Star Wars*, which had its own effect. During rehab he'd met a dozen people in his situation or worse (one girl, BeeBee Potrero, nineteen and stunning, with a fine-tuned body and plush swollen lips that intimated every sort of oral pleasure, had lost both her arms at the shoulders), the idea being to normalize the dis-figurement and accommodate yourself to the new reality, not hide from it. BeeBee never wore anything with sleeves if she could help it, and one of the other guys, who was missing both his left arm and leg, insisted on T-shirts and shorts as his way of saying everybody could just fuck off.

For his part, though, Cooper stuck to long sleeves because he was ashamed and humiliated and raging inside no matter what the coun-selors and therapists kept on saying or how his fellow freaks might have felt. They were damaged goods, all of them, and would be through all their days till they were laid in their graves, and that was something to contemplate: Would the bionics be buried with them? Would the

Hero Arm become one of the prized artifacts of the future, beggared tribes wandering a desert planet, scavenging what they could? *Alas, poor Yorick! I knew him, Horatio. And that there? That slab of battered but immortal Nylon 12 polymer? That was his arm.*

By the time he was done with the fitting and the rehab and the counseling and all the rest, it was fall, another fall. Everything was parched. The sky didn't know what clouds were, reservoirs shrank, wells went dry. On the opposite coast, Cat had given birth to twin girls in a hurricane, the streets flooded, trees down, his mother wielding the oars of an expropriated rowboat she'd found upside down on somebody's deck just to get her to the hospital. It was hard to imagine, given the conditions here. Here everything was withered and bleached of color, the ground cracked, the power grid exhausted, each day searing itself into the record books anew. He'd spent the afternoon with a cli-fi novel and a bottle of a local red, lying supine in the hammock strung between two live oaks in back of his air-conditionerless apartment and ignoring calls from his mother, Cat, Mari, and his physical therapist, Brewster Fanning, who left a message to say she was just checking in and to let him know that if he needed anything he shouldn't hesitate to give her a call.

At five he walked down the street to Dos Juanitos and had a veggie taco, a beer and two shots of tequila to liven things up. He was sweating in his long sleeves, but he wasn't anywhere near ready to start showing off the arm in public—or the hand attached to it, with its black mechanical grape-peeling fingers, which he mostly kept hidden in the front pocket of his jeans. He didn't want to see Mari or talk to her either—he was sick to death of her 24/7 solicitude and the way she lowered her head and braced herself when they entered any public place, as if she were there to run interference for him, which was just a way of shrinking him down to size whether she realized it or not. No, he was perfectly capable of raising tacos to his mouth and hammering shots of tequila all on his own, thank you very much.

He was doing that very thing, absently chewing a wad of beans and sauteed poblano peppers and sinking into oblivion while the tequila sang in his veins and the monumental faces of baseball players swelled across the screen behind the bar, when he felt a tap at his shoulder and turned to see a girl from the field station—the new girl, a conenose specialist—standing there grinning at him. "I see at least somebody's enjoying himself," she said.

She was a good six inches taller than Mari, her hair was the color of the Modelo he'd just ordered and she smelled of something sweet, like gum, Big Red gum, which she was chewing behind a set of front teeth as prominent as Mari's, a turn-on, a definite turn-on. Why that particular feature appealed to him he couldn't say—it was just one of the vagaries of attraction that kept the species going heterogeneously, one that the Japanese, in particular, prized. But this girl—her name came to him in that moment, Elytra—wasn't Japanese. Her ancestors, whatever their origin, had selected for buckteeth. And dirty blond hair. And height. And a whole lot more—she had BeeBee's body type, only with arms attached.

"Are the tacos as good as people say they are?"

"Elytra," he said, "right?"

She snapped her gum, widened her smile as if his reiterating her name were an attempt at levity, as if he knew her name as well as she did, as if everybody knew it and at any moment would spring up from their chairs and sing it out in chorus. "Well, are they?"

"I like the veggie," he said. "I'm not much for meat."

"Me either."

"My mother makes a mean mescal-worm taco."

"Wave of the future," she said.

He had one arm. He was semi-drunk. He couldn't help himself. "If there is a future."

She ducked her head, gestured to the seat beside him. "Mind if I join you?'

☀

SHE ORDERED A GRILLED VEGGIE tostada and a mescal negroni, a drink he'd never tried and didn't really want to, though she offered him a sip and he dutifully pressed his lips to the glass right where hers had been and, trying to be politic, proclaimed it interesting before going back to his beer. She didn't ask about his arm, though he saw her eyes register the glittering black fumble of his fingers as he tried to manipulate napkin, taco and glass in a succession of ordinary moves that should have been all but autonomous but still gave him trouble even after all these months of practice. To distract her he asked if Elytra was her real name.

She leaned back and laughed. She was wearing jeans and heels and she'd made up her eyes as if she weren't just here to beat the heat and take care of her nutritional requirements but to open herself up to the possibilities of an overheated autumn evening in a comfortably rustic setting that happened to smell of sizzling fajitas and tequila. "My parents named me Hermione, if you can believe it, but when I was twelve I changed it because beetles were my thing—still are."

"I love it," he said. "Too cool. Really, absolutely." He smiled. "But it's plural—shouldn't it be 'Elytron,' since there's only one of you? Unless I'm missing something." Was he staring at her breasts? Was he about to make a joke about pairs of things? Was he that far gone?

She showed him her teeth. "It just doesn't sound that feminine, right? And nobody knows I'm named after a pair of beetle wing covers anyway—except you."

"And everybody else at the field station. Which reminds me, where are they? Usually entomologists travel in packs—"

"Swarms, you mean."

He took a minute with that, nodding in acknowledgment. "Are you meeting anybody?" he asked. "Or are you just—?"

"I'm just," she said. "I needed to get out, see some new faces, eat something that didn't come out of a bag, and everybody was telling me about this place, so I decided to let the owls and coyotes have the field to themselves, for tonight at least. But Mari—you know Mari, right? She said she might drop by later for a drink, if I'm still here . . ."

"But you're not going to be here, are you?"

She looked into his eyes. "I'm not?"

"My apartment's three blocks from here," he said. "I've got a case of a pretty decent local pinot noir—Gainey? You know Gainey?"

She smiled, laid a hand on his arm—his real arm, the one made of flesh. "I don't think I can drink a whole case."

CONENOSE BUGS, A.K.A. KISSING BUGS because of their propensity to creep out at night and suck blood from the soft flesh around the lips of their hosts, were vectors of Chagas disease, a pathogen that had migrated north from Mexico on the hot winds of climate change. Elytra had migrated south from San Francisco State to collect and study them by way of completing her own dissertation. She walked with a rhythmic rolling gait along the shoulder of the dark macadam road, gesturing expansively and laughing at his jokes, and when they got to his apartment she settled into the easy chair by the window and kicked off her heels as if she'd already taken possession. She had an easy laugh. She liked the wine he poured, liked the music he played (Bebo y Cigala, in keeping with the Latin American theme of the evening). They talked bugs and academia and the various directions the social currents ran at the field station, though she was so new she was just working things out. Like with Mari. And him. He got up to refresh her wine, light a joss stick and a scented candle Mari had given him for his birthday. He watched her face as the flickering light played over it. He kept his right arm to himself.

As he was to discover after an hour or so, she was an aficionado of tattoos, of which he had none, his sole example—a red-and-black bracelet around his right wrist—having been sacrificed to Dr. Yang and his bone saw. She had a glossy goliath beetle tattooed between her shoulder blades, a single life-sized grasshopper on the swell of her left ankle and a kissing bug crawling up her abdomen, its long narrow blood-sucking proboscis thrust into the gap between her breasts. She showed them off for him in bed, dropping her clothes casually to the floor and using her epidermal etchings as a distraction from the awkwardness of the moment (they'd kissed to the point of combustion, he'd led her into the bedroom, she was willing and he was willing and he'd slipped out of his jeans and undershorts, but couldn't quite bring himself to unbutton his shirt and reveal the place where his Hero Arm attached just below the elbow joint he was fortunate—fortunate!—to have preserved). Even with Mari it had taken him months and here was this new girl naked in his bed and all he felt was a blackness inside him. It was like Melody Foster all over again.

"Should I turn out the light?" she asked.

"I don't care, sure," he said, and then she leaned across him, her nipples brushing his lips, to pull the cord of the lamp and plunge the room into darkness. Which was better. Much better. She hadn't asked about the arm and he hadn't offered any explanation, and now, in the dark, it just didn't matter.

IN THE MORNING, THERE WAS no escaping it. She woke beside him, her eyes roaming the ceiling and the high corners with their water stains and looping cobwebs before settling on his. "Hi," she said, and he said, "It was a tick. I almost died." He was still in the shirt, lightweight denim, Levi's finest, and he rolled back the sleeve and raised his right arm to show her the black fingers of his hand and the glistening forearm cover with the red highlights and the flap that concealed the battery. She didn't shrink from it, or not exactly, and of course she must have known something was off from the moment she sat down beside him at the bar, but here it was and it was out in the open now. "You hungry?" he asked.

"I've got to get back."

"Oh, come on, it's just coffee and croissants at this place over in Los Olivos, literally like five minutes away."

In the car she told him about her girlhood in Mill Valley and how from the earliest age she was more interested in nature—in opening her eyes up to what was around her—than in dolls and playing house or *whatever*, encapsulating the entire range of childhood activities in a single relative pronoun and a dismissive flick of her hand. Even as a teen she spent more time outside than online or at Starbucks or the movies or the mall, though there was that too. "Not a typical teen," she said, "but then what's typical? I had boyfriends, I went to the prom, all of that. College, dating, books, collecting. But for me? The best is just being alone in a wild place, decoding the world with my senses, you know what I mean?" She nodded, as if answering her own question. "Of course you do. We all do. We've got a planet to save."

"They used to call me bug boy," he said.

She laughed.

"What do they call you now?"

"Bug boy."

"No, really—"

"Nobody calls me anything. I don't really know anybody anymore, except bug nerds—even the vertebrate people seem strange to me. Like Carrie Stroh—you meet her yet? Our resident bat woman?"

"I haven't had the pleasure. But I say good for the nerds—at least we're not tearing the world down like everybody else."

"No," he said, "we're putting Band-Aids on it. And gauze, don't forget the gauze."

She was seated with her legs folded under her in the lotus position, the seat belt tugging at the fabric of her blouse, the first three buttons of which were unfastened so that the dark proboscis of her kissing bug was plainly visible in the gap between her breasts, not that anyone who hadn't seen the rest could make anything of it—it was a stealth tattoo and he appreciated that. They'd had sex twice the night before and once this morning and now they were going to sit across a table from each other and sip lattes and take delicate bites out of pastries while people murmured around them and the sun rode up the walls. Mari wasn't going to like it. If she found out about it. He wasn't going to tell her, that was for sure, because the way he was feeling at the moment he didn't owe her anything and if you came right down to it she was as much a vector of the bacteria that had taken his arm as the tick itself. Or close enough. She was the one who'd got him out there that day when he would have been doing something else altogether, in which case the tick would have had to find itself another host to feast on. A white-footed mouse. A rabbit. A deer. Or maybe it would have just starved and dried up, an innocuous all-but-invisible arachnoid husk clinging to a withered leaf.

Five minutes later he was standing at the counter of the café, manipulating his credit card, his latte and an almond-paste croissant on a tiny white plate, when his phone buzzed and he had to put everything back down to shove his left hand in his pocket and answer it. Elytra was sitting across the room at a table by the window, dipping her *pain au chocolat* in her latte and staring out the window, where a handful of well-fed, athletic-looking people with unassailable haircuts were going about their morning rounds. It was Mari on the phone. Feeling guilty, he took the call.

"Where are you?" she asked, a faint edge of hysteria in her voice, which made him feel all the guiltier, as if she were watching him on a wildlife camera.

"Home," he lied.

Her voice dipped: "Everything's weird here."

"What do you mean? Where?"

"Where do you think? It's ten-thirty in the morning. I'm out at the field station and it's like somebody flew over in the middle of the night with a crop duster."

"What are you talking about?"

"Everywhere you look there's dead bugs. Even the damselflies down by the pond, dragonflies, grasshoppers—and the oak moths in that grove of live oak out front of the ranch house?"

This had been an outbreak year for the moths, the worst in a decade (or best, depending on your point of view). The larvae had skeletonized the live oaks across the region, which would recover, mostly, depending on how severely the drought had affected them. It was a natural cycle and he was glad for it because it provided birds and predatory insects with a superabundance of prey and it cheered him just to see anything fluttering across the landscape.

"Yeah? What about them?"

"They're like this beige snow all over the ground."

He didn't want to go out to the field station. He didn't want to go anywhere. He wanted to eat his almond-paste croissant, give Elytra a farewell hug and go back to bed, and after that spend the afternoon in his hammock, in the shade, sipping wine and touching all the salient points of oblivion with each of his ten fingers, over and over again.

AFTER HE'D DROPPED ELYTRA OFF at her car and they parted with the faintest brushing of lips, all kissed-out, he went home to do just that, though the phone was buzzing in his pocket again. He shut it off and collapsed on the bed, falling instantly into a blackout sleep, his face buried in a pillow that smelled of her, the beetle-wing girl. When he woke, the sun was high in the sky. It was hot. Or not just hot, impossibly hot—the way it always was now that the Anthropocene was in its death throes and the whole world was a roasting pan in an oven somebody had forgotten to turn off. The sheets were sweaty and the lingering scent of Elytra had gone rancid. Or was it him? He gave his underarms a sniff and decided he needed a shower, but then showers used water and water was in short supply—better he should roll in the grass, but of course there was no grass either.

It was honorable to stink. You could stink for free. And if he showered, he'd have to remove his prosthesis, which he didn't really feel like doing. He was still a bit vague from the excesses of the previous day—and the day before that—and he felt light-headed as he leaned forward to tie his hiking boots, bringing his bionic fingers into play without even thinking about it. He realized he had no choice but to drive to the field station—out of curiosity, if not duty. Dead bugs? What was she talking about? No one used pesticides at the reserve, ever—that was crazy. He patted down his pockets—keys, wallet, cell phone—and started out the door, but when he got out into the full blast of the heat, he stopped himself. His eyes were drawn to the hammock. A mental picture of cold beer and a bag of Doritos came to him. He was thinking he could drive out to the field station later, maybe in the evening, when things cooled down a bit. Or tomorrow, tomorrow would work. What was the rush? He did not want to see Mari. Worse, Mari and Elytra together. Of course, once the day had drawn down and Mari was safely back in her apartment, it came to him that Elytra might just want to come back here, where there was a highly efficient ceiling fan and maximally chilled beer and two pillows that still bore the impress of their heads. All right. Okay. It was a plan. Hammock now, field station *mañana*.

It was then that he noticed the corpses littering the ground. They were on the hammock too, pale soft piles of them, moths, dead moths, moths uncountable, and not a single one gliding through the air or clinging to the branches of the trees. He was down on one knee, puzzling over the situation, when his cell buzzed again. It was his mother.

"Coop?"

"Yeah?"

"It's my bees."

He didn't have to ask because he already knew the answer, but he asked anyway. "What about them?"

"They're all dead."

14

THE TWINS

TODD WAS HAVING A GRAN RESERVA NEAT AND A BEER TO
back it up and she was sipping a tall rum tonic. People had told her it
was all right to drink when you were nursing (strictly in moderation, of
course), not only to save your own sanity but as a way of mellowing out
the babies just the tiniest little bit so you could get some rest—and they
could too. Beer, that was the thing. And she'd tried that the first couple
of weeks, just a beer, a single beer, but tonight the idea of a beer didn't
seem all that appealing, so she'd made herself a drink, and if one shot
equaled one beer, what difference did it make? Plus, beer made you bloat
and she had some serious weight to lose.

The twins were asleep in their bassinets in the bedroom and every
once in a while she'd glance at the baby monitor to see if there was
any change, but so far, so good, and she was taking advantage of the
moment to keep up with her social media because things had really
begun to take off for her since that insane night in the rowboat with
her mother. As terrifying as that night had been, she'd still managed

to record some of it on her cell, video and stills both, because it was a once-in-a-lifetime drama that people would really want to see and it took her mind off the pain to be doing something, anything. The screen kept misting up. She'd had to hunch over her bump with her raincoat flapping round her and since there was no light she had to use her flash, which flattened the pictures and gave them an edge of desperation. The wind never let up. It slammed at her shoulders till her body was like a kind of sail pushing them forward through the storm surge that had swallowed up the road and the front yards of the houses along the beach. Her mother, laboring at the oars, took the brunt of it full-on in the face. There was water sloshing around in the bottom of the boat. The bow rose and fell.

As if that wasn't bad enough, she'd begun to feel sick to her stomach, and on top of that she really had to go to the bathroom, urgently, and to hold it back was driving a stake right through her. She cursed Todd. Cursed babies and storms and hospitals. She had the feeling she was just going to go on like this forever, snarling her affirmations, fighting her bladder, pitching in a dark boat on a dark sea while she opened up as slowly and fitfully as one of those big sea turtles lumbering up on the beach to dig their holes and lay their eggs and the rain would keep coming and the boat would sail twice around the world and still nothing would happen. That was it. Game over. *With sorrows you shall bring forth children.* And then, like a miracle, the flashing lights of the ambulance appeared at the end of a long black corridor of the night and she saw the two paramedics there, wading toward her with a stretcher, and though she was as stressed as she'd ever been in her life, she filmed that too.

Todd was out on the deck, grilling steaks and lamb kebabs he'd marinated in yogurt, olive oil, lemon and rosemary, drink in one hand, tongs in the other, smoke rising round him. He was wearing shorts and a bright white tee. The sky behind him was clear and blue all the way to the limits of vision. There were no bugs. Everything glittered the way it did when you were high on drugs, though she hadn't touched pot, let alone pills, since she got pregnant. But the drink—the drink went right to her. Things shifted and shimmered. She felt glad, felt happy.

What she'd done that night, the real stroke of genius, was to take shots of the two infant car seats, wrapped in clear plastic, that her mother had insisted on bringing with them. Everything else was pure drama—and her followers doubled and doubled again on the insane power of it—but the car seats were a product and the amazing thing was, the manufacturer, Snug-a-Baby, had come to her and offered her a unique selling proposition and to collaborate on giveaways and contests, which meant that she was actually in demand and making money, or at least beginning to. Anytime she posted a shot of the twins, no matter what they were doing and whether they were in their car seats or not, she got a ton of likes and comments, and the people who made just about everything else for babies began to reach out to her. Which was amazing. But tiring too, so very tiring, because if you didn't keep up—all day, every day, religiously—you lost followers, and somebody else, somebody who lived only to cut you out, accumulated them. Before she finished the first drink, she knew she was going to have another.

Daria and her boyfriend, Miller, were the first to arrive and Todd made them drinks while they settled into the couch on either side of her so she could show off the twins, who were sleeping their little heads off, on the baby monitor. Daria and Miller made the appropriate cooing noises and used the standard adjectives, and she was proud and pleased, of course she was—this was the babies' coming-out party—but she wasn't going to be one of these obsessive first-time mothers who retool the world into a house of baby worship, and if she was, if she *was*, the girls were already online presences and how about that for your gratification threshold, measurable in likes? And dollars.

Miller—he was white, with teased-up electric hair, ink-black, just like Daria's, which was the thing they'd first noticed about each other when he walked in the door at Bobo's one night to meet up with a couple of male friends—came up with the perfect comment. He stared into the monitor a minute and said, "You better watch out or they're going to start charging you the excess cuteness tax," which was a sweet thing to say, and Todd, who'd just set down a tray of salsa, guacamole and tortilla chips on the coffee table, said, "Sure, why not, they're screwing me on everything else," and the doorbell rang and R.J. and his massive brother were coming up the stairs and she got up to put some music on.

Beyond that, things went a little hazy on her. This was a party, her first party, and she had the girls to show off, which she'd get around to in due time. For the moment, though, they were asleep, thank god for small mercies, and if that meant they'd be up six times in the middle of the night, she'd just have to deal with it. R.J. and his brother—Stoneman—stole the spotlight for a while with Willie II, lifting him out of the terrarium and handing him around so everybody could marvel over him, and then she was telling Daria and Miller about Stoneman and the amazing coincidence that he and her mother had shared a car on the way down here, a story she'd received like a wrapped-up baby gift from R.J. the last time she'd stopped in at Herps for supplies. (Rabbits, that is. Willie had graduated to rabbits now—bunnies—and because she had mixed feelings about that, so far she'd only offered him dead defrosted ones, which were like fuzzies, only bigger, a whole lot bigger.) The point of the story—the truly amazing thing—was that if it weren't for him her mother might not have got here at all and then who would have rowed the boat through the storm? Everybody looked to Todd, who really couldn't do anything but grin and shrug and wonder aloud if anybody wanted another drink. She held out her glass and he took it, but a look passed between them because she wasn't going to get drunk, was she?

They ate out on the deck. Todd took care of everything. He'd set the table with the original Fiestaware his mother had left him, including cups, saucers and serving bowls, all of it in pristine condition except for the saltshaker in cobalt blue that had a bald white chip at the base of it. Cloth napkins. Their good crystal. He even made the coleslaw and potato salad from scratch, baked his own pita for the kebabs, grilled the corn and made sure the wine—and rum—flowed.

She wound up sitting next to R.J., who acted as if nothing had ever happened between them, which of course, it had, and she reminded him of that by staring into his eyes for whole seconds at a time while he dropped his voice confidentially to tell her about his latest acquisitions and the middle-aged woman who brought back the ball she'd bought because it kept getting loose in the middle of the night and crawling into bed with her.

The twins—considerate girls, perfect girls—waited till Todd had served dessert before announcing their presence in a thin ascending duet that killed the conversation dead. Everybody looked to the monitor, which from this angle only she could see, so she turned it around so they could make out the bassinets and the squinched little faces and the mobile and the curtains with the seahorse pattern she'd picked out of a catalogue. "Another country heard from," R.J. said, and she got up, topped off her drink and went in to feed and change them.

Todd claimed he couldn't tell them apart, but that was nonsense, one of his little jokes. He was having a hard time wrapping his mind around the concept of fatherhood because fatherhood was a condition that required a serious readjustment of his self-image—how could Mr. Cool, Mr. Supercool, Mr. Ambassador, Mr. Host, be tied down like all those other clueless drudges out there? That was juvenile, she knew that, and knew too he'd come around as the girls began to take on form and personality. At the moment, they were just defined by their needs—and their needs were focused exclusively on her. She understood that. She was okay with it. For now, though, she was the drudge, and if she got five minutes to herself it was a miracle.

From the bedroom, she could hear the sounds of the party, laughter, music, arpeggios of intertwining voices running up and down the scale, more laughter, and she couldn't help feeling the anticipation. These were her babies. They were perfect. And she was going to go out there and show them off. She smiled to herself as she fed them, then changed their diapers and dressed them in one of the matching sets of onesies her mother had sent her—pink, with the same splash of cartoon seahorses as the curtains. She finished her drink, touched up her eyes and her lipstick, then cuddled Tahoe in one arm and Sierra in the other and made her entrance.

The deck was bright as a stage set and she blinked awkwardly against the glare while everybody grinned fixedly and Daria weaved back and forth with her phone, snapping one shot after another. R.J. said, "Wow, pretty impressive, they look just like babies—but how do you tell them apart?" and when she didn't answer, repeated the question.

"It's subtle," she said, sinking into the chair beside him. "But just spend some time with them—the way I do, like twenty-four/seven?— and you'll see all these little differences. And they've got distinct personalities already, believe me. This one?"—she glanced down at Tahoe. "She's going to be a warrior. And Sierra's going to be a peacemaker."

"Good thing there aren't three of them."

"Three? These two nearly killed me as it was."

"That's what I'm saying. If one's a warrior and the other's a peacemaker, the third one'd have to be a politician, right? What else is there?"

"They have Todd's eyes," Daria said, and that was true—shape and color both, a brown so pale and golden it was like honey.

"Special order," Todd said, and took off his shades so people could see the truth of it.

Stoneman was still working his fork around the dessert plate and taking measured sips of the Gran Reserva Todd had offered around when he brought the tiramisu out. His Kahala shirt was dark with sweat. "You know what?" he said, grinning up at Todd, then sliding his eyes to her. "I feel sorry for all the little boys out there. They're going to be in a whole lot of trouble in eleven or twelve years. Or sooner, maybe even sooner. I mean, I had my first crush in, what, fifth grade? How old are you in fifth grade, anyway?"

"Yeah, I can hardly wait," Todd said, but he was grinning too. This was his new role and he was just starting to ad lib his lines.

Stoneman turned to his brother. "Marcia Freeman," he said. "Remember her?"

"Little horndogs ringing the doorbell," Todd said. "What a joy that's going to be."

No one had anything to say to that, but Daria, who still had her phone in hand, framed Todd in the lens and said, "Come on, Todd, how about you hold the babies for a couple of shots?"

To swing the girls high over the table and hand them to her husband, their legs stiffening and hands slipping on the air, was a strange sensation, their heat gone, their solidity, and she felt released and anxious at the same time. This was the moment of truth for Todd because he'd hardly held them to this point. *I'm afraid I'm going to drop them*, he'd say, or *Please, I've never even seen a baby before in my life*, which was just part of the routine he was working up for public consumption, but here he was, cradling the girls against his chest as if he'd been doing it every day for the past two months, leaning up against the rail with the inlet as a backdrop so Daria could take pictures while R.J., still seated at the table, snapped a few as well. Which was fine. Todd could have been a model in a magazine—and of course, she got her camera out too. He grinned and posed and lasted all of maybe three minutes before he handed the girls back to her. "So the thing that amazes me?" he said, addressing R.J. and his brother. "The fontanel. You know about fontanels?"

They shrugged. They were bachelors. Snakes they knew, babies not so much.

"It's the soft spot? Where the bones haven't knitted yet? Like right here, see?" He leaned forward to run his palm over Tahoe's skull, then circled her fontanel with his forefinger. "You could poke right through it," he said, "Which, I have to admit, freaks me out. You want to feel it?"

"That's okay," R.J. said.

"Their skulls are flexible so they can get through the birth canal," she said. "It's like snakes unhinging their jaws."

"Unhinged head syndrome," R.J. said. "There must be a book about that somewhere, right?"

She wanted to laugh, but she didn't. She was just drifting, the

declining sun on her shoulders, the air so thick you could stuff a pillow with it. Behind her, in the living room, a slow blues was pulsing
through the speakers, part of the mix she'd compiled for the party, with
R.J. especially in mind. She was thinking one more drink but didn't
really feel like getting up to make it.

That was when an insect came sailing in out of nowhere—a big
black thing with furiously buzzing wings—and landed on Stoneman's
forearm as he was tipping the glass to his mouth. He jerked his arm
reflexively, spilling rum down the front of his shirt, then slapped the
thing and watched it fall to the table, where it lay on its back, still buzzing. She said, "No, wait," when he moved to crush it with the heel of his
glass, and in that moment they all saw that this wasn't an insect at all.

"Jesus," Todd said, "what *is* that?"

Whatever it was, it was spinning in circles and kicking out its legs
as if to right itself.

"A drone," R.J. said.

"A drone? Drones are like a hundred times the size of that thing."

"Not anymore. You know what this is?"

The term came to her then—it was something Cooper had been
talking about for years as bee populations steadily declined. "A
Robo-Bee?"

"Welcome to the future," R.J. said, leaning over his elbows to prod
the thing with one finger.

THE NEXT MORNING, SHE FELT like shit. Todd had slept on the
couch, which he was doing more and more lately, because he said he
didn't want the girls waking him up in the middle of the night. "I've got
to sleep straight through or I'm just destroyed the next day, you know
that," he said, and she said, "Well, what about me?" and he said, "You're
the mother," as if that settled it, point/counterpoint, end of discussion.
He also said—and had reiterated it at the party for everybody gathered

round—that he wasn't really all that enthused about the concept of diapers, of shit, that is, baby shit. "It's an evolutionary thing," he said. "Men don't mind killing things, gutting them, stripping off the hide or the scales or whatever—fish, I don't know, deer, wild boar, right?—and we've got no problem with worms, slime, cockroaches, piss and vomit and all the rest of it, but you got to draw the line somewhere. Known fact," he said, gazing around the table, "—women actually enjoy baby shit, isn't that right, babe?" he added, turning to her with his big toothy ambassador's grin.

He was being funny. Or tying to be.

"I don't know," she said, "but since Darwin isn't around to back you up, why don't we try an experiment and you change the girls ten times a day for the next week and see just how thrilling it is?"

He didn't answer, shifting his focus to R.J. and Stoneman instead. "Do either of you have a dog?"

R.J. shook his head. "Uh-uh, no way. Snakes and dogs don't make for a good mix."

"Because there's something I just don't get. The dogs keep turning over the garbage can to make off with the diapers—they just can't resist that mother's-milk-flavored shit. Or maybe it's the raccoons, I don't know, but somebody's really hot on it."

"Thanks for sharing that with us," Daria said.

"My pleasure." Todd, three-quarters gone at this point, tipped his glass to her.

If she felt embarrassed, Cat tried not to show it. He was striving to be just this side of outrageous, working up a routine as a way of dealing with his emotions over this sea change in their lives—parenthood, fatherhood, *babies*—and again, she could forgive him that, but for the fact that he left her out of the equation. She hadn't really been ready yet either, but once she got pregnant, she never looked back. He'd hounded her to have an abortion, day and night, but she kept throwing it back at him (*You told me you wanted a family*) and he countered with what would become his refrain (*Yeah, sure, in like ten years maybe*), but here they were, sitting round the table with their new Florida friends, the babies no longer theoretical but living breathing proof that the biology worked between them and there was no stopping it. *Really, how do you think all these people got on the planet?* she said, and he said, *Beats me.*

"What he means," she said, "is that he's just thrilled." She turned her brightest smile on him, where he sat across the table from her, glowing and beautiful and drunk in his crisp white tee that didn't even show any sweat stains. Which was amazing. He didn't sweat. Ever. She held it a beat. "Diapers and all."

He pushed himself up and leaned over the table then, pecking kisses to the tops of the girls' heads—their fontanels, yes—and then kissing her full on the lips. "I'm the luckiest man alive," he said, straightening up and making a muscle with his right arm. "You know what? I could even be persuaded to drink to that."

Daria applauded, thinly. The three guys just stared.

But now it was the next morning, there was a mess to clean up and she was hungover for the first time in a year, and what that was or wasn't going to do to her milk, she didn't know. Todd, who had an iron constitution, was already up. She smelled coffee, then she heard the shower, and in the next minute Todd was singing in there—*singing*—when she felt like she'd been hit in the head with a shovel. At least the girls were still asleep, but of course they were a time bomb ready to explode with their feed-me shrieks and the fuse was already lit and counting down. She was afraid to move. Afraid even to glance over at them. Her throat was dry. Her temples pounded. Alcohol dried you out, she knew that, and in the past she'd always been careful to drink a glass of water before bed, but this time she hadn't because she was out of practice and the rum had come up on her fast and the last thing she remembered was feeding the girls and then just passing out in bed while Todd sat in the living room with the music going and Daria and Miller still there.

She pushed herself up tentatively and found her feet still attached to her and her feet found the floor, small miracle, so she shifted her weight a couple of times and made her way to the kitchen for water, one glass, two, and because the Florida water tasted like shit—or, more properly, piss—she got a can of Dasani out of the refrigerator and downed that too. Outside, the morning was like a painting, or no, a diorama featuring gulls hanging by strings and immovable boats fixed on the sea, but it was bright, too bright, way too bright, so she slipped back into the bedroom, stole past the twins and eased into bed.

Next thing she knew, the sun had shifted, the girls were squalling and she was sitting up in bed, feeding them. In the interval, her headache had begun to recede and she felt she might want to put something on her stomach, maybe a soft-boiled egg and a muffin, not so much because she was hungry but because she was going to have to eat something sometime and it might as well be now. She called out to Todd, but Todd didn't answer. The smell of coffee had long since dissipated, losing itself in the general funk of decay that was Florida. The surf sloshed. The gulls cried. A series of pictures of the party came back to her, bright images that shuffled by like cards in a deck, and it made her smile—the party had been a success, their first step toward getting back to normal.

She changed the girls and put them down, then went out to the kitchen. Todd wasn't there. And he wasn't in the living room either. She put her egg on, made fresh coffee and began stacking last night's dishes in the dishwasher, puzzling over where he could be before it came to her: He'd told her he was taking the car in to the detailing place again. If he'd obsessed over the car before the storm, now he was even worse. The wind had raked various vegetative and man-made things across the finish after the cloth cover had been ripped off and the waves had reached high enough to splash the windshield, but no major damage had been done, which was lucky—the clips on the news showed a procession of totaled cars, roofless houses, downed trees and power lines, though everybody said it could have been worse since this was only a Category 2 hurricane. She could only imagine what a Category 3 would be like—or worse, a 4 or 5, which hardly ever happened, except maybe once every fifty years.

The egg timer dinged, followed by the double ding of the toaster oven, a little celebration of the usual. Most mornings she had breakfast out on the deck, but the table hadn't been cleared yet—it was a forest of wine bottles and dirty glasses—so she ate at the kitchen table. She was still there, hunched over her laptop responding to comments on her Instagram and TikTok accounts, when Todd came thumping up the stairs with the newspaper and a bag of beignets from a Cajun restaurant he liked that also happened to be owned by one of his regional clients who sometimes had him host events there. He was beaming. The sun duplicated itself in the twin lenses of his sunglasses till it looked as if it were pouring out of him. He must have drunk half a quart of rum the night before—and there was wine too—but you'd never know it.

"How you feeling?" he asked, dropping the beignets on the table. "I wasn't counting, but you were really going at it last night, wow, and when I came in to brush my teeth you were gone. And snoring, by the way."

"You snore too."

"Guilty as charged—but I enjoy my own snoring. When *you* start in, though—"

"But you can't hear it from the couch, can you?"

"No, or the babies either."

"Just wait till they get a little bigger."

He was hovering over her and he put his arms around her now and gave her a squeeze. "Come on, Cat, you know I can't wait to—it's been a while now, right? 'Babe, how do you call your lover boy?'" he said, quoting an old Lou Reed song he'd been fixated on since she'd got pregnant.

She leaned back. They kissed. He said, "Tonight, okay—for sure?" As if it were a duty. As if everything they'd had before were formalized now, sign on the dotted line, sex at ten, put it in, pull it out, the sheets sweaty, the air like a rolling pin flattening your skin till it was ready to bake in the oven of the night and the twins all set to start screaming any minute. He gave her nipples a squeeze, kissed her again. Then he was at the counter, pouring himself a cup of coffee, and she asked, "So how's the car?"

"I don't know. They do their best but their best isn't good enough.

And it's never going to be the same as it was before all that crap got blown all over it. There are these little hairline scratches and the finish feels, I don't know, bumpy or uneven or something if you run your hand over it—"

"Maybe we should sell it."

"Sell it? What are you talking about? I love that car—*we* love it, right?"

"Get an SUV," she said. "For the babies—and the flooding. You don't want to have to drive the Tesla through the ocean every time there's a full moon, do you?"

He didn't answer.

"And it's just going to get worse, you know that, right?"

"That car is part of my image," he said, swinging round on her, the cup in one hand, a beignet in the other. "I can't pull up at any of these high-end bars and restaurants in some boxy piece of shit with, what, *baby seats* in the back, for Christ's sake. I mean, how cool is that?"

Since the babies arrived, he'd been hosting events closer to home, though that still involved him coming in at three in the morning. He'd begged off on the longer trips by way of parental leave, but babies really didn't conform with the hosting image either and his boss didn't have all that much patience, so sooner or later he'd have to start flying around the country again—the world, Hong Kong!—and leave her behind. With the babies. She resented that. And she resented having to worry about the precious car every time she had to go out for groceries when he wasn't around. "Can't we have two cars?"

Well, no, they couldn't—he had enough trouble just maintaining one. And the expense, what with all the baby stuff now, just the *Pampers* alone, and you could double everything because there were two of them instead of the one most people had to deal with.

"Do you really want the babies in the backseat of the Tesla?"

"We'll cross that bridge when we come to it."

"We already came to it—like when I go to the pediatrician? Isn't it a pain putting the baby seats in the car every time? If we had an SUV they could just be in there permanently, because what difference does it make? We could get one of those Beemer X models, in black I was thinking—that's cool enough for you, isn't it?"

She was definitely making an impression on him, she could see that—he was giving her his out-of-focus look, as if he were studying a blackboard scribbled with equations that was located somewhere out on the bay. He rustled in the bag for another beignet, took a bite and shrugged, chewing. "I don't know," he said, flicking the crumbs from his lips, "we can talk about it when I get back."

"Get back? From where?"

"Didn't I tell you? Scott called yesterday while I was marinating the lamb? He wants me up in Boston next weekend—it's only a three-day trip, zip up the coast and zip right on back."

IT RAINED ALL WEEKEND. Not in Boston, apparently, but here in Florida where everything was already drowning. What was she facing? Boredom, with a capital *B*. She posted shots of her daily routine, with little self-deprecating but subtly hierarchical quips added, a mix she had down to perfection (woe is me, but woe is you too—or more woe because you're not living in a beach house with a Tesla Model S in the driveway and your babies aren't as good-looking as mine or your husband either) and she twice included video of the rain jumping on the deck and curtaining off the sea. The girls, at two months, were sleeping something like seventeen hours a day, but that was off and on, and though you weren't supposed to fall asleep with them in bed, she sometimes did, simply because she was too exhausted to move and by the time she could summon the energy to get up and put them back in their bassinets, she was already snoring, thank you, Todd. Everybody talked about postpartum depression—all that buildup, all that anxiety, and then your life goes on the way it was before, except with ten times the work and complication, no matter the joy of the babies themselves and the high of breast-feeding and all the rest—but she didn't think she had it. No, she was depressed for a very simple reason: Todd was gone. She wanted help and support. She wanted to get out. See something, go someplace, shake up the unbending daily routine that was making her feel more and more like a human cow.

If the rain would stop, even for half an hour, she could strap on her Weego and at least take a walk up the road with the babies, maybe even go as far as Bobo's and get some lunch and a glass of white wine . . . but the rain wouldn't stop and when she brought up the forecast on her phone it just showed the rain icon all day and into the night. It was two in the afternoon. She was bored out of her mind. She poured herself a drink.

She was sitting at the window, counting the raindrops, when the phone rang. It was her mother.

"Cat?"

"Hi, Mom."

"How are you holding up?"

"I don't know. Okay, I guess." She watched the rain draw patterns on the window. "Todd's gone again."

"What do you mean? I thought they gave him parental leave?"

"They did. But that was two months and the two months are up. He's in Boston for the weekend and I'm stuck here with the girls. And it's raining. Again."

"Rain? What's rain? It's absolutely scorching here and all the plants are stressed and the sundowners seem like they're constant now—what I wouldn't give for a little rain, even a shower. Your brother says it's never going to rain again in our lifetime."

"You're still coming for Christmas, right?"

"I wouldn't miss it. And your father's excited to see the twins in the flesh."

"I can't wait," she said. "And in the meantime why don't I send you a bucket of rain via UPS—that sound good? The supersize mailer?"

They talked for an hour, talked just to talk, and it made her feel better. As did the rum. She had two drinks before she even knew it, and after she hung up she put some music on and was about to go out to the kitchen and make herself a prosciutto sandwich before the twins woke up and called her back to duty, when her eyes fell on the terrarium. Willie II was pressed against the glass, his head weaving, the length of him coiling and uncoiling again till he might have been two snakes or even three, and it struck her that he was trying to communicate something to her. Did he want to be held? Released from the tank to glide around the room a couple of times? Or no: He was hungry, that was it, and when was the last time she'd fed him? She couldn't remember.

What with everything going on, she'd been neglecting him. Which wasn't right. He was helpless in there, totally at her mercy as if she were some kind of god, and letting him go hungry was just inexcusable, cruelty to animals, and she'd never been cruel to any animal, at least not intentionally. His bedding would need to be changed too—and water, did he even have water? Feeling guilty, she went to the freezer and extracted one of the frozen bunnies, which was just a gray anonymous lump of furred flesh, if you overlooked the ears and the flattened profile of the face. She put it in the microwave for a quick jolt, then laid it in her biggest saucepan, poured a can of heated chicken soup over it and set it aside to defrost, then went to the closet for the reinforced cardboard box she'd been using to feed him in.

The online forums advised against feeding snakes in the terrarium itself, lest they associate removal of the top with food, especially live food that had to be struck and killed, and she'd ignored the advice till the first time Willie struck at her when she was just opening the top to lift him out with her hook. So now—or last time, anyway, which had to be maybe a week ago?—she fed him in the box, which also allowed her time to clean the terrarium in the interim. Which was long overdue.

Willie reacted to her as she undid the fasteners, nosing at the four corners one after the other, and when she opened the top this time, he seemed even more agitated than usual—he was hungry—but he knew the hook and seemed to accept it as a condition of being fed. She balanced him a moment, then lifted him out and he flowed like a Slinky into the box, fully cooperating. Of course, as soon as she turned to clean the terrarium the twins woke up and started screaming, which meant she'd have to leave Willie in the box till she could see to them and be sure his dinner was defrosted all the way through, but it wasn't going to be a problem. The box was waist-high, the sides too smooth for him to get a grip. He'd be fine in there. And she really should have seen to him earlier, much earlier, while the girls were asleep or when she was talking to her mother or mixing herself the next drink. What could she say? Mea culpa.

15

THE NEXT-TO-LAST CHRYSALIS

COOPER COMMISERATED OVER THE LOSS OF THE BEES, BUT his voice on the phone was distant and dragged-down, as if he'd been drinking. In the middle of the day. She asked him, point-blank, because she was worried about him, and he said, "No, not yet, actually, but I'm planning on it."

"It's two in the afternoon."

"My arm hurts. Phantom pain—I'm getting phantom limb pain."

"Oh, stop it. This is no time for jokes."

"I'm not joking."

"Because the bees are all dead and I was really getting attached to them. Or the idea of them, anyway."

Over the past year Ottilie had become modestly proficient as a bee-keeper, which wasn't all that difficult since the bees did the real work and would have gone about their business whether she was involved or not. She collected honey in mason jars till the pantry was full and Frank said he'd already had enough honey to last him the rest of his days, at which point she began affixing labels to the jars—CULLEN'S FINEST—and giving it away to the people in her life she wanted to thank, Sylvie, the neighbors on either side of her and across the street, the postman, the hostess at the sushi restaurant. Nature's bounty. It made her feel good, ecologically sound, a habitat provider and a gift-giver too.

"Colony collapse disorder. It's an old story. We'll get you another hive."

"When?"

"I don't know, we'll go out and buy one, they're like five hundred bucks or something. But this is the tip of the iceberg—it's not just the pollinators, but everything else with wings too. I'm on my way out to the field station now to check it out, but just right here, in my backyard, it's like they came by in the middle of the night and sprayed DDT or something . . . What about you? Where are you, are you inside?"

"I'm out here by the hive."

"Look around—you see any insects in the air at all?"

THAT WAS THE BEGINNING OF what the press was calling the Bug Apocalypse, the phrase jumping out at you from every newspaper and magazine and the news crawl on the TV. Nobody could explain it. Neonicotinoids, systemic insecticides that first appeared in the 1990s and rendered every part of a plant poisonous, including the pollen, were among the suspects, but that didn't explain the die-off of insects that didn't feed on the targeted plants, like the oak leaf moths Cooper was so worked up over, though from her perspective it was good riddance to them since they'd denuded all the live oaks on the property and the trees were just beginning to come back. No, it went deeper. People were saying—Cooper was saying—it was some contaminant or combination of them they hadn't suspected or uncovered yet and that what was happening was a threat not only to bees and butterflies and the livelihood of entomologists but to the food chain itself. It made for good press, one more scare story to add to the mix, the sort of thing everybody would have forgotten about by the next news cycle.

Her bees were dead. She would get more. Five hundred dollars—that wasn't so extreme, was it? Though Frank would say five hundred dollars buys a lot of honey, a lifetime supply, really, and she would counter with her environmentalist's argument and serve up mealworm tacos for dinner and honey-drenched baklava for dessert, adding a cup of her cricket flour to the phyllo dough for emphasis. That was what she was thinking the first night, anyway, before the press got on the story and the true tenor of it came home to her. It was as if the bones of the earth had been laid bare and the windblown future would never cover them again, everything caught up in the death spiral Cooper had been gloomily predicting since he was a teenager. There might not be any bees to buy—and if there were, they'd just fly out into the world, into her garden, pick up the contaminant, whatever it was and wherever it was, and drop down out of the sky like so many flecks of lint. Insects were the food resource of the future, wasn't that how it was supposed to be? And they were all but infinite, weren't they?

The next morning, she took her swim, then went out to the far end of the garden and stood wrapped in her towel over the silent shell of the beehive for a long while, the dark shriveled corpses of the bees littering the ground all around it and ants—Argentine ants, translocated them-selves, like the European bees—making the most of the unexpected bounty. She stood there feeling desolate, nothing moving, not even the lizards or the yellow-cheeked birds that came to drink from the filter basket, and she had to hope they weren't insectivorous or their days would be numbered too. That was when she noticed that even the ants had begun to slow down, drawing back, hunching, twitching, curling up like stray punctuation marks in the dust. She didn't panic. It wasn't time for that yet. But since Frank was already at work—no matter how many bugs died, people still had to be treated for ailments major and minor and get their scrips for infections, allergies and the inexpressible sadness that was at the heart of everything—and because she needed to do something other than wring her hands and stare out the window, she put Dunphy in the car and drove up over the pass and down into the valley with the notion of taking her son out to breakfast and getting some answers.

A girl she didn't know answered the door.

"Hi," she said, "I'm Cooper's mother. Is he up yet?"

The girl was tall, blond, dressed in a T-shirt and panties, her feet bare and her toenails unpainted. She shook her head. "He's a late sleeper—but I don't have to tell you, right?"

There was a moment in which they stared into each other's eyes, then the girl pulled the door back and said, "I was just going to put some coffee on. You want a cup?"

They were sitting together at the kitchen table, the preliminaries over (her name was Elytra, her specialty kissing bugs), when Cooper came in, wearing running shorts and a long-sleeved shirt despite the heat. "I thought I heard voices," he said.

She smiled as he bent to peck a kiss to her cheek. "Don't tell me," he said, "it's the bees, right? They're still dead?"

"And everything else. Even the ants."

"I've been online half the night—it's not just localized, people are reporting it all over the place. And nobody knows what's going on."

"I can't believe it," Elytra said and she got up and went to the cupboard, with which she seemed casually familiar, extracted a bag of muffins, split open three and laid them on the rack in the toaster oven. "It's got to be just some blip."

"UFOs," Cooper said. He shifted to the counter to pour himself a cup of coffee. Dunphy, who'd been nosing around the corners, looked up at him expectantly. "Either that or the Chinese."

"But seriously," Ottilie said, "it can't be any more than that, some freak thing—radio waves or something, infrared rays, ultrasound, a new kind of virus maybe. There's just too many insects for them all to just disappear like that. Billions could die, trillions, and there'd still be trillions and trillions left, right?" One of the statistics Cooper was always touting was that the combined weight of all the insects on earth was seventeen times that of humanity, a staggering figure considering it would take millions of them just to equal the weight of even a single human. "Gnats," she said, "just take gnats alone—they bit me up in the garden day before yesterday to the point where I had to give up the fight and retreat to the house. See, right here"—she pulled up the cuffs of her jeans—"both ankles. And mosquitoes. They're so thick down where Cat lives it's like you're wearing a shirt of them every time you step out the door."

Cooper eased down in the chair across from her with a cup of coffee, selected a muffin from the platter Elytra had set in the middle of the table and began slathering it with butter and a dripping spoonful of Cullen's Finest. She noticed he was using both hands, though when he lifted it to his mouth it was with his left hand only, dropping the mechanical one to his lap like a tool he'd laid aside. "It can't be a pathogen," he said, "because it's cutting across so many different species. If it was a virus or bacteria or even a fungus you'd expect it to infect a given species or even a handful of related species, but this is something else altogether. And I tell you, it's got me terrified."

Elytra slid into the seat beside her and gave her a searching look, pouting her lips and arching her eyebrows. "You're saying it's the ants too? Which just seems incredible." She was pretty, with a natural wave to her hair—it was almost kinky—and her eyes were hazel shading to brown, like Cooper's. Plus, she had height—she must have been five-eight or -nine, which gave her an advantage over Mari. If anything came of the relationship, that is. Marriage. Grandchildren. That sort of thing. But here she was, getting ahead of herself again. The world was dying before her eyes and she was thinking of grandchildren?

"If that's true," Elytra said, "then there's really no figuring it. I mean, they're underground, they can survive anything, even nuclear radiation. The first thing scientists found after Krakatoa erupted back in the 1880s—the only thing, after the lava cooled, that is—was an ant."

"A spider," Cooper said.

"I thought it was an ant."

"Speaking of spiders," he said, "has anybody seen any—or are they gone too? Because that would tell us something if it's not just insects but the arachnids along with them." In the next moment, he rose from the table and crossed the room to fling open the front door on a blast of light and a whiff of overbaked earth. "No, look," he called, and she was on her feet now and so was Elytra, "they're here—*Pholcidae*! And a jumping spider—it's just climbing up the post as if nothing's wrong. Look at this! Look!"

For a long while the three of them just stared at the spider on the post as if they'd never seen anything like it, though it was common in its range, which took it from northern Mexico to the Great Plains and all the way up to southern Canada. The red-backed jumping spider, *Phidippus johnsoni*. Common as dirt. She'd seen thousands of them, yes, but not this one. This one was unique. This one was salvatory. She wanted to be amazed and relieved, wanted to be positive, but all she could think was, *What's it going to eat?*

IT WAS A LONG DAY, everything chaotic, the heat rising, the news baffling and terrifying in equal measure. She decided she'd go out to the field station with them and help sift through the brush behind the ranch house and bag and count specimens—to what end she didn't know. Cooper didn't seem to know either. There'd been a die-off, a once-in-a-lifetime event, and he was a biologist and what biologists did was collect, count and identify specimens against the expectation of some larger revelation. So she was there with him at ten in the morning, crouched over her hands and knees under the fierceness of the sun and picking miniature corpses out of the dirt with a pair of tweezers. She smelled sage and yerba buena and a dozen other things she couldn't identify. Her back ached, her shoulders, the muscles of her forearms. Though she was wearing a wide-brimmed straw hat and she'd smeared herself with sunblock, she could feel the skin tightening on the back of her neck and her face too every time she shifted position.

When they'd got out of the car in the dirt lot at the field station, Mari had been there to greet them, dressed in white jeans and a long-sleeved shirt, her eyes unreadable behind a pair of opaque blue-lensed sunglasses. "About time," Mari said, addressing Cooper. She didn't take his hand or hug him or acknowledge him in any other way than that and didn't say a word to Elytra, though she went down on one knee to ruffle Dunphy's coat and coo him a doggie endearment or two.

"Ottilie," she said, as if she'd just noticed her. "So nice to see you. You going to be one of our volunteers?"

"I am," she said, and didn't know whether to shake her hand or hold out her arms for an embrace till she did neither and the moment had passed.

"Crazy shit, huh?" Elytra said, but Mari didn't respond.

"It's not arachnids, as far as I can see," Cooper said, "so at least one of us is still going to have a job in the future."

"It was a jumping spider," Ottilie put in. "With the red back? And a couple of house spiders too, spinning their webs as if nothing was out of the usual. At Cooper's place?"

"So it's class-specific," Elytra said, "as crazy as that seems, but at least it's a starting point."

"Yeah, well, we'll see," Mari said, and then they went out to do their penance under the sun.

✳

SHE WAS SORE ALL OVER by the time she got home and the first thing she did, even before she flicked on the TV for the latest on the bug front, was jump in the pool. She'd tuned in to NPR in the car as soon as the station came into range at the top of the pass but learned nothing beyond the fact that scientists around the world were as baffled as anybody else. Various experts came on to make dire pronouncements about the food supply and speculate on what had caused the die-off but nobody really knew anything. Insect populations would rebound, they were all sure of that, or mostly sure, and even if they didn't the good news was that the grains that formed the foundation of the human diet—corn, wheat, rice—were wind-pollinated. Fruits and vegetables—nuts, berries, kiwi, zucchini, cherries, pumpkins, cantaloupe—were another story, and that was causing volatility in the futures markets, to say the least. Grapes? No worries there. The varietals that supported so much of the state's viniculture industry were self-fertilizing. People could do without almonds, peaches, even watermelon, but wine, never. At least that was what one zoned-out commentator proclaimed, which Ottilie thought flippant, given the magnitude of what was happening. But wine. Yes, wine. She toweled off and went barefoot into the kitchen to pour herself a glass of Viognier and sit in front of the TV.

When Frank came home she was in the kitchen making a salad, the radio tuned to the classical station. She halved cherry tomatoes, chopped romaine, cut thin strips of sweet red pepper and carrots from the garden, then swept them into her big ceramic bowl and added garbanzos, dry-roasted sunflower seeds and crumbled feta, each ingredient presenting itself in a whole new light, even the oil, the balsamic vinegar, the herbs. How much of what they were eating relied on pollinators? Of what they'd always eaten? Of what they'd taken for granted?

She heard Frank trudge up the stairs to the bedroom to change his clothes and then a moment later, preceded by the tap-dance of Dunphy's claws on the tile floor, he was there, dressed in his shorts and crossing the room to pour himself a glass of red, which involved the faintest circadian squeak of the cabinet's hinges and the soothing splash of the wine as gravity drew it into the glass. "You been following the news?" he said, swinging round on her, looking just exactly like her husband. Which was a good thing. A very good thing. "It's crazy, huh? Coop must be in heaven."

"Heaven? What are you talking about?"

"He's like Nostradamus. 'There will be scourges the like of which was never seen.' Our son, the prophet. He always knew everything was going to turn to shit and here it is."

"He's upset, just like everybody else, of course he is, and really, this is nothing to joke about—I mean, have *you* been following the news?"

"It's all anybody could talk about today. The whole practice was buzzing with it, as if the sky had collapsed. Then the commentators on the radio on the way home said we were going to be just fine because mankind's principal food crops don't need pollination, as if we were already moving on. In fact, one woman, an expert from some university I never heard of—Doofus U., you heard of that one?—said we'd be better off without insects because they take such a toll on crop yields, if you can believe the asininity of that comment . . . But Jesus, are you sunburned?"

"A little. I don't know. I was out at the field station with Cooper."

"Really? What does he say?"

"He says it didn't affect the arachnids, but all the insects, the bugs, they were dead on the ground—and, of course, my bees went yesterday, which is beyond disappointing but something I thought was localized . . ."

"Not the spiders, just the insects—what does that even mean?"

"He doesn't know. Nobody knows. I was on my hands and knees under that sun half the day, till the wind came up and blew everything away, dirt, bugs, seeds and twigs, stickers, burs. The foxtails are a nightmare out there."

"And the ticks, what about the ticks? They're arachnids. They must be in their glory." He tipped back his glass, puffed his cheeks, swallowed. "But seriously, I hope you checked yourself—"

"Mari gave me her eucalyptus-oil spray and when I got home I bundled up everything and put it in the wash—and then I got in the pool."

"Okay," he said, and he came across the room and wrapped his arms around her. "But just in case, I'd better inspect your body, especially those hard-to-see places, right? In bed? Later tonight?"

He squeezed her. She squeezed him back. She said, "Cooper's got a new girlfriend."

❁

IN THE MORNING, STILL NOBODY had any answers. She watched the news till she couldn't bear it any longer, then went out to work in the garden, though it was already pushing ninety, a temperature that would have been unheard-of for November only a few years back. For Cooper, over the hill in the Santa Ynez Valley, it was triple digits, which was going to make his fieldwork murderous, and how many bug carcasses did you really need to conclude something had gone very wrong?

Gradually, she fell into the rhythm of her work and it cleared her mind of everything but the most elemental imperatives, water this, clip that, build up the mulch here, reduce it there, and it wasn't until she dumped the clippings on the compost heap and turned the dirt over with her pitchfork that the news came back home to her: there was nothing moving in all that rich black loam, no earwigs, no beetles, no grubs or maggots or centipedes. Normally, they seethed and boiled with every thrust of the pitchfork, but nothing was moving in the soil today, not even pill bugs, which weren't actually insects but tiny crustaceans—and how could they be affected too? They couldn't. They weren't. She just wasn't seeing any today, that was all, because they were somewhere else, in somebody's else's compost heap or under a rock or the fence posts or cavorting in the leaf litter at the edges of the garden, mating and eating and defecating and dying as they always had, long before humans and their chemicals even existed. The whole thing was just as Elytra had said, a momentary aberration, a warning salvo from an overstressed planet, and maybe it would wake people up to what was happening. Or maybe not. Maybe nobody cared. Bugs, who needed bugs? Who even noticed them unless they were biting you?

When she moved on to the milkweed patch, she didn't know what to expect. Just a week ago she'd counted a dozen monarch caterpillars (and duly recorded the numbers for Cooper's study). Monarchs were the poster species for insect conservationists, an easier sell than, say, horseflies or dung beetles, obviously, and they were on the verge of extinction. The adults fed on the nectar of a whole smorgasbord of plants, but the larvae—the gorgeous plump caterpillars with their alternating black, yellow and white stripes—subsisted exclusively on milkweed, which allowed them to build up alkaloids toxic to predators. Over the summer she'd watched three generations of them form their chrysalises, emerge as butterflies and take to the air.

It was late in the season now, well into their migration period, when the adults of the western population would make their way here and points south to overwinter, but the persistent heat seemed to have thrown them off and they were still pupating, though Cooper had told her it was too late for the adults to be sexually viable, which seemed to her a terrible waste. She bent to inspect the plants, one after the other, but the caterpillars were gone. She went through them a second time, just to be sure, and this time she found two chrysalises, vibrant green waxy things that looked manufactured, like confections, like the mochi at the Japanese restaurant served up not on a plate but on a thread fastened to a slat of the fence. They were objects of beauty in their own right—so flawlessly constructed, so perfect, it was hard to imagine an insect had created them. Even more amazing: inside each of them was a caterpillar undergoing its metamorphosis into another form altogether, an imago that could dance on the currents of the air and soar hundreds of miles to a roost it had never seen or known before.

She got out her phone to take pictures and send them to Cooper—at least something was alive in the insect world and here was the proof of it. But then she noticed that the chrysalis nearest her was ever so faintly discolored, and when she looked closer she saw a dark spreading stain in the center of it like a bruise on a banana that had already gone rotten.

16

SIERRA

IT DIDN'T HAPPEN THAT DAY. NOTHING HAPPENED THAT DAY
but more of the same, more rain, more boredom, more rum, and
whether rum—Bacar-*dee*—was her drink of choice or not, it was free
and it was there and it helped render the endless parade of crap on cable
palatable, which in turn kept her from running down the street screaming her head off. Willie stayed in the box but she must have misread him
because he didn't touch his rabbit, which she finally had to put back in
the refrigerator when she transferred him to the terrarium. The rain
rained. The babies woke and she fed them and put them down, then
they woke and she fed them and put them down again. Todd didn't call.
Todd was in Boston, wearing his Armani tux and professionally flirting
with women in evening gowns with their boobs on display. *Oh, Todd,*
that is so fantastic! Oh, Todd, I really like the way you wear your tux,
so clean and crisp—and those shoulders—but what's that lump in your
pants? Do it again, Todd, same as before. Was he cheating on her? Their
sex life had gone down the toilet since the babies came so she wouldn't

put it past him. And it wasn't as if he had any real investment in them—
he hadn't even been there when they were born, which wasn't his fault,
really, but that was the fact. Was it last weekend when he took her out
for dinner and they got a little frisky after the girls had gone to sleep?
Yes, last weekend. That was good. That was like old times. But then he
spoiled it by saying, "Well, I guess this makes me a motherfucker now,
right? Literally?"

The next day she just couldn't take it anymore—her brain was dead,
her every post boring and formulaic, or worse, cheesy—and she waited
till the rain fell off to a mere downpour in the late afternoon, dressed
the girls in the matching miniature polyester microfiber rain jackets her
mother had sent them, backed the Tesla down off the ramp and drove to
Bobo's to see if there was anyone there she knew.

She was wearing sandals (anything else, other than maybe hip wad-
ers, would have been a decidedly poor choice in this weather; as it was,
mold was growing on all the shoes in her closet and half her handbags
too), which meant her feet got wet the minute she swung open the
car door and set them down in the parking lot. The lot wasn't flooded
exactly but pocked with puddles that were gradually creeping across the
macadam till before long they'd be one continuous puddle and McKen-
zie, the manager, could declare the lot officially inundated, park at your
own risk, chaos rules, etc., so what else was new? The girls were awake,
but mercifully quiet, as if they were awed by these strange new sensa-
tions crowding in on them, the drumming on the roof, the sizzle that
underlay it, the density of the air in their tiny lungs, *rain*. They appre-
hended it through their skin, their nervous systems, the looming white
flash of their mother's wet hands as she hustled them up the steps and in
the door, her hair instantly wet and hanging in her eyes and no way of
brushing it back till they were settled at a table and she could set them
down. Luckily, Daria was at the hostess stand and all she had to say was,
"By the window," and a minute later she was seated, the girls on either
side of her in their carriers and Daria making small talk as if there were
no such thing as rain and the restaurant wasn't all but deserted and the

tips she'd share with the waitstaff weren't even worth climbing out of bed for.

"The girls are getting big," Daria said. "Or is that my imagination?"

She laughed. "It's your imagination—but the way they go at me they ought to be the size of Godzilla by now."

"Todd gone again?"

"Boston. He'll be back tomorrow."

"Mojito?"

"You read my mind. And I'd better see the menu too."

She texted some people who'd transitioned from Instagram followers to bona fide online friends. Posted a couple pictures of the girls in their carriers with the rain-smeared window behind them and the overhead lights setting them aglow. She called Todd, but his phone went straight to message. The girls were perfect, drifting off to sleep as soon as she fed them (discreetly, right there at the table). The rain kept up. At some point, people began to wander into the bar, rain or no rain, but she didn't recognize any of them and it wouldn't have mattered if she did because she was limiting herself strictly to two drinks and then home. All she'd really needed was to get out and she'd succeeded, so hallelujah. For a long while, lingering over her second drink, she watched the people at the bar, guys mostly, but some couples too, all of them laughing, drinking, nibbling fried shrimp and oysters and calamari and chattering away like birds in the rain forest, living the stress-free life the way she and Todd had before the girls came along. Not that she'd change anything.

The point was, and she'd insist on it afterward, she wasn't drunk, not in the slightest—she was back to her former capacity, and two drinks, even if Ricardo knew they were for her and made them extra strong, were nothing. Plus, she'd had a steak with fried plantains and black beans and a salad because she was starving, and that gave her ballast, absolutely. And when the white Jeep came at her out of nowhere, she was able to avoid the worst so that the accident was just a fender bender and the girls were fine, and if they were screaming their lungs

out it was just a continuation of what they'd been doing from the minute she strapped them in, which admittedly might have been something
of a distraction. If they'd been quiet—if they'd been asleep—maybe her
reaction time would have been a hair quicker, but the point was the girls
were fine and so was she and it wasn't her fault because the guy pulled
right out in front of her.

He was older—fifty, sixty maybe. Dyed hair, but the giveaway was
white sideburns and a patch of white stubble on his Adam's apple he
must have missed while shaving. He was wearing glasses and a floppy
rain hat and maybe he was senile, maybe that was it. "You pulled right
out in front of me," she said.

You weren't supposed to admit fault in an accident—let the insurance sort it out—but he did, right away. "Oh, my god, I'm so sorry," he
said, standing there at the door of her car, which she'd pushed open on
the rain and the inescapable funk of Florida. "I just didn't see you, I
mean, with the rain and all—are you okay?"

She went outside of herself for a minute there, her hands trembling
with the rush of adrenaline as she pushed herself up out of the seat,
fought the catch on her umbrella and planted her feet on the rain-slick
pavement. She hadn't banged her head. She didn't have whiplash. The
airbags hadn't even inflated. It was a fender bender, that was all, but she
felt light-headed and the rain sang its songs in various keys, cars swish-
ing by with clusters of faces staring at her as if she were the star of her
own dramedy, into each life a little rain must fall—and should she snap
photos of the girls and show the world just how rock-solid an investment Snug-a-Baby seats were in an emergency like this with rain coming
down like a waterfall and logs turning into alligators and alligators into
logs? She wasn't drunk, not even close, and it wasn't her fault, but she
was careful to breathe shallowly since she didn't want him smelling her
breath—or the cops either, if the cops even had to be involved, and they
didn't, did they?

His face was like a peeled cantaloupe, if that was even possible—
could you peel a cantaloupe? His glasses—*glasses*, he was nearsighted,

half-blind, old—were steamed over. "The kids," he said, peering into the car. "Are they—?"

She didn't answer. She was inspecting the car while the rain made her clothes cling to her and she wondered what she was going to tell Todd—or no, she knew what she was going to tell him, *Some senile old guy with glasses an inch thick pulled right out in front of me.* And then she saw the damage, which was minimal, really, the headlight on the passenger side fractured and a gouge as long as her forearm in the front fender—which could be rubbed out or painted over or something, couldn't it? "They're okay," she said, "just a little shaken up maybe. It was—didn't you see me? I mean, my lights were on—they're still on, see?"

"I can't tell you how sorry I am," he said, and they both looked to his car, an impervious white monument shedding water like an elaborate sculpture erected there on the side of the road. Aside from a scratch on the bumper—a reddish scratch, tinged with her paint—it was undamaged. "Let me give you my information," he said, rain drooling from the brim of his hat. "We'll take some pictures, okay? But I don't think we really need to file a police report or anything since it's only a fender bender—just send me the estimate." He focused narrowly on her face. "You're all right, aren't you? The airbag didn't even deploy—or mine either."

"Yeah, no," she said, and she still couldn't quite bring the scene into focus because her nerves were destroyed and the rum was like a crimped wet blanket somebody had thrown over her shoulders, "we don't need the police."

BACK AT HOME, SHE HAD a long session with the girls, both of them fussing even after she fed and changed them, and she set them down in their carriers on the living room rug—*The moths, Jesus, look at the holes, just look at them!*—and rattled the bright plastic figurines on their mobiles to stimulate them and take their minds off their gas pains or colic or whatever it was. Or the trauma of the accident—could that be it? She'd inspected them minutely and there wasn't a bump or scratch on either of them, but there had been that single instant of impact that really couldn't have done them much good—milkshakes, they were little milkshakes, churn, churn, churn, even at the best of times. Tahoe seemed more upset than Sierra, but both of them cried and fussed and scrunched up their faces, and it went on forever even after she picked them up and cooed to them and paraded them around the room half a dozen times. Finally they both fell silent and she left them there on the rug where she could keep an eye on them and went to the counter to fix herself a drink.

She turned on the tube with the sound off and put some music on, a neo-soul singer she liked who had a hard-driving horn-inflected band behind him, and that made her feel better, but in the intervals when the dynamics dropped she could hear the rain on the roof, the eternal rain, and that depressed her all over again. And, of course, she was just putting off calling Todd and giving him the news about the car, which was going to send him through the roof, but she could already see turning it right back on him and using the whole episode to reenforce her argument about getting an SUV because it was an SUV that had hit her and if she and the girls had been in one themselves not only would they have been a whole lot safer and maybe even avoided the accident altogether but the damage would have amounted to nothing more than a scratched bumper. Or something like that. Theoretically, anyway. And on some level the whole thing was Todd's fault. If he'd been here, she wouldn't have been driving in the rain anyway, no matter what kind of car they had.

He picked up on the first ring. "Hey, babe."

"Hi."

"So it was pretty piss-poor tonight, older crowd, stupid jokes, some big regional restaurateur's premiere party for his new line of TV spots, all of which were beyond lame and kept playing on all the screens till you needed to get drunk just to stay alive. These rich people—they want what they want and they want it now, like I'm some sort of errand boy or servant or something. It was no fun, believe me. And you? You holding up? All good? So, I'll be home tomorrow—" he went on, without waiting for an answer, and then he reminded her of the flight number and warned her to be sure to call ahead in case of delays because he heard it was raining down there. Was it?

"It hasn't let up since the minute you got on the plane."

"Oh, no, Jesus, it's not flooding again, is it? What about the car—is the car okay?"

"Actually, that's what I was calling about—"

"Oh, shit, don't tell me—fuck, Cat, no!"

"It was a fender bender, that's all—some old guy pulled out in front of me. And in case you want to know, the girls and I are fine, though it was pure hell getting them to go down tonight . . ."

"But the car—what about the car?"

"If you'd let me get an SUV—"

"Fuck the SUV."

"You don't have to get worked up over it, it's just a scratch—I mean, they can rub it out or something."

"Rub it out? What are you smoking? Is it a dent, is that it? Is it dented at all?"

"Your precious car," she said.

"I can't believe you. I'm gone for three days—what did you even have to drive for? What, to go to the bar? Are you drunk? You sound drunk. Were you drunk behind the wheel?" He paused, trying to contain his outrage and find the perfect little envelope to cram it all into. "Jesus, I'm up here working my balls off—"

"Yeah," she said, "I'm sure you are. And how's that going for you? Don't tell me all the women were too old to screw. Poor Todd. I feel for you, I really do."

"You are out of your fucking mind. Really. Truly. Out-of-your-fucking-mind."

☀

THE RAIN WASN'T JUST OUTSIDE tapping at the roof and hissing in the gutters, it was inside her too, internal weather, insinuating things she didn't want to know and didn't want to hear. There was no way she was going to be able to sleep, not with the accident and Todd's level of animosity on the phone and the racket of the rain and that smell that seeped into everything, even the sheets and pillowcases. She just sat there at the kitchen counter, and if she had a couple of drinks, who was counting? Certainly not Todd. He drank even more than she did so who was he to criticize her? *Are you drunk? You sound drunk.*

She didn't feel like moving, so she stretched out on the couch and watched whatever on TV and though she'd been off pills of any kind since even before she got pregnant she took a Halcion and washed it down with the dregs of her drink, which tasted heavy and alien, as if somebody had snuck in and poisoned it on her. The girls slept on, oblivious, shooting out their little arms every once in a while in that falling-out-of-the-tree reflex, dreaming their baby dreams, sedated on the best drug of all, mother's milk. Her milk. Her daughters. Her house. Her house on the beach. What was wrong with her? She was just tired, that was all. And the rain. The rain made her crazy.

The last thing she remembered was some news story about bugs, about how there'd been a mysterious die-off of bugs not only in America but around the world, and she wanted to call Cooper and see what was going on, but she didn't. Her phone was right there in the back pocket of her cutoffs, but it seemed so remote, so heavy and unwieldy, so much trouble, she couldn't really muster the energy. The sleep that closed over her was absolute, a black hole that sucked in all the atoms of her body and brain and everything in her orbit, and if she was alive, if she was dreaming, she didn't know it.

What woke her was what always woke her—the girls—and what time it was, she didn't know, except that the windows were gray and not black. She pulled out her phone, which had gotten so much lighter overnight, and checked the time: 7:13. So she'd slept, finally, and that was good, but the girls—there they were, in their carriers, right there on the chewed-up rug in the shadow of the portable teak bar she'd bought to replace the ugly lowboy—were going to need her immediate attention . . . but there was something wrong, something radically wrong, a trick of her eyes, and only Tahoe was crying, screaming, and Sierra was wrapped up in some sort of bright shining blanket, which wasn't a blanket at all.

How long did it take her to realize the truth of the moment? To realize that her daughter's face was bright with spots of blood where Willie's teeth had tried to seize hold of her and that her daughter wasn't crying because she wasn't breathing because Willie's eight feet of constrictor's muscle was locked round her in the unbreakable utilitarian grip that had been an evolutionary force on this earth long before the arrival of humans, of mammals even? A nanosecond. And then she was on her knees on the floor, jerking at his head, pounding him with her fists, screaming herself. Willie wouldn't let go. His eyes were dead things. His coils tightened. In the next moment she had a knife in her hand, one of the chromium-molybdenum-vanadium steel Wüsthof knives Todd had insisted on getting because they were top-of-the-line, the best, and anybody who wanted to lay claim to being a chef on any level needed them as much as a Le Creuset enameled omelet pan or a Breville peel-and-dice food processor and how she'd gotten the knife from the woodblock in the kitchen she didn't know because she was here in the moment and she was slashing, she was stabbing, and still Willie wouldn't let go.

17

PYTHON MOM

OTTILIE WAS BACK ON AN AIRPLANE AGAIN, ONLY THIS TIME there was no anticipation, only dread, and this time Frank was right there strapped in beside her. They'd been planning on coming out for Christmas, but that plan had been derailed—obliterated, blown out of the water—and they were coming now, three weeks in advance, because at this point Christmas was all but meaningless. The flight attendant brought her a drink and she drank it and had another. The cabin hissed like a deflating tire. She could feel the throb of the engines through the soles of her shoes. An airplane. She was back on an airplane.

When the flight attendant came round with the menu, she just waved him away, though meals were one of the perks of first class, and they were in first class because everything else had been booked and this was an emergency and the expense never even factored into the equation. Frank wasn't hungry either and he didn't want a drink, didn't want anything, didn't want to talk or comfort her or even look at her. Half an hour into the flight he was asleep, bent over the tray table, his head cradled in his arms, his face turned away from her. He was in the aisle seat, his preference, because he had an enlarged prostate and had to get up and pee every half hour, so she had the window seat, rearing high above the clouds, the sun a constant, everything beneath her like the pale rippled corridors of a dream, and all she did was gaze out on it, unable to concentrate on a book or movie or anything else.

How could she? First Cooper, then the bugs, and now this. Her granddaughter was dead, a sweet little thing who'd barely had a chance at life, a two-month-old, an innocent, and her daughter was being flayed alive for it, the tabloids in full attack mode, twisting everything, and how do you deal with that? "Python Mom," the headlines screamed, and the networks ran endless footage of the house on the ocean with the red Tesla parked up on its ramp like a court exhibit, as if it were key to the character of the sort of mother who would keep a dangerous wild animal in the same house as her infant daughters. There were pictures of Cat from her social media, pictures of her with the snake, with the girls, with Todd, even pictures of the wedding, and how they'd obtained those Ottilie couldn't imagine because it meant someone they knew intimately had betrayed them, and for what, a couple hundred dollars? If that? Even worse, there was the question of child endangerment, of culpability, which involved the police and social services and the real possibility of putting Tahoe in protective custody, but what the world needed to understand was that this wasn't negligence in any way, shape or form, but an accident, a horrific accident, and far from being an unfit mother, Cat was totally devoted—what had happened could have happened to anybody.

Anybody who kept a snake in the house, that is. Really, what had she been thinking? It should have been in the basement, at least, but then there was no basement. Or out on the deck. Why couldn't it have been out on the deck? Why did she even have to have it at all? A snake. What kind of person kept a snake? What was wrong with a dog or cat—or one of the bunnies her daughter was feeding the thing now?

It was dark when they got to the house, but the narrow road was lit as if it were broad daylight, news vans canted like wrecks along the muddy shoulders in both directions, cameras everywhere, lights exploding, and here was action, the grieving grandparents, flesh and bone in motion, actual people slamming out of the rental car and ascending the outside stairway with startled faces and roller bags bumping along at their heels. "How do you feel?" one man in a short-sleeve dress shirt barked, jabbing at her with his microphone, and what was she supposed to say? No comment? I feel like a criminal? I want to grind you all underfoot like the human detritus you are? There were a thousand stairs. Her roller bag caught on each one. The air was so dense it was like meat. "Mrs. Cullen!" they shouted. "Ottilie! Frank!"

When they reached the landing, cameras rolling, voices clamoring, the night broken into jagged shards of light and shadow and the porchlight hanging over them like a grinning death's head, the door suddenly pulled open and she was startled to see Stoneman there, his chest and shoulders cordoning off the doorway. "Ottilie, I am so sorry," he said, shifting forward to embrace her while Frank looked on bewildered, and then they were in and he was shutting the door behind them. "You must be Frank," he said, taking Frank's hand.

The room looked the same as it had when she'd left two months ago, except that Cat wasn't in it or the babies either. Or Todd.

"Any of these hyenas gets in your face, you just let me know," Stoneman said. "That's what I'm here for."

"But where's Cat?'

"She said to call her as soon as you get in—and that she's got the guest room all set up for you."

"You mean she's not here?"

He was shaking his head. "She's back at the motel. But R.J.'s here with me—he's outside somewhere, poking through the bushes with a flashlight, trying to find Willie, because they won't let the kid back in till the threat's been eliminated, obviously. Not that he'd be much of a threat at this point—she stabbed him with the kitchen knife and he left a blood trail, but where he's got himself to is anybody's guess. The thing is, social services doesn't want Tahoe in the house till they're sure it's clear, so as it stands now, Cat just has to be patient till we can locate the snake, dead or alive."

Frank said, "That's ridiculous," but she realized it wasn't ridiculous at all—what was ridiculous was having the snake in the house in the first place.

"And if you don't find him?"

"We'll find him."

"But if you don't?"

"That's up to law enforcement."

From outside came a collision of voices underscored by the pounding of footsteps on the stairs. Stoneman froze and then the door pushed open and Todd was there, half-in, half-out, shouting down the stairway behind him, "This is private property, don't you get that? Fuck off, all of you, just fuck off!"

And then he saw them there and took her in his arms and she was crying even though she never cried because she was too strong for that, but there it was. Her nose was stopped up. Her eyes burned. "It's going to be okay," Todd said, rocking there with her in the middle of the room while Frank and Stoneman bore witness, but it wasn't going to be okay any more than Cooper's arm was going to be okay, and what was happening, what was going wrong with them? Where was the world she'd grown up in, where it rained when it was supposed to and there was a bee affixed to every white dot of clover on every lawn in the neighborhood and babies never died?

Todd released her and moved on to Frank, embracing him in that male way of quick clutches and back-thumps, and then Todd said, "Anybody hungry? I can make you something, no problem—in fact, it'd give me something to do, which is what I really need about now. No? How about a drink? Frank?"

"Bourbon," Frank said, and he looked displaced, weary on his feet. It had been a long day of travel and anxiety, anxiety especially—what was this doing to their daughter? There was nothing worse than losing a child, but then there was—this, this was worse, everything sharpened to a cutting edge, as if Cat didn't feel devastated enough as it was.

Stoneman said, "Whatever you're pouring," and she said, "Wine. A glass of that zin, maybe?" And then she went out on the deck to catch her breath and have a little privacy to call Cat, but that was a mistake—the minute she opened the door, the lights from below located her and a swell of voices crested and washed over her. There was the smell of the ocean, the grip of the night, and she wanted a minute to herself, a minute to breathe, but they wouldn't give it to her. She would have cursed them too, the way Todd had, but she didn't have the strength. She could see their upturned faces—and it wasn't just the reporters now but a milling mob like the protesters you saw on TV, which didn't make any sense at all. What were they protesting? Snakes? Death? Their own shriveled-up pathetic little lives? And why Cat? It wasn't as if she were a celebrity—but of course now she was, branded instantly, branded in a way she never could have imagined.

In the next moment she was back in the house and Todd was waving his drink at Stoneman and saying, "You know, this whole snake thing, and I'm sorry, but it wasn't my idea, and I'm not blaming anybody, not you, man, or your brother either," and she kept on walking, down the hall and into the guest room, where she settled on the edge of the bed and called her daughter.

"We're here," she said, stating the obvious. "And it's a nightmare. These people, these, these—"

"I know, Mom."

"Are you okay?"

"I'll never be okay."

She'd always thought of herself as an optimistic person, or at least forward-looking, but over the course of the two days since Sierra's death she'd been hard-pressed to find her bearings. She and Cat had had three or four long conversations over the phone, the words coming so slowly and reluctantly it was as if they were speaking a foreign language, and in a sense they were. She said, "We're coming over there now."

"Yes. Good. I want that. And I could use your help with Tahoe too because she's so upset, just crying and fussing—even though, I mean, she can't really know, can she?"

"No, she can't."

There was a long silence, then Cat said, "Just don't let anybody follow you."

THE VIOLENCE CAME AT HER like a spring released from a box, erupting right there at the foot of the steps where the sea oozed round the pilings and the sand had turned to sludge. Stoneman was its purveyor. He was in front of her and Frank, running interference, as he put it, and Todd on the step behind them, when a woman with inflated arms and a face deformed by rage rushed at her screaming, "Baby killer!," which was unaccountable in every way she could imagine even if the woman had somehow mistaken her in the uncertain light for her daughter. She couldn't have been more surprised if she'd been called an extortionist or a gambler or an astronaut. Nobody was a baby killer here except the snake and the God who'd allowed it to happen, but you'd have to believe in God for that sort of blame to accrue and she didn't believe in God, only the random shuffle of events, like this one unfolding right here and now. Stoneman seized hold of the woman to prevent whatever was going to happen next and then there was a man involved, a man almost as gargantuan as Stoneman himself, and the TV cameras recorded every moment of it, the curses, the thumps, the blood.

They took the rental car, which was all but anonymous, unlike Todd's sports car, and if anyone followed them she didn't notice. The motel was ten minutes away, a glare of excess light against a backdrop of night-black vegetation, and when she saw Cat in that little box of a room with her deadened eyes and the baby—*the survivor*—in her arms she was crying all over again. Todd and Stoneman loomed. Frank looked lost. The air-conditioner breathed for them all. Then Cat was hugging her father and Ottilie had the baby in her arms and everything slowed down.

Stoneman's right ear was bleeding. He reached up to assess the damage and came away with two blood-greased fingers before disappearing into the bathroom and returning a moment later with a scrap of toilet paper stuck to the side of his head. "You ought to disinfect that," she heard herself say.

Stoneman shrugged. Todd said, "I can't believe these people. If I had a gun I'd go out there and shoot them all. In the head. In the fucking head."

"Frank, why don't you take a look at that?" she said. "It shouldn't be bleeding like that, should it?"

"In a minute," Frank said. She saw that he'd misbuttoned his shirt. There was mud on his shoes. He hovered over the couch, as if asking permission, then eased himself down, exhausted.

The TV was on, the sound lowered to a murmur just below the threshold of intelligibility, a kind of electronic prayer, and the images—it was a cop show—flashing make-believe violence, actors, guns, faces distorted in mock outrage while the real thing played out on the steps of her daughter's house and Stoneman, the giant, stood there on the cheap motel carpet bleeding for it. The baby was asleep, oblivious to it all, to snakes and death and the sheer nastiness of the human tribe that got people off their recliners and out their front doors to gorge on somebody else's misery. Suddenly she was angry. And not just at the mob, but Cat for having let this happen—and herself as well because she hadn't said a word about that thing in the fish tank when they brought the girls home from the hospital riding a wave of ecstasy and relief and triumph too because not even a hurricane had been able to stop them. She'd felt it, though. Not a premonition, not exactly, but more a feeling of incompleteness, as if she'd gone through the whole checklist two times over—rowboat, birth plan, car seats, natural birth, a house that had been threatened but survived to welcome them back, the twin bassinets, the matching baby blankets and the mobiles—but had left out some essential element she couldn't for the life of her think of.

The baby was like nothing in her arms, like air, so light you wouldn't even know she was there. Staring down into the miniature sleeping face, she saw Cat, saw Cooper, maybe even a trace of Todd, if she was being generous. Her granddaughter, *her* genes.

Cat was watching her, her shoulders slumped, her face slack and worn. "It's one long nightmare," she said. "You wouldn't believe the woman from social services—she was like a pit bull. She had to see everything in the house six times over. Did I drink? Did I smoke? What did I do for a living? What did my husband do? Why wasn't he here? Whatever possessed me to have a snake in the same room as my babies and why were they in their carriers instead of the bassinets in the bedroom? Where was the snake now? How had it gotten loose? Was it going to come back?" She had a drink in her hand, something in a plastic cup with ice that rattled as she pressed it to her lips and tipped back her head to swallow. "You know what she told me? She could take Tahoe with her right then and there for a seventy-two-hour hold without even a court order, nothing, just her own judgment, and what I had to say about it, what I was feeling, was beyond irrelevant, zero, like I didn't even exist—"

"She called R.J.," Stoneman said, "and we came over and brought them here to defuse the situation."

"And now it's on us to prove the house is safe," Todd said, rattling the ice in his own drink, "or they're going to do whatever they want, which means we'd have to get a lawyer and the whole nine yards."

"But there are no charges, right?" Frank said.

"Charges? What are you talking about? It was an accident, they know that, everybody knows that."

Frank didn't want to put it into words and she didn't either. But the terms that came to mind were *child negligence, endangerment,* even abuse.

"You know," Todd said, turning to Stoneman, "if we can't find it, why don't we, I don't know, take one from your store, stab it in the head and hand it over to them, because how are they ever going to know the difference? And I'll pay, no problem. Happy to."

Nobody had anything to say to this. What good would that do? If the original snake was still in the house, hidden in the walls or a drain-pipe or the air-conditioning ducts, what was to prevent it from slink-ing out in the night and going after Tahoe? She tried to picture it, this uncoiling sheet of muscle with its vacant eyes and darting tongue, holed up somewhere till its wounds healed, waiting its chance. "Do it," she said, surprising herself. "Kill it, kill them all."

"Come on, Mom," Cat said, her voice strung tight. "That's just stupid."

"Stupid? I'm sorry, but every snake in the world isn't worth one hair of that child, your daughter, your own daughter—"

Cat stood there, three feet away, glaring at her. "You want to kill something," she said, "kill me. I'm the one. I'm the one that did this."

"Stop it," Frank demanded, rising from the couch to take her by the arm, but she couldn't stop.

"You know what we had in the house when you were this age?" she said. "Do you?"

Cat didn't say a word, just lurched forward, snatched the baby out of her arms and stalked across the room and into the bathroom, where she slammed the door so hard the air-conditioner rattled in its frame. "We had a *hamster*, Cat. A hamster!"

So she could watch it run round and round on its little wheel.

COOPER FLEW IN FOR THE funeral and he brought Elytra with him, not Mari, though what he was thinking she couldn't imagine because she hardly knew the girl, which just made everything that much more awkward. Not that it would have been any different with Mari—this was family only, or should have been. Frank picked them up at the airport in the rental car and brought them to Cat's house, where they were all staying as if it were a duty, as if they were there to keep the place safe from the ghouls and jeerers while Cat and Todd hid out at the motel and the snake lay low and social services processed forms. Two days had passed, the news cycle churning, and there was only a lone TV van parked out on the road when Frank pulled up in front of the house and Cooper and the new girl stepped out into the rain, the eternal rain that had felt like such a blessing when she'd got here but was just oppressive now—and wasn't this supposed to be the dry season? She'd been up all night, listening to the rain assault the roof, stewing in her own sweat, her mind locked out of her body as if it were sealed away in a safe. She'd had nothing for breakfast and nothing for lunch. The sky was made of metal. The sea pulled it down and swallowed it.

She watched from the window as Frank flipped open the trunk and Cooper reached first for Elytra's suitcase and then his own, his wet shirt-sleeve clinging to the nylon mold of his right arm and his hair shining like grease. Frank motioned as if to take the girl's bag for her, as if he were the one who was twenty-five, but she shook her head and hauled it herself to the base of the stairs, where she passed out of view. Ottilie was just getting up to greet them at the door when a movement caught her eye, a sudden flinging open of the doors of a squat car the color of rain stationed on the street. In the next moment the big-armed woman and the man who'd tangled with Stoneman were lurching out of the interior to shout something at Cooper and Frank as they hurried across the yard to follow Elytra up the stairs. She felt the hatred surge up in her. Furious suddenly, she jerked open the door, and instead of greeting the girl or inviting her in out of the rain or even working up a smile, she shoved past her to poise on the landing and shout over her son's and husband's bobbing heads to where the couple stood jeering on the verge of the property. "You're not even human!" she shouted and—she couldn't help herself—gave them the finger, which they gave right back to her, and how was that for human sympathy?

Inside now. Wet hugs all around. Cooper said, "Jesus, who are those people?," and Frank answered for her, "Animals," he said. "Just animals."

Then there was the unwinding, the dropping of the bags and a glance into the room where they'd be staying—Cat and Todd's bedroom—succeeded by a smokescreen of empty chatter about the flight and the weather and California and don't you wish we had some of this rain? Ottilie made cocktails and set out a platter of store-bought hummus and pita wedges and asked Elytra if she liked Cuban food because they were thinking takeout?

"Sure. I guess. I've never had it, actually."

At the door, after the initial moment of confusion, Elytra had said, "I'm so sorry," and Cooper said, "It's a fucking disaster, as if I didn't tell her right from the start," but nobody was ready to bring that elephant into the room and so here they were, sipping drinks and talking about Cuban food.

There was a straight-backed chair, one from the kitchen set, positioned where the hundred-gallon tank had been, and Cooper was slouched in it, sniffing his drink—Bacardí and tonic, with a slice of orange, which was what they were all having. He glanced at Elytra, who'd been vigorously drying her hair with one of the bathroom towels, and said, "It's meat-heavy, I'm sure—right, Mom?"

"The sandwiches are, but they have veggie fare too, fried yucca, tostones, salads, the goat cheese croquettes, which are to die for, right, Frank? We had them last night. And a salad. They make great salads."

The trivial stuff. The trivial stuff was easy.

Frank gestured to the window and the rain drilling the deck. "And they deliver, which is kind of key right now, what with this rain and the jerkoffs out there."

"What about Cat?" Cooper asked, turning back to her.

"She said not to worry about dinner, just get settled in, and we'll go over there later."

"She can't come here?"

She shook her head. "No," she said, "she can't."

✺

THE NEXT MORNING, THE MORNING of the funeral, she woke to sunshine and the fierce white underbelly of the clouds. Frank was asleep beside her, his breathing deep and rhythmic. There was the thump and release of the surf and the faintest tremor it communicated to the wooden structure of the house so that she could feel it through the floorboards, the bedposts, the mattress. It wasn't like the earthquakes in California, the last of which had hit in the middle of the night three months back and set the whole place swaying like a treehouse, but it was enough to remind her of it. The waves slammed at the shore, the house trembled, and she was here to register it. In Florida. Three thousand miles from home. Of course, it was just one more worry for Cat, rising seas, sinking shorelines, and what good was beachfront property if there was no beach?

She got up with the vague notion of fixing breakfast for everybody, but when she stepped out on the deck and saw the way the sun was floating up out of the ocean—the first glimpse of it she'd had since they got here—she decided to go for a walk instead and let them all fend for themselves. There were eggs in the refrigerator, oranges for juicing, English muffins, a loaf of sourdough—plus Todd was having the reception catered, so nobody was going to be in danger of starving anytime soon. She started off down the beach toward the inlet, the water faintly milky with the runoff of the rains, a smell of the open sea presiding. Birds coasted around her. The feel of the wet sand molding itself to her heels and toes was a small forgotten pleasure—and there were no bugs, no bugs in California and no bugs here either. She knew it was wrong, knew what Cooper would say, but she didn't miss them.

When she got to the bridge—no traffic, nobody around, not joggers or dog walkers or beachcombers, if anybody even called them that anymore—she crossed the road to the inlet, where there was more variety, where the dunes were crowned with sea oats and some sort of creeper. Palmettos thrust up out of the ground like spears. Pockets of mangroves crowded the shore and drooped over the water, darkening it with shadow. The day before, while the rain held steady, Sierra had been cremated. Her ashes reposed in an urn wreathed in flowers, which Cat had set on the particleboard bureau in front of the flat-screen TV in that generic motel room. Not that it mattered at this point, but Sierra should at least have been in her own home, even if she'd barely known it—the sad fact, crippling really, was that she'd been in the womb longer than in that house with its million-dollar views and shuddering beams and her mother and her sister and all of the world she would ever know. There would be no formal service, but Frank was going to say a few words and Todd would too, and since everybody hated the idea of the funeral parlor, Todd had reserved the shelter at a local oceanfront park for the reception. After the ceremony they would all wade out into the surf and commit Sierra to the waves.

Something rose and splashed out there in the water ahead of her, silken skin, the knife of the tail, and when it rose again she saw that it was a dolphin. In the next moment it was joined by two—no, three—others. She took it as an omen and stood there a long while watching them feed, undulant and acrobatic, until, as if at a signal, they vanished without a ripple. It was then—and she wasn't thinking about Cooper's disappearing insects or even the snake that could have been out here, could have been anywhere—that she felt a pinprick on the back of her neck and slapped at it automatically. In the center of her palm, splayed and flattened like a prepared specimen, was a dead mosquito. Even as she examined it, feeling, what—relieved?—the next one was alighting, singing its blood song.

WHEN SHE CAME UP THE last stretch of beach to the house, intent on giving Cooper the good news—the bugs were back, ready to suck blood and raise welts and deliver malaria, dengue, yellow fever and she didn't know what else—she was surprised to see a figure hovering at the base of the stairs, a man, spotlighted in the sun against the dark underpinnings of the house. At first she thought he must be one of the protesters or mental defectives or whatever you wanted to call them (the day before, in the driving rain, one of them had stood out on the road brandishing a sign that read FREE THE SNAKES!), but then she saw her mistake. This was R.J., Stoneman's brother, and he wasn't alone—wrapped around one arm and looped over his shoulder, was a snake, *the* snake, the one that would unlock the front door and let Cat back in her own house.

"I got him!" he called out to her as she slogged through the sand, which was deeper here, thrown up by the tide. She picked her way through the debris—bottles, driftwood, turtle grass, a child's Croc so pink it was like a dahlia blooming in the desert—and watched the way he held the snake, gripping it by the head while letting its tail trail down his back to swing loose at the level of his calves.

What did she feel? Anger. Here was this thing that had killed her granddaughter, a species brought all the way across the world from Burma by people like him—*Myanmar*, not even Burma anymore—to inflict all this pain, and from the way he was acting you'd think it was no more a concern than a length of garden hose. "Are you sure this is the one?"

Compared to her son—or Todd—R.J. was short, five-eight or -nine, maybe, which made the snake seem all the longer proportionately. He was wearing a pair of faded yellow board shorts, a Herps T-shirt and a bleached-out baseball cap that might once have been blue. "You see this?" he asked, pointing to a crusted black gash at the base of the snake's head. "This is where she stabbed him."

She must have looked doubtful, but then what did she know?

"Trust me, he's the one we're looking for, no question about it. And I tell you, I've never seen anything like this happen before, not even remotely, not in a thousand years."

"It didn't take a thousand years. Five minutes, that was all. Five minutes."

"I'm sorry, I really am. Truly." The snake shifted its head, sagged and shuddered down the length of it. The tail twitched, looped, twitched again.

"Are you going to kill it?"

He looked surprised. "They're going to want to see it—Cat, I mean. And the police, right? Isn't that what this is all about?"

Her voice caught in her throat. "Why'd you even sell it to her?"

He didn't answer. The rising sun—it was hot already and it wasn't eight o'clock yet—made the snake's skin shine like nail polish on a long extended fingernail. "You know where I found him?" R.J. glanced over his shoulder and pointed to the pilings that supported the house. "He was up in there, pressed flat to the underside of the floorboards. I must've walked by him five times and never even noticed him."

"You're not going to bring him in the house, are you?"

"Not if you don't want me to. I just want everybody to know we got him, that's all."

"Good," she said, "good. Because I don't think I could stand that."

"We can hold him at the shop, no problem—or take him over to Animal Control or the police or whatever Cat decides." He looked past her, out to sea, as if there were a whole raft of snakes out there that needed catching, every one of them culpable, every one a baby killer, then fished a pair of sunglasses out of his breast pocket and clamped them on. "You know, the amazing thing is how elusive these things can be—the balls especially, but all the constrictors, really. Any snake. Probably once a week we get one escaping in the shop. And this guy?" He glanced at the snake, gave its head a little shake so that its tongue stuttered in mid-flicker and its eyes hardened. "He could have been up under those floorboards the whole time and nobody would have known any different. Right, boy? Right?"

18

ASHES

HE GOT HIS PANTS WET TO THE CROTCH WADING INTO THE surf to toss a pinch of his niece's ashes into the sea, where they wouldn't feed anything other than bacteria and algae, the spirit gone and the flesh too. "Do you believe in the soul?" Elytra had asked him that morning as they lay sweating atop Cat and Todd's bed in the master bedroom of the Florida beach house that would be underwater in ten years, and he'd said, "I don't know, but there's pretty convincing evidence for James Brown and who, Aretha Franklin? Charles Bradley?"

They were both staring up at the ceiling, post-sex. She said, "I knew you were going to say something like that. But really, as a biologist, I mean?"

Soul—the soul—was an animating principle, that was all, life itself, and specifically, with regard to individuals like the dead child he'd never known or even seen except on FaceTime, the neurobiological mechanism that sets individual preference in motion, which gives rise to variation and personality. In the case of Sierra, unfortunately, there was little to go by, except, he supposed, in the discrete way she might have worked her lips to suck at the nipple or sent signals to her hands to clench and unclench. "As a biologist," he said, "I'm heartbroken for Cat. As a civilian too. But the snake was enacting the role of predator and Cat's kid was enacting the role of prey."

"You are so cold."

"No," he said, rotating his neck so he could see her in profile, her hair, her face, the long sloping field of her sweat-beaded flesh, "I'm hot."

The air-conditioner was cranked all the way up, though he despised air-conditioners because they were wasteful and ultimately conditioned the outside atmosphere to get progressively warmer and kill off everything that wasn't already extinct, but even so he was staggered by the heat here, even at night, and there was little choice. He wasn't in charge, anyway—his parents were. They were in the guest bedroom, sweating in their own skins and staring at the ceiling too for all he knew. They'd paid his airfare—and Elytra's, though they didn't know that yet. What they also didn't know was that he wasn't just here for the funeral, but that he and Elytra planned to stay on for a few days, searching for insects and recording which species were the first to come back and reseed their populations after the die-off no one was even close to fathoming yet. It was an opportunity he couldn't pass up. It would be like fifty years ago when Wilson and Simberloff famously tented and fumigated six tiny mangrove islands in the Keys, then recorded which species were the first to come back and recolonize them, the foundational study of island biogeography. And if there was any doubt the insects would come back, his mother was to present him with the evidence of it that very morning, a pair of Asian tiger mosquitoes (*Aedes albopictus*) she'd squashed in the palm of her hand, readily identifiable by their heroically striped legs. They were invasives. They carried Zika. But the point was, they were alive. Or had been.

Elytra had thought to bring a black skirt and blouse along for the funeral ceremony, but he'd been so focused on the idea of Florida and its remnant insects it never occurred to him to pack a dress shirt, let alone a black sport jacket (an example of which he didn't own in any case), so Todd had to loan him both, designer label, of course, and in place of a conventional tie he found a silver bola with a braided black leather cord in Todd's top drawer, his appropriation of which, for Todd, wasn't a problem. Todd had other problems. Obviously. He showed up just after breakfast, in a hurry, looking frantic, but somehow finding time to whip up a pitcher of mimosas before disappearing into the bedroom to dress for the ceremony and fetch an outfit for Cat, who was still confined to the motel with the baby.

Cooper had been outside on the landing, opening himself up to the possibility of insects, blood-sucking or otherwise, when Todd pulled up in the rental car. R.J., who'd stuffed the snake in a cloth bag by this point because nobody really wanted to see it, not now or ever again, shouted out to him, "Hey, good news—we got it!"

Todd looked baffled, as if the chain of events that had brought him to this moment in the front yard of the house on the beach where he couldn't even spend the night with his wife and child had slipped his mind, but then R.J. was advancing on him, waving the distended cloth bag in evidence, and his expression changed. "Get that fucking thing out of my face! Because I'll kill it, I will—"

"I'm just saying, problem solved, that's all. We got it, okay? I thought you'd be happy."

The beach winked and glittered under the sun. The temperature was already in the nineties and the air so saturated sweat wouldn't evaporate, leaving you defenseless against the heat. Mosquitoes track their hosts—mammalian, avian, reptilian, amphibian—through the CO_2 they emit in the process of breathing, and Cooper had been on the landing breathing in and out for the past five minutes, presenting himself as bait, but nothing was happening as far as that went.

"I know, I'm sorry," Todd said over his shoulder as he mounted the stairs. "I'm just worked up, that's all, but hey, great news. Really."

When he reached the landing, Cooper said, "At least it's not raining," and Todd gave him an outer-space smile before acknowledging him with a fist bump and heading on into the house to mix drinks and dress himself in black because black was the order of the day.

❀

THEY'D TOLD PEOPLE TO ARRIVE at the park by four because Cat wanted to arrange the ceremony so they'd be casting the ashes at dusk, which fell now at five-thirty or so. That left the afternoon to get through. The mimosas helped, but drinking so early in the day dulled him and made him morose—or more morose, if that was possible. He was sorry for Cat and Todd and his parents but even sorrier for himself because he didn't want to be there in that room through all those dragged-down hours, formally sweating despite the air-conditioning and repressing the urge to get out into the near-est patch of vegetation and comb it for insects. If mosquitoes had survived, what else was out there? Beetles. Beetles could survive any-thing. But what of butterflies, like the zebra longwing he hadn't seen and collected since Costa Rica? Or the Florida white? Or any of the tropical species that had been expanding their range northward as the climate warmed?

Todd, who was in a hurry, didn't actually get out the door for the next two hours. He emerged from the bedroom dressed in tailored black and with his hair pouffed up with spray, but he wound up linger-ing over the mimosas and after a while decided that everybody needed brunch, though they all protested since they'd just had breakfast. There was no stopping him. He draped his jacket over a chair, tucked his tie inside his shirt and started beating eggs in a bowl preparatory to mak-ing omelets filled with crème fraîche, grated parmesan and diced toma-toes, deciding halfway through that they'd need salads too and a glass of prosecco to wash it down, and where was Cat? Back at the motel. She called three times and each time he answered with the same line, "Be there in a minute, babe," though he acted as if it really didn't matter one way or the other. Call it avoidance behavior. Call it grief. Call it being an insensitive party boy stomping on his own emotions. A jerk. An asshole. Todd.

"I'll go over there with you," he heard himself say, and his mother said, "It's okay, I'll do it, just give me her outfit. Or no, I'll call her myself and make sure we don't forget anything."

R.J., though he was the subagent of the crime committed right here on the floor between the coffee table and the door to the deck, had invited himself in and was deeply involved with the omelet, the salad and the prosecco. His main topic, which he was now communicating to Elytra, was the capture of the snake. "Right there, right in front of my face. It's unbelievable the way they can blend in with their surroundings, even if it's some man-made structure it'd never come across in its native environment, I mean colors, textures. I had an anole once—"

And that was all right. They needed the distraction and though Cooper hated what the man did for a living—treating animals as commodities, breeding variations that would never occur in a state of nature, bringing invasives across state lines and more likely than not engaging in smuggling or at least fudging the rules, and you could just look at him and see he was a rule-fudger—he had to admit that on some level R.J. was as much a naturalist as he himself was. He knew his snakes. He was devoted to them. Even the ones that squeezed the life out of infants, coil by coil, breath by breath.

Elytra, going at the prosecco herself—on top of the mimosas—leaned in with a glowing face, happy to talk animals, especially given the circumstances. She was in her black skirt and a black silk blouse you could see through to her black brassiere, but she hadn't put her shoes on or her makeup or combed her hair—they had plenty of time yet, no problem there. The problem, as he began to realize, was going to be getting through this at all, the hours stretching before him in bleak parade. He wanted to go out and look for insects. He wanted a nap. He wanted to throw the ashes in the water and move on. As a compromise, he had another glass of prosecco.

At some point, his mother left to go to the motel, along with his father, and then finally Todd did too, but as the morning crept into the afternoon the family circle began to expand and the party, the pre-party, the *wake*, rolled on. Stoneman showed up, bringing a girl with him, and right behind him were Todd's aunt and uncle Cooper hadn't laid eyes on since the wedding and wouldn't have recognized on his own even if they were wearing name tags. Then there were two couples he'd never seen before, Cat's friends from some local bar. A trio of neighbors from down the street. A random old lady nobody seemed to know but who knew her way around the house well enough. They settled in, found glasses in the cupboard, prosecco on ice, Gouda and smoked trout in the refrigerator, and if their voices were muted at first in respect to the occasion, they went off-subject and off-key as the afternoon wore on and it was comical, really, like Finnegan rising from his bier anointed with whiskey and thundering, "Jesus, do you think I'm dead?" Except that ashes don't rise.

Cooper was too drunk to drive. Though he wanted to, if only to have a means of escape after the waves took the ashes and the caterers scraped the last plate into the trash, but then it came to him that he didn't have a car or even the faintest idea of where the ceremony was being held—and a final glass of prosecco wasn't able to illuminate him on that score. Elytra was no help. She was bugging out her eyes and waving her arms at R.J. and his brother, who'd joined him on the couch, saying things like, "You think that's bad, wait'll you see what happens when the kissing bugs are back and Chagas gets entrenched," and "You know, I welcome snakebites, I really do."

He thought about Mari then, and he wasn't making comparisons, not really, but Mari would have had a car. And she wouldn't have been so far gone, not this early in the day. But Mari had broken things off once she saw the way it was between him and Elytra, the first intimation of which she'd had on the day after the die-off when they'd gone out to the field station to survey the devastation. His mother had been there to provide cover and he didn't say two words to Elytra the whole afternoon, ignored her, in fact. Purposely. But there was some signal in the air, he supposed—pheromones, riding the currents—and Mari picked up on it.

He'd been out front of the building, standing in the flower bed so as not to squander the water he was gulping from the hose and running over his head and shoulders, his arm on fire and his throat clenched, when Mari loomed up out of the sun blaze and said, "Stop wasting water."

"I'm not wasting water," he said, already on the defensive. "Why do you think I'm standing in the flower bed?"

"*Rhamnus, Eriogonum, Asclepias*—you're going to drown them."

"You think I don't know my plants? I'm a butterfly guy, remember?"

"We're in a drought."

"A megadrought," he corrected, dropping the hose in the center of a clump of buckwheat and striding to the hose bib to turn it off. He was smoothing back his hair, enjoying the feel of the cool wet tendrils on his sunburned neck, when she said, "You're fucking her, aren't you?"

He didn't deny it, though he wanted to. "Just once," he said. "It doesn't mean anything."

Her features were bunched. She was sweaty and sunburned and her hair hung round her shoulders like a beaded curtain. "Just scratching an itch, right? Isn't that what you call it?"

He wasn't calculating. And he wasn't a liar, either, or not exclusively. "Something like that," he said.

And now? Now he was left to squeeze into the backseat of R.J.'s Silverado alongside Elytra, the girl who was helping him scratch that itch instead of Mari, while R.J. drove and Stoneman rode shotgun, everybody in sweated-through black and the sun swelling against the windshield until it looked as if it would burst through the glass and immolate them all.

THE PAVILION WAS EARTH-COLORED AND made of plastic lumber, which was insultingly ugly and destructive of the environment but resistant to the termites (invasive, Formosan, subterranean) that would commence converting any wooden structure to frass before the final nail was driven. It was open on all sides to the dunes and the ocean, which slapped at the shore as expected. *Ave atque vale.* Ashes to ashes. Or surf. Ashes to surf. He staggered out of the car, his shirt sweat-soaked, the jointure of his stump and prosthesis chafed and sore. He took hold of Elytra's arm to steady himself, but she was in heels now and no steadier than he. They advanced on the pavilion like eighty-year-olds, like cripples, but then he had to remind himself that he was, in fact, a cripple, and could be thankful only that the tick hadn't embedded itself in his leg. He saw faces, flowers, dresses, sport coats, ties. There were rows of folding chairs. Milling people. And a bar, except that the bar was closed and would remain so till the ceremony was over, which was another tragedy, a tragedy on top of a tragedy.

He sat in the front row, next to his parents. Elytra was on his right and Cat on the left, on the far side of their parents, with Todd and the aunt and uncle. He was surprised at how many people had turned out, fifty, sixty, maybe more, and chalked it up to Todd—everything was an occasion for Todd, an event, even a tear-fest like this, though he hadn't seen anybody actually break down yet, not even Cat. She looked to be in shock—and yes, there were a couple of hyenas from the tabloids back there keeping their distance in the parking lot, the sheer hideousness of the story its own raison d'être, at least until some other outrage came along to supersede it. Stoneman had stationed himself in the rear, along with R.J., to keep them at bay.

His father spoke first, leaving the peroration to Todd. The sun was in his face as it sank into the scrub behind the pavilion, isolating him as if a spotlight had been trained on him. He stood there a long moment, giving everybody a chance to settle down. The light was pink and soft, the heat off the scale. Birds hung in the distance. The waves clapped. When he had their attention he began a long anecdote about Cat when she was on the cross-country team in high school and how he'd gone to one of her meets on a baking afternoon and watched her disappear in the distance, trailing a pack of girls who ran like robots and feeling his heart sink because how could she ever hope to keep up with them, let alone make it to the finish line? It was a 5k race, with two wicked breath-stealing hills interposed along the way. The best of the runners, which included the fanatics pushing for college athletic scholarships, would run the course in nineteen minutes or so and the others might take half an hour if they made it at all. "And Cat, let's face it"— he paused to settle his eyes on her, grinning now, as if they were sitting around the table in the kitchen and nobody was dead—"was no fanatic and she didn't have a personal trainer or a pair of three-hundred-dollar running shoes and she was on the team only because it would fulfill her phys ed requirement for the semester. And it was hot, killing hot. Remember that, Cat?"

His sister raised her face like a platter with nothing on it, blank, zero, her eyes fixed and her mouth gone slack. It hurt him to see it. Crushed him. For the first time since he'd got off the plane he felt something outside himself, and it wasn't redemptive, not even close.

"You couldn't see around the bend on the final hill and the first girl to come into sight lurched to a stop two hundred feet short of the finish line, doubled over with her hands on her knees, and vomited, and I was thinking about heatstroke and whether there was a physician present and if I'd have to step in, when there was Cat, coming round the bend neck-and-neck with two other girls, all three of them looking as if their legs were about to go out from under them.

"What did I feel? I don't know, it's complicated. Pride, certainly— my daughter—but anxiety, horror, actually, over what she was pushing herself to do with the force of sheer will and doing it, just doing it." He paused, held the gaze of the crowd—the mourners, black-clad and sweating. No one stirred. They barely breathed. They might as well have been dead themselves. "She finished third, by the way, but the point is, she finished. Right, Cat?"

Then it was Todd's turn.

Todd talked about love. What he had to say, and he said it at length, was just short of sappy, but then that was what was expected—this was a funeral, after all. He took them step by step through his relationship with Cat, how they'd met on a double date with his best bud and his best bud's girlfriend, who also happened to be a friend of Cat's from high school, and knew from the start they were something special together ("She was so beautiful, look at her, she *is* beautiful, stunning, she's my Cat, but whip-smart too, smarter than I could ever hope to be, and for me that sealed the deal"), and how the wedding was the highlight of his life—until the twins came along. He choked up then and had to pause to take a drink of whatever he had in the plastic cup clenched in his right hand, his drinking hand, then gestured to Cat and the baby and said, "But this isn't about the past, it's about the future—hold up the baby, Cat, right, yeah, so everybody can see. We're mourning Sierra tonight, but here's the future!"

Somebody might have clapped, but then you didn't clap at funerals, did you? No, but in the next moment, release came and they were all trudging through the sand, Cat and Todd leading the way, and when they reached the edge of the water Todd handed each of the family members a silver memento cup engraved with Sierra's dates, a gray heterogeneous sprinkle of grit at the bottom of it. The fact was that funeral homes weren't all that particular about the ashes in their crematoria and a certain degree of intermixing was inevitable, the residue from the last cadaver swept into the urn for the current one, and what difference did it make in any case? The dead are dead. Better they should decompose in the ground and feed the life of the planet but that wasn't how Cat and Todd had seen it—and burial in Florida was problematic in any case because the water table was right there at the surface. So there were ashes. And the ashes were going into the sea like any other pollutant.

His parents barely got their feet wet, but he waded out, hand-in-hand with his sister, to commit his portion of his dead niece's mortal remains to the froth of the waves even as a gull swooped in low to try to make sense of the moment.

☀

TODD HAD HIRED A CELLIST to grind through the most harrowing pieces in the repertoire—Fauré, Dvorak, Bruch—while the caterer's staff trotted round with canapés and little plates and people gathered in groups of three or four and felt whatever they were going to feel. Relief, mostly. They weren't dead and never would be, though moments like these certainly must have made for a degree of reassessment. He found himself talking animatedly with a total stranger who'd worn an abbreviated skirt and sleeveless blouse to the funeral, her eyes flaring at the end of each phrase, like punctuation. He didn't catch her name. He was talking about bugs, how they'd be back, he was sure of it, absolutely, even if it took time, while her theme was the heat, how unusual it was for this time of year, which was normally the only bearable season in Florida and global warming was a fact, wasn't it?—when he felt a tap at his shoulder and turned to discover Melody Foster standing right there toe-to-toe with him and in the next instant leaning in to peck a kiss to his cheek. She'd flown in from New York—"Yeah, for Cat, just to be there for her"—and, naturally, the flight had been delayed, like all flights, and she was so sorry to have missed the service. How sad all this was, wasn't it?

He had a drink in his hand (rum, of course, Bacardí, as if this were just another of Todd's promotional events), and he gestured with it first to the girl in the too-short-for-a-funeral skirt and then to Melody. "This is Melody," he said, giving the girl an opportunity to identify herself, which she did, though he forgot her name in the time it took her to utter it because Melody was there and her lips had just brushed his cheek and Elytra was at the back of the pavilion with R.J. and Stoneman, waving her arms as if conducting her own private orchestra. "So how's California?" Melody asked and he said, "On fire. Perpetually." Her next sentence began with, "Do you remember when—" and the other girl excused herself and drifted off. At which point Melody mentioned that she was no longer seeing Stuart, the guy she'd brought to the wedding. "What about you? Are you still with that Asian girl, what was her name—Mari?"

"Uh-uh," he said, and left it at that.

"With me and Stuart it got to the point where there wasn't much there beyond the sex. I got tired of all these awkward meals in whatever restaurant where we both wound up staring into our phones—or getting in an Uber and finding the guy behind the wheel was more interesting than the one sitting next to me . . ."

The caterer had strung Chinese lanterns from the rafters and they glowed with increasing intensity as dusk settled in. He heard Todd's laughter rise up out of the buzz of voices and then two or three others joined in, as if a switch had been thrown. Ties were loosened, jackets draped over the backs of chairs. The caterer's people hustled, the cellist stepped up the tempo. And where was Cat? There, sitting beside his parents and the aunt and uncle, the baby asleep in her arms. He was about to go join her because Melody Foster was just a face and body at this point and if he needed a face and body he had Elytra, when the first mosquito landed on him. It was a juvenile, newly hatched from its pupal exoskeleton, and it settled on the slick shining polymer of his right hand as if confused by the signals it was getting. "A mosquito," he said to Melody in a wondering voice, raising his hand to show her. "How about that?"

She didn't answer, except to let out a curse, slapping now at her own hand, her forearm, the back of her neck. All at once mosquitoes were everywhere, consumed with purpose, and in the next moment everybody was in motion, writhing, cursing, ducking their heads and flapping their arms. The cellist cut off in mid-stroke. Cooper's mother, on the far side of the pavilion, beat frantically at the air with her napkin and in the next moment his father was pulling his sport coat up over his head as if he were caught in a rainstorm. Cooper couldn't see where Todd had got to, but Cat was crouched low in her chair, shielding the baby with her body. The mosquitoes kept coming—and what was this? Biting midges too, the no-see-ums that were like pinpoints of fire, and though it was almost dark, deerflies, whole squadrons of them. Within minutes the party broke up, people in full retreat, moving single-mindedly across the strip of sand to the parking lot and the refuge of their cars, hustling now, quick strides, jolting elbows, but he just stood there—slapping, yes, but too happy to move.

19

AFTER THE FUNERAL

EVERYBODY LEFT THE DAY AFTER THE FUNERAL, HER PARENTS
and Todd's aunt and uncle to fly back to California, Cooper and his girlfriend to go bug hunting in the Everglades. R.J. was at work, Stoneman
in Tampa overseeing accounts at the Herps shop there and Daria had
her own life, which involved working six days a week, for starters. The
flowers were wilting. The sun hung in the sky like a watch on a chain.
There was a smell of something rotting in the refrigerator but she
couldn't figure out what it was. At least Todd was home—they gave him
a week's bereavement leave—but even that wasn't doing a whole lot for
her because every time he glanced at her she felt so eaten up with shame
and self-loathing she could have dissolved right there on the spot. And
there was nothing to do to take her mind off it, absolutely nothing. She
had Tahoe to keep her going, diapers, feeding, up and down, back and
forth, but it was like walking on a treadmill. They got takeout, Chinese
one night, pizza the next. Todd made the odd meal. They started drinking at lunchtime.

She hadn't been answering her phone, just letting it go to message—and she wasn't responding to her messages either, wasn't even reading them—but three or four days after the funeral, when she was starting to feel marginally better, Daria called and she made the mistake of picking up.

"Jesus, *finally*. I must have called twenty times, Cat—how're you feeling?"

"Shitty."

"I've been worried about you—we both have, me and Miller both. I know it's hard, I can't even imagine, but if you want some company . . ."

"That's okay."

"A walk on the beach? Share a bottle of wine, watch a movie, whatever?"

"That's okay."

"You sound depressed."

"What do you expect me to sound like? People are sending me hate mail, I had to close down all my social media, every time I look at Tahoe I see Sierra and the way the ocean keeps rolling in and out is driving me crazy, like I'm on a sinking ship or something—"

"But Todd's there, right?"

"He was. He went out to the store two hours ago to pick up a couple of things. He's probably sitting in some bar."

She was staring out at the horizon and thinking of the VR headsets you put on when you want the world to go away—the ocean, she hated the ocean—when Daria said, "Okay, but I wanted to tell you something, just a heads-up?"

She didn't say anything. She reached down to scratch the bug bites on her legs, red welts that had bled and healed and bled again.

"This guy came into the restaurant yesterday? I thought he was a customer and asked him if he wanted a table but he flashed a badge and started asking questions—about that night, like what did you eat, how much did you have to drink, did I think you were a good mother, a good person, shit like that."

"That's insane. You've got to be kidding me."

"He talked to some of the others too, Ricardo, Kelsey, Whitney D'Orio, who I don't think you even know—"

"I wasn't drunk, not even close. And I ate. A full meal. You saw me."

"I told him as far as I knew you didn't have anything to drink and you would never drink and drive because that's just not like you, but he asked Ricardo for the receipts from that night, so I guess they know you did have, what—?"

"Two drinks. Two fucking drinks!"

There was a silence. Daria said, "Yeah, I just wanted you to know."

THEY ARRESTED HER THE NEXT MORNING. Todd was in the bedroom, on his laptop, working his accounts, and she'd just fed Tahoe and put her down when she heard footsteps and felt the faint vibration that ran through the house when anybody came up the outside stairway. There were two cops, one male, one female, and when she answered the door the female said, "Catherine Rivers?" and she nodded, thinking they'd come to inspect the house, though the woman from social services had already given the all-clear after R.J. found Willie, who was euthanized (not that it mattered to her, because he'd got what was coming to him, and if only he'd stayed where he belonged, in the environment she'd created for him, which was perfectly adequate, better than adequate, none of this would have happened).

Then everything shifted on her. This was no inspection, no inquiry, no follow-up, *Thank you, everything's fine, goodbye.* No. The woman, who was in her mid-thirties, chunky, wearing eye shadow and beige lipstick, which seemed totally incongruous, wrong, just wrong, announced in a voice so casual she might have been ordering lunch that they were arresting her on a charge of aggravated manslaughter of a child by culpable negligence and handcuffed her so quickly she barely knew what was happening. They were reading her her rights when Todd, in nothing but a pair of shorts, came out of the bedroom, looking puzzled. "Is somebody at the door? Cat?"

Her heart wouldn't stop. She couldn't swallow. Her hands were clamped behind her back and her head lifted off her shoulders and flew twice around the room.

The male cop shifted his feet so he was in between her and Todd even as Todd's face began to register what was happening and his eyes hardened. Though he never exercised and spent most of his time in bars and restaurants, he was naturally muscular—and tall—which must have made him a threat in the cop's eyes. The cop said, "Who are you?"

"Who am I? Who are you, is what I want to know."

Her voice was a squeak, as if the cuffs were locked around her throat too: "He's my husband."

"You're not arresting her, are you? I can't believe it. The woman from social services already inspected the place and said we were okay to bring our daughter back—"

"Where is your daughter?" The female cop put the question to both of them.

"Sleeping," Todd said. "She's only two months old, what do you expect? Seventeen hours a day, that's what she sleeps. Right, Cat?" And then he tried to defuse things—he was an ambassador, always an ambassador—adding, "It's tough work being a baby."

The cops weren't amused. The cops had a job to do. The female said, "You *are* capable of caring for the child while your wife is detained, isn't that right? Because if you're not, just let me know and we'll get Child Protective Services over here."

"You're kidding, right? You're really going to do this?"

They were already at the door, on the landing, the female officer guiding her with a hand at her elbow as they started down the stairs. Todd, barefoot, bare-chested, followed them out on the landing, his voice rising in anger and bewilderment: "It was an accident, don't you get it? An accident!"

☀

THE PRESS WAS RIGHT ON IT, though how they knew was a mystery unless the police had tipped them off. There they were, lined up out front of the station, eager and relaxed at the same time, pushing forward only when the police cruiser pulled up at the curb and they could verify who was inside, at which point they went into action, flourishing their cameras and calling out her name in a way that seemed almost jovial ("Catherine! Catherine! *Cat!*"), as if they were old friends there to see her off on a cruise or a flight to Maui. She stepped out of the car like a martyr. This was her perp walk, her public shaming, *aggravated manslaughter of a child*, guilty by virtue of being charged and handcuffed. She was the worst mother in the world. She was a criminal. She deserved everything that was coming to her.

"*Cat! Cat! Over here!*"

Moving now, head down, fixated on the shoes of the cop at her side because those shoes were all that mattered, those shoes were going to lead her up the walk and inside and away from the microphones and cameras and name-shouters because she was no longer herself but just an object on two feet with a firm guiding hand clamped under her armpit and what she was wearing or how her hair looked was so beyond irrelevant it never even entered her mind. But what she *was* wearing, what she'd see online and in the newspaper the next day, were flip-flops, white shorts that could have been cleaner and a milk-stained nursing top she hadn't had a chance to change. Bad mother. Dirty mother. Murderer.

"*Cat! Cat! Look at me, look this way! Cat, c'mon!*"

Inside it was like the eye of a hurricane. People stared at her, but they didn't have microphones and cameras and they weren't shouting and there was other business under way here too, other perps, uniforms, handcuffs. Light sat in the windows. She smelled Lysol, coffee, sweat. Her brain went numb. *Stand here*, somebody said. *Turn. Now the other way. Press your fingers here. And here.* Then they locked her in a cell and her brain started up again, harrowing her, defeating her, the seconds stretching to minutes and the minutes to hours, though she had no way of knowing how long she'd been confined in that concrete box since they'd taken away her watch and phone and there was no natural light to gauge by. They'd confiscated her ID too, which made her feel like a non-person, and the gold chain with the heart pendant Todd had given her a month after they'd started dating and which she'd never removed since, not even when she went in the ocean. They took her wedding ring too, though her finger was swollen from the heat and she could barely get it off.

But where was Todd? Why wasn't he here, why wasn't he bailing her out? Wasn't that how it worked? It came to her that he was out there someplace getting the money—but what money and how much? And what if he couldn't come up with it? Would he have to call her parents?

She paced the floor. Crouched on the edge of the bench, the cold metal frame cutting into the backs of her thighs. Stood. Sat. Stood. She could hear the breathing of whoever was in the holding cell two down from hers, the swoosh and squeak of footsteps in the hallway at the end of the corridor, the distant bled-out crackle of a radio, somebody somewhere sucking in their cheeks over and over in a way that managed to be worse than if they'd been sobbing outright. Did she nod off? Was that even a possibility? It must have been, because all at once a cop was there, another humorless woman with industrial makeup, and the cell door slid back. Then she was walking, the cop at her side, down the hallway, bars, suspended faces, snickering mouths—*Hey, what about me?*—until she was guided into a room dominated by a long raised table with the U.S. and Florida state flags arrayed on either side of it and Todd standing there just inside the door. He was in suit and tie, looking strong, and there was a tall square-shouldered woman at his side, the lawyer—*her lawyer*—who was going to straighten all this out.

Her legs felt the way they had in the race her father had talked up at the funeral, sagging and boneless, as if she'd run the 5k while standing in place, and she collapsed into the chair the cop led her to. She was leaking milk. She was starving. The first thing she said to Todd was, "Where's Tahoe?"

"Daria's watching her. At the house. She took off work, actually—"

The lawyer, Dodie Capistrano, her hair the color of aluminum foil and cut shorter than Todd's, leaned in to introduce herself and then, in a harsh whisper, said, "It's bullshit. That they should put you through this? A nursing mother?"

A fly flitted in Cat's face and she flicked it away. She'd been hurt and scared and defenseless, and now here was this woman calling it all bullshit, which it was, which it definitely was. She wanted to be back at home where she belonged, with her daughter and her husband and the waves, even the waves—she wanted to watch the waves and have a sandwich, soup, a salad, anything.

The judge was a woman who looked too young to be a judge. She wore a pair of Burberry glasses tinted just enough to obscure her eyes so you couldn't tell if she was looking at you or not. She read off the charges and asked, "How do you plead?," the answer to which was, "Not guilty." Dodie Capistrano immediately petitioned the court to drop the charges—"There's no crime here, Your Honor, just a tragic accident. The defendant has been put through enough as it is, having lost her daughter, and she sincerely wants to focus all her energy on the surviving child, who's only *two months old* and currently breast-feeding."

The judge was unmoved, but she did grant bail (in the amount of $100,000—"Excessive," Dodie Capistrano fumed under her breath, "way out of line"), and set the hearing, at Dodie's request, for the end of the week in order to get this over with as quickly as possible. "So you two can go back to having a life, right, Catherine? Or should I call you Cat?"

When it was finished, when bail had been posted with the intercession of a bail bondsman and the judge was on to the next hearing and the one after that, Dodie Capistrano led her and Todd down a hallway and out a side door that gave onto the back parking lot where there were no reporters, no spectators, nobody at all but for an overweight white-haired cop lowering himself into a police cruiser. The air was alive. Some sort of flowering vine cascaded from the chain-link fence that ran round the perimeter of the lot, the flowers so bright they overwhelmed her. There was a distant sound of traffic swelling and softening like music, forte, mezzo, pianissimo. The sun was sinking into the palms. And there was the Tesla, parked at the curb. Todd opened the car door for her, though he hadn't done that since their first date, and she slid into the seat and said, "I'm starving. Can we stop at a deli maybe on the way home? Just for a minute?"

Dodie Capistrano leaned in the open door. "They're going to drop the charges, don't you worry. And if they try using the drinking against you it just gives us something to negotiate with—AA meetings, right? They drop the charges, you go to AA. Sound good?"

THE FIRST THING SHE DID when she got home was pour herself a glass of wine, a full glass, not the exaggerated splash Todd always insisted on by way of appreciating the wine's nose. They'd stopped at the deli and got pulled-pork sandwiches, pasta salad and mango slaw, enough for Daria too, and she spent the better part of the next two hours with either a glass or fork in hand and the baby at her breast, giving a blow-by-blow account of the worst day of her life, excepting the one that began with Sierra lying there dead on the living room floor. Which goes without saying. But this was right up there on its own special scale and she was still so shaken she couldn't seem to stop talking. "They're the criminals," she kept saying, over and over, because it was true. "They're the ones that should be in jail, not me."

"Everything's going to be fine, I swear," Todd said. Dodie's the best." (It turned out he knew her through his contacts in the bar business, where encounters with the law—DUI, drunk and disorderly, assault, battery, indecent exposure—were hazards of the trade, but aggravated manslaughter? What did that even mean?)

The whole time, every minute she'd spent in that cell, she kept seeing Sierra with her bleeding face and dead white skin. How much had she known of what was happening to her? What must she have thought in her final moments? And the pain. Was it like drowning? Did she go into shock the way the antelope do in the nature films once the lion brings them down? It had to be. It had to be that way.

"It was so awful, I can't tell you. They put me in there and locked the door and it was like they took the whole world away. I didn't have my phone. Or my wedding ring even. And my daughter, my daughter with nobody to feed her, probably shrieking her lungs out the whole time. Can you imagine what that feels like?"

Todd could, or at least the lockup part of it, she knew that much. He'd been arrested as a teenager for drunken driving and then in college for something else, some fraternity prank that caught the attention of a passing squad car. She looked to Daria, who was holding her drink close, pressing the glass to one cheek as if it were the middle of the day and the heat was getting to her. "Have you ever been arrested? Have you ever had to go through that?"

Daria shook her head no.

"All I could think about was killing myself, really, I mean it—"

"That's why they take your shoelaces away," Todd said.

"I was wearing flip-flops."

Daria was the first to laugh, then Todd joined in and all of a sudden she was laughing too, trying to cover her mouth with her hand because this wasn't even remotely funny, was it? Or maybe it was. Maybe she was the butt of some whirling cosmic joke, tornado winds at the wedding, mosquito battalions descending on the funeral, her daughter squeezed into an urn and her jewelry molded out of steel at the handcuff factory. She got up to open another bottle of wine, and then, looking over her shoulder to where Todd and Daria sat in their individual pools of light cast by the mica lamps she'd got to replace the tacky ceramic ones Todd's mother had left behind, she had an inspiration. "Hey," she said, "what about a swim? Anybody up for it?"

"It's dark," Daria said.

Todd looked into his wineglass. "Two words," he said. "Bull sharks."

"No, I'm serious. I feel so dirty from that place—I just want to, I don't know, splash around and look at the moon, if there is a moon out there. Is there? Is there a moon?"

She didn't feel unsteady at all going down the stairs, the wine actually restoring her balance, physically and mentally both. She left the half-full glass on the bottom step, to refer to later, and let the night take her. A boat with a crimson running light was just barely creeping across the black chop of the sea, its engine a faint buzz over the advance and retreat of the surf. The sand was wet, dense, like cake batter, and it molded itself to her heels and worked its way between her toes. It felt good, felt normal. And there *was* a moon, or a half slice of it, anyway.

Todd and Daria had declined to join her, but there they were, on the deck, grinning and waving and toasting her with their drinks as she waded into the water, which wasn't as warm as she'd like, but that was all right, that was fine—what she needed was a cold slap in the face to wake her up from this bad dream she was inhabiting. Cooper had informed her the seas were acidifying as a result of all the excess CO_2 they were absorbing from the atmosphere, and that meant that eventually seafood would be nothing more than a fond memory, unless you were a fan of jellyfish, which would be the last thing to go, whereas clams, oysters, mussels, lobsters, shrimp, crabs—anything with shells, anything you'd actually want to eat—would go first, then the bony fishes, followed by the cartilaginous, if they hadn't already been trawled to extinction by then. Fish prices were already off the charts—she'd read that somebody had paid three million dollars for a six-hundred-pound bluefin tuna. But that was in Japan. And this was here. And now. And the water could have been warmer. Really.

She knew enough to shuffle her feet so as to avoid stepping on whatever might be lurking down there on the bottom, stingrays specifically—as far as she knew, they were still going strong. The water sailed in on her, parting round her knees, the beam of the porchlight fracturing in the wash of the surf, and she thought of splashing herself or ducking under to get used to the temperature (which was still higher even this time of year than it would have been in Malibu in the summer, so there was that), but in the end—on the tail of a catcall from Todd—she took the plunge. The spank of it, the release. She windmilled her arms, torqued her legs, stroking straight out from shore, feeling masterful and strong. When she flipped over on her back, the stars bloomed above her.

"How's the water?" Daria called, her voice disembodied, her face lost in the glare of the floodlights on the deck.

She didn't want to answer. She just wanted to drift.

"Babe? You still out there? The sharks didn't get you, did they?"

"It's amazing," she called. "You ought to come in."

But they weren't coming in and she had half a glass of wine waiting for her at the bottom of the stairs. She wouldn't sleep tonight, not with the trauma she'd been through, even if she swam ten miles, even if she took a pill, and she wasn't going to do that. For a while she treaded water, watching the moon, then knifed her legs and plunged down deep, where the pressure pounded in her ears and her lungs tightened and every stroke took her farther from all the shit of her life. She could have opened her mouth, could have breathed water instead of air, dissolving into the blackness like the jellyfish and the octopi and every other agglomeration of cells careening on the currents, but that didn't happen. Her body wouldn't allow it. At the last instant she shot to the surface as if she'd been ejected and all at once she was gulping air and then she was on her way back in, her stroke sure and steady. When the beach was there in front of her, cut out of the darkness like a jagged waistband, she made the mistake of feeling for the bottom with one foot, stepping down now, not shuffling, just stepping. That was when she felt it, right there, right under her heel, a thing as mysterious as the night, alive in its own skin, and whether it came equipped with teeth or a stinger, she never knew. Like a blessing, it was there and then it was gone.

❁

WHAT SHE SAID TO DODIE CAPISTRANO was, "I'm not an alcoholic and I don't have a problem," and Dodie Capistrano said, "That's not the issue here—the issue is how we present in court and since the DA already knows you were drinking the night all this happened and he's got a history too, I'm sure, of what bars you went to wearing that snake around your neck, what your average consumption was and Todd's too, we're going to give them a little contrition. You drank, you had a problem, there was an accident, you regret it. And"—she handed her a card—"you're willing to go to parenting classes. And AA."

"I'm not an alcoholic."

"Just *listen*," Todd said.

They were in the lawyer's office, which was standard issue, as far as she could tell, at least from the movies—she'd never actually been in a lawyer's office before. They were sitting at Dodie Capistrano's desk, in the supplicants' chairs, Tahoe asleep in her lap, Dodie seated across from them, her back to the window. There were bookshelves, filing cabinets, framed degrees, photos of Dodie with one grinning dignitary or another. And one thing more: an artificial Christmas tree perched on the windowsill, which was so sad it made her want to cry. Christmas. She'd been looking forward to it, her daughters, her parents, but Christmas was nothing now. Beyond the tree, the view was of Matanzas Bay, which jumped and sparked round Dodie Capistrano's silhouette while sailboats glided in and out of the silver frame of her hair.

"You have no priors, you're a good person, you're a nursing mother. There's no criminal case here. And if it wasn't for the press picking up on it you can bet the DA never would have got involved, and that's the unfortunate thing. People want to make a circus out of this and we're not going to let them."

Todd had been in a mood all morning, as if things weren't bad enough already. He'd been silent on the way over, playing the radio—the news, which was all bad all the time—just loud enough to stifle any conversation they might have had, as if what was happening in the world could have any shred of relevance compared to what she was going through. Let the bombs fall, let the refugees drown and the polar bears too, what was happening to her—*her*, not him—trumped it all a thousand times over. When she reached out and switched the channel to the music station she liked, he didn't even glance at her, just jabbed the button and put the news right back on. "Jesus, what's your problem?" she said.

He didn't answer. In a barking British accent, the newscaster read off the infection rates in India and Africa from the latest variant of the latest virus. Cars choked the road. The sun was giving her a headache. And when they got there and she needed to use the restroom he wouldn't even take the baby. "I got to go too, okay?" he said and turned his back on her.

Now, in the lawyer's office, while Dodie Capistrano went on about the bogus charges and what a charade the whole thing was, Cat found herself drifting. She didn't want to hear this. And she didn't like the way Dodie Capistrano was looking at her, as if the real charade were defending her to begin with, so she said the first thing that came to her: "You know, I almost got stung by a stingray, I think it was. Last night? I went for a swim, just to try to clear my head . . . ?"

Todd shot her a look. He was calculating what all this was going to cost, the hourly, the quarter-hourly, the ten seconds it had taken her to bring up the only non-negative thing to happen to her in the past two weeks, which, to her mind, was a sign that her luck was changing, the unseen leathery thing down there in the depths a talisman to lift her out of all this—it could have stung her, that was the point, but it hadn't. A week ago it would have and she'd have deserved it, but not now, not anymore.

"What are you *talking* about?" Todd thrust his hands up under his arms, impatient, angry, the muscles in his forearms like rods and pistons made flesh.

Dodie Capistrano gave her a blank stare. Then, recalibrating, she said, "I could see you going into the hearing on crutches, absolutely, but believe me we're not going to need it—all the sympathy's on your side already. The DA knows that, don't think he doesn't. And if it goes to trial, which it won't, it's a slam dunk."

"I hear it really hurts."

"What?"

"A stingray." She reached down to scratch at her bug bites.

Dodie Capistrano nodded. "Everything hurts," she said.

FOR THE NEXT THREE DAYS she barely moved from the couch. She fed Tahoe, fed herself, watched whatever the TV offered up. Todd was constantly on the phone, stalking from one end of the deck to the other, then he'd drive off someplace and drive back again, liquor on his breath. She knew she shouldn't drink, but she needed something to fight down the tension and she was scared and bored and hated the idea of having to go to AA, if only for show, so as a compromise she stuck to wine only and tried to limit herself to just two glasses, though that wasn't working at all. Dodie Capistrano might have made the whole thing sound like a game, like soccer—they kick the ball and you get it back and you kick it and then they kick it again—but the charges she was facing, which she made the mistake of looking up online, were no game. This was a first-degree felony and she was facing jail time, ten years at a minimum, as if she were the criminal here and not the victim, the bereaved, the one who kept crucifying herself over and over and couldn't even sleep for the weight of the guilt she imposed on herself—*she* imposed, not some court of law in a redneck state where they couldn't even speak English without making it sound like it was coming out of a distortion chamber.

On the third day, the day before the hearing, dinnertime, Todd hopped in his car and disappeared just when she needed him most, and by the time he came back up the stairs carrying a take-out bag from Captain's BBQ, she was in a state. "Don't leave me like that," she said.

"Like what?"

"You didn't say a word—do you have any idea what I'm going through? I can't sleep, I can't do anything. And you just disappear— what, to go out to some bar?"

He was at the kitchen counter now, rummaging around in the drawer for the corkscrew. "I wasn't at the bar, though I see you've been going at it pretty steadily yourself, so no criticism, okay? I got food." He brandished the bag. "Don't you want food?"

"What if they find me guilty?"

"Oh, fuck, not this again—I keep telling you it's not going to happen. They just have to flex their muscle a little, let the news outlets and all the rest see they're taking it seriously, but that's just for show. It'll all be over by this time tomorrow. Done. Finished. Finito."

She hated him in that moment. He was so sure of himself, so smug, walling her out with one cliché after another, none of which cost him a thing. "What about Sierra? What about her? She's dead and whether they screw me over or not isn't going to make a difference to her. She's never coming back. She's dead, Todd, *dead*. Do you even care?"

He was working the wine key in the cork, his wedding band glinting as he steadied the bottle. "Of course I care."

"You're probably glad she's dead. You never wanted her in the first place. You never held her, never changed her—not once."

From the bedroom came the thin choking wail of the baby waking up.

"Yeah, sure, make me the bad guy. But for your information I'm the one trying to keep all this shit together. You know what Scott Cozzens told me this morning?"

She didn't. And she didn't care. This wasn't about him, this was about her—and Sierra.

"They're nervous."

"Who? Who's nervous?"

"Corporate. They're afraid of bad press—can you blame them? If somebody puts the pieces together—that you're my wife or I'm your husband or however you want to slice it—it's all over. Image, that's what counts. They don't give a shit about anything else."

"So what are you saying, you're going to lose your job?"

He shrugged, toyed with his wineglass. He wouldn't look at her.

"I can't believe you. You're worried about your job, your image—your precious image? Jesus. I could be going to jail and you, you—"

"You're the one that bought the snake. You're the one that was drunk. And shit, had an accident on the way home? If they ever find out about that, yeah, it's not going to look good—for you or me either. For *us*. For you, me and Tahoe."

From the bedroom, as if she were fully cognizant of everything, Tahoe let out another shriek, and there she was on the baby monitor, red-faced, waking to a world in which her immediate needs were not being addressed because her parents were busy trading grievances over a bottle of wine.

"For you, you mean. You, always you."

The wine, red wine, the worst for stains, jumped from his glass in a looping arc in the instant before the glass hit the wall behind her. What was happening here came clear in that instant: he was bailing on her.

Right. And here he was, on his feet now, looming over her, being a jerk, his face as red as the baby's. "Are you going to deal with that fucking kid, or what?"

He left the rest unspoken, but she took his meaning. He didn't wait for an answer, didn't wait for her to shout back at him, make her own accusations, cry, plead, break down—he just scooped his keys up off the counter, went out the door and down the stairs. The last thing she heard before she went in to pick up Tahoe and feed and change her and pour herself one last glass of wine was the airtight suck of the Tesla's door as he slammed it shut.

PART III

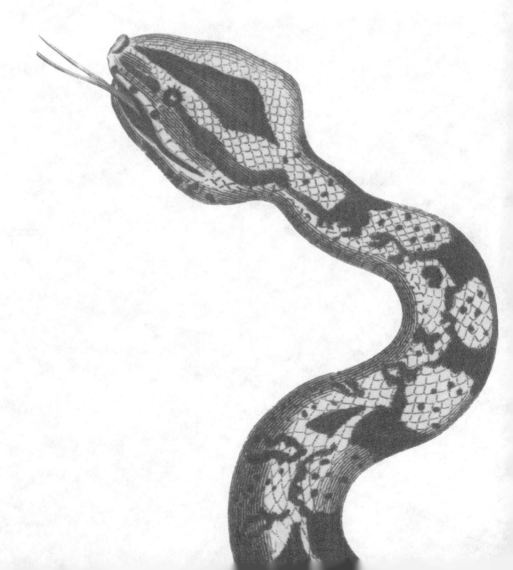

20

IN THE NIGHT, WHEN SHE COULDN'T SLEEP

IN THE NIGHT, WHEN SHE COULDN'T SLEEP, SHE COULD HEAR Sierra crying from someplace outside the door that gave onto the deck—Sierra, not Tahoe, who was asleep in her own bed across the hall, shielded by a force field of stuffed animals and grinning dolls. Or not crying, but mewling like a bird caught in a cat's claws. The first time it happened, she'd even got up to open the door and peer out into the night, but now she just lay there and took it. Most nights, there was the sound of rain, the hiss and trickle, the ferment, the house lowering itself to the surf like a giant going down on its knees, the rainy season the only season now. She didn't miss Todd anymore, though it had been hard at first, the way his personality changed, the way marriage and love and everything she believed in just got tossed in the trash. If it wasn't for R.J., she didn't think she would have made it. He'd been there for her when Todd wasn't, and when the peninsula was underwater and Todd on a continuous *Bacardí* odyssey, so far gone she didn't care if he ever came back, it was R.J. who brought her the skiff that had been sitting under a tarp out back of his garage so she could get to the store for diapers, meat, wine, toilet paper—had Todd ever even heard of toilet paper? The necessities? The bare necessities? There was no Tesla. No SUV. No Todd. She still didn't understand it—it was as if he'd been looking for an excuse to walk out on her.

She saw now that it went back even before Sierra, the little signals, the no sex, the way the babies seemed like an embarrassment to him whenever they were out in public, but the day of her court appearance, when her whole life was on the line, when she was seeing and hearing things that weren't there and so sick with dread she could barely get out of bed, that was the point of no return. She hadn't slept. Her hands trembled when she put on her makeup. She couldn't eat, couldn't think, and after she threw up the remains of whatever she'd managed to keep on her stomach the night before, she threw up again. But Todd? He was remote as a satellite. He didn't hug her, didn't kiss her, didn't do anything but avoid her eyes and try to pretend nothing was wrong. Wherever he'd gone the night before, he'd been back on the couch when it got light out, but he had nothing to give her except the same idiotic reassurances, which had no basis in reality at all, just fantasy, anything to shut her up. "Ten years, Todd," she kept saying. "*Ten years*," but he acted as if it were nothing, as if he could see into the future or had bought off the judge and the DA and the entire court system of the state of Florida.

They took R.J.'s car to throw off the reporters, slipping in the rear entrance of the police lot, where Dodie had arranged for them to park because everybody involved agreed this had been enough of a circus already, and still Todd acted as if he didn't know her because what if some paparazzo popped out of the bushes and snapped a photo that went viral and one of the up-and-coming young ambassadors for *Bacardí*, god forbid, wound up embarrassing the brand? She was furious and terrified in equal measure, clumping along in her block heels, head down, the air rotten, stinking, settling over her like a collapsed lung. They went in the rear entrance, retraced their steps through the inner corridors, Dodie Capistrano, a raging inferno of shoulders-back vigor and cockeyed assurance, leading the way, practically loping in her eagerness.

The night before, after Todd had slammed out the door, she'd called her mother so she could hear the same reassurances Todd and Dodie Capistrano kept giving her, only filtered through the first voice she'd ever heard—or felt, felt in the womb. If she was regressing, she didn't care. She needed her mother.

"What if it goes to trial?" she said the instant her mother picked up, but her voice couldn't seem to rise above a whisper.

"Cat? Is that you? Speak up, I can't hear you."

"I said, what if it goes to trial?"

"It won't."

"But if it does? I'd rather kill myself than have to go through that."

Her mother murmured something palliative, then murmured something more, but none of it meant anything.

"I just wanted to ask you, because this is so hard and I'm scared, I'm really scared—"

"Anything, honey, anything we can do, you know that."

The phone was heavy as a brick. Shapes wheeled at the periphery of her vision. "I mean, would you take Tahoe?"

"What are you talking about?"

"If I go to jail?"

"You're not going to jail."

She swirled the wine in her glass (the red, the good red, the Bordeaux, and why not?), watched it cling and subside. "Todd's hopeless," she said. "There's no way he could be involved or rise to the occasion in any way, shape or form. He wasn't cut out to be a father, I see that now, and we should never—I mean, I should never—have gone through with it in the first place."

She wasn't being emotional. Not in the least. She saw everything with perfect clarity. "You know what? I don't think I even like
him anymore."

THIS TIME IT WAS A courtroom, a big open high-ceilinged space with
rows of benches and clusters of people scattered round compartmental-
izing their own tics and miseries. Polished wood, flags, a smell of sweat
and deodorant and whatever it was they sprayed to keep down the bugs
that lived in the cracks and on the back side of the ceiling tiles. The
air-conditioner blew cold air. The windows were flecked with raindrops.
And there was the judge, presiding, her face jowly and sour, the too-
bright lights picking out each individual dyed hair on her head. Dodie
Capistrano ushered them into the first row of seats, front and center,
where the judge—and the DA—could get a good look at them, a family,
husband, wife, daughter. Infant daughter. In a baby sling, clinging to
her mother's chest. There was another case going on, the judge speaking into a microphone and addressing a man in a rumpled suit jacket
that was too short in the arms and wearing sandals instead of shoes, but
whatever it was all about meant nothing to anybody in the world except
maybe the court reporter and whoever paid the judge's salary.

She couldn't breathe. She had to use the restroom, desperately, a
burning finger poking her down low in the abdomen, but she couldn't
do that either because the judge and the bailiffs would think she was
making a break for it and the cops in the hallway would unholster their
guns and shout for her to freeze. Or shoot her. Would they shoot her?
A perp on her way to the restroom? She entertained that scenario a
moment—how much better it would be if they did just go ahead and
shoot her and get it over with, though she wouldn't want Tahoe to have
to see it because Tahoe was going to have a normal life, raised by her
grandparents in California, in the same house she herself had grown
up in, and go to school in the same schools and never have to appear in

court on such-and-such a date or live in anybody's shadow or breathe this putrid air again.

Then they called her name and she and Dodie Capistrano made their way to the podium where the rumpled-suit man had just stood with his shoulders slumped and his hands hanging at his sides and she studied her feet while Dodie Capistrano, her face locked in tight, radiated invisible beams at the judge seated up high on her throne. The DA rose. He was tall, aggressively bald, his suit cut as perfectly as one of Todd's. He was the enemy. He was an alien. He wanted to tear out her heart and eat it. Every bad thing she'd ever done in her life, even minor things like shoplifting two Linkin Park T-shirts she just had to have when she was eleven, right on up to driving drunk and backing into a car at the mall and just driving off and leaving the heartbreak for somebody else to deal with, came roaring into her skull. She'd always thought of herself as a good person, but now she understood how wrong she was. She was guilty, guilty as charged, and she deserved everything coming to her. And more, and worse. What about the time she went on for a full drunken hour trashing her mother to her college roommates just to make herself look bigger? Or her grandmother's funeral—she didn't even go to her own grandmother's funeral because she was on spring break in Arizona and too selfish, too much of a self-involved shit. A little shit. That's what she was.

Everybody was staring at her. She didn't know where to look. If she raised her eyes, the judge was right there front and center with her executioner's face; if she looked to either side there were clusters of tight-jawed strangers—and the press, the press, of course, who only wanted to see her destroyed because they were hateful and measured themselves against her and wanted everybody's life to be as hopeless as their own. Wasn't it supposed to be hot in hell, but cold, cold at the very center? She was a heartbeat from losing control of her legs—or rising right up through the ceiling like a rocket and leaving all this unendurable *shit* behind . . . but then the DA opened his mouth and what he was saying was so extreme she couldn't even begin to process it: "Your Honor, in light of our investigation"—two beats, three—"we are electing to dismiss this matter in the interest of justice."

The judge, her voice crackling and alert, freighted with a thousand reiterations, pronounced, "Case dismissed," then turned to her and said, "Bail is exonerated and you are free to go."

Dodie Capistrano, still towering, still locked in, leaned forward and said, "Thank you, Your Honor," and the whole world came careening back to life.

TODD HUGGED HER. DODIE CAPISTRANO hugged her. Whatever reporters were still following the case tapped out their eviscerated stories and in the next moment she was moving again, walking, but more briskly now, Tahoe snug and tight and riding the swell of her belly, which she hadn't lost yet but was going to now that she'd got her life back, eating right, exercising, cutting down on her drinking, she swore it . . . except not today. Today she was living in the moment. She'd gone from zero to a hundred, from nothing to everything. She wanted champagne. She wanted to laugh and shout and cry, get shit-faced and smear her lips with guacamole and lobster salad and profiteroles and éclairs and not even think about dieting. And, of course, Todd had arranged a party, the one thing he could be counted on to do without fail, a surprise party, a get-out-of-jail-free party, which she had no hint of till they pulled up in front of the house and the crash of the surf gave way to the *whomp-whomp-whomp* of the big speakers in the living room. "I told you, babe, didn't I tell you?"

The first glass of champagne (Moët & Chandon, Todd's touchstone, which he also just happened to get a deal on through the same distributor that handled his accounts) tore off the door of the cage they'd tried so hard to keep her in. The second glass had her going round the room hugging everybody, R.J., Stoneman and his girlfriend, Daria and Miller, people from Bobo's and the Cornerstone, a bar owner friend of

Todd's whose name she didn't even know. She needed to call Cooper, call everybody, but here was Todd, bottle in hand, topping off her glass. "I can't believe it," she said, rocking in rhythm to the music and trying to hold her glass steady while dandling Tahoe on one knee. "How did you know? I mean, what if it went the other way? What were you going to do with all this champagne?" She laughed at her own question. She was giddy. The answer was obvious: they would have drunk it all the same, in joy and sorrow, in sickness and health.

"Don't be ridiculous. It was never going to go the other way. Dodie told you that from the beginning—weren't you listening? No prosecutor was going to put you on the stand with a baby in your arms. For an *accident*. It was an accident, or did you forget that?"

A tune she loved, bass-heavy and flaring with horns, burst out of the speakers and flooded the room. R.J., his hair hanging in his eyes and his glass held high, got up with a quick fluid roll of his hips and started dancing with his brother's girlfriend, but his eyes were on her, and she thought he would have asked her instead if Todd hadn't been standing right there. But he was. With a bottle of champagne in his hand. Todd. Her husband. The love of her life. He might have had his limitations, might have made himself his number one priority, but he'd got her Dodie Capistrano and her house on the beach and he sure knew how to throw a party.

Later, when the music got softer and gravity began to exert itself and people sank into all the available chairs and held fast to their glasses even as Todd kept circulating with the bottle, she found herself sitting cross-legged on the rug with R.J., Stoneman and the girlfriend, Loralee, staring into the baby monitor as if it were one of the eagle cams she liked to watch online, and was it really all that different? Mother and baby, the bassinet standing in for the heaped-up nest of sticks, except that she wasn't perched over the rim of it with a fish clamped in her talons. Or a snake. Eagles loved snakes.

Somebody opened the door to the deck and a pair of big mottled moths sailed in to fling themselves at the mica lamps, a scene which would have pleased her brother. He'd gone back to California the day before they'd arrested her and been spared all this, thankfully, though her mother must have given him a stimulating version of events. He'd tried to call her half a dozen times but she'd just let the phone buzz because she couldn't face dredging everything up all over again. But now it was different. She'd already called her mother—in the car on the way back from the courthouse—and she'd call him too. But not yet, not yet—the moment was too delicious to let go of.

She watched the moths beat at the lampshade, fooled into thinking sunrise had come early. Stoneman said something disconnected from what the conversation was or had been, "Energy like you can't believe," and she liked the phrase and held on to it and missed what came next because she was in a special place now. The moths' wings carried a powder that was actually composed of tiny scales, like a lizard's scales, which was why they were classified as *Lepidoptera* (*Lepido*, scale, and *ptera*, wing), a fact Cooper had taught her, along with a thousand other things about the natural world, most of which she'd forgotten or filed away in an internal folder to be retrieved only if she found herself on a TV quiz show, *Name the order to which butterflies and moths belong and translate its meaning into English.*

Three girls came up the stairs and joined the party, friends of Todd's. The music pounded and she couldn't hear what Todd was saying to them or they were saying to him, but they were all sunshine and grins. And legs and eye shadow and earrings. Cocktail waitresses, no doubt—Todd knew a lot of cocktail waitresses. R.J., who'd been right there at her side for the last half hour, talking mostly about music, but books and movies too and just life in general—conversation, patter, give-and-take, anything to take her mind off what she'd been through— glanced up at the girls and said, "If you're going to need anything, just let me know. Whether I'm at home or the shop, don't worry, you can call me anytime."

She looked to Todd, then back again. "No, I'm good. *Finally*," she said.

"I mean when Todd's gone."

"Gone? What do you mean?"

An awkward sliver of a moment. The champagne had deadened her legs. She couldn't have got up off the floor if she wanted to, but she didn't want to. She was perfectly fine here.

"His trip, I mean?"

She didn't want to pursue it, didn't want to ask, "What trip?" as if she wouldn't have been the first to know, but R.J., seeing his opening, said, "You know, next week. He said he was going up to Atlantic City and then the Hamptons, isn't that right?"

THERE WAS AN END TO all that, though it dragged on over the course of a year, every day poisoning the next till she and Todd couldn't be in the same room for five minutes without fighting over something, whether it was who's going to take out the garbage or where's the money for the phone bill or what's for dinner, not to mention what to do about the mold creeping insidiously up the walls and the pilings rotting under the house. He took it and she took it and Tahoe shrieked and filled her pants and the ocean tore at the beach and rocked the house and then one day he went off in the Tesla and didn't come back.

That was a day. The sun was out, but it was like a probe tracing every gouge in the walls and scrape in the floor. Tahoe was running a fever and she'd fussed all night (not that it bothered Todd out there on his couch), so she took her to the pediatrician first thing in the morning, and no, he was too busy to go with her, okay? "I've got a life," he said. "Does that come as a surprise? How you think the bills get paid?"

When she got home, Tahoe asleep in her arms, he walked right on past her without even asking what the doctor said—past her and out the door, a suitcase in each hand and his garment bag riding the spread of his back like a pair of folded wings. "Where're you going?" she demanded, even as the door stood open and he swiveled round to give her a look that had nothing in it, nothing whatsoever, null and void. "Don't tell me you've got another event? Where is it this time, huh? I mean, you couldn't even tell me?"

He just shook his head, very slowly, as if it weighed more than he could bear. "I'm sorry, babe," he said. "I really am." And then he started down the stairs.

When she looked back on it, she saw how inevitable it had been, a mistake from beginning to end, and whether Sierra died or not it wouldn't have made any difference. But she didn't look back, or tried not to, even when the noise she woke to in the morning was the cry of a dead and cremated infant shaping itself around the standard complaint of the gulls while the sea sluiced in to carry off their leavings and keep the cycle of life right on track. Guano. It was everywhere, striping the roofs of all the houses on the peninsula, whether they were occupied still or abandoned to the water that just kept on coming, seasonally, daily, whether the moon was waxing or waning or the rain spigot on or off.

ON THIS PARTICULAR DAY, MID-OCTOBER, Halloween coming on and Tahoe soaring with excitement over her costume ("Gulpy Gator, can I be Gulpy Gator?," the answer to which was yes, though Gulpy Gator was male and didn't have a female counterpart as far as Cat knew), they were going to have to take the skiff because the road was inundated and the car, a used Nissan EV her parents had given her the money for, was parked in the lot at Bobo's because you couldn't trust the driveway here or even the peninsula road, a whole section of which kept washing out as fast as they could repair it. She was up early, as she was every weekday morning, getting Tahoe ready for school. It was overcast, drizzling, the deck slick and the birds lined up on the rail to haunt her. She soft-boiled two eggs, one for Tahoe, one for herself, toasted muffins, set out the butter and the jam and poured herself a cup of coffee. The TV weatherwoman informed her that it was drizzling, which she could see for herself, and would go on drizzling all day long and probably for the rest of everybody's life on earth and that the king tides they were experiencing would keep the streets flooded and people in low-lying areas should take precautions while boaters should be aware that bridge clearances would be lower than usual.

Tahoe was old enough to dress herself—six, first grade, a big girl, as she liked to call herself—but she did need supervision or she'd dawdle forever picking out what top to wear or which pair of Crocs, the lime-green or the pepper-red or the cotton-candy-pink, and she did tend to forget one thing or another, her backpack, her umbrella, her snack, her lunch, her thermos, her workbook with her drawings and puzzles and blocks of painstakingly reconstructed letters, so it was always a trick making sure they got out the door in time for school, whether they had to use the skiff or not. And this morning they most definitely did. As they had the day before and the day before that—all week, really.

It was warm out, warmer than it should have been for this time of year, but she had to remind Tahoe to keep her raincoat buttoned up— if she got herself soaked, no matter how warm it was, she'd be shivering and crying and insisting she didn't want to go to school and why couldn't she just stay home in bed and do puzzles and read her books and color? "I hate the rain," she'd say. "Why does it always have to be raining?" Down the stairs now, the sky and the land and the sea all one composition, Tahoe pestering her to let her steer the boat and she giving the standard answer, "We'll see."

When it was flooding like this she kept the skiff in front of the house, facing the street, moored to the salt-killed pine in the middle of the yard and braced by lines she drew taut to a pair of eyebolts R.J. had screwed strategically into the frame of the house. Which meant they had to wade just to get to it, which Tahoe always thought was a real adventure, and what was that swimming in the water, a turtle—was that a turtle? Mom? It was. Yes, it was. "Good eye," she said, amazed that there was anything alive out there anymore, and then they were unfastening the cover and Tahoe was bailing out the accumulation in the bottom of the boat while she dropped the lines and pulled the cord to start the engine with a low coughing rattle and they were off.

This was her favorite part of the day, the school ritual, which brought her back to her own childhood when her mother walked her the six blocks to Twin Oaks Elementary every morning, though there'd been no boats involved or cars either. Just two pairs of legs, her mother's and her own. She cut a V through the played-out water, focusing just over her daughter's head but watching her too, the way she hugged her shoulders and hunched forward over her seat in the bow, the ends of her hair whipping in the breeze, the rain misting round her, the out-of-control world in control for once. Her own hair barely fluttered. She'd cut it short and dyed it just after the hearing (golden copper, which was a good match with her coloring), but kept the bangs longish, and the beauty of it was, nobody ever recognized her, beyond the odd encounter where someone would say, *Don't I know you?* and she'd respond by shaking her head and saying, as casually as she could, *I don't think so.*

The engine did what it was supposed to ("You can steer on the way back, I promise, but we're in a hurry now"), pushing the skiff through the water till the water gave out and they could beach it and walk up the glistening wet blacktop and into town, where the beach houses gave way to condos and shops and restaurants. Then they'd get the car at Bobo's for the two-mile drive to school. Normally, she'd go back home, unless it was one of the two days a week she was waitressing (at Bobo's, lunch crowd only, though she occasionally filled in for Daria or Whitney at dinner, when she could get a babysitter, that is), but this morning she had errands to run, after which she was going to go over to St. Augustine and meet R.J. for brunch and just kick back and enjoy the day.

They'd arranged to meet at a café that served breakfast all day and had the added advantage of possessing a liquor license so you could have a Bloody Mary or mimosa with your crepes and egg scramble and get a little head start on the afternoon. Which was fine with her. Better than fine. Just what she needed to break the monotony of the drizzly days and the burden of all that mold encroaching on everything in the house, no matter how much she scrubbed and sprayed and fought it back with bleach and scouring powder. She dropped Tahoe at school, watched her splash through the ankle-deep water in the yard and disappear through the front door without turning to wave because she was in school mode now, then drove to the supermarket and pushed a cart up and down the aisles for half an hour, relying on her memory to fill in the gaps of what they were out of, which was practically everything. The perishables went into the two big Igloo coolers she kept in the back of the car, for transfer to the skiff when school was out. Then it was the ATM and the gas station and her responsibilities were over till she had to pick up Tahoe after school.

Just as she was rolling into the lot out front of the café, which was flooded, like just about everything else—*king tides*, she'd never even heard of king tides till she moved here—R.J. called. He was having car trouble—could she pick him up at the shop?

"No problem," she said, but of course it was a problem and always would be. To actually step inside the shop was beyond her, but there were times when she'd meet R.J. or his brother on the sidewalk out front or across the street at Cora's, which was better. As much as she told herself she had to face up to the reality and get beyond it—especially since she was dating the co-owner of the place—the sight of it froze her. *How can you go out with him, of all people, after what happened?* her mother kept demanding, at least in the beginning, and she didn't have an answer for that herself, except that R.J. made her feel good and he treated her a whole lot better than Todd ever had. As for the shop, every time she pulled up outside it was like taking the smallest dose of poison in order to build up resistance—*Mithridatism*, she'd looked it up—though it wasn't really working. She called him when she got there and he said he'd be a minute because the tow truck hadn't shown up yet and why didn't she just go over to Cora's and wait for him there? They could have lunch there too, which might be easier.

Though the tide was up, the street was clogged with cars nosing along like boats on the bay and the parking was limited because the

county had put pylons up all over the place, as if that would make a difference beyond just creating an extra level of aggravation, and the only
spot available was right in front of the store. She got out, the water up to
her shins, cold but relatively clean, unlike the black water in places like
Miami that was so contaminated with fecal matter and industrial waste
you didn't dare let it touch your skin. The drizzle had thickened to rain,
which got her hair wet before she could unfurl the umbrella, and here
came a car moving just fast enough to compact a wave and fling it at her,
which got her cursing aloud. That was when she glanced up and saw the
window there, right in front of her, the one with the canted artificial
branch and the snake in possession of it. Willie's mother. Just there, just
being. And bigger than it was possible for any snake to be.

A new awning descended from the top of the window, which
R.J. might have told her about in the course of things—for shade, to keep
down the heat, wasn't that it?—and under the awning was a woman her
age clutching three or four bright magenta shopping bags and shelter-
ing from the rain, which was coming down harder now. Cat could have
gone inside, but that wasn't really an option, not in this lifetime, and she
didn't want to just sit there in the car—what she wanted was to cross the
roiling inlet of the street, perch on a stool at the bar and wait for R.J. in
comfort. The rain wouldn't let her. It exploded around her, every drop
like a BB, like a ball bearing, and in the next moment she found herself
under the awning with the woman and her magenta shopping bags as
the rain beat down and the big snake melted into the branch.

"Jesus, this weather," she said, just to say something.

The woman—girl, she was a girl just like her, if early thirties still
qualified, which it did because it was a matter of how you thought of
yourself and how you dressed, especially how you dressed. This girl,
transparent raincoat (Lululemon?) over white shorts and collared blouse
topped off with a black bucket hat, certainly looked the part. She was
shopping, no matter the weather, and here she was temporarily stranded
under the awning out front of a pet shop specializing in reptiles in a
neighborhood that didn't really have a whole lot more to offer.

"They say the king tides are with us for the rest of the week, if not more," the girl volunteered. "And the rain too."

"The Sunshine State," Cat said, and the girl laughed. It was a moment of mutuality, cozy almost—the storm, the floodwaters, the interruption of routine that forced everybody into a new mode of being, deadlines softening, plans abandoned, the hours mutating the way they did when you were a kid and school was canceled—and she was about to ask the girl if she wanted to dash across the street to Cora's and have a drink or a cup of coffee, when the girl said, "What's with that snake? I didn't even know they could get that big. It's humongous—I mean, what do they even feed it?"

She looked up at the window and saw her reflection there, her face cold and bloodless, the world just a transparency, a simulacrum. There was nothing she could say, and even if there was, she couldn't trust her voice.

"I can't believe the pattern," the girl said. "It's like living art, don't you think?"

THE FOOD WASN'T MUCH AT Cora's, but Cora's was easy. She sat at the bar waiting for R.J., scrolling through her messages and the news of the day, and though it wasn't even noon yet, she ordered a drink. Not a mojito, but a Bloody Mary, which made her feel less guilty because she wasn't a morning drinker and Bloody Marys were just juice with a kick, perfectly acceptable with brunch, which was what they were going to have as soon as the tow truck came, and if she wasn't really hungry she'd fake it for R.J.'s sake. There was hardly anybody in the place, what with the rain and the flooded streets, and after Cora mixed the drink she came round the bar to sit beside her for a chat.

Cora had a new boyfriend, a former college basketball star in his mid-fifties who'd been good enough to play in the European League for a decade or so before he gave up and opened a string of shops to sell plastic bags of authentic coquina and seashell art to tourists, and just the mention of his name—Mel—was enough to get Cora going ("Socks, the man has never worn a pair socks in his life, not since he left the bas- ketball court, anyway"), and if that subject petered out there was always the weather. And Tahoe, how big she'd gotten, how cute she was, how proud of her Cat must be and how Cora envied her because she'd never had any children herself, which was actually the saddest thing in her life. At first, after what had happened, the few times Cat had been in, always with R.J. or Stoneman and Loralee, Cora had fumbled around for what to say, giving her long forensic stares as if she were some kind of freak—which, of course, she was, *Python Mom*—but that was so long ago now it wasn't problem. Or not for Cora, anyway.

She was on her second drink by the time R.J. came in, dripping, and they moved to a table in the corner and ordered food, a fruit plate for her and a breakfast burrito for him. He was worked up over the car and what it was going to cost him ("It's not the battery—it's like two years old and still under warranty—but who knows with all this fuck- ing water we have to drive through all the time, everything shorting out and rusting up, and I hope that's all it is, a short"), but the food calmed him and when he saw she was having a Bloody Mary he ordered a beer and after that another beer and a shot because there was nothing any- body could do about anything so they might as well enjoy the afternoon, right? Besides which, he'd closed up the shop for the day because who was going to come out in this to buy their kid a bearded dragon or a cha- meleon or anything else?

Time slowed. There was soccer on the TV, of course, ubiquitous soc- cer, infinite soccer, soccer on top of soccer, but muted, and when she glanced up from time to time she saw how essential it was to have these particular figures in their bright bicolored jerseys drifting across the screen over the mahogany glow of the bar and the golden glint of the bottles, as if the whole thing were an art installation in a museum some- where. It was raining out. It was dry in here. She felt as if she were asleep and awake at the same time. She sipped her drink, set it down, sipped it again. Three months back R.J. had joined a retro cover band and they talked tunes and set lists for a while and had another round of drinks and then it was time to go pick up Tahoe.

It was still raining. He drove, both because she was feeling the effects of the alcohol and did not want to get pulled over and have to deal with the law—never, never again—and because he was going to take the car once he'd dropped her and Tahoe off and helped her load the groceries into the skiff. "You know what's funny about the set list?" he said, still ruminating over this new toy in his life, a four-piece band called Loco that might even start to get some gigs before long. "As many times as I've heard a given song I never catch the lyrics because I always take it in as a whole, the intensity of it, the emotion, and so I wind up having to write them out on a crib sheet as if I have some sort of brain glitch . . ."

Everything was gray, the car windows, the streets, the storefronts, the palms. He was a good driver, a careful driver, negotiating the swamped streets as if he could see through the swirling opaque surface of the water to the pavement beneath—and the curbs, which were like hidden shoals waiting to punch out your tires and tear off your exhaust system. She said, "I know every word to every song you guys do."

"I wish I had your brain."

The first time she had sex with R.J. was the week Todd left. She was the one who called him because she was feeling as if she'd been snapped in two like one of the brittle stars that washed up on the beach and she was calling everybody—Daria, her mother, Melody—and talking, talking, talking till she had no more breath left in her body. He listened. He said the right things. And then he asked her to dinner, and if it was strange to absorb his scent and the taste of his tongue and feel that his shoulders weren't Todd's or his hands or the rest of him either—his dick—it was good, more than good, and as time went on it just got better.

She smiled. Here in the moment, with R.J. at her side, it was almost as cozy as Cora's. The windshield wipers kept track of everything. They were safe in their steel shell, on their way to pick up Tahoe with plenty of time to spare. "All things considered," she said, "I think I'll keep my brain—if you don't mind, I mean."

"I wasn't really up for a brain transplant, anyway," he said, casually swinging the wheel to the left to avoid a tangle of floating debris even as the radio murmured over the chorus of a song she liked and the sky opened up ahead of them and the sun, the actual sun, which she hadn't seen in a week, built itself a cathedral of light right there in the middle of the street.

SHE LET TAHOE RUN THE skiff on the way back (*You promised*), which was only a ten-minute ride in any case. It was a small enough reward for putting up with things like having to live in a house that smelled like a toilet and was constantly shifting underneath you as if it were floating out to sea. Or having a divorced father who showed up once a month with one girlfriend or another for a rocket-express trip to the toy store and a three-star restaurant, *You be good now, see you next time, you're the best, honey, aren't you the best?* Tahoe would come home talking about *pannequets* and *confit* and *écrevisse* and why can't we have that at home? (Answer: Because this isn't a restaurant and I'm not a gourmet chef and how about if I make turkey burgers for dinner?)

The sun felt good on her face, though she worried about exposure since she hadn't bothered with sunblock, for either her or her daughter, because there was no hint of sun when they'd left the house in the morning. Which was okay—a little sun never hurt anybody. And it gave you vitamin D, which was essential for something or other. Nothing to worry about. Fortunately, enough residual alcohol lingered in her veins to bring the right tone to the afternoon and there was wine at home and the promise of R.J. joining them later for dinner, so she just sat astride the seat and watched the clouds bunch at the horizon like big clusters of white grapes and enjoyed the ride. Tahoe was a serious child, rock-steady, and that was evident whenever she was given responsibility, like now—she kept her

hand fixed on the tiller and her eyes focused ahead to pick up on any hazards the flood tide might have dredged up out of the sea.

They were almost home, three or four houses away, when her daughter suddenly cut the throttle and let the skiff swing round on the current. "What are you doing, honey?" Cat asked, pivoting in the seat
and holding a hand up to shield her eyes against the glare. "Why are
we stopping?"

Tahoe pointed to the house in front of them, a two-story clapboard
place like theirs, with the same floorplan and outside stairway, probably
built in the early seventies by the same contractor. The wood was weathered an opalescent greenish gray, just like theirs, but the difference was
that this house had been red-tagged and deserted for the past month.
"Look, Mom, up there in the window?"

At first she didn't see it, the window glazed with sun, and then she
did: movement there, a shadow stroking the glass and stroking it again.
She'd seen reports on the news about vagrants moving into abandoned
houses, just wading in and taking possession, animals too—raccoons,
opossums, rats, snakes, iguanas and whatever else could swim or climb
or crawl. Not to mention birds. And bats. "What is it? Is somebody
in there?"

It was then that the thin muffled complaint of the cat came to them
and the shadow took on shape and dimension, all head and ears and
mouth, the pink palate, the white spikes of the teeth, yellow eyes burning holes in them. In the next moment, the cat rose to its haunches and
began pawing at the window.

"We have to save it," Tahoe said, the skiff rocking beneath them, the
engine gabbling in neutral, the sky fleeced with sunburnt clouds.

"We can't go in there," she said automatically. "It's somebody else's
house. It's against the law. It's trespassing." Of course, even as she said it,
she knew they were going to tether the skiff to the railing, mount the
stairs and try the door, which would be locked, then go round to each
of the windows in succession until they either found one ajar or had to
break the glass.

She didn't trust Tahoe with maneuvering in close—that was just begging for trouble—so she took over the tiller and eased the skiff up to the stairway and secured it to the rail with the bowline knot R.J. had taught her. The steps seemed secure enough, in better shape than their own, actually, but she was on high alert—the house had been red-tagged, after all, which could have meant anything from water damage to the disintegration of the pilings, *Danger, Keep Out*— and it took her a moment to work up the courage to take hold of the railing and pull herself up onto the first step above the waterline. She shifted her weight experimentally while Tahoe, rocking just below her in the boat, gazed up at her with a solemn face. The cat was louder now, more plaintive, its cries rising till they broke off in a confusion of catarrhal growls that made it sound as if it were choking. "I want to come," Tahoe said. "Please?"

"Give me a minute. I just want to make sure it's safe." She started up the stairway, holding fast to the railing and testing each step as she went, and all seemed solid. She didn't ask herself what she was doing and didn't wonder if she'd be here at all if she was strictly sober, but just let her feet guide her until she reached the landing and tried the door. "It's locked," she said, calling down to her daughter as if that would be the end of it, but Tahoe was out of the boat now and running up the steps, all knees and elbows and the sunlit shine of her hair, a tiny figure expanding in time and space. Tahoe didn't say a word but went straight to the window, pressed her palms flat to the glass and tried to raise it, and when that didn't work, went to the next one.

All at once the cat appeared on the other side of the window-pane, materializing so suddenly it startled her—a Bengal, wasn't it? A pet, definitely a pet. She didn't want to think of the diseases it might be carrying or fleas or mites or ringworm either, because none of that mattered—she was going to break that window and rescue it and take it home with her and give it to her daughter to raise, a normal pet, as her mother might say, a proper pet, sanctioned and approved. And that girl at Herps? Cat hadn't said anything more to her before wading across the street to Cora's, but if she had she would have nodded at the snake in the window, and whether R.J. ever made another sale or not really didn't factor into it, because she would have said, without hesitation, "Don't even think about it."

21

THE HEAT

DID PEOPLE EVEN GIVE DINNER PARTIES ANYMORE? WHAT was the point? Half the world was flooded and the other half parched and the crops kept failing and failing again. People were starving, even here in California. There were refugees everywhere. The wine tasted of ash. It hadn't rained in as long as she could remember. But Frank was retiring and she was giving a party, albeit a modest one, just eight: her and Frank, Cooper and Elytra, Sylvie and Peter, and Frank's PA, Allison, and her husband, Gerald, whom she barely knew but was happy to include. If you gave up on celebrating the milestone events, you might as well give up on life, which was how she justified it to Cooper, who raised all the usual objections: the waste of water and electricity, not to mention the food resources, even if she was going vegetarian with an overlay of *cuisine de divers insectes*, plus lab-cultured chicken for Peter, Sylvie and Frank. Which was cultivated from cells and you could eat without guilt. Chicken. Real chicken. No animal suffered, no animal was killed. And there were no shellfish allergies to worry about or chitin either.

At the moment—mid-September, nine a.m., already ninety-six degrees and climbing—she was out in her garden, or the remnants of it, picking cherry tomatoes. She'd let everything else go—the wildflowers, the penstemon, the milkweed for Cooper's butterflies (which were all but extinct at this point anyway), her zucchini and corn and green beans, no water to spare—but she couldn't live without tomatoes. She'd planted them in whiskey barrels to keep them away from the gophers, which were desperate themselves. The gophers were migrating down out of the foothills to the oases homeowners had unwittingly created for them and bringing their predators with them, coyotes and rattlesnakes in particular. She had to worry about Dunphy, who was arthritic and half-blind, every time she let him out in the yard.

Like now. She picked tomatoes and kept an eye out for him as he nosed around in the stiff dead brush and lifted his leg, then limped to the door in the expectation of being let in out of the heat. "Good boy," she murmured, "just be patient, I'll be there in a minute." Not that it was all that much cooler in the house. Years ago they'd sprung for an air-conditioner because life had become unlivable without it almost year-round now, but the electricity kept faltering under the weight of the demand, which, of course, surged just when you needed it most. Brown-outs gave way to blackouts on what seemed like a regular basis, which in turn led to spoilage and food waste and a refrigerator that never had a chance to maintain a safe temperature, necessitating more trips to the market, which burned more fuel and kept the cycle spinning. And the pool, which should have been her salvation during the heat waves, had turned soupy because when the electricity was down the filter was filtering nothing. She fought the algae with jug after jug of chlorine till the pool smelled like a chemical factory, but still she wound up with ropy green filaments of it pasted to her shoulders and interlaced in the strands of her hair, and the water, even in winter, always seemed tepid. Her biggest regret was not having installed solar panels when she had the chance—now they were impossible to come by because everybody had the same idea, the whole world sweating as one.

Just as she was heading back in, the colander of tomatoes cradled to her chest and the dog slipping past her into the refuge of the darkened kitchen, the UPS van pulled into the driveway. Setting the colander down on the wicker chair just outside the door, she circled back round through the gate, waving to catch the driver's attention. This would be the grasshoppers for her *chapulines*, which she'd waited for all day yesterday only to find a printed note stuck to the front door informing her that the driver was sorry to have missed her and as a matter of company policy couldn't leave the package without her signing for it since it contained perishable items—her livestock, that is. She'd long since given up on the crickets and mealworms, which tended to die off on her no matter how conscientious she was with feeding and maintenance, though she still used cricket flour and for special occasions ordered grasshoppers from Entomo Farms. Frank had lost his enthusiasm for insects years ago in any case and everybody else she knew, aside from Cooper, couldn't seem to overcome their prejudices, but *chapulines* were different, as irresistible as potato chips and a whole lot healthier. And now that lab-cultured meats were widely available (and coming down in price), she didn't feel it was quite so crucial to include insects in her diet—or serve them at parties.

The driver was a man she recognized from past deliveries, though she didn't know his name. He looked to be in his fifties, pouchy eyes, dried-up skin, hair drawn back in a milk-white braid fastened with a silver clip that caught the sun and flashed it at her when he turned his head to greet her. "Livestock?" he said, handing her the package with a grin. "What is it—Fish? Frogs? Bugs?"

"*Chapulines*. Grasshoppers, that is."

"You got a pet lizard?"

"No," she said, "uh-uh," and didn't bother to elaborate. It was too hot to elaborate. She shook her head and sighed. "This heat, huh? Half the time I can't even think, it's so hot."

"Just like yesterday and the day before that. And next week's supposed to be hotter yet." "I tell you, this thing"—he tapped the side of the door—"it's like a furnace, even with the air cranked. And just when I get some cold air on my face, it's the next stop and I've got to open the door again."

"Stay hydrated," she said, which was like saying, "Have a nice day," in former times when there was a whole range of other considerations in people's lives besides the heat. He saluted her with a liter bottle of water, took a long swallow, slammed the door and backed down the driveway.

Once she'd put her grasshoppers in the refrigerator—not the freezer, not yet—she topped off Dunphy's water bowl, then drove to the supermarket before the heat built toward the afternoon and the hundred and ten they were predicting, with another ten degrees on top of that for the other side of the coastal range, where Cooper must have been dying.

THE SUPERMARKET HAD ITS OWN generator, which was a good thing, because the minute she stepped in the door the lights went out. She stood there a moment, just behind the line of cash registers, her eyes trying to adjust while the silhouettes of her fellow shoppers flickered past her on the extended shadows of their carts, and then the generator kicked in, light solidified the aisles and the hidden speakers resumed cranking out ads as if that were all that mattered. There were specials on products she'd never heard of, displays of things she didn't want. The shelves were haphazardly stocked, shortages of one thing or another leaving gaps the management tried to fill by overstocking squat clear bottles of kimchee, pickled onions, sassafras tincture and Dr. Delahanty's Authentic Creole Gumbo, whatever that was. The meat was bloodless and gray, not that she was in the market for it, and the nuts—almonds and pistachios, especially, which she found herself craving—were so pricey nobody could afford them. She couldn't find the heavy whipping cream she needed for dessert or the capers for her pasta *fredda*. There was bread, though, fresh-baked on the premises. She laid three sourdough baguettes in her cart, then went to select her cheeses in the deli.

When she'd gone through her mental checklist and scanned the items in her cart twice over, she wheeled into the liquor department to pick out the wines (six red, six white, avoiding anything from Napa, which was the most likely to be smoke-tainted), and the first thing she encountered was a sake display, which made her think of Mari. Mari had been prescient, at least when it came to sake, which, according to the magazines and what few dwindling pages were left of the local newspaper, was emerging as the drink of choice for the cognoscenti, or whatever they were called nowadays. The strivers. The people who thought making an impression meant something. Gourmands. Foodies. The world was collapsing like a punctured balloon, but there were still foodies out there. And sake was their drink of choice because the smoke of the wildfires didn't affect the rice it was fermented from, though nobody bothered to mention how water-intensive the crop was.

Of course, with Mari, sake had been part of her heritage . . . and what had she heard? Was it from Cooper? Or Elytra? Mari had been offered a position at one of the universities up north—in Eugene or Boise or someplace. Which was a whole lot more than Cooper could say for himself. He was still a grad student, at least nominally, and getting by doing maintenance at the field station (lifting, hauling, weed-whacking) while trying to recalibrate his dissertation—or a dissertation, any dissertation—to reflect the cascading series of crashes and explosions in the local insect populations. And the heat stress that was driving species north even as the plants they relied on to survive dried up and died, providing yet more fuel for the fires. Fuel for dissertations too. She didn't want to nag him, considering what he'd been through, but it was time he bore down and got on with his life. Past time. Way past.

She was heading for the checkout when, in one of those coincidences that made her wonder if she wasn't controlling the world with the flow of her own thoughts, she glanced up and saw Mari right there in front of her, pushing her own cart. There was a man at Mari's side, white-haired, diminutive, his glasses catching the reflection of an energy-drink display in sheets of color. Even before she smiled and said, "Mari, how great to see you," she realized that this was Mari's father and that Mari was in town to visit him, because the mother was dead, wasn't she? And the father retired now? Hadn't she read something in the paper about that?

Mari introduced her father not as Phillip, but as "My dad," then asked about Cooper. "I hear he's still doing work out at the field station?"

"Yes, and still working on his dissertation." She wanted to elaborate, but that would have involved excuses—or worse, criticism—so she changed the subject. "And you, I hear you're a professor now?"

She was.

"And your ticks? How are they doing?"

Mari let out a laugh, displaying her teeth. "They're moving north. I guess they couldn't stand to see me go."

"The environment's stressed to the limit, isn't it?" she said.

"Ticks don't thrive in a desert."

They'd thrived long enough to deprive her son of his arm, that was what she was thinking, but in that moment she glanced down at Mari's cart and saw that she was buying fish—and not just any fish, but the New Sea brand of lab-cultured bluefin tuna, which was something like sixty dollars a pound. Mari registered the look on her face. "It's my father's birthday," she said. "We're splurging."

"Happy birthday," she said, addressing the father. She watched his smile animate and die and saw what he was in that moment: sad, wifeless, lonely, a widower limping toward the grave in a city by the sea that used to be lush and smokeless, with public gardens instead of homeless encampments and offshore breezes that kept everything cool and allowed you to sleep at night without soaking the sheets in sweat. Worse, she saw herself in him, if anything should happen to Frank, and it would, of course it would, nothing to look forward to but the surcease of the grave, where tuna didn't register, whether fresh-caught, cultured in a lab or dug out of a can stamped with an expiration date. "How's the quality?" she asked, putting the question to him instead of Mari—it was his fish and his birthday. "My husband and I haven't tried it yet, but I hear it's good . . ."

"Almost real," he said, the smile flickering to life again. "Quasi-real. The ersatz of the ersatz. But what else is there? Tilapia? Have you ever tried tilapia sashimi?" He brought a hand to the frame of his glasses, as if he were about to slip them off and polish the lenses on his shirttail, which hung loose over khaki shorts and a pair of exaggerated calves, which made her decide he must be a bicyclist. Well, good for him. He wasn't dead yet.

Mari said, "So how's Cat?"

"Cat?" She tried to freeze her expression exactly as it was a beat ago when the subject was sushi. "Great," she said. "Really great."

IN FACT, CAT WAS A disaster, but that was none of Mari's business—or anybody else's. Cat should have moved on long ago, but for some unfathomable reason she insisted on staying there in the only place in America where anyone would have remembered anything about who she was or what had happened to her. And why was that? Why did she have to go on punishing herself? How could she live in a house whose every feature was a reminder of the worst night of her life and why did she have to go out with a man who, of all things, sold snakes?

Because it's my home. This house is the only thing I've ever owned, can you understand that, Mom? Can you even begin to?

Well, no, she couldn't. It was a wonder the house hadn't been red-tagged by now, half the other places on that vanishing strip of sand already abandoned, feral cats making themselves at home in the cabinets, anoles climbing up the walls and those other things, the black-and-white ones, tegus, that grew to the size of a beagle and bolted down anything they came across, animal or vegetable, perched on the decks and rooftops as if they'd sprouted wings and flown there. Property values were nil. No insurer would touch Cat's place or anything within five miles of it (which no doubt was why Todd had so magnanimously parted with it in the divorce settlement). The schools were fairly good, she'd give her that, but to get out to the street and catch the bus, if there even was a bus, Tahoe had to ride in the skiff that had been sitting out back of R.J.'s garage for twenty years, which meant that Cat had to pilot it both ways—and become an Evinrude mechanic in the process.

No different from the suburbs anywhere, Mom, like in California, where the boats are SUVs—except that we're not on fire all the time.

THE ICE IN THE COOLER had turned to slush and before she could transfer the perishables from her cart she had to crabwalk it over to the median and pour off the meltwater. Her sandals squelched on the black-top, which seemed to be oozing tar, and the air was stitched with the faintly sweetish odor of petrochemicals and something else too, something burning somewhere. The mall owners had planted shade trees throughout the parking lot, but the drought had killed off the better part of them, so there really was no relief, the trip from the car to the store and back as harrowing as a trek across the Sahara, only without the sand. The windshields of the cars flashed like comets. Everything seemed to float up off the ground and she floated right along with it, but her skin felt tight, as if she were wearing a blood-pressure cuff over her entire body, and when she slid into the front seat and caught a look at her face in the mirror she saw the telltale redness there, the first sign of heat exhaustion. She drained her water bottle, cranked the air-conditioning and sat there in the poor striped shade of a dead pepper tree till she came back to herself, then put the car in drive and kept her foot on the accelerator all the way home.

The first thing she did, even before she unloaded the car, was strip down to bra and panties and plunge into the pool. Then it was all right, then it was fine—just a little heat, that was all, and she felt lucky to have the pool, luckier than most, even if the chlorine burned in her nostrils and reddened her eyes. She'd swum her laps that morning, so she didn't do much more than rise to the surface, prop her elbows on the coping and hover in the shade of the diving board till things evened out, at which point she reminded herself she had guests coming, just like in the old days, and climbed out of the pool to quickstep across the patio and into the house. She didn't towel off, but let the evaporation cool her as she put the groceries away, then went about cutting romaine and halving her cherry tomatoes for the green salad, boiling fusilli for the pasta *fredda* and making the broccoli-quinoa patties she planned on serving along with the cultured chicken as a main course. She thought of the dog then—he hadn't come to greet her at the door but just lay there stretched out on the tiles beneath the air-conditioner, panting and twitching in his sleep. She filled his water bowl, which was nearly empty, and saw that he hadn't eaten the cup of kibble she'd given him that morning. "Too hot to eat, huh?" she said, and he responded by lifting his tail and dropping it, once up and once down, no wasted motion.

She steamed the broccoli, patted it dry, then put it in the food processor with two eggs, fresh-grated parmesan, chopped scallions and the quinoa, and pulsed the ingredients till they were combined. The recipe called for almond flour to bind the mixture so it could be shaped into patties and she was briefly tempted to substitute a cup of her cricket flour before thinking better of it: What if Peter and Sylvia tried them? Or Allison's husband? She had no idea what allergies he might or might not have and it really wasn't worth finding out. She had a brief vision of him, bony, anemic, balding, with a dandruff-flecked beard and a powder-blue dress shirt buttoned up to the collar as if every occasion were a formal occasion, crouched over the downstairs toilet, vomiting. A tragedy at any time, but in this heat? The thought made her laugh aloud, which made her think she needed a glass of wine. She flicked on the classical channel, poured herself a glass of Chardonnay and measured out a cup of almond flour to add to the mix.

As prearranged, Sylvie showed up at five. This wasn't a surprise party, but Ottilie thought it would be more dramatic, more of an occasion, if Frank were occupied all afternoon, so Peter and Cooper had taken him out for lunch and then a movie at a theater that was reliably air-conditioned except when it wasn't because the brownouts came without warning, like today, like now, when the electricity had died just after four and showed no sign of coming back on anytime soon. Sylvie was here to drink wine and help with the arrangements. She brought flowers with her—a bouquet for the centerpiece of the table and another for the sideboard, though it was a real extravagance, the price of flowers gone astronomical given the water restrictions and the cost of pollinating by hand or courtesy of the Robo-Bees you saw everywhere now as if nature were no longer necessary. Or available. (Which it wasn't, at least as far as the bees were concerned, since they'd never really come back after the first big die-off. Unlike the mosquitoes. Or Elytra's kissing bugs. Was that ironic? Anything that fed off blood was thriving, while the beneficial insects, from ladybugs to butterflies to bees, were barely hanging on. But then, as Cooper was quick to remind her, we were the biggest food resource left on the planet, so what would you expect?)

The first thing Sylvie said was, "I didn't know the party was going to be so informal or I would have just come naked," and for just a fraction of a moment Ottilie didn't know what she was talking about until she realized she wasn't in her two-piece but her still-damp bra and panties.

Was she embarrassed? No. Sylvie was too close a friend for that, and if her hips and thighs could have used a little reduction and her abdomen was maybe a bit slacker than she'd like, what difference did it make—she was seventy years old and in better shape than ninety percent of the women her age. At least she could still walk. And swim. And try out new recipes, like the broccoli-quinoa patties she was going to fry in avocado oil till they were golden—if the electricity came back on, that is. And if it didn't? She didn't want to think about that. Takeout at Frank's retirement party? How reduced the world had become.

"Sure," she said, "why not? If the heat keeps up like this we'll all be going naked. But you look as if you could use some liquid refreshment—white or red?"

The flowers found their way into her two most cherished vases, with just a finger of water in the bottom of each (why waste it: the flowers would be wilted by tomorrow anyway), then they set the table and retired to the pool with the Chardonnay till she had to go in and get dressed for the party. She'd told everyone to come at seven when she hoped it would be cooler, but as she put her makeup on and tried to do something with her hair (which, she saw, was still decorated with the odd streak of spirogyra), it felt hotter than ever, if that was possible. Her phone app informed her that the outside temperature was 116. And that was here, by the sea—she could only imagine what it was like out where Cooper was. "I'm dying," she said to Sylvie and Sylvie laughed and poured them each another glass of wine.

The lights flickered to life around six, which meant that the air-conditioner kicked in and gave them some relief, though the thermometer in the front hall still read 97—that couldn't have been right, could it? She wiped the sweat from her temples and forced herself to drink yet another glass of water, though she was feeling bloated and faintly nauseous as it was. At least now, though, the range was operable so she could cook the veggie patties and the chicken, which came in the form of pan-ready nuggets—and no, she wasn't about to deep-fry them the way they did at the fast-food places, but sauté them in the avocado oil she'd use for the patties. Or cakes. She'd call them cakes, which sounded more upscale than patties, didn't it?

"Call them croquettes," Sylvie said, fanning herself with the Style section of the newspaper.

"And the *chapulines*? What do I call them?"

Sylvie made a face. "I don't know, how about *bugs*? *Fried bugs*?"

"*Insectes frits*?"

"No," Sylvie said, "it's an insult to the language. Let's just call a bug a bug and get it over with."

✻

THE HEAT DOMINATED THE DINNER conversation, what records were being set, would it ever relent, how many of Frank's patients—*former* patients—had suffered heatstroke in the past week and how the first generation of CO_2 scrubbing plants were going online by way of a too-little, too-late attempt at mitigating the problem, but you had to start somewhere, didn't you?

"They're building one in Goleta, where that defunct mall was?" Frank said. "You drive by and they're enclosing the whole space, which must be two acres or more, and it's still just a drop in the bucket."

"How I'd like a drop," she heard herself say. "And a bucket to put it in."

She was feeling the effects of the wine—and the heat, which made her dizzy, the electricity having cut out again halfway through the meal and the candlelight blurring the edges of things—but she was content in the moment, the croquettes a hit and the nuggets too, though every bite was analyzed and debated, especially by Frank and Peter, who found them unconvincing, too tender and yet not tender enough, bland, tasteless, unchickenlike, and where was the muscle fiber? The fat? Allison's husband—he was English, how could she have forgotten that?—fingered his way through the *chapulines* as if they were popcorn and helped himself to second portions of both the croquettes and the chicken and had nothing but praise for the chef. ("Quite savory," he said. "Delectable, really. And these *chapulines*, you say they're bugs? Is that right?")

"Forget the bucket," Cooper said. "Latest long-range forecast is for another catastrophically dry winter in a state that's already in exceptional drought, and what terminology are they going to come up with next—exceptionally exceptional? Extremely exceptionally exceptional?" He'd been sour all evening, everything he had to say a kind of jeer, as if things weren't bad enough already. His face was flushed. His voice was too loud. Was it the heat? Was that it? This was supposed to be a celebration, wasn't it?

"The problem is," Frank said, "what to do with the carbon dioxide these plants capture. You can only carbonate so many cans of Pepsi, right? Pump it underground? Sure, where? How deep? And I read that we'd have to build two hundred and fifty thousand plants like the Goleta one worldwide just to remove one percent of annual emissions. Better we should all just go around in air-conditioned suits—"

"*Fireproof* air-conditioned suits," Cooper put in.

"At least that would solve the mosquito problem," she said, but nobody laughed.

Elytra, loose-limbed and pretty, her hair kinked with sweat and her mascara smudged where she'd been rubbing at her eyes—allergy? the heat?—leaned into the table on her elbows and gave them all a serene smile. "The solution's simple. You go up twelve miles in a fleet of jets and spray sulfuric acid, which combines with water vapor to form sulfate aerosols to reflect sunlight back into space, like happens when you get a major volcanic eruption, and the whole earth cools down because it's got this big umbrella over it."

Cooper swung sharply round on her, angry suddenly, angry again. "Who you going to put in charge of that? The government? Meta? The Chinese? That is just plain asinine."

The subject was depressing. And her son was embarrassing her.

"It's beyond useless," he said, "can't you see that?" He glared round the table, belligerent now, on his high horse. "And if you think technology's going to bail us out of this with some feel-good shit about carbon capture or spraying acid in the stratosphere then I'm sorry but you're all fucking delusional!" He punctuated this by slamming his fist down on the tabletop. His plate jumped. The silverware rattled. His glass, filled to the top with his umpteenth glass of wine, swayed and righted itself.

"You know what's happening here?" he demanded. "You know what this is all about?" In the next moment, he was tearing at his sleeve as if his shirt were on fire, exposing the arm he insisted on keeping hidden even after all these years, even from his family, his father, his mother—his own mother. He raised his arm high, as high as he could reach, and flapped the black mechanical fingers back and forth as if signaling to someone across the room.

Frank said, "Coop."

"Nature bites back," he said. "That's what this is all about. Literally, in my case."

"Stop feeling sorry for yourself," Frank said. "There're plenty of people out there worse off than you. Grow up, already."

Cooper dropped his hand and made a point of slowly wrapping his nylon fingers round the stem of his glass, finger by finger, then raised it in a slow dramatic gesture and drained it in a single gulp, which was embarrassing all over again—what was wrong with him? You sipped wine, he knew that. You savored it. Especially with what a bottle cost these days.

She turned to Elytra, trying to redirect things, and asked her how her research was coming.

"Me?" Elytra looked startled, as if she were still in the stratosphere with her fleet of regulatory planes.

"I mean, with this heat? You're still on kissing bugs, right?"

Kissing bugs—*Triatoma sanguisuga*, properly—fed on the blood of anything they could attach themselves to. They liked heat. And they liked the nests of wood rats, where they were protected from predation and had ready access to their rodent hosts. Elytra collected them by seeking out the nests, briefly evicting the rats and sifting through the litter for the bugs, which were the size of a paper clip and decorated with red, orange or yellow stripes, depending on the species.

"Their numbers are up," Elytra said, "and the percentage carrying Chagas is way up too, close to ninety percent in the samples I'm taking out at the field station."

"Which means what?" Sylvie said. She looked half-asleep, the effect of the wine and the heat, which made everything so hard. *Dinner party.* What had Ottilie been thinking?

"It's a parasite, a trypanosome, formerly rare in California and now right here with us. If you get bitten and it gets into your bloodstream— at night, when you're asleep, so most people don't even know about it, just that here's this itchy bump at the corner of your mouth or eye, like a mosquito bite—it can be serious."

"Myocarditis," Frank said. "I saw a handful of patients with it and mostly we were able to treat them with antiparasitics like nifurtimox and benznidazole, but if you don't catch it early you can wind up with heart failure. Digestive tract problems too, enlarged colon, chronic esophageal swelling. It's not pretty."

"You're scaring me," Sylvie said. "Especially since I don't even know what to look out for—kissing bug, what is a kissing bug?"

"Show her, why don't you?" Cooper said, and here the mechanical fingers came into play again, jerking at the button of Elytra's blouse, which fell open to reveal the outsized tattoo of a bug rendered in two colors, its head and proboscis a solid midnight black, the thorax and abdomen striped with alternating bands of red and black. Elytra wasn't wearing a bra, and who could blame her in this heat? She didn't seem embarrassed, though, except by Cooper, who really was making a spectacle of himself.

"It's pretty," Sylvie said. "Almost, I mean. For a bug."

Peter, leering, said, "Very pretty."

It was then that Allison's husband—Gerald, seated at the far end of the table—murmured, "Sorry," and went slack in his chair, his arms flopping at his sides even as his head thumped down like a cannonball not inches from his dessert plate. There was a moment of stunned disbelief, as with any sudden eruption of the unexpected: Was he joking? Was he going to pop up with a grin and a comment about the potency of the wine or the bite of the *chapulines*? But then Frank was on his feet and ministering to him and Ottilie saw what it was in that moment:

heatstroke. She'd been nervous about it all week, the news full of it, people dying in their bedrooms, on their couches, in lawn chairs and behind the wheels of their cars, and here it was in her own dining room. Rapid pulse, that was one of the signs—and the face, the red face, as the body tried to cool itself by pumping blood to the extremities. Frank propped him up, pressed a thumb to his wrist, then peeled open his eyelids on pupils that were shrunk down to nothing—miosis, another sign. "The pool," Frank said, his voice calm and even. He'd seen it all before and he was seeing it now. "Get him in the pool."

Frank worked an arm under one shoulder, Cooper the other, and then they were all out on the back patio, people holding up their cell phones for the light, the only sound the scrape of their shoes on the Saltillo tiles. They moved in a body to the shallow end of the pool, where Frank and Cooper slid into the water, easing Gerald down between them while Allison, looming over them to direct the beam of her cell phone, kept repeating, "He's going to be all right, isn't he?"

"He'll be fine," Frank said, "just give him a minute."

Gerald was a bundle of wet rags. His face lacked structure. He was breathing fast and hard—*tachycardia*, that was the term, she knew that much. They sank him up to the neck and held him there, Frank splashing water in his face and crooning his name, "Gerald, Gerald, wake up, Gerald," until the crisis was past. After a minute—no more—Gerald shook his head and took command of his limbs, trying to rise to his feet even as Frank pushed him back down. He said, "I must have—" and Frank said, "Yes. And here"—reaching for the glass of water Allison handed him right on cue—"drink this. And no more wine—it just dehydrates you."

The night settled, no light anywhere but for the narrow beams of their cell phones and the muted reflection of the candles glowing behind them in the house, which seemed miles off. Frank cocked his head to scan the dark shapes gathered round the pool, their friends, their dinner guests, all of them hushed and tentative. The stars reared above them. The owl that had recently taken up residence in the eucalyptus grove out back began an intermittent commentary on the state of things. "In fact," Frank said, "that goes for all of you. And while we're at it, I want everybody in the pool, come on, strip down, everybody in."

One by one, they shed their clothes and slipped into the water, laughing softly, at ease now, embraced by the element that had given rise to life in the first place, no sweat, easiest thing in the world, and who needed clothes, anyway? "Pool party," Peter hooted, planting his elbows on the coping and thrashing his feet, his penis bobbing and plunging against a pale flash of pubic hair and the green silk of the water. Sylvie swam the length of the pool and back again, her head and shoulders rhythmically fracturing the faint scrim of light that clung to the surface. Elytra rose and sank and rose again. Gerald, guest of honor by default, stood upright to fish his wallet and car keys out of his pocket, slapping them down on the coping behind him and wondering aloud about his remote—how was he going to start his car? Nobody responded. What was a remote? He could always get another one—he was alive, wasn't he? But Cooper was the one who really came to life, as if the crisis had been orchestrated to set him free. He was transformed. He laughed and shouted, lurching out of the pool and cannonballing back in, over and over, and if his arm was malfunctional, if the batteries shorted out and the components broke down, it really didn't seem to matter anymore.

LATER, WHEN EVERYBODY HAD GONE, she and Frank cleaned up together, gliding round the kitchen in perfect sync, as if they were dancing at a remove. She felt good, he felt good. They'd had their party and no one had died—how about that?

"I should have called the whole thing off," she said, bent over the dishwasher, inserting plates, saucers and cups in the slots designed for them, an activity that always calmed her, form and function, technology at its finest. And yet the machine used water, 2.4 gallons per cycle, and that water went down the drain. Better she should just let Dunphy lick them clean—or prop them up at the base of the orange tree and hose them off.

"It was a great party—one of our best ever. And you know what? The pool made it."

"Poor Gerald," she said.

"Yeah, well, get used to it. This is just the beginning." He set a pan in the sink, squirted it with dish soap and gave it a quick shot of hot water. "Coop's right. In twenty years it'll look like Saudi Arabia here. All the car dealers'll be selling camels."

"And Macy's will have burnooses on special."

He laughed. "Yeah, something like that. I'm glad I'll be in my grave by then."

"Don't say that."

"Give my minerals back to the earth. And your bugs—your bugs can have my flesh."

"You'll live to be a hundred. Easy. And I'll be right there with you."

She was scraping one of the plates into the dog's dish—Cooper's, he'd hardly eaten anything—when a picture of Dunphy came to her, fat, golden-eyed, a connoisseur of people food, and where was he? He might have been old now, clumsy and swaying over the attenuated props of his legs, but he never missed a meal. She called his name. Called again. She turned to Frank. "Have you seen the dog?"

He wasn't under the table, wasn't in the living room or in his bed either. She found him in the laundry room, where he sometimes liked to spread himself out on the tiles where the cold-water pipe climbed up the wall by the washing machine. "Dunphy?" she said. "Come on, boy, it's dinnertime."

He didn't move. And because he spent most of his time asleep—twenty hours a day, at least—there wasn't really all that much she could tell from his posture. Dogs didn't sweat, dogs panted, she knew that.

That was their release, that was how they got rid of excess heat. They died when people locked them in their cars in the parking lot or chained them in the yard with insufficient shade or water, thoughtless people, people who didn't deserve to have a pet.

"Dunphy?" she called again, but Dunphy didn't thump his tail or perk his ears or flick open his eyes—no, he didn't move at all.

22

WHAT IS FLAMMABLE
AND WHAT IS NOT

THE DOG WAS DEAD, NEWS OF WHICH CAME IN THE FIRST text he opened that morning, and so was his $80,000 Hero Arm, and while there was nothing he could do about the dog, reanimating the arm was pretty straightforward—dry out the components, replace the battery, hook it back up and hope for the best. He kept a spare battery and toolkit in the back of the closet for just such an eventuality, though he was going to need the coordination of at least one additional hand to complete the task and Elytra was sleeping late, deep into the furnace of the morning. The night before, in the intensity of the moment, he hadn't been aware of what he was doing—Gerald was unconscious, Gerald was dying, Gerald needed to cool down ASAP. *Get him in the pool,* his father said and he reacted without thinking, the arm so integral to him now he wasn't even aware it was there unless he was in some public place and feeling everybody's eyes lasering in on him.

Once he realized what he'd done, once he was in the pool and his father was in control and Gerald coughed and spat and shot out his arms as if to catch himself in midfall, it was too late to do anything but let the alcohol sing in his veins and get every last lick of enjoyment out of the situation. He set himself free. The heat had its claws in him, but the pool—the release of it, the regeneration, memory of the flesh, childhood, inner tubes, splash fests and diving contests with Jerome and Cat and her friends, *Melody Foster*—put an end to it. And not only to the heat, but whatever it was that had made him so angry and hopeless all day, which of course had more than a little to do with the occasion, his father stepping down after tending to three generations of patients while he himself didn't even have a real job. Or prospects. Or butterflies to catch and tag and study. Or protect, because that was the crux of it. Habitat. Habitat was all. If he only had a spare hundred million—or a billion, make it a billion—he'd buy up every scrap of viable land and plant it with wildflowers and milkweed and find a way to neutralize the pesticides in the soil, create his own private bugtopia, keep out, no trespassing, no Roundup here, no Ortho or Hot Shot or Talstar P. Just dirt. Just life.

It was quarter past seven and he was in the kitchen, frying eggs, when Elytra came in and dropped into her chair as if she'd fallen off a cliff. "Is there any coffee left? Or half-and-half? And would you put an egg on for me—or is that what you're doing?"

He felt . . . not good, not exactly, but all right, given the circumstances. "*No hay problema.* These are things any one-armed man can do with ease."

She looked up at him then, at his dangling sleeve, and asked, "Is it really ruined?"

"I sure hope not," he said. "I've got it out on the picnic table in the sun, which ought to dry it out in short order because that sun is just fucking relentless. I'm just praying I don't have to spring for a new microprocessor."

"Ouch. What's that going to cost?"

"I don't know, too fucking much. Like everything else."

The plan for the day was work. It was Saturday, but he was doing brush clearance out at the field station and she was going back down over the hill to work in the lab at the university, examining field samples in light of the fact that the Chagas trypanosome had been showing up in the blood supply locally, contaminating it, that is, which meant that the parasites didn't even need the kissing bug to infect their hosts anymore—the Red Cross was doing it for them. Or had been until somebody thought to test for *Trypanosoma cruzi*.

She got up to pour herself a cup of coffee while he maneuvered around the hot pan with the spatula. The kitchen was cramped and dirty. Everything was dirty, the whole apartment, which depressed him because this wasn't the way he wanted to live. *You're not much of a house-wife*, he'd said a week after she moved in, and she said, *Neither are you*, and he said, *I'm not a wife*, and she said, *Don't look at me.* Now, stirring honey into her coffee with a spoon that had been stuck to the counter since she'd left it there yesterday morning, she said, "You sure you really want to go out there in this heat?"

"What heat? It's only going to be one-fifteen. I'll probably need a sweater."

"Wear that big straw hat," she said. "And think electrolytes or you're going to wind up like Gerald."

"Poor Gerald."

"And the poor dog," she said. "We should have put him in the pool too."

THERE WAS A GATE AT the entrance to the field station, where the county blacktop ended and the dirt road began, and you needed to have the code to gain access. It was a way of keeping people out, people who would otherwise bury the place in a drift of broken glass, shit-stained diapers and discarded mattresses while blasting away at anything that moved with their assault rifles and 3-D-printed Glocks and Berettas and whatever else they had tucked in their waistbands. Cooper appreciated the gate. He was all for it. And he felt privileged every time he punched in the code and it swung back for him, one of the consolations of the terms of his employment that had seen him devolve from researcher to tool-sharpener and handyman, though he'd never been particularly handy, even before his abridgment. Still, once he drove through the gate, he was in another world, the kind of world he wanted to abide in, where the flora and fauna had a chance to survive without interference. Immediate interference, that is—there was no escaping the climate catastrophe, which was stressing everything, leaves hanging limp on the trees, water sources exhausted, the grasses waving like a hundred million match heads awaiting the moment of combustion. Which was why he was out here today, despite the heat—because of the heat—to do his part to mitigate the fire danger.

The reserve that incorporated the field station was a former cattle ranch donated to the university thirty years ago, six thousand acres backing up to Los Padres National Forest. Before that it had been home to the Chumash, who'd inhabited this very ground for some eight hundred years before they were evicted in the 1820s, which was a crime, a shame, one more black mark in the annals of colonialism and all the rest of it, but the point was the land had never been given over to development—there'd been no oil wells here, no chemical plants or shopping centers or pavement even, and that made it as close to natural as you could find along the California coast. The cattle, in their day, had browsed and trampled the native plants and kicked up dust and contributed their flatus to the stew of greenhouse gases superheating the world, but the cattle were long gone and the ranch hands with them, and today, here in the killing heat, he had the place to himself.

There were a couple of cars parked in the shade of the oaks out front of the main building, but no one was stirring, and he really wasn't feeling very social anyway, so no loss there. He was going to get social later, meeting up with Elytra in the tavern at the top of the pass to knock back rum and Coke in a plastic cup, dance till he was sweated out and consume barbecue chips fresh from the foil-lined bag and then maybe a Cobb salad (hold the meat) from the self-consciously rustic restaurant next door where everybody was a California cowboy or the best friend of one. He had a gallon jug of water with him, which he transferred to the pickup someone had donated to the field station in a time before his time, then laid his tools in the bed—weed whacker, chain saw, hoe, mattock, rake—and drove out past the moribund pond into which they were obliged to pump precious well water to keep the fish, frogs and aquatic insects alive. (And everything else too: the tracks of bear, bobcat, wild boar, deer, coyote and mountain lion were intaglioed in the mud all the way around the shoreline and the trail cam one of the researchers had set up routinely captured their ghostly manifestations on film, the paw raised, the hoof planted, eyes hungry and hard and focused.)

There was a radio in the truck but he didn't want the radio. He wanted to hang his left arm out the window in the crucible of the sun and watch the way the irradiated grasses staggered up the hills till the dark tourniquets of mesquite and toyon choked them off, everything still and golden and nothing to distract him but the crunch of the tires and the way the light sat in the trees with the equinox coming on. The good news was that his right arm seemed to be working the way the manufacturer intended, which meant the microprocessor hadn't been damaged and he wasn't going to have to park himself in a chair and stare into the TV screen till Amazon delivered a replacement. His hand was on the wheel, the tires crept in and out of the potholes, the chassis swayed. Behind him the dust pooled and swirled and went airborne, smelling of pulverized earth and the oils the sun leached out of the plants.

He was no more than half a mile from the field station when he came around a bend and saw the tree there blocking the road, a gray pine that had given way to the twin imperatives of bark beetles and gravity, with an assist from the drought. This was a stretch where the vegetation needed to be cut back, which he'd intended to do since spring but was just now getting around to, having concentrated his efforts on the growth nearest the buildings and then radiating out from there. He decided to deal with the pine first, then take the weed whacker to the grass—at least he'd be in the shade of the trees, for what it was worth.

He was wearing jeans and a denim shirt (long-sleeved, always long-sleeved, no matter the heat), but before he was halfway through his second cut the fabric was clinging to him and his socks were nothing more than sponges oozing in his boots. His toes felt amphibious. His hair dripped. The shirt was pointless, actually, so he peeled it off and flung it through the window of the cab, nobody out here to see him anyway, but there was nothing he could do about the socks—you couldn't wear sandals, not unless you were okay with poison oak blisters erupting between your toes or the venom of pissed-off rattlesnakes racing for your heart. He took a long swig of water, then went back to work on the tree, supporting the weight of the saw with his left hand and guiding it with his right. He was deep in the dream of work, seeing nothing but the sectioned pine and hearing only the screech of the saw, when he glanced up at a sudden movement on the road ahead of him.

It wasn't a deer. Wasn't a bear or boar or mountain lion—it was a human being. A female human being, dressed all in white, coming like an epiphany toward him with her face flowering in surprise, a smile now, a wave, and he saw in that instant that this was Mari, *here was Mari*, out for a reminiscent jaunt in the preserve where she used to work on a day when the temperature was already pushing a hundred. He killed the saw and set it down without thinking, right there where the dead yellow pine needles flecked the dust of the road and the dead yellow grasses ran back from the verge and all the way up to the underskirts of the mountain. But he wasn't thinking about that—or how hot the saw blade might have gotten as it tore through the trunk of the tree or the way the tank dribbled fuel because the cap, which had come from another model altogether, didn't fit as snugly as it might. No, he was thinking about her, about her gaze and her reaction and what she must have been thinking about him. And his arm. She'd seen it before, back when he'd first got it, when they shared things and went places and she woke up in his bed a couple of days a week, but that didn't matter because this was now and he felt vulnerable and weak and always would till some alpha-geek bioengineer came up with the formula for growing it back again.

Her eyes never left his face (*Arm? What arm?*) as she waded through the slew of lopped-off branches and found her way to him. "Another tree down," she said. "I saw it when I was hiking out and I was thinking, well, at least it's one less thing that's going to burn, right?"

He gave her her smile back. She was looking good, looking strong, as if she could hike another twenty miles, right on up over the mountain and back, heat or no heat. She didn't need makeup, had never needed makeup. Mari. Her legs. Her breasts. Her lips. Her teeth. "Bark beetles," he said. "*Ips spinifer* the suspect in this case."

Neither of them noticed what was happening with the saw and the thinnest vaguest noncommittal wisp of smoke it was generating among the pine needles lying thick in the roadway, the moment awkward in the extreme, both of them sending out feelers along the lines of how've you been, how's work, I saw your mother in the store the other day, yeah, she told me, what's it like up there in Oregon, must be tick heaven . . . Just as he was about to say, "You want to have a cup of coffee or a sandwich or a drink or something, because I can always do this tomorrow," the wind swooped down the funnel of the road to rattle the trees and enliven the tinder beneath the saw, sending a perfect little ribbon of flame fanning across the dirt and into the grass.

It was like a trick of the eye: there was no fire, then there was. They both registered it in the same instant and in the next instant they were on it, stamping and kicking up dirt, and never mind the look of panic on her face or the fact that the joke was on him. "Shit!" he said, or maybe he said, "Fuck!," one of those monosyllabic expressions of anger, dismay and horror that was as automatic as a dog's bark. She echoed him as the flames got up and jumped into a clump of chamise that was interlaced with another clump and another and the wind fed them oxygen, snapping and crackling, and was he going to be the one to burn down the entire preserve and destroy everything they'd all worked for? No, absolutely not, because here he was with the mat from the driver's side of the truck, beating at the flames, and she was right there beside him with the mat from the other side. Adrenaline ruled. The mats rose and fell. The fire didn't stand a chance, did it?

Reconstructing it later, he wasn't sure if he stumbled into her or vice versa, but at one point they both went down together and by the time they got back up the Nylon 12 of his Hero Arm was singed and her blouse desecrated with soot, yet it was a small price to pay when you took the larger view because it was their bodies, their knees, groins, chests and backs that definitively knocked the fire down, drop and roll—the whole thing, from ignition to extinction, couldn't have taken more than five minutes.

"Jesus," he said, "what was that all about?"

She didn't answer, just bent to scoop up dirt with her bare hands and drop it on anything that looked even vaguely questionable. Feeling guilty, feeling stupid, he got the rake out of the back of the truck and gave the whole area a savage going-over until he felt her eyes on him and glanced up. "If I'd known," she said, "I would have brought marshmallows."

There was a black smudge under her left eye. Her sweat ran dark, then clear, dripping from the tip of her nose. He looked down at the saw, which was undamaged as far as he could tell. Blackened leaves and grass stalks fanned out from it like abstract art, charcoal on dirt. "My bad," he said. "But it was a good thing you were here—you saved my ass."

She acknowledged this with a nod, then clapped her hands and wiped them on the flanks of her jeans before reaching up to push the hair out of her face. He wanted to ask if she was dating anybody, some fellow bug nerd up there at the U of O, somebody negligible, but he had no right to do that. Or at least not till they'd gone through the preliminaries.

"This is insane," he said. "It's too hot to work, way too hot, a million times too hot. Really, I don't know what I was thinking." He ran his fingers over the rough spot on the prosthesis where the Nylon 12 had blackened and melted, a scar there, and how about that? Not flesh, but scarred all the same. "You want to grab a cup of coffee or a beer or sand-wich or something? Or iced tea, how does iced tea sound?"

IT WAS TOO EARLY FOR a beer, but after they'd cleaned up at the field station, she thought it sounded like a good idea to have a sandwich, and yes, iced tea, anything cold, right?, and he followed her in his car over to Dos Juanitos and a table tucked inside by the air-conditioner. She ordered a breakfast burrito—with ham, though she knew he disap-proved or maybe she'd forgotten or didn't care because what he thought or felt or declaimed to the world meant nothing to her under the present circumstances—and he had the same thing, only without meat, because meat was murder, for starters, and it was the carnivores who'd destroyed the earth, fueling the Auschwitz of the slaughterhouse and lining up at In-N-Out Burger with their motors idling for as long as it took for the animal matter to sizzle on the grill and the air to turn to poison. She saw the look on his face and said, "I like ham once in a while, so shoot me."

"I don't want to shoot you," he said, holding it beat and letting his eyes settle on hers. "I want to fuck you."

Almost all the tables were occupied and people were backed up at the cash register for takeout though it wasn't yet noon—Saturday, brunch crowd, nachos, pico de gallo, enchiladas, tostadas, tacos al car-bón, the smell of singed meat like a ticket to the fiesta, and Mari giving him a long look of concentration. She didn't flinch. Didn't even blink her eyes. "You blame me, don't you?" she said.

He said, "No," automatically, though that was the truth of it. He could never be like BeeBee Potrero or that other guy in rehab, whose name he didn't even remember, the one who flaunted his protheses as if they were a fashion choice, because his self-image had never been all that rock-solid to begin with. *Bug boy, science nerd, geek.* If he had to rate his own looks on a scale of one-to-ten for a psychological profile, he would have assigned himself a seven or so, though his mother—and Melody

Foster and maybe Elytra—would have given him a nine, a nine at least. Irrespective of his mutilation, that is. In the bedroom in his apartment, on a white oak stand he'd got online from IKEA, was the memento he'd been left with, his totem in a jar of formalin, the puckered etiolated arm with its fading wrist tattoo. *Why don't you get the same design on your other wrist?* Elytra had asked him after she'd added a blood-engorged anopheles mosquito to her epidermal gallery (in her left armpit, where nobody could see it unless she raised her bare arm, sexiest thing in the world) and he told her he was waiting for his arm to regenerate.

"You have to move on," Mari said.

"Grow up, you mean? Take it like a man? Get a life?"

She was studying him with that maddening scientific objectivity, her eyes rinsed of anything like emotion. "I'm engaged," she said.

"Congratulations. But tell me it's not a biologist."

"He's a politician. Councilperson, actually. Ward Five."

"I don't know what's worse," he said. "But then you've always liked bloodsuckers."

She didn't react, which somehow disappointed him. He was joking, of course, but then he wasn't. They'd just been through something climactic out there at the field station, transformational even, her blouse still damp and discolored where she'd dabbed at the stains with a wet paper towel, and when he'd chosen the term *fuck* instead of *make love* or *get naked together* or any of the other half-ass euphemisms, he was trying to provoke her, yes, but still it was an overture and she'd shot that right down. Which made a flare of anger rocket through him, anger compounded by his own guilt and venality and the fact—he just noticed, just now—that some bozo at the bar was wearing shorts so he could show off a leg prosthesis as crude and in-your-face as a pogo stick, and what was the guy thinking, what was wrong with him?

"I want a beer," he said, rising to his feet. "You want a beer? Or a margarita? How about a margarita?"

"I don't know," she said, "it's early yet. And I've got to be going at some point, but you go ahead—"

"Is that a yes?"

She shrugged.

"What about more salsa, some of that chipotle or the super-hot stuff, you like that, don't you?"

"Sure," she said, "okay. The green one?"

Their waitress was a harried scrawny blonde who looked all of twelve and was clearly over her head with the brunch crush, so on his way back from the salsa station he squeezed in at the bar and ordered two margaritas by way of expediting matters. When the bartender set them in front of him, along with the check, instead of just pointing to his table, he dug in his pocket for his wallet, which involved balancing the two little plastic ramekins of salsa on his right palm, which should have been routine, no big deal, nothing at all, except that the guy showing off his prothesis, who was sitting two stools down, was giving him a look he didn't appreciate. The guy was forty or so, beefed up with the evidence of the hours he devoted to the gym, the paneled chest, biceps like tortured animals, his head shaved to stubble and his face looking as if it had been painted on, damage there, war damage, no doubt, and how many times had he been mistaken for a vet himself? And sure enough, here it was: the lips drawn back in a bitter mocking all-hail-the-freaks grin, and what unit were you in? It was a real shitstorm over there. Mazar-i-Sharif, Herat, Kandahar.

Just as he slapped open his wallet on the bar with his left hand, his good hand, the one that worked without mechanical assistance, without stint or worry, the Hero Arm gave out on him over there on the dextral side. He didn't have time to reevaluate vis-à-vis the viability of the microprocessor or whether the battery still held its charge or if the working parts had oxidized, because the arm was hanging dead at his side and the two varieties of salsa, one red, one green, were decorating the lap of the woman he'd shoved in next to at the bar. She was middle-aged, with an enormous head and a fluffed-out nimbus of hair that just added to the effect. There was a smear of guacamole at the corner of her mouth. She looked like a man, might have been a man for all he knew.

"What are you doing?' she demanded, her eyes burning with out-rage as if he were pulling some sort of mean-spirited prank on her.

He was going to say he was sorry, make apologies, offer to pay to have her dress cleaned, all of it, everything, get right down and abase himself if only he didn't have to own up to his abridgment, here, now, in public, but then the pogo-stick guy—was he with her?—burst out with a laugh even as he could see Mari at the periphery of his vision in the act of getting up to come to the rescue as if she were his minder still. All right. Fine. Mari wasn't going to fuck him anyway, or he her, however the grammar went, so what did he care? What he cared about was the guy with the pogo stick for a leg who should have known bet-ter, should have been laughing at himself, and so he took his drink in his good hand, leaned in carefully over the woman's back and flung it directly in his face.

23

EATEN FROM WITHIN

SO THEY HAD A CAT ("CAT'S GOT A CAT," R.J. QUIPPED, "HOW cool is that?"). He peed and crapped in a plastic kitty litter pan, crawled under the sheets to sleep with Tahoe at night, ate roaches, kibble and two three-ounce cans of Fancy Feast a day, ate constantly, making up for the privation he'd suffered in the abandoned house where he must have subsisted on a thin diet of whatever he could catch—rats, she supposed, mice, bugs. Tahoe named him Hambre (not Hombre, but Hambre, because he was hungry all the time and she was picking up words and phrases from the kids at school and the cartoons on TV and inserting them in whole strings of sentences as if Spanish and English were interchangeable). Most days the yard was flooded, so they really didn't have to worry about the cat going any- where and Tahoe was good about keeping the front door closed in any case, letting him out only on the deck, where he could get some fresh air and harass the gulls and deposit the occasional coiled turd in back of the gas grill but couldn't get down to water level even if he wanted to. Unless he could fly.

The cat was a positive thing, absolutely, a thing they bonded over and felt good about ("We rescued him, Mom!"), and if the camouflage pattern of his coat reminded her, unfortunately, of Willie II, she could live with that. Call it karma. You could breed a thousand generations of snakes and they'd still be wild, still be snakes with snake brains, but the Bengal was a hybrid created by cross-breeding wild and domestic cats so you got the best of both worlds. It knew humans. It was affectionate. The wildness was in its coat, though like all cats it was a killing machine. Hambre got a bird once in a while, which she didn't like at all, but he was discreet about it and never left anything but feathers behind. And he was hell on cockroaches.

One morning, after she'd dropped Tahoe at school, she came home to find him outside on the steps. It was one of those increasingly rare days during which the ocean stayed where it was supposed to and the yard was above water—he could have taken off if that was what he'd wanted but here he was, flattened to the tread of the third stair up, his eyes fixed on her, tail twitching. All she could think was, *He needs to go back in the house*, but when she leaned forward to pick him up, cooing to him, nice cat, good cat, *gatito bueno*, the step suddenly gave way beneath her and she lurched forward, giving herself a scare and scraping her forearm in the process. Hambre, startled, shot past her and disappeared around the corner at the base of the steps, the flag of his tail furled for speed. That was bad enough, but this, right here before her, was worse: the wood of the step was eaten from within and it was alive with bugs, little white pustular things with orange heads, and where the step met the wall she could see the same damage there, working its way inside. Her arm was bleeding. The cat was gone. But her house, her beach house, the only house she'd ever owned or was likely to own unless she won the lottery (which she'd never played and never would, only suckers need apply), was under siege.

You didn't need to be an entomologist to know that these little

white things were termites, Formosan termites, a kind of metastasiz-
ing arthropodal cancer that would devastate everything if she didn't get
right on it. Which would require tenting and the spraying of poisons—
sulfuryl fluoride, for starters, fipronil in direct application for backup—
and what was that going to cost? Todd already balked at the alimony he
had to lay out each month and he wasn't going to be happy about this at
all, as if it were her fault, and she could already hear him, *Don't tell me
you didn't have it inspected all this time?*

She made some phone calls. She was coffeed up, the words coming so fast the people on the other end of the line just listened till they
broke in to say they could send somebody out next week or the week
after, which wasn't good enough, not even close. Finally she thought of
Roger Tish, who owned Bobo's and Le Matin down the coast in Day-
tona Beach and who'd come on to her in an overt way a couple of times
when she was working her shift, which made her feel uncomfortable in
the extreme, but she couldn't think of anybody else, so she called him
and he put her in touch with a company called BugOut, which sent a
representative that afternoon—at low tide, thankfully. By the time the
representative arrived—a woman, not a man, who came up the stairs
with Hambre in her arms as if cat-fetching were part of the service—
she was so agitated she'd opened a bottle of wine. She knew she was
going to have to eat something before she went to pick up Tahoe, yet the
mood she was in required a straight application of vino rosso, unadul-
terated, and so she might have been just the slightest bit off-kilter when
she pulled open the door.

The fact that it was a woman standing there was the first surprise
(bug-killing was the province of men—killing anything, for that matter), and then, of course, the cat, which she'd called repeatedly and left
the door ajar for and was on the verge of going down to look for under
the house, but hadn't quite . . . She took the cat from the woman as if it
were a bouquet and let her smile blossom. "That step down there? Did
you see that step?"

The woman was in her mid-twenties, dressed in a beige uniform tailored to emphasize her figure, and she wore a cap with the logo of the company printed on the crown. She was pretty, striking even, but her skin was blotchy and red, as if she'd been exposed to too much sun—or chemicals, poisons that ate away at the fabric of life and persisted in the soil and the fatty cells of the human body, and what would Cooper have to say about that? Her name tag, gold lettering against a black background, read LANI.

"Termites," she said. "But you already knew that. You got dry rot too."

"Dry rot? With all this flooding—and the rain, *Jesus*—shouldn't it be, I don't know, wet rot?" She was trying to be flippant, make a joke, ingratiate herself because this woman was here to help her correct a problem that was seriously freaking her out, the whole house being gnawed out from under her, and were they in the walls, the ceiling, behind the refrigerator and the countertops? The cabinets? And the floors—were the floors going to give way like that step?

"You probably got wet rot too, but we won't know till we do a complete inspection, top to bottom. I mean, from the looks of it, you could have structural damage here."

"Dry rot, wet rot—are you serious? What's the difference?"

Lani just shook her head. "It's all bad. We're seeing a lot of both lately—and, of course, the termites too. Dry rot and wet rot are both funguses, just that the wet rot is more likely to occur where there's direct contact with water, people's bathroom floors, that sort of thing. Basements, if they have them."

"But you can fix it, right?"

"We don't give estimates till we know what we're dealing with—the extent, I mean. But we can treat it right away, that's our job, that's what we do."

They were still standing in the doorway, Hambre clinging to her shoulder, Lani holding up a brochure featuring a magnified photo of a termite, which she handed her by way of illustration. "I can do a preliminary right now and schedule the full-scale inspection for tomorrow. Is that okay with you?"

She didn't like what was happening, didn't like the diagnosis, didn't even want to think what this was going to cost. She just nodded.

"Okay, so what we do if we find what I'm pretty sure we're going to find judging from what I've already seen, is we're giving you top priority on scheduling, because these things can chew through a five-foot length of two-by-four every three weeks"—she paused to level her gaze on her—"and you don't want that, do you?"

TODD SHOWED UP UNANNOUNCED three days later. He looked good, she had to admit, his chest and arms buffed out and his tan so uniform it might have been lathered on, which, maybe it was. He'd never used a spray-on tan, but she wouldn't put it past him—looks, appearances, that was Todd to a T. He wasn't driving the Tesla, but a new black BMW X3, exactly the car she'd wanted, which she might have called ironic, except that ironic didn't apply—this was more a slap in the face. He didn't have a girlfriend with him, though, so that was something, and she wouldn't even have seen the car except that the floodwaters had finally receded and the county had repaired the washed-out section of the road so that he was able to drive up to the house and park out front on the street. It was a Saturday, noonish, the sun shining and the temperature in the eighties—all in all, a nice day. She'd spent the morning getting the place ready for the fumigator, sealing foodstuffs and clothes and sheets and pillowcases in the Nylofume bags BugOut had provided and packing for a three-day vacation in the Bahamas with R.J. and his brother.

"You've got to be out of the house for seventy-two hours, right?" R.J. had said. "And Stoneman and I want to see a man about a snake down there, so . . ."

"Tahoe's got school."

"She can miss a couple of days, can't she?"

It took her all of ten seconds to agree that Tahoe could, in fact, miss a couple of days, especially since she couldn't be at home anyway, and then she called Daria, who said she'd take the cat, and that sealed the deal.

And now—she wasn't looking her best, just wearing an old pair of shorts and a sweatshirt, her hair unwashed and her eyes like two pits dug in the middle of her face—she went to answer the doorbell and there was Todd leaning against the rail, his arms laden with shopping bags. He'd brought toys for Tahoe, as he always did (a Zoe doll and a Creator Cam so she could make her own videos), but he'd brought champagne too and takeout from Sakada—three *poke* bowls and an assortment of sushi, including *ebi*, Tahoe's favorite. "Hi, babe," he said, flashing his ambassador's grin, and in the next moment they were hugging and it was as if she'd gone back in time.

He breezed right into the house like he still lived there, still owned it, and she thought he was going to comment on the state of the place— it could have been cleaner and there were thumbtack holes in the walls where she'd taken down Tahoe's summer drawings and hadn't got around yet to putting up the autumn ones (not that they were all that much different, since there were no autumn leaves to depict and Tahoe, to be honest, didn't seem destined to have a future as an art- ist, though that wasn't for Cat to say)—but he didn't. He went to the kitchen, extracted the two bottles of champagne and slipped them into the refrigerator, then pushed through the door to the deck and began arranging the food on the teak table they'd bought together to replace the funky wrought-iron one his mother had left behind. That was . . . well, interesting, in a way that tugged at her just the smallest little bit. Todd. Being domestic.

She followed him out with a pair of champagne flutes and the cloth napkins. "This is a surprise," she said. "What's the occasion? I mean, it's been *months* . . ."

"I was here just last month, remember? To take Tahoe to Gator-World? And I was in the vicinity so I figured why not, let's do it up." He maneuvered round her to duck back inside and fetch the Fiestaware bowls because it just wouldn't do to eat out of a plastic take-out box, and then he was back again, easing the *poke* into the bowls and arranging the sushi on a platter.

She watched his back, the muscles there bunching and releasing. She said, "You saw the step, right?"

"How could I miss it? You can spot the yellow tape from the street." Was that a critical comment? Was he going to break the mood now and start criticizing her? But no—he was smiling as if it were nothing to get excited about, as if termite damage were part of some elaborate comedy routine. "You get an estimate?"

"Not yet. Just for the tenting. She'll have the inspection report by the end of the week, she said."

"She?"

"You'd be surprised what women can do," she said. "We can pack our fat cells with pesticides just as easily as any man can."

He gave her a lingering look—not unfriendly, far from it. "But you and Tahoe'll be out of the house, so no problem, right? And it takes, what, a couple of days for the spray till it's safe to come back, and then, what, you hire somebody to wipe down all the surfaces? Or does the exterminator do that?"

"Seventy-two hours," she said. "And yeah, they're going to do it."

"Package deal, huh?"

"She already mentioned somebody for the repair work, once they find out how extensive it is, and she's not trying to push it, just a local company, father and son, she likes—"

"You contact the insurance?"

"Not yet."

"Because the deductible's ridiculous. And they don't do mold, nobody does mold. Termites, I'm pretty sure, but I really don't know. If they can screw you, they will."

"Maybe we get lucky and it's just the step and that hole where they got into the house."

"Fat chance."

Here it comes, she thought: *Why didn't you?* and *I told you so*, the old resentments, the anger, and what *was* the name of the latest girlfriend, the one he was living with in Miami, the one who was far from imperfect? But he didn't say a word and the moment slid away. He gave her a smile, the flawless teeth, the dimples, Todd. "Let's crack that champagne," he said. "And where's my big girl—she in her room?"

LATER, AFTER TAHOE HAD COME charging down the hall shrieking, "Daddy! Daddy!" and clung to him till he released her and forked over the presents, after they'd sat at the table like a family, working their chopsticks and sipping their drinks while Tahoe alternately cooed to her new doll and chattered about everything she could think of, school, friends, toys past, present and future, music, TV, her tablet and her bike and the skiff she was allowed to pilot on the way to school when the streets were flooded, after Hambre slunk out the door and sprang to the table and then the railing and Todd's eyes watered and he sneezed and had a coughing jag, they opened the other bottle of champagne and let the day settle over them like a down comforter.

For a long while she just listened to him talk, the intonation and rhythm of his voice inhabiting some deep part of her, real and present in a way nobody else's was. "You remember Tanya?" he asked.

"I don't know, which one is she?"

"Come on, Cat—we were living together the past two years?"

"Yeah, so?"

"So we broke up like three months ago and you know what? It's a relief. She was"—he waved a hand in extenuation and left it at that. "I don't know," he said. "I'm not seeing anybody, I'm really tired of all that shit. What about you? You still with R.J.?"

She didn't answer, just reached for the bottle, which was almost empty, and filled her glass to the top. She knew what was going to come next. They were going to have cocktails and at some point go out to dinner at one of the nice places on the water, a family, a family still, because that's how the biology worked, then come home so he could read Tahoe her bedtime story. They'd sit on the couch and watch something on Netflix and they'd start fooling around and he'd spend the night and if the termites were in the walls they could chew away to their hearts' content. If they even had hearts.

SHE'D NEVER BEEN TO THE Bahamas—Hawaii, yes, Acapulco, Cabo, but never anything off the East Coast—and she was looking forward to the trip, just to get out of town, see something different for a change. Her life was nothing to complain about—she had Tahoe, the house, R.J., her parents were still alive and going strong, the beach hadn't vanished yet and she'd gotten used to the idea of running errands in the skiff when the tide was up, almost as if she were living in Venice, which was exotic, which was cool—but there were days, too many days, when she felt the heavy gravitational creep of boredom and started drinking earlier than she'd like. She had no hope of being an influencer anymore, that was over, but she kept her hand in under a pseudonym and posted pictures and commentary on beachfront living, cuisine and fashion, and had attracted 2,500 followers, which was better than nothing and was a way of justifying the time she spent online (2,521, actually, as of last count).

She and Tahoe flew to Miami with R.J. and his brother, then connected for Lynden Pindling Airport in Nassau, and the whole trip took just over five hours and cost $350 round trip, though you could fly there direct in an hour and a half for $16,000, if money was no object, but of course money was an object. In any case, R.J., whose business must have been doing better than she thought, paid for her and Tahoe's fares and the hotel too. Tahoe loved it. There was a mob of sunburned kids jumping in and out of the pool all day long and when she got tired of that she made a playhouse of the room, tenting the sheets on her bed, scrolling through the TV channels as if she'd never seen a remote before, and no, they were not ordering room service because it cost a small fortune, so let's just content ourselves with the restaurant, okay? Or, better yet, McDonald's? At least for lunch?

For her part, she spent most of the day sitting by the pool with her iPad and a cocktail, diving in every once in a while to refresh herself, and that was nice—the pool, the Black barman with his shirt open down the front so you could admire his six-pack—but otherwise the view out to sea wasn't much different from what she got at home. Clearer water maybe, but the waves were more or less the same, washing in and out like some bodily function, ditto palms, the sun, the sailboats bobbing at anchor. Gulls, buzzards, parrots in the trees. Lizards. R.J. and his brother spent the three days cruising out to one of the smaller islands, chasing after snakes, something she wanted nothing to do with, thank you very much. When they got back, though, they all got together for some lively dinners and washed everything down with rum punch—and so what if it was fattening, she was on vacation—and on the second night, Stoneman babysat so she and R.J. could check out the clubs and go dancing under the stars and have a good time.

No, everything was great, no complaints. Until they flew back to Miami.

There was a dog at customs, an ordinary mutt you might see anywhere, black with a white banner down the middle of its snout, floppy ears, nothing threatening, not a German shepherd or Doberman with their edge of unpredictability, just a dog. Cute, almost. But it keyed on Stoneman, which at first she thought was kind of funny till she saw the look on his face. The dog sniffed him, its ears cocked, then glanced up at its handler, a man in uniform with a regulation mustache and hair shaved tight to his skull, before settling down on its haunches, eyes fixed on Stoneman. "He's cute," Tahoe said. "Is he a boy or girl?"

"No petting," the handler said—the cop, that is, whatever sort of cop he might have been, NSA, DEA, CBP, but not ordinary police because she didn't recognize the uniform. And then, to her: "Ma'am? Please restrain your child."

Tahoe loved animals, loved dogs, and Cat had promised to get her one someday, but wasn't Hambre enough for now? And if she'd leaned forward to stroke the dog's ears, where was the crime in that?

The handler repeated himself, "Ma'am?," and she said, "Tahoe, no."

The dog never moved, never even blinked. It just sat there staring up at the great mountain of flesh that was Stoneman. And then the handler said, "I'm going to have to ask you to step over here," indicating a hallway across from the customs desk even as R.J. thrust his face in and said, "Is there a problem?"

But here was the thing: He knew there was a problem and knew exactly what that problem was and he never gave a thought to the repercussions, which entailed all four of them, their group, their party, being escorted down that hallway and into a smoked-glass interview room. And searched. Like criminals. Even Tahoe.

THERE WERE TWO AGENTS NOW, same mustache, same haircut, same build, and when they insisted that Stoneman remove his shirt, the problem—Stoneman's problem, R.J.'s problem, and now hers too—was revealed. Looped round his midsection in two long tubes of flexible plastic, the kind you might use on an aquarium filter, only bigger in diameter, considerably bigger, were a pair of identical silver snakes—boas, from the look of them. Perforations over their mouths and nostrils allowed for the passage of air; the tubing was fastened to Stoneman's bare skin with strips of clear surgical tape. And the snakes? The silver boas (*Chilabothrus argentum*) that were, as she was soon to discover, among the rarest snakes in the world, if not the very rarest? They were squeezed in those tubes like sausages and couldn't have moved if they'd wanted to.

The second agent produced a pair of handcuffs and in a voice that might have been a recording for all its lack of inflection or emotion, announced, "I am hereby placing you under arrest for violating the Lacey Act, 16 USC 3371–3378," then fitted the cuffs around Stoneman's wrists and read him his rights. Stoneman said nothing. He just stood there while the agent photographed the snakes against the dead-white sweating rolls of his flesh, then stripped off the tape without ceremony and carefully set the snakes—the contraband—on the stainless steel counter behind him.

All this time—three minutes, four, five?—she hadn't said a word, either in denial or protest. She was sick with fear, feverish, drowning in the moment: Was she going to be charged as an accomplice? Were they going to handcuff her too like they'd done that catastrophic day in her own living room? Charge her with smuggling, animal abuse, knowingly and willfully bringing contraband into the country, being a bad mother, a bad influence, the worst? And why did it have to be *snakes*, snakes of all things? They were searching R.J. now, not that it mattered, because all she could focus on was the specter of Child Protective Services and the voice screaming in her head: *Unfit mother. Python Mom. Jailbird. Perp.*

She stood there rigidly, clutching her daughter's hand as they patted R.J. down, in shock, yes, but then the shock exploded into fury—what had he been thinking, dragging her into this? The jerk, the fuckup, the moron. Him, of all people? The man who'd lived through the trauma with her, lifted her up during the worst period of her life, slept in her bed, treated Tahoe as if she were his own daughter, tucked her in, read her stories, made her feel special. And then the thought came to her that he'd set the whole thing up purposely, coldly, with forethought and calculation, using her and Tahoe as cover, the happy family, the vacationers, father, mother, child and the big innocuous uncle in the shirt so outsized it could have been a tent.

It was a female agent who searched her and Tahoe. She directed them to a screened-off area at the back of the room that contained nothing but a single plastic-top table and a poster on the wall that listed, in both English and Spanish, the items you were prohibited from bringing into the country, along with their symbolic representations. There was the outline of a pistol, a monkey in a cage, seeds, plants, pills, a hypodermic syringe. Tahoe, who was never at a loss for words, no matter the circumstances (she was a talker, just like her father), was strangely silent, as if she'd caught the cues from the men who'd searched first Stoneman and then R.J.—as if she knew she shouldn't say anything, as if she was *scared*. It was outrageous, unforgivable—to put a child through this? She wanted to protest, tell the woman they didn't know anything about it, about the snakes and whatever else Stoneman—or R.J.—might be carrying on their persons or in their luggage or what their motives were, but she didn't. She'd learned her lesson the first time around, when they'd come to the house and took hold of her wrists and clapped the handcuffs on her, no mercy, no extenuation, no pleas.

The agent didn't make a single concession to her or her daughter, didn't even speak beyond issuing her terse orders, *Stand here*; *Empty your pockets*; *Put your personal items on the table.* Her hair was up in a bun. She wore a face mask. She took a moment to snap on a pair of Nitrile gloves, then announced, "I'm just going to pat you down, okay?" And it was like what happens at security if you set off the alarm when you pass through the scanner, a pat-down, that was all, and then the wand too, up and down their bodies, their limbs, and it was a good thing the woman didn't attempt to touch her daughter anyplace beyond that because she wouldn't have been able to tolerate that no matter what it cost her. That was the point of no return. Her face might have been drained of blood and she might have looked compliant, ashamed, whipped, but inside she was on fire. She hated this woman, hated this place, but most of all, she hated R.J.

The silver boas lay motionless on the table beyond the curtain, the rarest of rare, all but forgotten in the moment because the moment was about human beings and their deception and greed. The species was found only on the Conception Island Bank in the Bahamas, and hadn't been discovered till 2015, when a team of researchers spotted an individual clinging to the fronds of one of the silver palms that was to give it its name. It was primarily arboreal and had evolved to match the color of the palm itself so it could evade predators while feeding on birds and birds' eggs in the treetops. No one knew how many of these snakes existed, but given the scant range the species enjoyed, its numbers had to be minuscule, which accounted for its critically endangered status, which, in turn, made it all the more irresistible to herpetologists, collectors and, especially, traders. One of the two specimens that had been concealed in Stoneman's adipose folds was a gravid female; the other was a male.

BOTH STONEMAN AND R.J. MISSED the flight back to Jacksonville, and as far as she was concerned it was no loss. R.J. had been cleared—he was carrying nothing but his own flesh and bones and the ten thousand or so microbial species everybody routinely carries around with them—but he had to stay behind to bail out his brother. "We'll catch a later flight," he told her, "no worries."

The tip of his nose was sunburned, his eyes were climbing a rope. They were standing just beyond security, their bags at their feet. People passed by, oblivious, as if nothing had happened, as if all the silver boas in the world were still out there on those islands where they belonged. "Can we have pizza?" Tahoe asked, still clutching Cat's hand—or clutching it all over again, as if she were a clingy child, which she definitely wasn't, another strike against R.J.

"Sure," she heard herself say, "just as soon as we find our gate."

"It's going to be in D Concourse," R.J. said. "I'll walk you over."

Tahoe was wearing the pink Glitter Kitty backpack the customs cops had rifled and X-rayed. She lifted her left hand to her mouth to chew her nails, a habit Cat was trying to discourage. "Are they going to put Stoneman in jail?" Tahoe asked, addressing R.J. because he was the apparent authority on issues of snakes and cops and airports.

"Yes, but not for long—I'm going to help him. We'll both be home tonight."

"But why?"

He looked to her, then back to Tahoe. "Because we weren't supposed to have those snakes—you saw them, right? They're very special snakes and we wanted to bring them back with us and give them a good home . . ."

"For pets?"

Again the look to her. "Yeah," he said. "For pets."

A heavily accented voice announced a flight over the loudspeaker. A woman pushing a cart overloaded with luggage wheeled past—atop the suitcases was an animal carrier with the face of a dachshund staring out at them, as if on cue. "I'll walk you over," R.J. said, reaching for the handle of her roller bag.

She waved him off. "Don't bother," she said.

"You sure?"

"Yeah," she said. "I'm sure."

24

THE FIRE THIS TIME

SHE WAS TIRED OF SYLVIE, TIRED OF SEEING HER FACE ACROSS the kitchen table, tired of her conversation, her complaints, even her accent. And empathy. She was tired of empathy too. It was ungenerous of her, she knew that, disloyal, selfish even, but after three weeks of having to tiptoe around her own house, she'd had it. With Peter too. And their cats. The insurance would pay to house them once things were sorted out, but every room in every hotel, motel and Airbnb within a hundred miles was booked solid in the wake of the latest round of wildfires. The governor had declared a state of emergency. The National Guard was patrolling the streets. Where there'd been trees, shrubs, businesses, homes, now there was only ash.

Of course Sylvie and Peter were welcome to the guest room for as long as they needed it, that went without saying, but at this point it had become a question of privacy more than anything, more than the cats shredding the furniture or the extra burden of shopping and meals and cleanup and the dishwasher running 24/7. The last time she and Frank had lived with another couple—two couples, actually—was close to half a century ago, when life was a door propped open with a broomstick and connection was what she wanted above all else, shared meals, shared music, shared minds. Or so she'd thought till it all broke down in pettiness and recrimination. She couldn't imagine living like that now—or even in an apartment, where you were forced into intimacy with people you'd never know otherwise. Or want to know. Her son would have accused her of being an elitist and maybe she was, but at her age all she wanted was clean and quiet and everything in its proper place. Including people.

Out of guilt, she'd spent the better part of the afternoon with Sylvie, helping her sift through the ashes in the hope of turning up whatever the fire might have missed, which didn't seem to be much. The ash lay in an unbroken plain that ran from yard to yard as far as you could see, houses gone, trees gone, only twists of blackened pipe and the remnants of chimneys to break the monotony. Some of the houses had had pools, the outlines of which cut dark debris-glutted rectangles out of the earth. There was wind, of course, there was always wind, fanning the ash, swirling it in miniature cyclones that choked the air so they had to wear face masks to avoid breathing it in—particulate matter, the ultrafine grains that work their way deep into your lungs and lodge there permanently— and they both wore swim goggles too, to keep it out of their eyes.

By noon the temperature was in the high nineties and within the hour it broke a hundred for the thirteenth consecutive day. She was sweaty. Her back ached. She felt dizzy. But she kept working her colander through the drifts in the approximate place where the master bedroom had been—the fire had come on them so suddenly Sylvie hadn't had time to take much of anything, not her clothes or passport or the enameled jewelry box that contained the family heirlooms, including a pair of diamond drop earrings she'd inherited from her mother and an Edwardian brooch in the shape of a butterfly that had belonged to Peter's grandmother. So far all they'd turned up was a blackened hose nozzle.

"What about a metal detector, Syl? Wouldn't that be easier?"

Sylvie was twenty feet from her, down on her knees in the ash, work-ing her own colander through the debris and coming up with nothing but pebbles—not stones, not precious stones, just pebbles. "I wouldn't know where to find one, would you?"

"We could google it—"

Sylvie didn't answer. Her clothes—blue jeans and a navy blouse Ottilie had loaned her—were flecked with ash the consistency of Gold Seal flour and her hair was streaked with it, as if she were going back to her natural color. She looked like a refugee—she *was* a refugee. All she had were the things Ottilie had given her when she and Peter moved into the guest room with their two Siamese cats and whatever they'd been able to salvage in the dark with the smoke detectors screaming and the electricity out, poles burned, wires down, every tree in their garden a torch.

This time the fire had come in the middle of the night, a vast cordillera of flame that swept out of the chaparral with a roar like the exhaust of a rocket. One couple—young, in their twenties—had been overtaken in the street, running for their lives after their car broke down, and Ottilie couldn't get the image out of her head. Did they hold hands? Urge each other on? Scream? Sob? The fire sucked the air from their lungs and left them lying there facedown on the pavement, untouched but for the spatter of blood that marked the impact of the wife's fall. They'd been married six months. They didn't have any children. Mercifully. Others burned in their beds, or if they'd got out in time, in their cars, which were jammed bumper-to-bumper on the back streets, tires exploding, gas tanks going off like bombs. Twelve dead and how many yet to be discovered in the debris no one knew.

"What's the use?" Sylvie flung down her colander, rotated her hips and sat heavily, the ashes fanning out around her. "Our whole life is gone. Everything we've ever owned. We are done. *Terminé.*"

She wanted to be positive, but there was no upside to this. What was she going to say: *At least you're alive? At least you have each other? At least you got the cats out?* She and Frank had been the lucky ones—just as with the last fire, the one that put a cap on Cat's wedding, this one shifted with the wind, but this time it kept on going, burning its way across the city house by house, block by block, till it reached the sea and there was nothing left to feed it.

What if it had been them? What if it was their house that was gone? She was a saver, a historian, an archivist of the life she and Frank had built together, and even the smallest things—the finger paintings and misshapen ceramics the kids had made in elementary school, report cards, high school and college essays, photo albums going back two generations—were signposts to her, heartbreaking, beautiful. The furniture she'd collected piece by piece over the years. The carpets she'd bargained for in one shop or another, Bokhara, Yasmin, Aditi, the merchants delivering their spiels and all the while the sinking feeling that she was being cheated. Her mother's china. Her own jewelry. Her books. Her clothes. No matter what she said or understood about the venality of clinging to material things, there it was. People said, "You can live without that," and she'd nod and agree, but the truth was, she couldn't. Anytime a siren screamed out on the street she prayed it was for an accident, a heart attack, a police shooting—anything but fire.

All at once, she felt ashamed of herself. This was Sylvie, her best friend, who'd lost everything, and here she was thinking only of her own convenience—Sylvie could stay on as long as she liked. Of course she could. Absolutely. She was going to say something along those lines, something encouraging, when the edge of the colander struck home and there it was, the brooch, the butterfly, the diamonds and opals intact and its wings unbent, shedding ash. She rubbed it between her fingers, then laid it across her palm and dipped her head to blow it clean with a puff of air. "Hey!" she cried out. "Look what I found!"

☀

THE FIRST THING SHE DID when they got back was take a swim. Sylvie declined to join her, opting for a shower instead, which was thoughtless, the water bills well over a thousand dollars a month now—and penalties on top of that for exceeding the limits of the tier they'd been assigned to, which was calculated on the usage of a two-person household, not a four-. She tried not to show her irritation—"My hair, it's filthy," Sylvie complained, "*I'm* filthy, and I'm going to need a good shampoo, and conditioner, is there any conditioner left?"—but she couldn't help herself. "There's plenty of conditioner," she said, "but what we lack, Sylvie, is *water*, remember?" Her own hair could use a good shampoo too, but she limited herself to one three-minute shower a week—wet the hair, twist off the faucet, lather up, then turn it back on for a quick rinse and forget the conditioner. And yes, she kept two five-gallon plastic buckets in the shower stall to catch the rinse water, but Sylvie didn't seem to take the hint. What did she think—they were decorative? And the towels— Sylvie used three or four every time she showered, leaving them wadded up on the floor, and maybe that was a French thing, but it just meant yet another cycle of the washing machine. She used a single towel herself— and reused it till began to stink.

By the time she climbed out of the pool, any sense of charity she'd developed out there in the ash pit had vanished. The pool towel was stiff to the touch, but she used it anyway and put it back on the hook in the sun where it would dry and stiffen all over again. The night before, they'd gone out for Chinese, which Peter had made a show of paying for, waving Frank's card away ("Please, you've done so much for us"), and tonight she was planning on cooking, though it was no fun with Sylvie looking over her shoulder, never shy about offering her opinion on the optimal way to cut endive or bake Brie or poach scallops. Tonight, though, she was keeping it simple, pasta and salad, with turkey meatballs on the side to keep the carnivores happy.

Sylvie had her hair up in a towel and she didn't offer to help—
or interfere—which was just fine with her. They had a glass of wine
together, but didn't say much. Sylvie had had a good cry over the brooch
in the car on the way back and she was settled in at the kitchen table
now, working a pad of polishing cloth over the setting. "Yes, it is coming
back, don't you think?" she said. "Good as new, right?"

Ottilie glanced over her shoulder—she was slicing mushrooms
at the counter while the onions caramelized in the pan. "Diamonds
are indestructible, but I don't know about the gold—you're lucky it
didn't melt."

"Oh, yes," Sylvie said, "I am the luckiest woman in the world. Tell
me that. Tell me again."

The meatball mixture—two pounds of ground turkey into which
she'd worked three eggs, fresh breadcrumbs, grated parmesan, thyme,
oregano, diced onions and a judicious shot of Worcestershire—was in the
mixing bowl on the table, ready to be molded in her cupped hands and
browned in the pan she was heating on the stove. Out the window she
could see Frank and Peter stretched out in the chaise longues by the pool,
dripping dry and chatting amiably, beers in hand. The shade of the oaks
out back had begun to creep toward the house, a continent on the move.
There wasn't a cloud in the sky. The sun was a furnace. The air-conditioner
strained. "I didn't mean it that way," she said, "you know that."

Sylvie didn't answer.

She was thinking she'd like to hear a little music—by way of
distraction, of clearing the atmosphere, bringing a little lilt to the
proceedings—and she turned round to dry her hands on a paper towel
before digging the phone out of her front pocket, and would it be jazz
or classical? Or rock, though Sylvie hated rock, or so she said every time
Ottilie put on Maclovio Pulchris or even Bowie or Dylan. (*Why couldn't
we have just silence? What's wrong with silence?*) That was when she saw
the cat on the table—one of the cats, she couldn't tell them apart—its
head in the bowl of ground turkey. Right there in front of Sylvie, as if
she'd gone blind.

"Get out of that!" she shouted, startling Sylvie, but the cat didn't even look up, just kept gorging. She snatched the first object that came to hand—the spatula—and flew at the thing, whacking its bony rippled backbone with everything she had. The cat went spinning across the table like a cue ball, plunging over the edge in a scramble of limbs and raking claws before letting out a single outraged yowl and disappearing down the hallway; unfortunately, in its umbrage, it managed to take her T. G. Green gripstand mixing bowl with it, a bowl she'd had since she and Frank first started dating.

The tile floor was unforgiving. The bowl lay there at Sylvie's feet, shattered, the meat bristling with ceramic splinters. "Don't you dare hit my cat," Sylvie said, her mouth drawn tight.

Ottilie was locked in on the recoil, ready to swat again—and bring it on, go get the other one too, because she'd had it, she'd really had it. "You know something?" she said, her voice right on the margin of breaking. "You're being a bitch, a real bitch. Didn't you see the cat right there in front of your nose?"

"I did not see the cat." Sylvie slapped the brooch down on the tabletop. "I just lost my house, everything! And you're the one—you're the bitch."

"Yeah, well, it's your mess," she said. "You clean it up." Then she crossed the room and went up the stairs to her bedroom, slamming the door behind her and flinging herself down on the bed. She lay there for a time, but it was hot upstairs, too hot, and she pushed herself back up, still fuming—what were they going to do about dinner now? Go out? And have to sit across the table from her as if nothing had happened?

Her phone, which she kept in the back pocket of her jeans, began to give off a thin annunciatory bleat—if it was Sylvie calling to apologize, she wasn't going to answer. But it wasn't Sylvie, it was Cooper, his voice filling the space in her head like gas in a beaker.

"I just wanted to tell you," he said, "so you'd be the first to know—Elytra and I are getting married."

She almost said, *It's about time,* but caught herself. They'd been living together for years now and they'd never been officially engaged, never even mentioned the institution of marriage as far as she could recall, but that was Cooper's way. Anything conventional—like actually finishing your degree and getting a university position—he just shook off. "What great news," she said. "Congratulations."

"Well, yeah, we just thought it was time. Or Elytra did—not that I'm not thrilled, I am, she's it, she's the one."

"We can have the ceremony here," she said, and as soon as she said it she thought of the water situation and immediately regretted it. "Of course, I'd call up the weather service in advance and have them shut off the wind that day . . ."

"We're going to do a civil ceremony. At the courthouse."

She couldn't hide her disappointment. "That's no fun." She was picturing the bride, tall and clean-limbed, with her embroilment of hair and her tattoos, coming down the steps of City Hall in a satin gown, a bouquet in her arms and the proboscis of her kissing bug glinting in her cleavage. "What does Elytra say?"

"She's just like me: no fuss. Weddings are just a huge waste, all those resources down the drain. Water, did you think of the water? All those people flushing the toilet? Those days are over. Long over."

"What about her mother?"

"Her mother's in Burgundy, getting shit-faced with her boyfriend on a gourmet wine tour."

"You're not thinking of doing it, what, *now*? How long's the wine tour? You're not even going to wait till she gets back?"

"They're estranged, I thought you knew that? Her mother went off the deep end a long time ago. Anyway, you're the first to know about it, okay, so be happy for me."

"I am happy, but—"

"Good. Perfect. We're thinking Saturday."

"Saturday? What about Cat?"

"We'll FaceTime her."

There was so much wrong here, she didn't know where to start. "Why don't you just elope, if that's how you feel about it?"

"Because you wouldn't be there. Mom, I'm doing it for you, that's why I'm calling. To give you a heads-up."

"I'm just stunned."

"It's good to be stunned sometimes, isn't it? Breaks the pattern, don't you think? By the way, you still on for tomorrow?"

He'd asked her if she wanted to help him with the monarch count out at the field station and she'd jumped at the chance, if only to get out of the house and away from Sylvie, and she said, "Sure, yes, of course," but she wasn't quite ready to let go of the wedding business yet, because couldn't they put it off even for a week so Cat could come? "What about your nose?" she asked.

His nose had been broken in a bar fight, which was hard to fathom, since he was going to be thirty-five in a month and he'd never been violent, even when he was drinking, which, apparently, he had been. Apparently, too, he was the aggressor. Something had set him off and he'd thrown a drink in a man's face and the man got up off his barstool and punched him hard enough to break the bridge of his nose and empurple his right eye till it looked like a damson plum grafted to his face. "No worries," he said, "the swelling's down and it's not even going to have to be realigned, so I'm good to go, pretty much."

"What time tomorrow?"

"Early. Before the heat sets in? Say, seven or so? If I don't answer my phone, just bang on the door, okay?"

SHE DRESSED IN WHITE, WARY of ticks (or more than wary—paranoid, actually), made goat-cheese-and-roasted-pepper sandwiches for the two of them and brought along a liter of water each and a bottle of wine, which made her day pack heavier than she'd like, but of course it would be that much lighter on the way back. It was still dark when she'd got up, the house silent but for the faint rattle of Peter's snoring from down the hall—or maybe it was Sylvie's. Which was strange, their presence in the house, their bodies and emanations and whispers of sound, their psyches ticking away like remote calculators constructing their own realities, sleeping and waking in a space that was hers, a reduced space that didn't even have Dunphy in it anymore. This was the hour when she missed him most. He'd been there to greet her every morning for seventeen years, part of her ritual, put the coffee on, fetch the paper, take him for his morning walk, then back home to feed him and sit down to breakfast and let the day uncoil around her. Frank had buried him in the far corner of the yard, where the remains of his predecessor— Cappy—had been reintegrating with the earth longer than Dunphy had been alive.

The big surprise was the weather. It was almost cool—mid-sixties, anyway—and for the first time in weeks the sun was obscured by an unbroken band of cloud that curtained off the mountains as if they'd never been there. She went out the back door and stood in the yard, her face raised to the sky. And what was this? Moisture. The faintest touch of a mist that couldn't even be called drizzle, that wasn't measurable, not even a trace, but enough to register on her skin. H_2O. It was a kind of miracle. She felt almost giddy—were they finally going to get a break?

When she backed out of the carport, there it was on the windshield, pinpricks of moisture, material and present, and so what if it wasn't enough to merit flicking on the wipers? She let out a laugh— what a world they were inhabiting, where a few drops of moisture could make her mood soar the way music did, the way love did. She just sat there, the engine running, watching the way the pinpricks gathered and the world softened around her, from the shining pavement to the leaves of the shining trees. She had an impulse to turn on the radio or bring up the weather on her phone, but fought it down—she didn't want to be disappointed.

25

IT WAS A SKIFF

THE WATER WAS UP AGAIN, CREEPING IN UNDER THE HOUSE and slapping at the pilings with a slow steady protracted pulse. Why it was up, no one could say. The moon was in its quarter phase, which generally meant lower tides, though there was a storm moving in to counter the effect. According to the meteorologist on TV (Brenda Fassero, who'd twice been in Bobo's while Cat was there, the first time while she was on duty, though she didn't get to wait on her, the other time when she was having a cocktail at the bar with Daria after her shift), it was likely to impact their weather as the day wore on. So yes: The seas were running a little higher than normal. Boaters beware. Watch the bridge clearances. Stay tuned.

She'd had to use the skiff to take Tahoe to school that morning—the skiff R.J. hadn't come to reclaim yet, a sign he was still hoping to get back together, which absolutely was not going to happen, not in this lifetime—and she'd had breakfast at the Cornerstone and lingered over the free paper and her phone before going back home to clean up after the exterminators. They'd wiped everything down to remove any residue, but she didn't trust them, not with Tahoe in the house, so she was giving everything a second go-over. She'd done the kitchen and Tahoe's room the day before and today she was planning on getting to the rest. Outside, the sun was shining, but the sky was dense and pale, as if the rain clouds had already moved in, and yet when she stepped out on the deck she saw it wasn't overcast at all. The sun was right there, unimpeded, but it seemed duller somehow, as if she were seeing it through a panel of frosted glass, and the sky that supported it was like a blank page, not gray, not blue, but white. She noted it and moved on: At least it wasn't raining. Yet.

The estimate for repairing the termite damage—and the rot, wet and dry—was more than double what she'd anticipated even on the high end. Todd, despite his spending the night a week ago and for once acting like a real father to Tahoe, the funny Todd, the charming Todd, the Todd she'd fallen in love with, told her flatly over the phone that it wasn't his responsibility. "I gave you the house, okay? Free and clear, no mortgage, no nothing. Upkeep is your problem. End of discussion."

"What about Tahoe?"

"What about her?"

"It could be dangerous—they've already red-tagged six other houses. What if it collapses, how would you feel then?"

"It's not going to collapse."

"What, you're a structural engineer now? Read the report I sent you."

"Sell the place, then."

"You're joking, right? Who's going to buy it, the Termite Preservation Society?"

"Talk to the insurance."

"I already did. They say they don't cover termite."

"Talk to them again. Write your senator. Get a job."

"I already have one."

"Listen," he said, and what she heard in the background was live

music, bar chatter, a TV voice announcing a soccer game in Spanish—
fútbol!—"I gotta go. I'll talk to you later, okay?"

The conversation with her mother was even harder (*Why don't you
give up on the beach fantasy and come back home? Right*, she countered,
where everything's on fire all the time?) but in the end her mother promised to send her the money, which she, in turn, solemnly promised to
pay back. She was a failure, they both knew that, a fuckup who'd lost
her child and her husband too, who was working a part-time waitressing job that was so far beneath her, she was losing whole banks of brain
cells every day and clinging to home ownership as if that were going to
redeem her in the face of all the forces arrayed against her, beginning
with, but not limited to, rising seas and termites that had migrated all
the way from Asia to undermine whatever little she had left.

She was using an old washcloth and a spray bottle of Murphy Oil
Soap on one of the shelves in the pantry prior to restocking the canned
goods and the rest of the foodstuffs—pasta, condiments, grated parmesan, capers, pickles—that had been sealed in the Nylofume bags and
left out in the middle of the room while the sulfuryl fluoride penetrated
the walls, when the plank tilted forward and a rain of frass the color of
gunpowder fell to the shelf below. Behind it, the wall was honeycombed
with the galleries of the now-dead insects, and when she inserted a finger in the hole where the shelf had pulled loose, the wood gave way in a
crumble of powdery flakes.

Which was just great. Perfect. Now she couldn't even put the food
back. The whole pantry was going to have to be rebuilt first—and what
was wrong with metal, steel, let them eat through that, beams and struts
and flat gray impenetrable shelves only rust could disintegrate—and in
the meantime the food was going to have to stay right there on the floor
in the bulging double plastic bags while she dodged around them every
time she stepped into the room. She felt like giving up. Felt like screaming. But she just left everything where it was and took the spray bottle
and the rag and went into the living room to rub down all the surfaces
and then start in on the walls.

The second time Brenda Fassero had come in, Cat got a good look at her because she wasn't hustling from table to table to the kitchen and back but just relaxing at the bar after her shift. Brenda looked smaller than she did on TV and her makeup wasn't as extreme, but she had presence and the kind of glamour celebrities seemed to radiate as if they were plugged into their own portable sockets. Not that she was such a big deal—the local weatherwoman, that was all—but people noticed, nudging each other at the bar and snatching glances over their shoulders, trying not to be too obvious, and one guy went up and asked her for an autograph and then sent a round of drinks to her table. Brenda had lifted her face to him and beamed the kind of smile she might have used to introduce a high-pressure system over the Gulf, signed a Bobo's coaster for him and went back to chatting with her (date? husband?) as if being recognized and signing autographs were as natural as drawing breath. Which gave her all the more power. It was expected. Her due. She was a celebrity and you weren't, that was how it was.

What did it take to be a weatherwoman, anyway? It wasn't as if you needed a degree in the meteorological sciences to pout and grin and wave your arms at the camera while reading your lines off a monitor. Brenda Fassero was eye candy, that was all, and she wore killer outfits, that went without saying, and probably made a healthy salary, and she got free drinks and had a hunky boyfriend or husband to show off in public and get confidential with right there at the table anytime she wanted, tête-à-tête over autographs and grilled scallops alike. What Cat was thinking—that day and now, as she wiped and scrubbed and tried her best to remove any trace of insecticide from her furniture and the walls and floors and anywhere else it might be lingering—was that she could do that job. Easily. She was about the same age as Brenda Fassero and just as pretty—prettier, actually, and taller too—and give her a couple hours' practice in the bathroom mirror and she could perfect the whole gamut of TV facial expression, from the clenched-brow gravitas of the hurricane warning to the radiant joy of unmediated sun-and-surf weather. Sure she could. But she wasn't doing it. Wasn't doing anything but scrubbing and polishing and holding her breath till the next storm hit. And who was going to hire Python Mom anyway, no matter how many times she changed her hair color?

The water was still coursing through the yard when she went to pick up Tahoe after school, but at least it wasn't raining, so there was that to be thankful for. It should have been low tide, but lately it was hard to tell the difference since the water seemed to do whatever it wanted irrespective of the moon or the tilt of the earth or any other force she knew of. She got the car out of the lot at Bobo's, made a quick stop at the grocery for frozen lasagna—the family size, which would last them two days, maybe three—and a pre-made salad in a cellophane bag to go with it, then picked up Tahoe, deposited everything in the skiff, drove back to Bobo's to leave the car there and walked her daughter the ten blocks to the skiff, nothing out of the usual—or the new usual, anyway. She'd never been to Venice, but she'd spent a week in Amsterdam once, long enough to slow down, park herself on a bench and see what the life of the city was like, the locals using the canals like backstreets to run their errands in skiffs and rowboats, and if that had seemed romantic— or quaint or backward or exotic—she was living it now. The car sat at Bobo's. The skiff was her conveyance.

It started to rain by the time they got to the boat, but they were old hands at this now and the groceries, which were plastic-bagged in any case, were tucked up under a tarp in the bow and the perishables stowed in the cooler, on ice. She was always afraid someone would come along and see the cooler there in the skiff and make off with it, but that hadn't happened—there wasn't a whole lot of traffic in the neighborhood anymore, what with the red-tagged houses and the street inundated half the time, and she always left the boat where you had to wade to get at it and locked a cable around the steel post the city had erected in drier times to announce the speed limit (25, which would be like waterskiing if you tried to do that now, even in the biggest SUV on the market).

The rain got heavier as they were coming up the stairs, but it was just rain, sans wind, not a hurricane or even a tropical storm, as per Brenda

Fassero's facial-tic assurances on the morning news. The cat met them at the door, mewing for food, and in the interval in which the door swung open and they struggled in with the groceries and schoolbooks and their dripping raincoats and hats, he never even made a feint for the door. It was dry inside. There was food. He was a stray no longer. Tahoe had renamed him Leopard, which proved a mouthful, and so she'd shortened it to Pard. *Which is like a pardner, right, Mom? Like he's my pardner?*

Nothing happened. The rain fell, the sea washed the pilings like an enormous dishwasher on rinse, lasagna baked in its own foil tray, saving on cleanup, there was wine, there was rum, there was music on Spotify. It was the third week of November, and what she was going to do for Thanksgiving, she didn't know, especially since R.J. and his herpetological circus were out of the picture now and forever, but she thought she might bake a turkey anyway and see if anybody from work wanted to have a little adventure in the skiff on the way to dinner, *Over the backwash and through the seaweed to grandmother's house we go.* Or something like that. She even sang a verse or two aloud for Tahoe, experimenting with the lyrics, grandmother in this case all the way across the country in a dried-up house where the doors never stuck and the woods were incinerated stalks against a fiery sky. Grandmother had sun, though. And she didn't have mold. Or termites. Or the stink of the muck that made the whole world smell like an open grave.

She felt like reading Tahoe a bedtime story, though Tahoe was at an age when she really didn't want one—she had a phone and TikTok and Instagram and her own taste and predilections, her own life, or the beginnings of it—but she insisted, so the two of them sat on the couch while the rain rapped at the roof and read *Matilda* for maybe the twentieth time (*"Because we are playing with mysterious forces, my child, that we know nothing about"*). Then Tahoe went into her room to text her friends till she fell asleep and Ottilie made herself a drink and paged through *Elle* while watching an episode of a Finnish cop show on Netflix that was exactly like an American cop show except that the streets were laminated with ice and the food and fashions were slightly off, aside from the wine—every woman, whether cop or suspect, clutched a wide-bowled glass of red in one hand unless she was either skittering across the ice after somebody or, as the case may be, skittering away.

Then it was midnight and she woke with a start on the couch to the rain and the Finnish dialogue and went on into bed, exhausted from having done nothing all day, or practically nothing—nothing like what Brenda Fassero must have done, Brenda Fassero, who would no doubt be getting up in four or five hours to head for the studio in one of the cute little outfits she must have spent half her life shopping for and have the makeup artist go to work on her. And what was this exhaustion? Was it the alcohol, was that it? Maybe she should try to cut back, maybe that would be a good idea. She pushed herself up from the couch, feeling as if she were carrying a medicine ball on her shoulders, just wiped, absolutely, and she skipped brushing her teeth and barely got her clothes off before she was asleep.

The noise that woke her was like the snapping of a bone, only amplified a thousand times. It was a rupture, a breach, and before she could react the bed tilted radically to the left and a weight descended on her, sudden and savage and pinning her to the mattress like an insect on a mounting board. Everything hurt. There was no light, nothing, just blackness. She heard Tahoe, somewhere, crying her name.

WHAT SAVED HER WAS THE headboard, which caught the falling beam and redirected it by a matter of inches, crucial inches, inches that kept it away from her head and face—that and the mattress, which gave way just enough to cushion the blow. She'd been sleeping on her back, her legs akimbo, and the weight, which turned out to be the overhead beam—rotted, wet, scrawled with the signature of the termites—had come down across her left thigh. The pain jumped and settled and she tried to get up but the weight wouldn't allow it. Tahoe cried out again, closer now: "Mom? Mom, are you all right?" Struggling, pushing against the pain and the splintered immovable bulk of this thing that held her fast, she stretched her full length to reach for the flashlight on the night table, but the night table was gone, flung all the way across the room on the downward slope of the buckled floor, but she didn't know that yet.

"Mom?"

"Can you turn on the light, honey? I can't see. If I could see . . ."

There was the snap of the light switch, but nothing happened. "It's broken."

"Can you find a flashlight?"

"*Mom*, are you *okay*?"

"I'm okay, I'm fine, I just need some light, that's all, so I can . . . But listen, we have to get outside as soon as possible, okay?" She tried to keep her voice under control. "And I'm going to need a flashlight—or your phone, what about your phone?"

Then everything shifted again and there was a crash from the other end of the hallway. A window popped. Then another. There was a long frictive groan. She felt a trickle of water on her face.

"Don't move, honey, just stay right there—you're in the doorway, right?"

She was flashing on the earthquake drills in elementary school, get under your desk, stand in a doorway, cover your head, but this was no earthquake—there were no earthquakes in Florida. But there were doorways, there were doorways everywhere.

"I can't see anything, I can't *find* my phone, Mom, *Mom*!"

"Just a minute, give me a minute, it's okay, it's going to be okay—"

"And Pard, where's Pard?" Tahoe's voice broke. "Pard!" she cried, a thin knife of desolation that cut right through her. "Pard!"

Cat fought the beam, forcing herself down against the recoil of the box spring, gaining an inch, then another, and all she could think was that she'd lost one daughter and she wasn't going to lose another. The bed, the beam, the dark, the smell. "*Pard! Pard!*" The weight was on her knee now, flattening her kneecap, and then it was on her shin, raking at the skin there, and now her foot, and in the next moment it let go of her and she was up off the bed and fighting for balance, walking, groping, stumbling, the pain all on the surface, nothing broken, or she didn't think so, and here was her daughter's clenched form in the doorway and she was clinging to her and if her bare feet—their bare feet—were cut and bleeding because there was glass on the floor that wasn't a floor anymore it barely computed because all that mattered was getting down the hallway, through the living room and out the door before the house buried them alive.

All the things familiar to her—the furniture, the TV, the kitchen counter and her collectible Fiestaware and the pots and pans and anything else in the cabinets, wine bottles, the smacked-down refrigerator— were arrayed like weapons against her. She was in her nightgown, the thinnest of skins, slamming from one thing to another, holding fast to her daughter's hand until they reached the door that wouldn't open because the doorframe had shifted and she had to smash out the window and work around the teeth of the glass as she stepped through it and lifted Tahoe out and onto the landing to grab hold of her wrist and pull her down the gauntlet of the rotten steps that were pitched into the side of the house now and forget the railing, forget the rot, just get down and get away.

At the bottom, in the yard, the water surged violently around their knees, the sting of the salt seeking out every least cut and abrasion. It wasn't dawn, not yet, but the sky had lightened enough to give form to things. The dead tree. The skiff. And the house canted above them, wearing a fragment of its roof like a hat knocked askew. Tahoe's face was too dark to read, just a shadow, and she hadn't let go of her wrist because it wasn't over yet, not till they were in the skiff and cutting a swath through the water, out and away, clear.

"*Mom*," Tahoe whined, "you're hurting me." Only then did she let go.

☀

IT WASN'T COLD, BUT SHE was shivering. The palms gathered the darkness. The other houses on the street were invisible. She would have called 911, but she didn't have her phone. Or purse or ID or even a pair of pants and a tee. Her nightgown, soaked through, clung to her, blossoming where she was bleeding, and Tahoe, beside her in her wet pajamas, was crying softly. They were a hundred feet from the house, in the drive, far enough away to be clear of any falling debris, but not in the skiff, not yet. "You stay here," she told her, warned her, "while I get the boat. Okay, honey? Are your feet cut?"

Her daughter didn't answer. "Pard," she said. "We have to get Pard."

"He'll be okay, don't worry. We'll come back for him, I promise."

The house chose that moment to shift again, jerking forward with a harsh grating roar that annulled the thump of the waves, and Tahoe cried out as if she'd been stabbed. "Mom! Mom!"

She was going to tell her it was too dangerous, tell her that cats have nine lives and he could take care of himself, she knew that—didn't all the books say so?—but then they heard him, the cat, Pard, give out with a single thin desolate wail and Tahoe took off running, her arms waving in the air and her knees high-stepping through the froth of the water. Cat made a snatch for her and missed, and then she was running herself.

It was still too dim to separate the shadows, the house a factory of dark crushed angles, black on black, but her daughter's pajamas were a pale flutter that stood out against the backdrop and she saw that flutter at the base of the stairs and heard herself shouting, "No!," until she was there and climbing, frantic now and cursing herself and why had she ever let go of her, why, why, why?

The stairs quaked and the flutter was gone, absorbed suddenly by the black hole of the broken window above the landing. She heard Tahoe calling, "Kitty, kitty," and the image of the snake and the baby on the floor came gushing up out of her mind, hateful, inadmissible, and she cut herself again on the shattered glass, back in the house now, in the darkness, shouting Tahoe's name.

The moment expanded till it took in the whole universe. She was blind and groping and every hidden festering odor of the house was out in the open now and her heart was tearing a hole in her chest all over again. She screamed her daughter's name till her throat clenched. Something crashed to the floor, and then another thing, and another. . . but all at once a thin amputated wail rose up out of a blackness that was absolute and here it was, delivered up like a miracle: the cat. And her daughter. Because her daughter was right there, flesh and blood and the cold wet touch of her skin, *Tahoe, Tahoe*. Then she had the cat in her arms and the cat was clinging to her, its claws digging in even as the glass stabbed at her feet, and she didn't feel a thing. Down the stairs one more time, the last time, last time ever, each step stressed and canted and groaning under her weight and Tahoe's too—Tahoe's too. The skiff bobbed there in the darkness. She braced it against her hip so her daughter could climb in and the cat could huddle under the seat till she released the lines and climbed in herself to jerk at the cord and bring the engine to life.

She revved the motor, the throb of it rising through the throttle and up into her fingertips, her hand, her arm, the power all hers now, and what she was seeing was California, a rental there until the insurance could sort things out, Tahoe enrolled at Twin Oaks Elementary and herself working a job that took more than half a brain or applying to grad school or doing something in fashion or design, no Todd, no R.J., no Herps, no beach, no waves, no rain, no rot. They were out on the belly of the flooded street, facing forward, slicing through the water, when the house gave way behind them, collapsing with a clatter that was like the sustained applause at the end of a concert. Tahoe saw it, swiveling to look over her shoulder from where she sat balanced in the middle of the bow seat, but Cat never turned her head—all she wanted to see was right there in front of her.

26

IT ALL PALES

COOPER WAS WAITING FOR HER WHEN SHE PULLED UP IN front of his house. He was wearing khakis, pants and shirt both, which made him seem like an official of some sort, as if he'd got a job with the Park Service or Fish and Game, and he looked good, lean and tall and fit. But for his nose. His nose was discolored still and the eye too, though not as obviously as when he'd stopped by the house to show it to Frank the morning after it had been rearranged for him by that stranger in the bar. He smiled and bent to tap at her window, making a corkscrew motion with his good hand, a vestigial gesture from the era when vehicles had roll-down windows. Ottilie was flustered for a minute, fumbling for the button—*technology*—and then the window sank into the doorframe and his smile went up a notch. "I was thinking we'd take my car?" he said. "Because we're going to be driving the whole length of the dirt road to the end of the ranch property and hike in from there, okay? And the road's pretty rough—you wouldn't want to scratch up your shiny new vehicle, would you?"

The car, which they'd just bought a month ago, was the newest model of the Olfputt hatchback, fully electric and with photovoltaic panels on the roof to take advantage of the relentless California sun (what the Swedes, who manufactured it, got out of that particular feature, she couldn't imagine, though climate change was searing Stockholm too—or more so, since the poles were heating three times faster than anyplace else).

"Sure," she said. "Fine with me."

"It's going to be a pretty fair hike, maybe three, four miles? You okay with that? There's this grove I want to check out ahead of the Thanksgiving count where I've found monarchs in the past and nobody really knows about, so I'm curious. And hopeful. Can I be hopeful?"

She pushed open the door, got out and gave him a hug. "I'm hopeful too," she said. "And don't worry about me, I'm not as old as I look—I can make three or four miles. Easy. Maybe even five, do I hear five? It's your father who could use the exercise. And Dunphy, if he was around still. I miss him. Especially in the morning when the first thing I'd do is take him for his walk."

"Yeah, he would have liked this, a chance to wallow in poison oak and stick his nose in a pile of coyote scat—or, what, roll in it? But really, it's amazing he lasted that long. What was he, fifteen, sixteen?"

"Seventeen. You were in college when we got him." The memory carved out a pit inside her and suddenly she was on the verge of tears. Was it morally defensible to grieve over an animal when the world was such a vast sink of loss? When children were starving and the sun burned hotter every day? She'd loved the dog. So go ahead and crucify her.

"He'd just be tick bait out here, anyway," Cooper said, taking her pack from her and stowing it in the back of his car. "What about you, you need bug spray? We're going off-trail, so be prepared."

☀

ANY SIGN OF THE MIST along the coast was lost here—once you climbed up over the pass and descended into the valley it was always hotter and drier, at least in summertime, and summertime seemed to last longer and longer now, which was disastrous for the cool-climate wines like pinot noir and Chardonnay the region was famous for. As were the fires. And the drought. Frank's joke came back to her—*In twenty years it'll look like Saudi Arabia here*—which wasn't really that far off. Maybe they should have bought a camel instead of a car. What was the one with two humps—the Bactrian? Or was it the dromedary? No matter, better two humps than one. Economize. Save on electricity for the car. And have fresh camel milk to pour over your cereal in the morning and a nice bowl of camel yogurt and blueberries for dessert. She was going to tell Cooper about the morning's moisture, the miracle of it, but he was in the middle of a convoluted story about the politics of the field station, and the moment passed. By the time they got to the entrance gate the sun was hanging over the oaks in a cloudless sky—and yet the heat wave had definitely broken. It was almost cool. Should she have brought a sweater along? A sweater. What a concept. She'd almost forgotten what a sweater was.

Cooper drove faster than she was comfortable with, especially on a dirt road, skirting dips and outcroppings as if he were on a racecourse— the term *gymkhana* came to mind—and she would have told him to slow down, but she didn't want to nag, at least not yet. There was the issue of the wedding they needed to discuss—certainly they'd have a reception, wouldn't they? And if he didn't want to have it at the house, she'd already come up with a list of places she thought might work, from the courtyard at Casa Lorena to any one of three beachside parks she could think of where you could reserve picnic tables for the day and bring in caterers to set things up. She had a fleeting impression of that pinch-faced woman who'd catered Cat's wedding—the one who refused to cook on an electric range, and what kind of thinking was that when they were phasing gas out everywhere in the interest of the environment and clean air?—but this wouldn't be anything like that. Keep it simple. Cooper was opposed to any kind of display—display equaled waste—and she didn't blame him. If it was at Casa Lorena, it would just be the waitstaff, which was basic enough, and if Cooper wanted the beach she'd ask around about a down-to-earth caterer and not some prima donna who owned her own restaurant and treated everybody who didn't as if they'd just emerged from a mud hut.

The road ran through fields of pale yellow grass broken by dark patches of mesquite and coyote brush, then dipped into a grove of pines. The light was restrained here, softer, and the way the road looped gracefully round the trees made it seem like a natural feature, as if it had been here forever, before there were cars, before there were people, though of course that wasn't possible. At least it blended in—it wasn't concrete or macadam, just dirt. Low-impact. When people were gone, the scrub would grow back in and eradicate any trace of it. *When people were gone.* Where were they going? Ask Cooper and he'd tell you—they were going the way of the thylacine, the great auk and the aurochs. Then the macadam would crumble in the parking lots of all the malls across the country and the skyscrapers would topple and there'd be no consciousness big enough to worry about restoration or climate change or whether it was ever going to rain again.

The immediate problem, though, was dust. The windows were rolled up, but she could still taste it in the back of her mouth. Skeins of it spun out behind them and she saw that the bushes on both sides of the road were smothered with it, a problem they could have helped minimize if they'd walked instead of taken the car, but then despite what she'd told her son, she wasn't a hundred percent sure she could make the whole distance on foot as it was—and off-trail, no less. She was more a swimmer than a walker and though she was in better shape than most women her age, her left knee had been flaring up lately and she was going to be sore, she knew that, especially on the way back.

Cooper was still on his monologue—he'd told her about Carrie Stroh, right? The bat woman? Who happened to be bat-shit crazy and kept her guano samples in the refrigerator with the sign on it that read PEOPLE FOOD ONLY in three-inch-high letters? Red letters? In Magic Marker?—when he suddenly jerked the wheel and the car veered left round a bend and they flushed a pair of deer, a buck and doe, which vanished into the brush like a conjuror's trick, as if they'd been born and matured and died in an instant. Fighting the wheel with both hands, he rumbled over a snarl of dead branches that whipped at the undercarriage, then slowed to point out the trunk of a fallen tree and the rounds that had been cut from it. "That came down in the last windstorm. Hey, you need any firewood?"

"Firewood? Half the town's already been converted to charcoal."

"Just asking."

"We haven't used the fireplace in as long as I can remember. Plus, it pollutes the air, right? Isn't that what you always said?"

The other topic she wanted to take up with him, beyond the wedding—*and please, please, please put it off till Cat can get here*—was his arm. She'd found two articles online about the revolutionary advances in limb regeneration through the use of stem cells and intracellular electrical pulses. People could regenerate their livers, so why not the rest too, if technology—good technology, technology applied to people instead of the endless parade of new and improved products you just couldn't live without—could unlock the formula? Salamanders could regrow limbs, planaria spontaneously regenerated their heads and tails as need be, and what about starfish—cut off the arm of a starfish and toss it in the ocean and the amputee grows it right back and in some species even the severed portion is capable of reproducing another specimen. Entire. A new being to cling to the rocks at high tide and pry open clams and mussels at will. She'd printed both articles and brought them along in her backpack. When the moment was right, she'd give them to him.

They lurched in and out of ruts, trees loomed and receded, quail shot away on both sides of the car, crows screamed at them from the trees. Everything had begun to look the same—familiar, that is—when Cooper pulled over along a stretch that opened up on an expanse of chaparral and the sun-bleached buttress of the mountains that were right there in front of them now. "Okay, this is it. Ready?"

She was. And what she was thinking was that she should come out here more often, just to break the routine at home where every day was like the one before, right down to the tic of irritation she felt every morning when Sylvie drifted into the kitchen for her coffee or the way Frank would settle himself in his chair with his iPad and the TV on mute for hours at a time. ("I'm in training for the nursing home," he'd joke, which wasn't funny, not at all.) Even as the thought came to her, she stepped out of the car and the morning burst open around a flock of turkeys—she counted fourteen—bobbing their way across the road, a species common here now, but still a sight that always made her smile. How bad could things be if you had turkeys to admire?

Cooper was pointing to the ridge ahead of them. "You see that grove of pines up there? That's where we're going—it's a really special place, you're going to love it. And maybe we get lucky, what do you think?"

"Lead on," she said and followed his shoulders through the chaparral, trying to avoid contact with the vegetation as much as possible and glancing down every few minutes to inspect her jeans for ticks, which really shouldn't have been a problem till the rains started—if that was even a possibility anymore the way things were going. They were mostly silent, bound up in the immemorial rhythm of ambulation, one foot in front of the other, a rock there, a bush, swivel your hips, skip forward, duck that limb, and it was deeply meditative, beautiful really, but she couldn't stop thinking about the wedding—which was good news, great news, but why so sudden?

"So why now?" she asked, breaking the silence.

"Why now what?"

"Getting married. And what's the rush?" And then, half-jokingly, "She isn't—?"

"Ma, no, uh-uh, no way." He swiveled his head to look back over his

shoulder and make eye contact. "We just thought it was time. Or, actually, Elytra was the one." He ducked round a sandstone boulder the size
of a sedan, animal tracks in the dirt, his boots doing a little waltz step.
"And no, there aren't going to be any children, not now or ever, if that's
what you're thinking—we both agreed on that. Not when we're pushing
the envelope of nine billion on this planet. Are you kidding me?"

She had nothing to say to this but she couldn't help thinking it was
a waste, the two of them such superior people, strong, bright, handsome,
alert, the final expression of a specific set of genes transmitted through
all the generations since the species got up on two legs and ambled across
the savanna. A loss. A real loss. And there was no sense in trying to convince Cooper otherwise, but then who knew? Birth control failed. And
once that happened, once Elytra was pregnant and the hormones were
flooding her system, she might feel differently—and so would he. He
was always talking about living a natural life—well, what could be more
natural than that?

She was moving right along, no problem—her knee was fine, her
hiking boots felt snug and the rubber bands she'd stretched around the
cuffs of her jeans to inhibit the ticks were still firmly in place—and she
did a little dance around the boulder herself. Three or four miles? Piece
of cake.

"Is it selfish of me to want grandchildren?"

"You already have one."

"That's not even replacement value."

"Yes," he said.

"Yes what?"

"Yes, it's selfish."

WHEN MOUNT PINATUBO ERUPTED IN the Philippines in 1991, it
was the second largest volcanic event of the twentieth century, exceeded
only by the eruption of Novarupta, in Alaska, seventy-nine years earlier.

So much debris was heaved into the stratosphere that for the next two years the worldwide temperature declined by a full degree until gradually the particles dissipated and it began to climb back up again. That was fact. That was what Elytra had been going on about the night Dunphy died. The albedo effect. Put a chemical umbrella over the planet to deflect the sun and slow the warming that was accelerating out of control. Of course, it wasn't natural (but then the burning of fossil fuels wasn't natural either, unless you considered anything humans did a function of natural processes) and there was no telling what unforeseen consequences might arise, disruptions in already disrupted weather patterns, too cold in some regions, not cold enough in others, crop failures, international disputes, war. It needed study. It needed statutes. It was either inspired or purely crazy.

Was 1991 that much cooler than 1990 or 1989? She couldn't recall. They'd just moved into their house and she was trying to furnish and remodel it and help Frank establish his practice and pay the bills. Weather was weather. Maybe you consulted the newspaper or turned on the TV to see if rain was in the forecast or if the winds were going to kick up, but there was nothing you could do about it in any case. It was enough to get through the day. The apocalypse was offstage, so distant at that point as to be the stuff of sci-fi, drones, mother ships, hyperspace, catastrophically bad weather, but it wasn't offstage any longer. The heat was real. The glaciers were going fast, the drought was bottomless, the seas rising.

What she didn't know—or Cooper either—not yet anyway, was that two days earlier, all the way across the world in Luzon, a Philippine billionaire she'd never heard of had taken it upon himself to solve the problem independently, sans consulting the military or the UN or climate scientists or anybody else. The press, which would break the story by the time they got back to the car, invariably inserted the descriptor *rogue* in front of *billionaire*, as if that could explain or excuse what he'd done or as if all billionaires weren't rogues to begin with. It was as simple as Elytra claimed. The billionaire, a close ally of Sara Duterte, the country's ruler, who allowed him to make use of a military airstrip, no questions asked, retrofitted six Gulfstream corporate jets and sent them up into the lower stratosphere, where they dispersed droplets of sulfuric acid, which in turn combined with water vapor to form sulfate aerosols. These particles, like the ones the eruption of Mount Pinatubo produced, had the effect—were having the effect, even as she and Cooper dodged ticks and started up the slope to the pine grove—of reflecting one percent of the sun's energy back into space. One percent, that was all it took, and the cooling was under way, though it had nothing to do with the heat wave breaking, or not this one, anyway, and if the particles interfered with the scattering of electromagnetic radiation so that the sky would appear more white than blue, it was a trade-off everybody could live with. Wasn't it?

THE CLIMB WASN'T ESPECIALLY DIFFICULT, but halfway up the ridge she began to feel things drifting on her, the rocks and bushes reshaping themselves like images on a screen, Cooper's head and shoulders and the neat rectangle of his day pack—which was blue, sky-blue—beginning to blur at the edges. An image flickered through her brain—a face, her mother's face, rising up before her as if it were painted on a helium balloon and sailing away, higher and higher into the pale nullity of the sky, and then another balloon started to rise, but it was faceless and she lost track of it. Her throat was dry. Her feet felt as if they belonged to somebody else. She didn't want to appear weak, especially after scoffing at the distance, but she just . . . needed . . . a minute to gather herself, that was all, and she called out to him, breaking the silence again. "Coop, can we take a break?"

He turned to her in slow motion, ten feet away, naked stone and a bleached struggle of dun vegetation framing him, his expression shifting from neutral to a kind of awakening alarm. "Are you okay?"

"I'm fine."

"You sure?"

There was a squared-off boulder the size and height of a coffee table right there in front of her. She sat down on it, dug her water bottle out of the backpack and took a long swallow. She wiped her mouth with the back of her hand, took another swig. She hadn't realized just how thirsty she was. "All good," she said.

He was right there now, easing down beside her, setting his own pack on the ground between his feet and searching through it with his good hand till he came up with an energy bar and handed it to her. "Mom, a little sugar fix," he said. "You don't realize how many calories you're burning through out here—you did have breakfast, right?"

"I'm fine," she repeated. She could see what he was thinking, having brought his mother all the way out here under a pale sun and paler sky, miles from the nearest road, his seventy-year-old mother who was just then having some sort of episode, which was probably just nothing, dehydration, the gradual erosion of age, a spell, a moment.

"We can go back if you want, no big deal."

"I want to see butterflies, don't you? And count them. I want to count them too."

"Don't get your hopes up," he said.

FIFTEEN MINUTES LATER THEY WERE atop the ridge in the shade of the trees, pines like the ones below, but denser and greener, as if someone had stopped by and watered them with the longest hose in the world. It was cool under the trees, almost sweater-cool. There was a strong smell of the terpenes they used as part of their arsenal in the war against bark beetles, the smell of Christmas wreaths and Pine-Sol. Cooper was visibly excited, racing along ahead of her until remembering himself and slowing his pace. The branches flared like wings, the trunks shone with a muted light. She didn't see any butterflies. "Is this where they're supposed to be?" she asked.

"Not quite. There's a clearing up ahead where the trees provide a windbreak but also let the sun in so they can be active in the daytime, and if they're here, that's where we're going to find them. Of course, who knows what that heat wave did to them."

She'd had her annual physical a month ago and everything was normal, blood pressure, cholesterol, EKG. Her doctor—a woman half her age—had praised her, as if she'd had anything to do with it beyond eating right and getting her daily exercise, when it was actually out of her hands, a dice-throw of the genes she'd inherited. And luck, that too. She was lucky to have her health, lucky to have Frank, her children, her house, her life. So if she felt just the slightest bit off-kilter, whatever it was wasn't serious, she was sure of it—and she'd consult Frank when she got home, just to be safe. At the moment, though, she was walking through a forest with her son and the world was sufficient, radiant even. One foot in front of the other, the trees, the light. If there was a heaven, it would have pines in it, pines like these that made sense of the ground and propped up the sky without the slightest effort. Her head cleared. Her breathing slowed. She quickened her pace. Then all at once the clearing opened up around them and Cooper said, "Yes!"

At first she didn't see them, or she did, but only the few that were separated from the mass and drifting free against the silken scrim of the branches. But Cooper, grinning, pointed straight ahead and there they were, long garlands of butterflies descending from the treetops, their wings folded, each a link in the chain. A wind stirred the trees—or maybe it was something else, a disturbance in the atmosphere, a ghosting of the new reality—and they began to separate, falling and rising like leaves if leaves could rise again. She tried to count them, because that was what she was here for, but there were just too many.

Acknowledgments

I WOULD LIKE TO THANK THE FOLLOWING FOR THEIR KINDNESS and generosity in sharing their expertise: Giovanni Martinez, Kate McCurdy, Hillary Young, Katja Seltmann, and Nicole Evans.